TWO OF A DEADLY KIND

The Candy Man—He is a chameleonlike maniac whose true face is a puzzle. His life's work is sadistic murder, his diabolical dream is a world where dementia rules, and his sworn enemy is the one man who put him away.

The Ferryman—He is perhaps the most lethal super-agent ever activated. A man without a past. A killing machine sworn to combat evil. When his superiors betrayed him, he brought them down. Now they want revenge, and he is alone against an organization he thought he'd destroyed—*and* a madman he thought he'd imprisoned forever.

THE NINTH DOMINION

A heart-stopping novel of the world trapped in the shadow of apocalyptic evil, by the bestselling author of *The Eighth Trumpet* and *The Valhalla Testament*.

THE
NINTH
DOMINION

Jon Land

FAWCETT GOLD MEDAL • NEW YORK

For the Barrington Middle School
Where you can go home again

A Fawcett Gold Medal Book
Published by Ballantine Books
Copyright © 1991 by Jon Land

Library of Congress Catalog Card Number: 91-75836

ISBN 0-449-14775-4

Manufactured in the United States of America

First Edition: February 1992

ACKNOWLEDGMENTS

Mention on this page is hardly adequate thanks for those whose names appear. Without their efforts on individual parts, the whole formed by this book would be considerably weaker and less enjoyable.

I start as always with Toni Mendez, an agent who has been there every word of the way on this one and all the others. To insure those words are the best they can be, I rely on Ann Maurer whose diligent work continues to spare my readers exposure to lines not fit for public consumption.

Of course there wouldn't be any public consumption, if not for the Fawcett family headed by Leona Nevler, Clare Ferraro and Susan Petersen. Daniel Zitin *is* the best editor in the business and I continue to be amazed at his ability to figure out what I'm trying to do and tell me how to do it better.

With Emery Pineo, the impossible continues to be only a phone call away. From picking locks, to moving mountains, to blowing up buildings, he outdid himself on this one and holds on to his title as the smartest man I know.

Morty Korn makes his twelfth consecutive appearance on this page for once again trudging through an early draft. And Tony Sheppard deserves special mention for trudging through all of the early drafts.

For help with armaments and explosives, my thanks as always to Walt Mattison. For technical advice on all things aviational, I am indebted to Richard Levy of Corporate Air Newport. Thanks also for help received from Mitch Reiter, Dave Zucconi, Dianne Serra, Mike Paul, and Professor Elmer Blistein.

Others who helped in the technical research for this book requested that their names not be mentioned. I still wish to thank them for their innovative thinking and professional expertise.

And finally thanks to Mitch, Stephanie and everyone at the *real* Camp Towanda, my new second home.

Easy is the descent to hell:
Night and day the gates of dark death stand wide open;
But to climb back up,
To retrace one's steps to the upper air,
That is the work,
That is the difficulty.

The poet Virgil in the *Aeneid*

THE FIRST DOMINION

The Locks

Wednesday, August 12; 11:00 P.M.

CHAPTER 1

"**I**'LL be leaving now, doctor."

Alan Vogelhut, chief administrator of Graylock's Sanitarium for the Criminally Insane, gazed up vacantly from the papers on his desk. "Yes, Miss Dix?"

"I said I'm leaving," his secretary replied. "I don't want to miss the last launch, with the storm and all."

Only then did Vogelhut notice the rain slapping the office windows. It was as though the world beyond the walls of "The Locks" did not exist for him at all. As the institution's first and only chief administrator, he had in his charge the most vile and heinous of criminals, committed to The Locks by courts that had no fonder hopes than to forget about them forever.

"Yes," he said, "I quite agree."

"I'll see you in the morning, then."

And Miss Dix was gone.

Vogelhut looked at the mounds of paperwork on his desk and knew he wouldn't be getting off Bowman Island that night. He kept a small apartment inside the facility for times like these, and lately he had been using it more and more. Leaving The Locks for even the briefest of periods was becoming increasingly difficult for him. He sometimes thought that he was as much a prisoner of this place as were his charges.

"The time," he muttered, "the time . . ."

He was late for his evening rounds, woefully perfunctory but

3

nonetheless carried out each and every evening. Vogelhut moved away from his desk and caught a glimpse of himself in the rain drenched window. His gray hair hung limply. His face was pale, almost ashen, the face of a man for whom the sun was a long forgotten memory. Was it old age, he wondered, or just The Locks itself?

Vogelhut stepped into the corridor and locked his office door behind him. At this time of night, he had the halls to himself, and the quiet soothed him. Quiet meant routine, and routine had become the only security he could find refuge in. Given the hour, he would skip the more docile wings and head straight for the maximum security section known as MAX-SEC.

Alerted to his presence by surveillance equipment, the MAX-SEC guards were waiting for him when he approached the central monitoring station.

"Good evening, doctor," one said, while the other two continued their vigils before the dozen television screens that constantly scanned the tombs where America had buried eighty-four men and women alive.

Everything was computer keyed and controlled. The dozen screens rotated the pictures from seven cells each. Vogelhut often watched the inmates in their cells for long periods at a time, transfixed by their every mannerism. He felt like a voyeur, peeking into worlds that were both fascinating and incomprehensible. Each in the space of his or her cell behaved differently. At least three of the inmates in this wing never slept. Now one of them was gazing at the camera as if he knew Vogelhut was watching.

The prisoner flipped him the bird. Vogelhut trembled and turned away. How many deaths had these men and women caused? How much pain and suffering? Vogelhut tried never to consider such questions. MAX-SEC was built to accommodate 144 prisoners, but the present number was the largest ever to populate it.

He had retraced his steps down one hallway and swung onto another when the lights around him flickered once and died. The power failure, Vogelhut reasoned, was undoubtedly caused by the storm. He was reassured seconds later when the emergency system kicked in to restore a measure of light. Vogelhut pivoted on his heel to return to the MAX-SEC area. A power failure at The Locks was a matter for serious concern, and again he took refuge in the routine to calm his jittery nerves. Even now, two dozen guards would be rushing to the MAX-SEC wing—standard procedure in the event of a power outage. Vogelhut was taking no chances with his eighty-four most important tenants.

Halfway back to the monitoring station, the emergency lighting died, plunging the hall into utter darkness. Fear gripped Vogelhut's innards. This could not be. Sophisticated precautions had been employed to prevent against losing both the primary and backup systems. He could hear the pounding rush of the oncoming guards now, could see the darkness splintered by their flashlight beams. Vogelhut put his left hand against the wall and kept moving.

"That you, doctor?" asked one of the MAX-SEC station guards when he rounded the corner into the spill of a flashlight.

Vogelhut shielded his eyes from the glare and edged on. "Are they quiet?"

"Can't tell. All the monitoring systems are out."

"That's right. Of course."

"What the hell happened, sir?"

Vogelhut reached the monitoring station just as the first of the two dozen emergency guards hurried down the final stretch with flashlight beams leading.

"I don't have any idea," was all Vogelhut could say.

He knew there was nothing to worry about. In the event of a power failure, a secondary locking system in the MAX-SEC wing automatically took effect. Cobalt bars extended across all three of the twelve-inch-thick doors one had to pass through to gain entrance. Not only could the prisoners not get out in such an event, but no one could get in, and that included the guards.

Two dozen of them, flashlights aimed low, crowded behind Vogelhut. They carried M-16 A2 machine guns outfitted with sensor triggers rigged to a certain thermal signature. No one else but the individual guard could fire his own weapon unless it was reprogrammed. This added security precaution was to prevent the prisoners of MAX-SEC from ever turning the guns against their captors.

"I can't raise anyone in main control," reported the monitor, who was still wearing his headphones.

"Keep trying," Vogelhut ordered.

The minutes passed. Five was stretching toward six when the primary power snapped back on. Vogelhut's own sigh of relief was drowned out by a larger collective one. Yet instead of clear pictures the twelve television monitor screens showed only garbled, static-filled displays.

"What's wrong?"

"I don't know, sir," the headphone man said, flipping every switch in his reach back and forth. "I'm not getting any signals from inside MAX-SEC."

Vogelhut didn't hesitate to make the decision required for just such an emergency. He yanked a strangely shaped square key from his pocket and handed it over.

"Open the doors."

"Sir, procedure—"

"Damn it, there is no procedure for this!" Vogelhut's insides felt like barbed wire was scraping against them. "You have your orders. Open the security doors. On my command."

From his pocket, the monitor extracted a matching key that was affixed by chain to his belt. He inserted both his and Vogelhut's into the proper slots on the black console and waited. Vogelhut turned to the guard captain at his rear.

"Level one first. Twelve cells, two of you to a cell. Captain, we'll communicate by walkie-talkie. Give me the signal when you're in position."

"Yes, sir."

"Questions?"

"No, sir."

"Let's get on with it then."

The captain and his team moved to the black steel entry door. The captain punched the proper code into the keypad and the vaultlike door swung open. The guards crowded together outside the first of the additional three access doors permitting entry to MAX-SEC.

Vogelhut turned back to the monitor, who was ready with the keys. "Now, son."

The guard turned both keys simultaneously. An ear-splitting wail began to pulse at one-second intervals. Vogelhut's face was awash in the glow of the red entry lights now flashing on the control board. Inside MAX-SEC the three access doors were swinging open one at a time, the guards surging from one door to the next the moment each was opened. They bunched together, sprinted forward, then bunched again until they had at last entered the first of the four levels.

"We're in, sir," Vogelhut heard through the walkie-talkie. "Dispersing now. Everything looks normal."

"On your mark, Captain."

"In position . . . now, sir."

Vogelhut looked back down at the monitor control. "Open level one cell doors."

The guard flipped the proper switch, finger trembling the whole time.

"Report, Captain."

"Jesus Christ . . ."

"Captain, report!"

Silence. Vogelhut could hear some kind of commotion through his walkie-talkie but no discernible words.

"Captain, I did not copy your last comment."

More commotion. Shouts now and footsteps, but still no words.

"Captain, what is going on?"

"They're gone."

"What?" Vogelhut knew he had heard wrong, he must have heard wrong.

"The prisoners are gone!" the captain of the guards confirmed. "Every fucking cell is empty! . . ."

CHAPTER 2

JARED Kimberlain rested his elbows on the table and leaned closer to the woman across from him. When he spoke his voice was soft.

"Do your superiors know you came to see me?"

"Unofficially," replied Lauren Talley. "It wasn't easy to convince them."

"It'll be even harder to convince me, Ms. Talley."

Lauren Talley propped her elbows on the table as well, straddling her cup of cooling coffee. The FBI Learjet had brought her to Vermont at an expense she'd better be able to justify upon returning to Quantico. The behavior science department, that part of the FBI with jurisdiction on serial killings, was located there on the grounds of the bureau's academy. Talley was a special agent who, after a rather spectacular rise through the ranks, was number three on the section's totem pole. She took great pride in that fact, but today there were other things occupying her mind.

Kimberlain had chosen this diner for the meeting. Even though Talley had arrived twenty minutes ahead of schedule after a two hour drive from the airport, he was already waiting for her at this corner table. Her eyes went to him as soon as she stepped through the door. Jared Kimberlain's file picture didn't do him justice. Nor did the ominous descriptions passed on by those in the bureau who had crossed paths with him before. Even among the diner's population of truck drivers and construction workers who needed to roll up their sleeves to let their forearms breathe, Kimberlain stood out. His crystal blue eyes mesmerized her, then beckoned her over. She accepted his hand after he rose to greet her. His touch was like ice. Her grasp went limp within it. She felt instantly drained and uneasy, as if he had stolen her strength as quickly as that.

"How much do you know?" she asked him now, turning away from those dagger-sharp eyes to stare at the counter. Those eyes belied the full, almost soft look of the rest of his face. Dark brown wavy hair long enough to cover the top folds of his ears framed that face. It surprised Talley that he didn't wear it shorter.

"I know there's not an eye in this diner that hasn't been locked on you since you walked in. I know you've made a lot of truckers' mornings. You should have warned me."

A waitress came and the two of them leaned back to allow the woman to set Talley's breakfast on the table before her. Scrambled eggs and three strips of bacon battled each other for space. The toast came on a separate plate. The waitress refilled Kimberlain's coffee cup.

"Bring me a cheese danish, too, will you?" Talley asked her.

The waitress seemed surprised as she jotted it down on her pad. Kimberlain smiled.

"They keep Special K behind the counter for the few women who come in here," he said by way of explanation.

Talley slid the first forkful of eggs into her mouth. "I eat when I'm nervous."

"Do I make you nervous?"

"The fact that you might say no does."

Lauren Talley shook the hair from her face. Though a year past thirty, she could have still passed for a college student. That fact had proved a hindrance as much as a help at Quantico. People didn't take her seriously. Many still thought she was a secretary, unable to picture her hard at it on the trail of some vicious serial killer preying on America's heartland. She had thought about cutting her hair, adding glasses maybe, anything to make her look older and more serious. But she had dismissed it as a bad idea. None of these cosmetic changes would help her discover what role she was expected to play. She was making it up as she went along.

"How much do you know?" she repeated.

"What's been in the papers, on the news. Small towns. Two of them."

"He killed the entire population of both. Six days apart: 108 in the first, 115 in the second. The second was two nights ago. I've got the files in the car. They don't say anything more substantial because we haven't got a single lead."

"Not exactly. There's the thing about one of his feet not being whole."

Lauren Talley nodded. "We could tell from his boot imprint that his left foot was malformed. We're still trying to figure out if it was congenital or caused by an accident. Press got ahold of it."

"And thus his nickname . . ."

"Tiny Tim," Lauren Talley said. "I told my superiors I could get you to help. I don't plan on leaving here empty-handed."

"In that case you could take your cheese danish to go."

"He's going to do it again, you know."

"Unless you catch him."

"We won't be able to. He's too good for us."

"Maybe too good for me."

"The others weren't. Not Leeds. Not . . . Peet." Talley gave up on her eggs and leaned forward. "I want to try something out on you. Peet escaped from The Locks three years ago and was reported drowned. What if he made it to shore? What if he lived?"

"To be reborn as Tiny Tim?"

"It's possible."

"Not unless the victims all had their heads torn off their shoulders."

"What I mean is—"

"Listen, Ms. Talley. Peet killed individuals: seventeen in seventeen different states. He killed them up close and personal. Tiny Tim is a wholesale slaughterer."

"You sound like you're defending Peet."

"Just clarifying things. And I'm done hunting monsters, Ms. Talley. I leave it to the professionals now. I've got better things to do."

"Your file was rather specific on that count. A number of incidents I believe you call 'paybacks.' "

"*Alleged* incidents. Otherwise, I'd imagine someone else at Quantico would be investigating me."

"You have powerful friends, Mr. Kimberlain."

"Well earned over the years I assure you, Ms. Talley."

Kimberlain fidgeted, drained the rest of his coffee, and slapped his cup back into its saucer. Talley knew she was losing him.

"Just let me tell you about the towns. Hear what I've got to say while I finish my breakfast."

"Go ahead."

"Daisy, Georgia was his most recent stop. Population 115. Dixon Springs, Montana, population 108, was his first."

"What'd they have in common besides size?"

"Isolation and nothing else. Dixon Springs is a seasonal ski resort. Not many stick it out for the summer. Daisy has lots of small farms."

"Population makeup?"

"Daisy was almost all black. Dixon Springs was a hundred percent white."

"Survivors?"

"A few kids out camping in the woods. Infants."

Kimberlain's eyebrows fluttered. "He let the infants live?"

"Only the ones he didn't find."

Kimberlain cleared his throat. "Weapons?"

"Pretty much what the papers said. Bare hands, knife, silenced pistol and machine gun, poison gas in Dixon Springs but not Daisy."

"Indicating . . ."

"Military background almost surely. Also availability. He uses stuff he can get his hands on. That should narrow the field down considerably."

"Except you've run your checks on men with military backgrounds, looking for one with a deformed foot perhaps as a result of service, and those checks haven't yielded anything."

"The injury could have come postservice."

"You could send a memo to every hospital in the country. Ask them to check their records."

"We have. We are."

The cheese danish came, and Talley lifted it to her mouth but didn't bite. "You were in the army, weren't you?"

"What does my file say?"

"It doesn't, not specifically anyway."

"And your point is . . ."

"That some people with military backgrounds don't have files."

"Like me, for instance."

"I thought you might have a few ideas on possibles."

"Drawn from my nonexistent years of military service, you mean."

"Yes," Talley said. "Exactly."

"I didn't serve with Peet, Ms. Talley."

"Anyone else come to mind?"

"I worked alone. Always."

"Like Tiny Tim. He doesn't leave any prints, blood, saliva, not even any sweat, Mr. Kimberlain. We've got no physical evidence, besides size fifteen boots, to pin on anyone even if we do get lucky."

"Running into a guy this size won't exactly qualify you as lucky."

Talley hesitated and leaned back. The rest of her eggs had gotten cold and she seemed to have lost interest in her danish.

"Like you running into Peet in Kansas."

"That's wasn't lucky, and I've got the scars to prove it."

"You quit after that."

"I stopped hunting the sick sons of bitches who fester in America's underbelly. I didn't quit."

"You got Leeds."

"Somebody had to."

"Somebody has to get Tiny Tim."

Kimberlain's blue eyes caught fire. "It's not going to be me. You're wasting your time."

"I brought the files. They're in the car. I was hoping you could look them over, tell us what we're doing wrong."

"Not praying enough maybe. Might be the only thing that stops Tiny Tim."

"If the two towns have nothing in common, how did he choose them?"

"They have something in common, Ms. Talley. There's always something. The trick is finding it and figuring out the pattern so you can break into it."

"That's how you caught Leeds. And Peet. I think it's him we're after. I think he's Tiny Tim."

"Peet's dead."

"No body was ever found."

"The search didn't extend to Newfoundland. That's where the body probably ended up."

"There are tens of thousands of other towns that fit Tiny Tim's pattern. We can't watch them all, and no matter what steps they take, they won't be able to stop Tiny Tim."

"So you'll have to stop him."

Talley stopped her danish halfway to her mouth again. "Tell me how."

"Try licking the icing off first," Kimberlain said, as he stood up and slid out of the booth.

"You haven't finished your coffee."

"Caffeine spoils my day."

"I think we can ruin it anyway. Take a look at this memo that crossed my desk yesterday," Talley said, pulling a neatly

folded set of pages from her handbag and handing it up to him.
"We're not planning to release it to the press."

Kimberlain unfolded the memo. His eyes turned to stone as
the first line jumped out at him:

> *The escape of eighty-four prisoners, including Andrew Harrison Leeds, from the maximum security wing of Graylock's Sanitarium is being termed . . .*

"When?" he asked.

"Night before last."

Kimberlain read a little more and then looked down at Lauren Talley. "Tiny Tim's the least of your worries now."

"And what about your worries? Leeds was yours."

"All I did was catch him."

"That makes him yours. Now that he's out you'll have to catch him again."

Kimberlain didn't bother denying it. "I'll need access to The Locks."

"For a price."

"Tiny Tim?"

Lauren Talley nodded. Kimberlain retook his seat.

"Your eggs are getting cold, Ms. Talley. Finish them so we can talk."

CHAPTER 3

THE machine gun accepted the weight of the ammo belt grudgingly, the extra bulk of it nearly tipping the pedestal over. Hedda steadied the assembly and eased it closer to the missing window. She gazed down across the street at the former holy residence in the Moslem quarter of Beirut near the Hippodrome, just five blocks from the location of the U.S. marine barracks that had been destroyed by a terrorist bombing in 1982. Her binoculars dangled from her neck, but she did not lift them; her mind worked better when she absorbed the scene this way.

None of the Palestinian guards on duty inside and beyond the fence gave this apartment building a single glance. By all accounts it had been bombed out twice in the civil war, and even the city's many homeless were smart enough to avoid it. Still, the terrorists should have been less lax in their duty. She supposed overconfidence was to blame. They had not lost a single western hostage to the kind of operation she was about to execute.

But this was the first time they had dealt with The Caretakers.

Hedda had learned from her control, Librarian, that the son of a high ranking American in Saudi Arabia's Aramco oil conglomerate had been kidnapped by a Palestinian group calling for the complete withdrawal of American capitalist influence from the region. No ransom demands for the boy or opportunity for negotiation. He was just a symbol, kept alive only to furnish videotapes and perhaps a severed ear or finger if things took a turn for the worse. The boy's father had managed to reach the proper parties and proved both willing and able to meet the nonnegotiable fee. The rest had fallen into place swiftly.

Hedda did not know how The Caretakers had uncovered the boy's whereabouts, nor did she care. Her job was to get him out and reach the rendezvous point. Her job alone. Caretakers never worked in groups and only occasionally in pairs. Twice she had been coupled with Deerslayer; in their last teaming, he had lost an eye. Only fast intervention by Hedda had saved his life, and she had heard that he became even more deadly after donning the black eye patch.

Hedda checked her watch. She had seen the boy escorted outside to play in the sun the last two days at precisely the same time. His captors had tried to get him to kick around a soccer ball, but he resisted, moping and avoiding them.

The boy had still been dressed in his school uniform, the white shirt grimy and one of the legs of his gray flannel pants torn through at the knee. Hedda had raised the binoculars then and focused on the boy while he sat alone on a bench within the once well-sculptured courtyard of the holy residence. Tear stains ran down both his cheeks. His upper lip was swollen and showed traces of a scab. His long hair hung wild and uncombed.

Hedda pulled a snapshot of the boy from her pocket. Crinkled now and poorly focused to begin with, it pictured him smiling in the same school uniform.

Christopher Hanley, age twelve . . .

Hedda's mind returned to the scene in the courtyard from the previous two days. The terrorist pair trying to interest him in a game of soccer, the ball kicked the boy's way and left there. That scene was about to be repeated, and this time she would make use of it.

Hedda pulled what looked like a transistor radio from her duffel bag and began the task of affixing it to the machine gun.

* * *

Fifteen minutes later she was hidden among the remains of three burned-out cars on a side street bordering the compound. She checked her watch.

4:20.

According to routine, the boy would be emerging with his captors in the next twenty minutes. It was time to move.

There were only two perimeter guards on the outside of the six-foot-high stone wall to complement those within the courtyard. All of them wore standard PLO khaki uniforms and baggy Arab headpieces that draped down over their shoulders as well. She had viewed their motions closely enough to see the yawns and disinterest. Eliminating one to allow access would not be a problem; the only issue was timing.

Hedda tucked the headpiece over her head and readied herself to move. The duffel bag she had brought with her contained a uniform that matched those of the Palestinian guards. She was big for a woman at just over five-foot-ten, so a glaring discrepancy in size would not be a problem in the plan she was about to enact.

4:30.

The holy residence stood as a virtual ousis in the midst of a desert of destruction. This part of Beirut was mostly abandoned, except for a few homeless and beggars who came to these dead streets to avoid the shooting war. Hedda had decided while observing the residence from the apartment building to launch her strike from the holy residence's right flank. The guard who stood between her and entry had a beard, so her final action before leaving the apartment building had been to affix a false beard to her face.

Hedda slid as close to him as she dared and crouched behind an ancient stack of garbage cans rank with flies and maggots. A Palestinian spotter watched over the street from the circular dome that topped out the holy residence, but the sun was in his eyes from the west now, which accounted for her choice of the right flank.

The guard was passing by her. Hedda sprang.

She covered the width of the street in a single breath, bouncing on her toes to stifle any sound, knife already in hand. Hedda clamped a hand around the guard's mouth and plunged the blade through his back into his heart. His body spasmed, feet kicking as he rasped a scream that her hand swallowed. He was still twitching when she dragged him across the street to be hidden amid the garbage.

After stripping off the dead Palestinian's machine gun and making sure he was sufficiently covered, Hedda grasped the soccer ball she had wedged between two fly-infested cans. The ball was an exact twin of the one the boy's captors had attempted to interest him in the day before, right down to the dirt stains on its panels. She picked it up and held it in plain view as she made her way back across the street. On the sidewalk, she bounced it a few times and then hurled it casually over the fence. Her target was the part of the courtyard where the captors had been kicking their own ball the day before. To anyone who bothered noticing, her action would have looked perfectly harmless. A ball lost over the stone fence retrieved and tossed back in.

Hedda heard the ball bounce twice before it started rolling. When no commotion or shouts came from within, she breathed easier. All was ready now.

4:35.

Christopher Hanley would be emerging any minute. Hedda continued on the appointed rounds of the guard she had slain.

The gate permitting entrance to the courtyard from the right flank of the wall was located two-thirds of the way up and forward. It was locked from the inside even now, but she had studied the lock's construction long enough through the binoculars to have her pick ready for what would take eight seconds at most. She would time her entrance to the courtyard with the perfect distraction as cover, something sure to draw all interested eyes to it: the appearance of the young hostage in the courtyard.

Hedda did not have to see Christopher Hanley's emergence; she heard words spoken loudly, followed by the thud of a soccer ball being kicked.

Hers or theirs? she wondered.

She reached the gate and had the lock picked in under seven seconds. She swung it open and locked it behind her.

Hedda walked briskly through the courtyard toward the rear of the house. The boy was sitting as before on the bench, stubbornly kicking at the ground with head down while his captors kicked the soccer ball about.

No, *two* soccer balls. They were kicking both hers and theirs. One landed far off in the bushes and Hedda lost a breath thinking it might have been hers. But the one they began exchanging, trying to coax Christopher Hanley into joining them, she recognized as her own, its black squares slightly darker. Perfect.

She passed within two yards of the boy and would have been tempted to meet his stare had he not been gazing forlornly into the ground beneath him.

You'll be out of this before you know it, she thought, trying to push it into the boy's head. *I promise. . . .*

Christopher Hanley's head came up slightly, as if in response to a call of his name, then sank again. Hedda made her way around behind the house. With the boy outside now, all eyes would be focused his way, leaving the back clear.

Two guards patrolled the rear of the holy residence, a third maintaining a vigil near the back door. Hedda yanked her silenced nine-millimeter pistol from her belt and concealed it by her hip. Not hesitating, she walked straight toward the door guard. Either of the other two could have observed her if they had bothered to notice.

"What are—"

They were the only words he managed to utter before she shoved the pistol against his ribs and fired twice. Then she shoved him backward against the door as he died. Supporting the guard there as if he were feather light, Hedda worked the door open and brought him in alongside her. There was a small alcove off to the right, and she dumped his body in it before sealing the door again.

She heard a door close on the floor above her. Hedda reached the majestic staircase that spiraled upward, just as a slightly older man in uniform started down. Their eyes met, and his told her enough. She shot him in the head, and the man crumpled. The commotion drew a Palestinian from the front of the house, turbanless, starting to go for his gun as he moved. Hedda shot him three times in the chest and pressed on.

Another guard lunged out from a doorway and grabbed for her pistol. She saw his mouth opening to form a shout and slammed her hand over it. The force of the blow cracked his front teeth, and the man's eyes bulged in agony. Her right hand let him have the pistol, trading it for a grip with her iron fingers around his wrist. She twisted, and the resulting *snap!* was louder than any of her silenced gunshots. The man's agonized scream was lost to her hand, and she rotated her palm under his chin. Hedda could see his eyes watering in pain as she snapped the chin back. A crunching sound came this time, muscle tearing away from ruined vertebrae. The man's neck wobbled free and then flapped down near his shoulders. Hedda let him slump and pushed him into the doorway he had emerged from. Then she crept to a window that looked out over the front of the holy residence.

Christopher Hanley was off the bench now, hands wedged in his pockets as he kicked stones about the ground. Nearby, but not too near, his would-be playmates continued kicking her soccer ball about. Hedda pulled the detonator from the small pouch at her back and activated it. Two of the three lights upon its black exterior glowed red.

A button rested beside each of the glowing lights. One would trigger the explosive gases pumped into the soccer ball to mix with finely milled pieces of glass. Harmless until they were sent rocketing out under explosive force. The second button would remotely activate the Russian-made 7.62mm machine gun she had set up across the street in the apartment building, aimed dead center for the courtyard. Even if it didn't claim a single victim, it would succeed in drawing the remaining guards' attention to the apparent point of attack, this an instant after the soccer ball had laid waste Christopher Hanley's nearest captors.

Chaos would result, and Hedda would be able to approach the men from behind while their attention was focused entirely on the apartment building. She would make it seem as though she were coming out to get the boy back inside and then take them all out from the rear.

Hedda's fake beard was starting to itch horribly and she wished she could strip if off. The Kevlar bulletproof shirt she wore inside her uniform top was baking her with sweat that had soaked through at her underarms and midriff. But the beard was still important to her plan, and the time when she might need the Kevlar was fast approaching.

Hedda judged the Palestinians kicking her soccer ball to be comfortably away from Christopher Hanley. She raised her detonator and moved a pair of fingers to the top two buttons.

Wait! The main gate was being opened, a Jeep ready to enter the complex with what looked like a troop-carrying truck squeezed behind it. Reinforcements? Replacements? It didn't matter. Her last guard count from the apartment building had numbered fourteen, with five of these dead already and most of the rest hers to take from the rear. But now there were additional troops entering from the front as well. Her plan was blown, *everything* was blown!

But there was still a chance for success, if she acted fast enough. The gate was just now swinging open. The troops in the truck were still outside the complex, and she was in. Hedda pressed the top button on her detonator.

The soccer ball exploded with a *poof*. A brief scream followed in the instant of hesitation she gave herself before pressing the second button. The rapid fire of the 7.62mm commenced immediately, echoing nonstop through the sifting breeze. The hundred-shot burst would be good for between ten and eleven seconds.

Instantly Hedda spun away from the window toward the front door. She threw it open and rushed down the steps into the chaos she had created.

Magnificent! Everywhere terrorist gunmen were firing into the empty apartment building, none looking her way. The Jeep that was barely through the gate was equipped with a heavy-caliber machine gun in its rear, and one of its occupants was trying to slam a belt home to join the battle. Those that had come in the truck had been effectively pinned outside the gate. Some were already firing their own barrage as well, which added to the staccato symphony. Others had merely dived for cover.

Christopher Hanley, meanwhile, was crouched behind a nest of bushes, trembling, his back to it all. The guards who had fallen to her soccer ball lay twisted in misshapen heaps just yards away from him.

Hedda knelt over the boy.

"No!" he wailed at her.

"I'm here to rescue you," she said, and her perfect English made the boy turn her way.

His face was dirt-stained and scared. Hedda reached down and hoisted him to his feet.

"Stay near me! Whatever happens, stay near me!"

Shielding him with her body, she rushed for the house in the last seconds of blessed chaos provided by the machine gun. Inside, uniformed figures were charging down the spiral staircase.

"I've got him!" she screamed at them in a voice lowered to sound like a man's.

Her disguise wasn't meant to hold up to close scrutiny, but it didn't have to. The onrushing guards didn't notice anything was wrong until they were right on top of her, and by then her machine gun was firing, the boy shoved behind her. When it was over, she yanked him back to her side and dragged him away from the windows, in case her gunshots had drawn attention from the outside. Hedda figured escape through the rear of the residence held her best hope now. She reached the back door she had gained entry through and stopped.

Alone I could make it. But with the boy, chased by the reinforcements in the truck through an unfriendly city . . .

There was no hope for them beyond the residence, beyond these walls—not yet anyway. Their best chance for success and survival now lay within.

"This way!" she said, and started to drag Christopher Hanley back toward the front of the house.

"No!" he protested, trying to hold his ground.

"It's the only way," Hedda said in as soothing a voice as she could manage. "You've got to trust me."

CHAPTER 4

"**I** TOLD them I didn't want you here," were Dr. Alan Vogelhut's first words to Kimberlain. "I told them we didn't need you."

"Have you found Leeds and the others?" And, when Vogelhut made no reply, "Then maybe you do need me."

"I've got a call in to Talley's superiors now."

"They're busy with other things, Doctor, like cleaning up the mess you let spill out of here. Don't wait by the phone."

They were in Vogelhut's office in the small administrative wing of The Locks, notable from the outside by the presence of windows much of the rest of the structure lacked. Vogelhut hadn't offered him a chair, and Kimberlain hadn't taken one. The office smelled of strong, stale coffee. Vogelhut's clothes were rumpled and his face drawn. If he was sleeping, it wasn't doing him much good at all.

"You stand to lose your job over this," Kimberlain said suddenly.

"I don't need you to remind me of that."

"I can help."

Vogelhut opened his mouth but didn't speak.

"We want the same thing, Doctor: Leeds and the others back here where they belong."

"There's an army out there already looking."

Kimberlain shook his head. "They don't even know where to start."

"Everything is under control."

"Is it, Doctor?" Kimberlain stepped closer until his thighs squeezed against the front of Vogelhut's desk. "Interesting group that walked out of here the other night. Care to call the roll? Why don't we start with C. J. Dodd, who machine-gunned the occupants of three separate fast food restaurants? Or Jeffrey Culang, the auto mechanic who cruised freeways in his tow truck searching for stranded motorists who needed help. He made a museum of their body parts in his basement. I believe you testified as an expert witness at his trial."

Vogelhut said nothing.

"You didn't testify at the trial of Dr. Alvin Rapp, though. Lovely gentleman who drained and drank the blood of nine of his patients. Almost as nice as Mary Conaty, or Mary Mary Quite Contrary, who buried the remains of fifteen drifters in her backyard garden."

"That's quite enough, Mr. Kimberlain."

"No, there are still eighty more to go, including Leeds." Kimberlain's stare made Vogelhut look away. "We do this one of two ways, Doctor. Either with your help or without it. I'm here on FBI authority. I don't need to be talking to you, but I thought I'd extend the courtesy in the hope that the favor would be returned. I'm going to head toward MAX-SEC now, whether you accompany me or not."

The Ferryman was halfway to the door when Vogelhut stood up.

"You'd fit right in with them, Mr. Kimberlain," Vogelhut said, as their heels clip-clopped down the hallway toward the maximum security area.

"Is that your professional opinion?"

"I've been around them long enough to know the scent."

"Must like that scent, Doctor. Burnout in jobs like this

usually comes on pretty fast. Replacement's a built-in ritual. Strange that you've been here since the beginning. Not even a single vacation.''

"I've got a job to do."

"Exactly why I'm here."

They exchanged no further words until they reached the monitoring station that marked the official entry point of MAX-SEC. Kimberlain had expected it to be crawling with investigators, but it was deserted. Bright fluorescent lighting burned on, used by no one. Over at the control board the television screens were black and dead.

Vogelhut pushed some buttons and Kimberlain heard the distinctive clicks signaling that the doors leading into MAX-SEC were now open.

"This is exactly the way my guards found it. Nothing has been disturbed."

Vogelhut's words caught Kimberlain after he had crossed through the open doorways. His heels echoed on the tile as he walked the corridor deliberately, trying to sense, to feel. The residue of the madness that had lurked here remained thick in the air. The Ferryman felt he could almost smell it. The vast filtration systems could not cleanse the air of the mustiness. A dank scent of mold and spoiled food.

"Let's start with the notion that the escape occurred in the roughly six-minute interval of total blackout," Kimberlain proposed. "What possible escape routes were available?"

"The doors on all levels were sealed by cobalt, as I mentioned."

"Leaving?"

"The MAX-SEC wing is totally self-contained. There are emergency exit doors at the end of each hall, yes, but the cobalt seals would have extended over them as well."

"But no one could swear they actually did. I mean from your vantage point, you only knew they were activated. Since the exit doors weren't checked until *after* power was restored, you don't know for sure that they worked."

"But we do know that the only other access door all the other doors lead to on the top MAX-SEC level *was* secured and manned by guards within one minute of the original power failure.''

Kimberlain nodded his understanding. "Air conditioning ducts, chutes of any kind?''

"None any wider than the width of a man's arm.''

Kimberlain thought for a moment. "What if the prisoners didn't actually escape during the blackout? What if they waited until the doors were open afterward and got out somehow in the midst of all the chaos?''

"I thought of that,'' Vogelhut told him. "I had the guards search every potential hiding place, every corner and crevice, in MAX-SEC. And I resealed the doors before the search commenced in case they found something.''

"Assume the prisoners somehow slipped by. What then?''

"They'd still have to get off the island, and we made sure it was covered by guards and a trio of helicopters. This isn't a single man we're talking about here like it was with Peet. Eighty-four prisoners could never have gotten off the island without being seen.''

"But you put a net over the entire Cape Stone area just in case.''

"Along with a slightly less effective one around the bulk of Lake Ontario. They yielded nothing.''

"Thorough searches of both The Locks and Bowman Island have been conducted?''

"Ongoing even as we speak.''

Kimberlain was grasping at straws now. He walked about the hallway and listened to the echoes of his own shoes. At last he approached one of the high-tech cells and focused on the door.

"This slot here,'' he said, feeling about a double-locked square cutout, waist level high and six-by-twelve inches in size. "For feeding the prisoners, I presume.''

"Built to the exact specification of the trays, of course. The trays are composed of paper specially treated to be pliable, impossible to twist into edges.''

"What time were the prisoners fed dinner the night of the escape?''

"Between six and six-thirty as always."

"You're sure?"

"I checked."

"The power failure occurred just before eleven-thirty."

"Correct, yes." Vogelhut tried to grasp Kimberlain's train of thought and failed. "But the prisoners were in there when I made my rounds. I told you I saw them. What happened here is impossible. We've had two hundred investigators through MAX-SEC in the past two days, and not a single one has been able to convince me otherwise."

"You try dogs?"

"MAX-SEC spooks them too much to focus. A few were ready to attack their masters when they were commanded to go in. Damn dumb animals."

"Maybe they're smart," Kimberlain ran his hand briefly along the wall. "I'd like to bring my own bloodhound in on this, someone who specializes in the impossible."

"Is he cleared?"

"He doesn't exist anymore, if you get my drift."

Vogelhut tapped his shoe nervously while considering the prospects. "I can buy him twenty-four hours. That's about it."

"He works the impossible, not miracles."

"It's the best I can do."

"Let's hope he can do better."

Kimberlain had started back down the corridor on the first level of MAX-SEC when Vogelhut's voice stopped him.

"Can I ask you a question?"

"Go ahead."

"Would you be doing this if Andrew Harrison Leeds wasn't one of the escapees?"

"We'll never know, doctor, will we?"

Andrew Harrison Leeds was the latest of the monsters the Ferryman had tracked down. He would say the last, just as he'd said about Winston Peet, except he understood well enough now that such pronouncements were meaningless.

It was food tampering that formed the basis for Leeds's reign of terror. The poisoning of baby food, soda, frozen dinners, over-the-counter medications, and candy had led to the deaths of forty-one individuals from coast to coast. The killer's preference for chocolate bars led the tabloids and rag sheets to christen him the "Candy Man." The Ferryman became involved after a mother from Peekskill, New York had died in full view of her children while munching a candy bar.

The FBI had been able to pinpoint thirteen sites in ten different states where the tampered goods had been purchased, no particular pattern to discern among them. Department, convenience, grocery, as well as drug stores—the Candy Man was apparently choosing the points from which to distribute his death with uncharacteristic randomness. Kimberlain read the files over and over again until the crucial piece fell into place.

The Candy Man wouldn't be satisfied merely with depositing his poisoned products on the shelf and leaving. His satisfaction would lie in being present to watch his victims purchase the product, maybe even tear off the candy wrapper on the way back to the car. That was where the pleasure of the act for him lay. Without the witnessing, his deed bore no purpose.

The Candy Man had worked at the stores, damn it, all of them!

The FBI had fingerprinted each and every employee at all of the sites and hadn't drawn a single match. But Kimberlain knew that lacquer could be painted over someone else's fingertips, allowed to dry, and then carefully peeled off. With a little bit of glue at the right time, anyone could have new prints long enough to fool any check. So Kimberlain carefully read the transcripts of the interviews the bureau had conducted with all the employees at the thirteen sites. He had the Candy Man pegged by the time he had finished the batch from the fifth site. Calls the next morning to all thirteen confirmed that the man in question had indeed left his job almost immediately after each incident. Different names, social security numbers. No pictures.

Behavioral science obtained detailed descriptions of the clerk in question from the stores. Not surprisingly to Kimberlain, they were wholly dissimilar outside of general size. Different eyes and hair color; a limp in one, a stutter in another. The Candy Man would never let anyone see his true self.

There was enough in the descriptions, though, to form a general composite. Within three days the rough sketch had been sent to every store manager in the country, and two days after that the call came in.

The Candy Man was in Key Biscayne, Florida, working as a checkout clerk at a Winn Dixie supermarket. Kimberlain was face to face with him in line when the FBI closed in with guns drawn.

Five hours later, three Evian bottles were found to be poisoned. The Ferryman cringed as he thought of this monster ringing them up with a smile on his face, saying "Have a nice day," while he placed his victim's shopping bag in the wagon.

The Candy Man was later identified as Andrew Harrison Leeds. Leeds pleaded no contest and was sentenced to The Locks following psychiatric evaluation. That should have been that, but gazing into his snow-cold eyes from the checkout line, Kimberlain felt certain that product tampering was only the tip of Leeds's hellish iceberg. Indeed, the findings Kimberlain made during the months Leeds had spent in The Locks made him count his blessings that the world would never hear from this monster again.

But it would now, and not just from Leeds either. Eighty-three others had found their way out with him, out once more into the world they had once terrorized and would terrorize again. Eighty-three, plus Leeds . . .

The prospects made Kimberlain's flesh crawl.

The man hidden amid the trees of the Cape Stone waterfront watched the launch approaching the dock. Its sole passenger stood in the center, defying the wind and waves. The concealed man raised a miniature video camera to his eye and depressed the record button. He had to rotate the camera only slightly to follow the launch to its mooring. As the passenger stepped onto the dock, the man zoomed in for a close-up, capturing as much of the angular face as the lens would give him.

The man's car was parked off to the side of the road, just beyond the trees that rimmed the shoreline. He removed the tape from his camera and popped it into a video machine resting on the passenger seat. The machine was connected to the microwave parabolic transmitter on his roof. The man hit the SEND key, and instantly the contents of the tape were beamed via satellite to the waiting downlink.

The machine beeped twice to a signify a successful transmission, and the man returned to his vigil at the water's edge.

CHAPTER 5

HEDDA waited in the darkness. Next to her in the closet the boy Christopher Hanley was shivering again.

"Just a little longer," she said with as much reassurance as she could manage.

It was the one place the Palestinians would not, *could* not, think to look: the holy residence itself, the very place in which Christopher Hanley had been imprisoned.

The terrorists had been charging through the front door when Hedda and the boy ducked into an alcove. The alcove led into a central room, from which all furniture and fixtures had been removed. A vast expanse of polished wood bordered by dull areas indicated that there had once been a large rug in the room. At one end Hedda found a door that led to an empty storage closet. Inside Hedda had stripped off her beard.

"Who are—"

"Shhhhhhhh," she had cautioned the boy.

"I want to know who you are," he whispered. "Did my father send you?"

"Yes," Hedda told him.

"I knew he would. I knew it!"

Christopher spoke bravely, and she didn't want to spoil things by saying nothing had been accomplished yet. Everything that remotely related to success was on the outside of the fence; a hundred yards away that might as well have been a thousand. But since the Palestinians would be massing their search beyond the walls, under cover of darkness she and the boy could make it out. Hedda had cars stashed at three separate locations. Reach any of the three and the required distance could be put between her and the men now determined to catch her. Then she would get to a phone and arrange for pickup from Librarian.

And now that darkness had come, Hedda could judge the level of light by the amount that sneaked through the crack at the bottom of the closet door. She and the boy sat on the floor, close but not too close. He had wrapped his arms around his knees and was rocking slightly back and forth.

Hedda mapped the logistics out in her mind once more. The room was situated in the front of the residence, with the main entrance to the complex a hundred yards away. In just a few minutes now she would lead Christopher through one of the windows and then escape through the nearest gate. At last she slid over to him and whispered her plan.

"I'm scared," he responded.

"So am I. But if you do everything I tell you, *everything*, you'll be home playing football tomorrow."

"Soccer," the boy corrected.

Something warm slid up through her heart, forming a stark contrast with the icy perfection with which she had killed today. She wanted this boy to live. Damn it, she was his only hope. Somewhere deep a memory stirred. Another boy, about the age of Christopher Hanley. Her memory struggled for total grasp of it, then faltered as the calming recollections of her childhood took hold. She had grown up on her grandparents' farm. She saw it now on a midwinter day. Snow coated the meadow. Breath misted before her grandfather's face as he returned to the house from his morning chores in a plaid mackinaw jacket, white wisps of hair left to the whims of the wind. The memories made her feel warm. They came when she needed them most, always vivid and never far away.

"I'm ready," Christopher Hanley whispered, bringing her back to the present.

"Good. Just a little longer."

With that she thought of something and unbuttoned her khaki shirt, dripping with sweat now. The bulletproof undergarment was just over a quarter-inch thick, its Kevlar woven into incredibly dense strands. She pulled it over her head and wished the sweat hadn't added so much to its weight.

"I want you to take off your shirt and put this on under it," she told the boy.

"What it is?"

"It stops bullets."

Timing was critical now. Wait too long and the troops would return to the residence. Move too soon and the night would not be dark enough to cover their movements.

"How many of them did you kill?" Christopher Hanley asked as he strained to button his shirt over the Kevlar.

"I don't— It doesn't matter."

"Yes, it does. When they took me, they killed my teacher. I saw the man who did it."

"I know."

"I hate them. I knew someone would come. I dreamed it. If I had a gun I would have done the same, and I don't care if you believe me or not."

"Eight," Hedda answered.

"Huh?"

"And I believe you."

* * *

The soft grass cushioned their drop out the window. Hedda went first and then raised her hands to help Christopher. The cover of the once well-manicured bushes hid them for now, but the floods sprayed more light than Hedda had expected. A dash in any direction risked them being trapped out in the open, Hedda powerless to offer further resistance. She had a fresh clip snapped in the machine gun, yes, but bullets were useless to her if it meant drawing all the opposing forces to them. For now, though, the perimeter guards were scattered casually about, any reason for vigilance gone with the apparent escape of their young hostage.

Bright beams sliced through the night and nearly caught them. Hedda grabbed Christopher and drew him down closer to the ground. The light passed over them and was gone. A vehicle, a Jeep it looked like, had pulled into the residence through the main gate. The darkness of the night grew more complete again when the Jeep's high beams switched off. Hedda heard its engine rumble briefly and then shut down as well. She judged it to be parked along the circular entry drive halfway between the gate and the house.

"Stay by my side," she whispered to the boy. "Move as I move."

On knees and elbows, she kept her pace slow so he could keep up. It was hardly necessary. The boy was young and athletic and crawled across the ground like a monkey. They stayed within the dying garden that rimmed the house all the way around the front. The Jeep was parked just where she had expected it would be. A pair of guards remained on duty near the gate, one each on either flank.

The Jeep was thirty-five yards from them. A quick dash to it would be too risky because of the attention it might draw. It would be better to keep using the night for cover. Attention would be drawn only once they had appropriated the Jeep.

She gestured toward the Jeep and the boy nodded. He was an amazing young man to be able to maintain such control after what he had been through. Again her mind stirred. Another boy . . . Another time . . .

When?

Who?

Other matters demanded her complete concentration now. There was some degree of ground cover en route to the Jeep, but not much. Necessity dictated they be in the stark open for the last stretch, and Hedda could only hope the night would be enough to shield them. The cold dirt quickly turned to the warm asphalt of the circular drive, and then this gave way to damp grass. Thirty yards covered before she knew it.

The boy's enthusiasm carried him past her, and he reached the Jeep while she was still on her stomach. She caught up and positioned him under cover of its front bumper, then slid on toward the driver's side. It was the same Jeep that had arrived just prior to her triggering the plan that afternoon. Its fifty-caliber machine gun hung barrel down, sleek and all but unnoticeable in the night from even this slight distance. Using the frame for cover, she climbed into the driver's seat and hunched low beneath the dash.

The keys were in the ignition. Rapidly Hedda calculated the time lag of starting the engine, shifting into gear, and crashing through the front gate. The risk was there, but it was considerably smaller than that posed by chancing flight from the residence on foot.

"Now!" she rasped, and instantly heard the boy crawling across the stone pavement.

She guided him up into the passenger seat, signaling him to stay down, low as he could.

"Then search it again!"

The words emerged through the open entrance to the holy residence. The occupants of the Jeep were returning! No wonder the gate had not been closed upon their arrival.

Hedda instantly turned the key and slammed down on the accelerator, almost in one motion. The Jeep shot forward, tires kicking stones in its wake. She spun the wheel to the left, climbing up on the grass briefly en route to the front gate.

Screams and shouts followed her every move, but bullets did not follow them until the Jeep bore down on the gate.

"Stay down!" Hedda ordered Christopher Hanley.

One of the guards rushed her from the left, and Hedda shot him in the face. The second Palestinian lunged out directly before her and the gate. Orange flared from his machine gun barrel, the staccato bursts drowned out by the Jeep's revving engine. Hedda ducked low enough to avoid the spray of glass as the windshield exploded inward under the barrage. She still held her own machine gun, but the Jeep itself was an infinitely preferable weapon.

She flinched at the thudding impact when the bumper smacked into the Palestinian. He was pulled under the Jeep, and a thump followed as one of its rear tires rolled over him.

"Keep your head down!" she ordered Christopher Hanley. But a glance at his huddled form told her the boy was already doing just that.

Bullets traced them from within the courtyard, but it was too late. She knew these streets well, had memorized their layout as part of the preparation for this mission. She had deposited the nearest car on a street called Javinta, where there would be enough traffic at this hour to provide sufficient camouflage. She allowed herself to breathe easier. This mission was drawing to a close. The rest of the escape route was all worked out. Routine from here.

She swung the Jeep left and then right. A brief stretch down a one-way street gave way to Javinta. Just past the stop sign up ahead the car would be waiting. Hedda slowed the Jeep, so as to blend with the normal traffic. Her eyes sought out a place to abandon it even as she peered into the night for the reassuring sight of her plant car. Just after the stop sign, just—

The harsh revving of an engine made her swing to the rear. A Jeep was coming up on them fast from the other end of Javinta. Gunmen began opening fire from its open cab. The few pedestrians in the street scattered, diving for cover. Bullets chewed her Jeep's steel frame. Christopher didn't need to be told to duck down this time. Hedda joined him beneath the dashboard and returned the fire with her own machine gun. The pursuing Jeep skidded to a halt, unwilling to chance the temporary fusillade of her bullets. There was no reason to do otherwise. They had her outgunned, over-matched. Unless . . .

Hedda's eyes locked on the fifty-caliber attached to the Jeep's built-in pedestal. She hurdled over the seat and jammed the gun upright. She locked the bolts and feed mechanism into place, and stood there defiantly against the hail of bullets splitting the air around her.

She was vaguely aware of Christopher screaming at her in the last instant before the heavy *rat-tat-tat* began. It stunned her ears, and the gun pulsed in her hands. The burst slammed into the enemy Jeep's side and pummeled the gunmen firing from within it. There was no time for celebration, though, as another pair of Jeeps screeched down Javinta Street following the path of the one she had destroyed. Hedda readjusted her aim, not liking the odds.

"I can drive," Christopher yelled up to her from his position of cover.

"What?"

"My father taught me. I could—"

"Do it!" she ordered just as the new Jeeps' gunmen seemed to find them in the night.

He slid into the driver's seat and gave the engine gas, testing both it and himself. He was barely big enough to see through the remnants of the windshield. Hedda felt the Jeep lurch forward, sputter, and then lurch again. The pursuing Jeeps drew within range. She opened fire just as their Jeep jolted forward and picked up speed.

The second pursuing Jeep wavered out of control. The driver of the third deftly avoided it and charged on, a twin of her fifty-caliber offering return fire as Christopher tore through the Beirut streets, heedless of traffic signals or pedestrians. There was no need to honk the horn; the gunfire was klaxon enough. He drove better and faster as his confidence grew. Suddenly Hedda feared a quick turn or stop might upend or send her flying.

Hedda saw her clip was nearly expended. A quick search of the Jeep's rear found no replacement. She had forty rounds left at most and began firing much shorter bursts to keep their pursuers honest.

Honest . . . Yes, that was it!

She abandoned the fifty and grabbed her machine gun from the front seat. Then, still straddling the Jeep's front and back sections, she draped one of her powerful hands between the boy's on the steering wheel.

"Hold on," she ordered. "I'm going to crash us."

"Wha—"

She had spun the Jeep into the sideways skid by then, ramming them against a parked truck. Christopher bounced in his seat. Hedda was thrown into the steel frame of the windshield. Breath gone, she nonetheless opened apparently desperate fire with the machine gun still dangling from her shoulder, as the final Jeep bore confidently down upon them.

She lunged back behind her fifty-caliber when only thirty yards separated the Jeeps. Her hand found the trigger and squeezed in the same motion. The remaining bullets in the belt punctured the engine block and blew out the pursuing Jeep's front section. Flames jumped from its hood. She saw it waver from side to side briefly, before it careened over and went skidding by them down the street. Sparks from the resulting friction seemed to fuel the flames further, engulfing the Jeep in a massive fireball. The final blast came before it impacted with anything. Steel shards blew outward, and she covered the boy to shield him from them.

"Now let's get you home," she told him.

They abandoned the Jeep for one of the escape cars, which brought them across the city to a small restaurant she knew possessed a public phone. Christopher stayed by her side the whole time, both of them drawing stares from the puzzled patrons.

"Station sixteen."

"This is Hedda. Retrieval complete. Require pickup."

"Position?"

She gave it.

"Litani River Bridge in the Bekaa Valley. Twenty-five miles east of you."

"I know it."

"One hour. Librarian will be there."

The phone clicked off.

The boy spoke nervously for much of the ride, Hedda paying little attention to what he was saying until some of the words tugged at her mind.

"What did you just say?" she asked, interrupting him.

Christopher seemed confused. "That I couldn't understand why—"

"About your father."

"That he doesn't have anything to do with them, so why did they kidnap me?"

"But he works for Aramco."

The boy shook his head. "No, he doesn't. He's a chemist, an organic chemist."

Now it was Hedda's turn to be confused. "In Riyadh?"

"No—London. That's where I'm from."

Hedda tried to keep her mind on her driving. The information Librarian had provided pertaining to Christopher Hanley was all wrong. Her people never made such mistakes, unless, unless . . .

The mistakes were purposeful.

"They kidnapped you in London," Hedda resumed.

"I only saw one of them."

"Was he at the residence?"

"No. He was just at the school." The boy's head lowered. "He shot the teacher who tried to help me." His eyes glistened. "He was big and only had one eye."

A chill swept through her. "One . . . eye?"

"He had a patch on the other."

Hedda went numb.

Deerslayer! The only other Caretaker she knew, a man whose life she had saved . . . This boy was describing Deerslayer!

But how could that be? Why would The Caretakers arrange

a kidnapping, only to thwart it in the end? It made no sense. There was something she was missing, something she hadn't been told for whatever reasons.

They lied to her. . . .

The possibility was unnerving. With trust lost, everything was lost. Again, where was the reason, the sense? Perhaps she was overreacting, her rapidly depleting supplies of nervous energy causing her to think incoherently.

"We're here," she said a few minutes later, after pulling the car off to the side.

"Aren't you going to drive across?"

"No," she told the boy, not exactly sure what she was doing.

The bridge was dark and secluded. Hedda and Christopher reached the west side, and instantly three sets of headlights flashed on from the east. Hedda squinted into the brightness. The boy raised a hand to shield his eyes.

"Come on," she instructed, and together they began to walk across toward the light spilling their way.

The bridge was a hundred yards long, stretching across the width of the Litani River, which ran north to south. Christopher's pace slowed as they drew nearer the middle. Hedda sensed his reluctance.

"You're going to leave me with them," he assumed, quite correctly.

"They'll take you back to your father."

He's a chemist, an organic chemist.

Across the bridge waited those who had lied to her. They sent her to retrieve the boy for reasons they did not honestly divulge . . .

He was big and only had one eye.

. . . after Deerslayer had kidnapped him and delivered him to the Arabs. Coincidence maybe. Or perhaps the boy was wrong.

Somewhere deep within Hedda a memory fluttered. Another boy, another time. Lights, gunshots, and blood, so much blood . . .

They had passed the halfway point when Hedda first saw the

men standing outside all three cars. Just shapes really, barely visible through the blinding glare of the headlights. But their spacing was all wrong for a simple pickup. Hedda slowed. She eased a hand back toward the boy.

"Stop," she ordered.

"What?"

Her hand touched his shoulder. "When I tell you, we're going to turn around and run back to the other side, to the car."

"But—"

"When I tell you."

Hedda had barely started to swing round when gunshots split the night. She dropped prone instinctively at the initial sound. A pair of bullets thumped into the boy's chest, stopped by the Kevlar undergarment she had given him. She lunged his way and thrust him backward, trying to shield him. The ancient wooden bridge coughed splinters at her. A bullet grazed her shoulder and spun her away from the boy. She had jumped back for him, when a shell slammed into his thigh and sprayed her with blood. She heard him scream and then gasp.

Hedda grabbed firm hold of Christopher and pushed off the railing into the night, the two of them airborne in the same instant. The sound of bullets continued until the very last when the cold waters of the Litani River dragged her under.

"I think we got her, sir," the man reported to the figure seated in the car.

Librarian had not exited the middle sedan's backseat during the ambush, not even when the remainder of his men swept across the bridge to gaze down for signs of drifting bodies. Now he plugged what looked like a three-pronged adapter into a flesh-colored receptor that protruded from his throat just beneath the Adam's apple. When he spoke, his mechanically synthesized voice emerged from a speaker resting on his lap.

"Did you find . . . a body?" The voice was a wet gurgle,

the way a person would sound with a mouth full of water that somehow stayed put while he spoke.

"Not yet, sir."

"Then you did . . . not get her."

"There's blood, sir."

"Not enough."

"I can send the men to the shoreline."

"Won't matter."

"If you had let us post men on both sides of the bridge—"

"One side should have . . . been enough, Stur-ges."

Sturges seemed about to argue the point when he thought better of it and moved back to his post. Librarian watched him with a smile trapped just behind his lips and a shallow sigh emerging from his speaker.

CHAPTER 6

IT was after midnight by the time Kimberlain pulled into a parking lot adjacent to Sunnyside Railroad Yard, a resting place for mothballed railroad cars just outside of the tunnel under the Hudson River to Penn Station in Manhattan. His first task was to uncover how the escape from MAX-SEC had been pulled off. Only one man he knew could help in solving that puzzle, and Kimberlain was approaching his home now.

He danced across dead railroad tracks as if current might still have been pumping through them. The gray and brown steel corpses of Amtrak and New Jersey Transit cars were lined up for a good eighth of a mile, rows squeezed so close together that there was barely enough room for Kimberlain to shoulder his way between them. The pair of rusted brown cars he was heading for had carried cargo in their time, not passengers. They were off to one side, apart from the neighboring lines of Amtrak cars relatively new in appearance.

"Knock, knock," he said softly into a small slit cut at eye level on the side of one of the rusty cars. The car's rear door opened with a familiar *whooosh* of hydraulic power.

"About fuckin' time," Captain Seven said.

Of course, Seven wasn't his real name, and Kimberlain couldn't have said what his real name was. He knew him only as a spaced-out tech whiz who'd made his mark in Vietnam as a brilliant flake from the seventh planet in another galaxy. Captain wasn't his real rank, either, but it sounded nice when the Seven was placed after it. He seemed content never to return to his own identity, and Kimberlain never pressed him about it.

"What the fuck?" Captain Seven demanded inside the car, as the door *whoooshed* closed again behind them. "You told me you'd be here an hour ago. I been waitin', man, I been waitin'. . . ."

The captain's hair had hung past his shoulders, wild and unkempt, for as long as Kimberlain had known him. The only difference was that recently the locks that rimmed his face were turning gray. He wore cut-off jeans that exposed his thin, knobby legs and a leather vest over a black Grateful Dead T-shirt. A medallion with a sixties peace sign embossed upon it dangled from his neck, even though he'd spent much of that era fighting in Vietnam instead of protesting about it.

"Not like you to be so nervous, Captain."

"Yeah, well times change. People, too. You wanna see why I'm nervous? Come here and I'll show you."

Captain Seven led Kimberlain through the technological expanse of the first railroad car. Everything was dark and sleek, shiny black leather furniture built precisely to fit its allotted slot. The carefully arranged interior was filled from floor to ceiling with flashing lights, diodes, CRT screens, monitors, switches, and assorted electronic equipment and data banks. They passed all of these en route to the second of the connected cars. Seven slid the doors open and led Kimberlain in.

The captain's living quarters didn't look appreciably different from the preceding car. A single bed and chair battled for space with more of his equipment that had overflowed from next door. A television screen that curved sharply at the edges dominated one wall. Seven had made a three dimensional projection system for Kimberlain that surrounded him and allowed him to watch films as though he were a part of them. The only reason Captain Seven had not devised a similar system for himself was the limited space available in his railroad-car home.

"What's this?" Captain Seven asked him, holding up a plastic contraption bristling with tubes and dominated by liquid-filled chambers.

"Your favorite bong for smoking your Hawaiian lava-bed pot. As I remember, it doesn't have to be lit."

"So right. Breathing in supplies all necessary combustion. What I did was mix up a compound that reacts with oxygen. Formula was tricky, but I had some free time. Notice anything else?"

"It's empty."

"Fucking A right it's empty. Know why?"

"Your supplier blow town?"

"I quit, Ferryman, and it's fucking killing me. I smoked that stuff for thirty-three years, since I was nine, and never had a problem. Now I give it up and I'm a fucking basket case."

"Then why quit?"

"Prove to myself I could do it. Like a challenge."

"More like a mid-life crisis," said Kimberlain, eyes fixed on the captain's graying locks.

"Sorry, man. I skipped right over that just like I skipped adolescence and young manhood. Spent my adolescence in juvie for blowing up a school and my young manhood in the Nam 'cause I did the job so good they had to build the fucker up from scratch. Fucking recruiters got a strange screening system."

Captain Seven sat down on the bed with his bong, cradling it as a young girl would a doll. Kimberlain took the chair.

"SF boys want those who can get them results," he said.

"Yeah, Special Forces was a good tour. They don't ask how, they just say do. More results the better. Nobody asks questions. Then they busted up the unit, reassigned me. To light infantry or some shit like that. I gotta write reports all of a sudden, you believe it? Get approval from cherry lieutenants ain't never seen blood 'fore I can drop Alka Seltzer in water. Came up with this perimeter defense system once, like claymores only you plant the explosives on trees instead of in ground. Thing I'm figuring is the lead gook trips a normal wire, he gets blown to shit while his buddies hit the ground firing. So I come up with a system where all the lead guy does is trip an activator, and maybe five seconds later, when his gook buddies are in the kill zone, my mines kick in. Effect would be like ten .50 calibers sweeping the Z and none of our boys within a half mile."

Captain Seven was still cradling the bong in his lap, like a napping child.

"So I go to one lieutenant who sends me to another lieutenant who sends me to a captain who says, 'Gee, that's an impressive idea, but it sounds too excessive.' Can I come up with anything he can sell easier to the colonel? So I tell him to aim his ass at the gooks and light a match to his farts. See if that's less excessive enough for him."

Kimberlain laughed.

"Hey, Ferryman, I ever tell you my shit story?"

"Plenty of them, Captain."

"I mean *the* one. Goes like this. Course you couldn't know it 'cause it was before your time, but one of the big problems in the Nam was what to do with all the shit. I mean camps could get pretty raunchy if they didn't watch themselves. So I came up with a way to turn the shit into a methanelike gas that would make napalm look like sunscreen. This time I get to see the colonel himself. Says he likes the idea and hands me a dozen forms to fill out. One of the items says I got to send a sample of materials for testing. Jesus Christ, it's like they didn't know there was a war on. So I figured fuck it and did what they asked: I sent them a bag of shit.''

"And that's what got you sent home," Kimberlain thought he remembered.

"Not exactly. Took the fucks two weeks to figure out what it was."

"You got twenty-four hours to figure out what I got for you today."

Captain Seven's eyes glistened. " 'Nother locked room murder?''

"Better. Mass escape from the MAX-SEC wing at The Locks."

"How many?"

"Eighty-four."

"Leeds?"

"Yeah."

"Oh, fuck."

Captain Seven bounced off the bed and dashed to the black clothes chest. The top drawer yielded a plastic bag that he opened to reveal a pile of finely milled, greenish-black marijuana.

"Hawaiian lava bed," he pronounced. "World's finest."

"I thought you quit."

Seven began packing the pot into the proper chamber. "Yeah, that was this morning. But I need my wits about me now."

Captain Seven sucked in on one of the chambers. The water pulsed and bubbled, and suddenly smoke was everywhere, churning through the labyrinth of passages en route ultimately to his lungs. The captain moved his mouth away and held the smoke in with his eyes squeezed closed.

"Ahhhhhhh," he exulted seconds later, eyes coming open. "That's better. I'm ready now. Talk."

Kimberlain told him the story as Vogelhut had related it, describing the physical logistics in detail and stressing the time constraints involved.

"Fucks sure pulled off a lot in six minutes of darkness."

"Head man is certain that's all they had. So what we got is a highly fortified installation on an island in the middle of a raging storm. Even if the inmates *had* walked out of their cells, where the hell did they go? How did they get off the island?"

Captain Seven took another long hit off the bong. When he spoke again, his voice sounded nasal, hoarse from the happy fire in his throat.

"Go home and get some sleep, Ferryman. Leave the impossible to me."

"Twenty-four hours, Captain."

Seven reached over for a battered jean jacket planted on a hook. "Get there by dawn if I hit the road now. See you for breakfast the day after."

Kimberlain headed back for his cabin in the woods of Vermont as soon as his business with Captain Seven was completed. He hated long drives, because they left him with only his thoughts to keep him alert. Tonight those thoughts had trudged backward to the origin of the Ferryman.

He had finished training with the Special Forces and been accepted for a tour with the antiterrorist commandos composing Delta Force, when word of his parents' death reached him. He was granted an emergency leave to attend the funeral. He would be the only relative there, the only one left besides a sister who had fled the strict Kimberlain home and had never returned. To his father she had no longer existed. His mother had cried a lot over it. Kimberlain, only a boy at the time, barely remembered her.

The base commander at Fort Bragg had hinted that unusual circumstances were behind the deaths of his parents, and Kimberlain found out the truth in the hours before the funeral. Apparently they had been touring California in their recently purchased RV when mechanical problems forced them to pull over. His father must have stubbornly insisted he could fix it himself, and the problems had dragged on past nightfall when the aging couple became prey for a gang of bikers. The gang decided to expropriate the RV for themselves. Shots were exchanged, and by all accounts, his father put up an incredible fight. But in the end the sheer number of the bikers won out, and both his parents were killed.

Kimberlain had been given the day of the funeral plus two additional days leave from the base. At the grave site he ignored the clichéd phrases of the unknown minister, his mind on other things. He had smuggled a .45 off Bragg in his duffel, and if he needed more than a single clip to finish the job, he deserved whatever fate awaited him.

The plan he would use developed quickly. He remained in the civilian suit he had worn to the funeral and pulled a cap over his standard army haircut. He rented a huge Lincoln at the nearest Hertz, paying cash for the iron monster. He drove to the bar that was the known biker hangout and from the outside found it packed with an unruly crowd of leather-clad drunkards and roisterers. Judging that it would be at least midnight before the crowd began to disperse, Kimberlain bided his time.

He left the bar around 11:30 and drove south. All the bikers lived in a housing development just off Route 15, and he picked a spot in the meager spill of a streetlight to pull over. He jacked up his car and yanked a rear tire off as if it were flat.

Dozens of bikes flew by him without stopping. A few slowed. Obscenities were shouted. Kimberlain started to consider what he might do if the night finished this way.

He didn't have to consider long. Seven of them pulled up. They had driven by initially, then circled back. It took all his self-control to wait for them to make the first move, and when they did it was over very quickly. Kimberlain killed the first two and the last one with his bare hands. In between he used the .45, connecting on every shot. Inspection of the bodies when he was finished revealed the gang leader not to be among them. Kimberlain returned to the bar and barged into the back room where he found the gang leader meeting with a tall well-dressed man.

"Fuck!" the leader roared when he saw Kimberlain coming.

But it was the well-dressed man, strangely, who drew a gun. By then Kimberlain had managed to grasp the beer-slowed leader and spin him into the line of fire. The biker took four of the gunman's bullets, then crashed backward against Kimberlain, separating the Ferryman from his pistol. With bullets still coming, Kimberlain tore a chain from around the dead man's chest and lashed it outward. The jagged edge tore into the gunman's throat and shredded it. Kimberlain left him there in a puddle of blood, gasping toward death.

Kimberlain left California without giving the bikers another thought and drove the Lincoln straight through without sleep to Fort Bragg, where he confessed to the MPs. Military jurisdiction won out, and he was placed in the stockade to await summary court martial. Hanging was a very real possibility, life in the stockade a certainty. Or it would have been, if the man from The Caretakers had not come calling.

"You have skills that are perfectly suited for a special group I represent."

"What group?"

"You've never heard of us. Very few have. We're called The Caretakers. Capital *T*, capital *C*."

"And what exactly do you do?"

"We take care," the man had said. "Of the country."

And for nearly three years after being "removed" from the stockade, that was what Kimberlain had done. Each Caretaker was expert in the trade of killing, but none more so than he. The enigmatic blind leader of the group who called himself Zeus christened Kimberlain "Charon" after the mythological ferryman who took the dead across the river Styx. The anonym couldn't have proved more fitting. His first two years were marred by not a single mission failure. All those chartered for passage across the river Styx completed their journey.

But in the end his own ticket had proved one-way. His last assignment culminated with him being left for dead by his own people; by Zeus, by all of them *goddamn it* ! The long days of flight alone through the jungles of Central America crystalized his predicament for him. To destroy evil he had become evil. The Caretakers themselves were evil. By alerting the proper authorities, Kimberlain forced the issue. Having their existence revealed in the wrong Washington quarters was more than The Caretakers could take. They were dissolved as quietly as they had been formed.

He had managed to avenge himself on those who had wronged him. Yet he remained unhappy and unfocused. He desperately missed the action of the field and the purpose it gave him. Despite its falseness, it had at least provided a center for his life, and without that center he felt out of balance, useless. He needed to feel worthy again; he needed to matter.

The initial solution came to him quite by accident. A former Caretaker he had worked with had become a sheriff in Southern California. His Orange County district was being plagued by a series of stranglings, and he asked for the Ferryman's help. Kimberlain overcame his initial reluctance and found that taking up the chase allowed him to employ the skills so long a part of him and so sorely missed. Yet now *he* was in control. His work resulted in the strangler's capture, and his reward was a deeper understanding of himself. He was a hunter, and a hunter needed to hunt. More than that, he was a monster, and only by tracking down other monsters could he atone for his past. He began working on his own, uninvited, to track down the most loathsome of criminals.

And yet this, too, left him unfulfilled before very long. To track down these monsters he had to enter their thoughts, and even before his encounter with Winston Peet the hate was telling on him. He had thought that pursuing the deviants who own the underbelly of America would somehow vindicate him for his actions as a Caretaker. Yet their victims were still dead, just as his were. He lay in the hospital those long weeks after his encounter with Peet and considered the track his life was on, no longer satisfied with it. Everything was death, his entire existence still defined by it. Nothing had changed, and nothing would until he found a way to breathe life back into himself.

But how? The Ferryman gazed out at the world and saw pain. Everywhere he looked were people who had been wronged and were helpless to avenge themselves. Their lives had been taken from them. Often the system was to blame, a system he had once been part of. A system he had killed for. He realized that the best means for him to live again was to help others do the same. Offer them a lifeline in the hope of grabbing hold of it himself.

And so the paybacks began. Slowly at first, irregularly spaced until word leaked out and he was flooded with more requests than he could fill. There was no set procedure to reach him. But word continued to spread. People with a need for his services always seemed able to find him somehow, and he helped them because the process allowed him to help himself. How many lives had he taken or destroyed as a Caretaker? Kimberlain hadn't counted back then, just as he didn't now count the specific number of people helped by his paybacks. He knew there was a balance to be achieved, and he would feel it when he got there. Until then, the paybacks would continue.

He was spared further thinking when the private road leading to his cabin appeared two hours before dawn. He snailed down the upaved road in his four-wheel-drive Pathfinder, careful to check his portable perimeter monitoring system at various junctures along the way. None of the alarms had been triggered, none of the traps sprung. The cabin would be as it had been when he left.

He was halfway between the Pathfinder and the porch when he saw the crinkled piece of paper stuck to the cabin's front door. It flapped in the breeze like a shirt tossed over a clothesline, and the bold print grew clear in the moonlight just before the Ferryman was close enough to touch it:

Came here as soon as I could. Sorry I missed you. Will call again.

The words made little sense until the next breeze lifted the top flap to reveal the note's signature:

Andrew Harrison Leeds

THE SECOND DOMINION

Trails

Saturday, August 15; 6:00 A.M.

CHAPTER 7

"**W**E'LL be out of here as soon as we can." Talley promised.

"There's no rush; so will I."

"For good?"

"Until this is settled. My security's been broken. If I stay here, Leeds or one of the others is bound to come back."

Talley had made it up to Vermont in record time, three hours from the time Kimberlain's call reached her. She had traveled in the same Learjet as the day before, once again, she claimed, to the bureau's chagrin.

"You're getting good at bending the rules, Ms. Talley."

"Only slightly, Ferryman."

Kimberlain's eyes narrowed. "I see you've been checking files."

"Just one. I was especially interested in the more complete details of your paybacks."

"Really?"

"For personal reasons. We have a deal, remember? I give you free access to The Locks. You help me with Tiny Tim."

"Meaning . . ."

"A visit to the town he hit three nights ago to tell us what we're missing."

"Later."

"That's not good enough."

"It'll have to be for now. I want to hear what you've learned."

The forensics team that had accompanied her was still inspecting the grounds when they stepped from the porch into Kimberlain's cabin.

"Whoever it was came alone," Lauren Talley reported.

"It was Leeds."

"We don't know that for sure yet."

"I do."

"The handwriting doesn't match what we have on file."

"You really don't know much about Andrew Harrison Leeds, do you? I can show you five different examples of his handwriting, all different."

"That's impossible."

"Not for Leeds. Any traces of a vehicle?"

Talley shook her head. "None we've been able to find. He could have parked it off on the road and walked."

She let her eyes wander about the cabin's interior. It was ordinary in all regards except for two things. The first was an entire wall devoted exclusively to weapons. Pistols, muskets, ancient swords, sabers and knives hung in no discernible pattern, some as good as the day they were made. The second was an odd contraption that looked like a movie projector with dozens of lenses extending out in all directions.

"Multidimensional television," Kimberlain said by way of explanation. "Friend of mine designed it for me, the same friend who's up at The Locks now trying to figure out how Leeds and the others got out."

Talley's eyes gestured toward the far wall. "And the weapons?"

"I restore them. It's very soothing. You should try it. Civilized weapons for more civilized times."

Talley gazed over the impressive array. "Some would take issue with that." She hesitated. "Do you really think Leeds might come back here? I could have a team sent up . . . Set a trap."

"That would be the surest way to insure he never reappears."

"These men are good."

"So is Leeds. He'd sense them from a mile away."

Talley's dark eyes flashed beneath her flowing auburn hair.

"How much do you really know about Andrew Harrison Leeds, Ms. Talley?"

"I read the file, the trial transcript."

"They were based only on what could be proven. They tell only a fraction of the story, one-fifth at most and very probably less."

"The identity business you mean."

"Leeds had five of them we know of. Before the killings that earned him the nickname Candy Man, he was a professor of forensic pathology at the Brown University medical school. Like to hear about that one?"

When Talley made no reply, Kimberlain continued.

"Class was dissecting cadavers one day, Leeds demonstrating every step of the way on a raised platform. Trouble was his cadaver wasn't dead, just anesthesized. He performed an autopsy on a living coed."

Talley's eyes wavered.

"His third identity was as a physician, family doctor as a matter of fact. Killed twenty-two of his elderly patients twenty-two totally different ways."

"My God . . ."

"Number four was a psychiatrist. His patients swore by him. Then seven failed to return home the same day. They were all found in his office, seated as for a group therapy session. They were all dead. Leeds strangled them, then cut out their eyes, ears, and tongues."

Talley wavered. "Can I sit down?"

"Be my guest."

She sank into the couch. "Why wasn't any of this in his file?"

"I followed it up on my own. You don't publicize what you can't prove."

"You tracked all of this down yourself?"

"I followed the trails, the patterns."

"He wanted to be caught, is that it?"

"Not at all. He wanted to be *noticed*. The act is meaningless, without recognition. People like Leeds live off raw emotion. What they bring about feeds their ego, and in turn their ego needs to be fed more. They're almost like infants in that respect."

"People like Leeds," Talley echoed. "What does that mean?"

"Monsters. Behavioral science can call them any psychiatric term you want, but that's what they are."

"What about his fifth identity?"

"Private school teacher. Seventh grade somewhere in Florida. Took his class on a field trip one day. . . ."

"Oh no . . ."

"Not a single body was ever found."

Talley was looking very pale. "He was the worst, wasn't he?"

"Or best. Depends on your perspective."

"Jesus . . . How do you do it, go after them I mean?"

"Because I have to . . . just like they do."

"And in this case you've got to get him before he gets you, is that it?"

Kimberlain moved closer so that he was at the center of the glare reflecting off the many lenses of the multidimensional television apparatus. For just an instant Talley imagined he was actually a projection, a ghostly specter projected in six hundred horizontal lines of resolution, instead of a man.

"Not at all," he told her. "If Leeds came here, it's because he's secure in the notion he's got the perfect place to hide."

"Meaning . . ."

"Meaning a sixth identity I never uncovered, a sixth identity he can safely disappear into. And once he does, we'll never find him."

"Where will you start?"

"With an expert," the Ferryman told her.

* * *

The day was more than half gone by the time Kimberlain pulled his Nissan Pathfinder off the road and drove it as far as the Maine woods would allow. The walk that would follow was all of two miles. There had once been a road a four-wheel drive could negotiate easily. But that had long been camouflaged to cover the cabin's existence and current resident from unwelcome scrutiny.

Kimberlain reached the cabin, careful not to conceal his presence but also not to announce it too boldly. It looked considerably different from when he had occasionally used it himself. The trees and undergrowth had been unopposed in their attack. Vines slid across its roof and wrapped about the front porch beams. The cabin looked more as though it had grown out of the forest now, rather than having been built within it. Kimberlain wasn't surprised.

Whuck!

He instantly pinned the sound's origin to the rear of the house. Circling round, he heard it three more times before his eyes locked on the massive bare shoulders and bulging arms that wielded the ax effortlessly.

Whack!

Another log splintered in two and dropped from the cutting board. The neatly stacked pile that formed most of the open area between the cabin and the woods was enough to last two winters, even three. Still, Kimberlain knew it grew bigger every day.

"Hello, Ferryman," Winston Peet said without turning, as he brought the ax slamming downward again. "I knew you'd be coming."

Strange to call this man a friend now, since the first time they had met six years ago each had tried quite determinedly to kill the other.

Fifteen murders had been committed before behavioral science called in the Ferryman. All the bodies had been found with their heads missing, ripped from the torsos *by hand*, explained pathologists, following death by strangulation. Impossible strength was clearly involved. Don't look for a man, the advice went, look for a monster.

In the end, Kimberlain found the answer to the question of how to catch him had been right in front of everyone's eyes all the time: each killing had taken place in the previous victim's birthplace. The first had been killed in Boston. That victim's birthplace was Gilford, New Hampshire; the victim there was born in White Plains, New York. And so it went in state after state.

The sixteenth victim had been born in the town of Medicine Lodge, Kansas. It was there, in the kitchen of the town's bar and grill, that Kimberlain first met Winston Peet. He stood over the corpse of the bar's lone remaining waitress. Kimberlain had met plenty of giants in his time, either abnormally tall or abnormally well muscled, but had never laid eyes on a creature who was so much of both.

The monster grinned from beneath his bald dome and slid the pretty waitress's head across the floor toward the Ferryman's feet. The fight that followed made history of a sort, lasting exactly the fifty-seven seconds it took for the bureau men to be attracted to the sounds of a struggle. They found Kimberlain standing over the giant with pistol in hand. The arm holding it hung crooked from a dislocated shoulder. His other wrist was broken. He was already coughing blood from numerous internal injuries, including a severely lacerated kidney. The monster, for his part, was bleeding badly from around the collarbone, courtesy of the meat cleaver Kimberlain had driven deep, the wound that had ultimately toppled him.

Kimberlain had steadied the gun as he heard the FBI charge through the entrance of the bar.

Fire, he told himself.

Shoot me, the monster's sagging eyes seemed to beg.

The Ferryman held the gun rigid, and then the FBI men took over, their pistols and rifles ready as if this were a wild beast finally cornered in the jungle.

Not far from that, was the judgment of the court. They found

Winston Peet to be totally incapable of distinguishing between right and wrong and sentenced him to The Locks. Kimberlain figured he was done with Peet at that point, but then the letters started and kept coming.

Two of the letters concerned an especially brutal series of murders and it was this that had drawn Kimberlain to The Locks three years before. Peet seemed to have insight into the latest monster the Ferryman was pursuing. Less than a week after the meeting, Peet escaped from The Locks and appeared in a hospital room Kimberlain was temporarily confined to. He claimed to have been renewed, reborn, his former self slain by the Ferryman's spiritual bullet. He wanted to help and insisted he was the only man who could.

As it turned out, Peet was right. The turn of fate cast them as allies, and when it was over, Kimberlain owed the giant too much to return him to The Locks. So he had brought Peet here to a cabin he had built himself in the woods of Maine to live out his life alone and in peace. He visited the giant at sporadic intervals, more for his own needs, he had to admit, than Peet's.

Winston Peet was turning around now, facing him with ax in hand and massive bare chest muscles rippling.

"Let's talk about Tiny Tim, Ferryman."

CHAPTER 8

"**H**E's not what I came about."

Peet rested the ax against the log pile and started forward. A man his size should have pounded the earth with each step, but Peet's stride was light and graceful, the moccasins he had sewn himself barely grazing the hardened ground. His bald dome glimmered with sweat. He stopped a yard away from Kimberlain and didn't offer his hand.

"But he is out there, Ferryman, and only you can bring him in."

Kimberlain gazed up at the giant, and his eyes locked briefly on the neatly lined scar that he had put through the left collarbone with a meat cleaver. "How'd you know I was coming?"

"You need me again. Your need reaches me like a rope that would pull me back into the world you helped me leave."

"The FBI came to see me, young lady from behavioral science with her own theory about Tiny Tim. She figured out you may be still alive. She thinks you're him."

"Does she?"

"Yes."

"And what do you think?"

"Like I said, that's not what brought me here."

"You can check my feet if you want." He gazed at the ax

still held by his side. "Perhaps I chopped part of my left one off by accident since I've been here."

"Someone clever wouldn't need an ax to leave behind whatever clues they wanted."

"Someone like you, Ferryman."

"Except the young lady doesn't suspect me."

"Because she doesn't know you as well as I do."

"Meaning?"

Peet's face was expressionless. "Accept what you are, Ferryman. Stop using me for scale to place yourself at the level you desire. Even the young woman from the FBI looked at you and knew."

"Knew what, Peet?"

"That she was facing what she was after. Perhaps not in name, but certainly in feeling. The other level, Ferryman. She knew that only one who dwells there could do what her quarry has done. You, me, and now Tiny Tim. She accused me, but she might just as easily have accused you."

"I don't want to believe her."

"Why?"

"Because it would mean I was wrong about you."

"No—because it would mean you were wrong about yourself. Your misjudgment of my character would mirror your misjudgment of your own. If I could still be guilty of such an act, then so could you."

"And could you?"

The faintest hint of a smile crossed Winston Peet's lips. "My eyes, however strong or weak they may be, can see only a certain distance, and it is within the space encompassed by this distance that I live and move. The line of this horizon constitutes my immediate fate, in great things and small, from which I cannot escape. Around every being there is described a circle, which has a midpoint and is peculiar to him. It is by these horizons, within which each of us encloses himself as if behind prison walls, that we measure the world. . . ."

"And how does Tiny Tim measure it?"

"The evil of the strong harms others thoughtlessly—it *has* to discharge itself; the evil of the weak *wants* to harm others and to see the signs of the suffering it has caused.''

''You're saying Tiny Tim is weak.''

''Physically, he is a match for us, but in no other way. How many now?''

''Over two hundred. Two separate towns in less than a week.''

Peet seemed to dwell on that briefly. ''He likes what he does, Ferryman. I have felt him out there, a black vacuum sucking in what little it can accept.''

''But you didn't send for me. You didn't want to . . .''

''Help?'' Peet completed. ''I didn't because I can't. I can't help you with Tiny Tim because the dark world he inhabits lies on the fringe of our own. To pursue him I will have to cross over, and once over I fear I will never come back.''

''In other words, you're afraid of becoming the man you used to be.''

''Because I never stopped being him, Ferryman. I merely redefined his essence. To pursue Tiny Tim, I would have to redefine it again.''

''In hunting a monster, one must avoid becoming one,'' said Kimberlain, paraphrasing Nietzsche.

The giant smiled broadly. ''And when one stares into the abyss, the abyss stares back.''

''I've just come from there,'' Kimberlain told him. ''And it's empty.''

''Leeds is out,'' Kimberlain said when they were inside the cabin, watching as Peet's features became tense. ''He escaped from The Locks three days ago with the rest of the population of MAX-SEC.''

''How many?''

''Eighty-three.''

''I did not feel them, Ferryman. Strange.''

The cabin's interior was furnished with a combination of the furniture Kimberlain had built before abandoning the project and that which Peet himself had constructed. The lines of

Peet's pieces—a couch with handmade cushions, a kitchen table made of birch, bookshelves only sparsely filled—were much rounder and softer. Kimberlain realized the hard squareness of his own work mirrored the difficult times that had seen its construction. He sat on the couch, dwarfed upon it. Peet, of course, had built everything to his own massive scale. The giant stood motionless in the open kitchen area, suspended between the task of making breakfast and the chore of accepting Kimberlain's words. On a nearby counter lay a powerful shortwave radio that was Peet's only contact with the outside world. Kimberlain figured the batteries would probably last him a lifetime.

"Leeds came to my house," he continued. "Walked right up to my door and left me a note."

"And how do you feel about that?"

"Violated."

"Yes, Ferryman, but not because he invaded your property as much as your mind. Have you forgotten everything you have learned from me, Ferryman? For Leeds the end is without worth. His essence lies in the means. Not the kill, but the chase leading up to it. Only a game, but no fun unless there is someone to play with."

"You're saying he wants me to go after him again."

"More, that he expects you to and he wants you disadvantaged by the illusion of his own superiority."

"Maybe it's not an illusion."

"And that's what this is about, isn't it? For the first time you, the Ferryman, must face someone getting the better of you. If anyone given a whole sack of advantages finds in it not even one grain of humiliation he cannot help making the worst of a good bargain. Leeds has humbled you not once, but twice."

"Twice?"

"A man like Leeds, once beaten, would never taunt the one who bested him. He would taunt him only if he wanted the other to know he had not been bested at all."

"Meaning . . ."

"We sit within our web, we spiders, and we can catch nothing at all in it except that which allows itself to be caught."

"You're saying I caught Leeds because he *wanted* to be caught? So he could end up in The Locks?"

"And now, Ferryman, he is out of The Locks with eighty-three others."

"Then he leaves me a note. . . ."

"His way of letting you know he was the better all the time."

The sense in Peet's argument was twisted, perverse, but undeniable.

"Why?" Kimberlain asked.

"A purpose we cannot see."

"Why me, I mean."

"Predictability. A great strength but also a profound weakness. There is more, though. Leeds would never have bothered with his taunting visit unless he feared you. You occupy his thoughts because of that fear. Sometimes one attacks an enemy not only so as to harm or overpower him but perhaps to test how strong he is."

"He could have just killed me."

Peet smiled. "Just as you could have killed me when given an even better opportunity that lifetime ago. Simple, Ferryman. He who lives for the sake of combating an enemy has an interest in seeing that his enemy stays alive. Leeds needs you. You provide him with an object of hate that drives the madness within him."

"How can I make that work for me?"

"By finding his purpose, the truth behind what brought him into The Locks . . . and what brought him out. It lies in his past, and it is there you must go."

"Alone, Peet?"

The giant's expression looked suddenly sad. "I'm sorry I cannot help you."

"I understand."

"Do you?"

"Enter that void and maybe you revert to the monster you used to be."

"Or simply redefine the monster I am now."

"So you could have been Tiny Tim?"

"As easily as you could have."

Kimberlain started for the door.

"You could stay for breakfast," Peet called after him.

"I'd better get started," Kimberlain said, looking back at him.

"But you'll come back."

"I already have. You gave me your answer, and I accept it. It was wrong of me to come here."

"I am here because of you."

"A payback, Peet. I owed you. We're even. We can leave it at that."

"We can never leave anything, Ferryman. You swore I was your last hunt, but then Leeds came along. Now Leeds is loose again, and you must take up the chase. And after that you will come here seeking my council with another."

"Tiny Tim, Winston?"

Peet came out of the kitchen area, his huge bulk blocking a measure of the light shining from inside. "We are so much the same, Ferryman. Doomed by qualities we alone share. Doomed to live apart in the shadow of society's judgments of us. Doomed to grow in power that others don't understand and thus fear. Accept that and beware of it."

"Beware of what, Peet?"

"The higher we soar, Ferryman, the smaller we seem to those who cannot fly."

Librarian sat in the darkened room, gazing up at the camera mounted on the ceiling above him.

"You disappoint me, Mr. Chalmers," said a voice through an unseen speaker.

Chalmers made sure his own speaker was facing the camera before responding. The cord connecting it to his throat dangled limply down to his lap.

"It was . . . unavoidable."

"Really? Then I am to believe that Hedda's escape was due to your negligence."

"My men should . . . have opened fire . . . earlier."

"You should have ordered them to."

Chalmers remained silent.

"Do not play me for a fool, Mr. Chalmers."

"Do not play . . . me for one . . . either."

"I'm afraid you leave me no choice. There is, after all, the additional matter of the remainder of your operatives having not arrived at the island yet."

"Recalling . . . them has taken . . . longer than . . . expected."

"I'm losing my patience, Mr. Chalmers."

Chalmers's hands tightened on the arms of his chair.

"Your operatives are important to me. I need them. They are vital to my plan. You will send them to the island, Mr. Chalmers."

"Yes."

"And you will dispose of Hedda."

"Yes."

"Do not disappoint me again."

Chalmers stared into the camera and said nothing.

CHAPTER 9

"**A**RE we going to die?"

The boy's question shook her alert, and Hedda tried to sound sure when she answered him.

"We've come too far for that."

"I'm scared," he said as he tightened his pants belt. His leg was stiff and lame from the wound and ached with pain.

"We'll be safe soon. I promise."

Hedda made herself smile confidently and shook her head. Her mind spiraled backward, struggling to keep the last twenty-four hours clear.

That was what it had been now, almost to the moment, since she and the boy had taken their plunge from the bridge.

She had lost her hold on Christopher as they fell, then heard him hit the water an instant after her. He had already slipped below the surface when she reached him. He was unconscious yet trembling, evidence of shock. She knew the Kevlar shirt she had given him had prevented what would have been instantly fatal wounds, but depending on where the bullet had lodged in his leg it might not matter. She swam to the boy and tucked an arm under his throat. The water could not hide the scent of blood, both his and hers. Ignoring her own wound, she began to swim away. She supported the boy so his face rode even with the surface. As for herself, a breath every thirty seconds or so was all she required.

With the breaths came glimpses of the activity occurring upon the bridge above. The gunmen struggled for sight of her first and then searched for a quick route down to the river bank. By the time they found it, Hedda was well downstream.

Her own shoulder had begun to throb. Worse, she knew that Christopher Hanley's blood was still flowing from his leg wound. Immediate action was required if he was to survive the night.

He was still her responsibility, after all. In Hedda's mind her assignment had not ended with the bizarre turn of events at the bridge. The plunge into the icy waters might have saved their lives, but it was only temporary. Librarian would know they were alive, *she* was alive, and respond accordingly. The thing Hedda had to do was seize the advantage the enemy's present confusion provided.

The enemy . . . her own people.

Why? And why had they lied about the boy to begin with? Deerslayer had kidnapped him, and then she had been charged with getting him back. It made no sense!

For the moment all that mattered was treating Christopher's wound. Hedda gently dragged him up on shore into a covering nest of shrubbery. The night was warm and breezeless, a blessing for the necessity of maintaining their body temperatures at levels required for survival. There was also a half moon, which would aid her significantly in her work.

She removed a leather pouch strapped to her belt and then yanked the belt free of her pant loops. Resting the pouch on a rock beside her, she tied the belt around the boy's thigh above the wound to form a makeshift tourniquet. Almost instantly the flow of blood was stanched. Hedda then opened her pouch to reveal various swabs, suturing equipment, and a number of painkillers and sedatives. The small penlight tucked against the pouch's bottom was a hundred candlepower strong in an adjustable beam. Hedda wiped an alcohol-rich towelette across her hands to clean them as best she could. Her right hand closed on the penlight, and she checked the boy's vital signs. The pulse was slow but active. His skin was horribly pale. If she wasn't too late, it was very close.

The bullet had entered his thigh on the outside eight inches above the kneecap and exited midway on the leg's front. That meant two areas to be sutured instead of one, but at least no bullet to remove. A fair exchange. Hedda cleansed the wound and readied her suturing needle. She did not want to risk giving the boy a sedative in his weakened condition. If he showed signs of coming awake, she would have no choice, but until then she would rely on his unconscious state to be her anesthesia. Exhausted, she completed the suturing job through sheer force of will. She dressed and wrapped the leg. Already Christopher's color was coming back. He moaned softly. Hedda stroked the boy's forehead.

Abruptly something made her yank her hand away. The memory of another boy had stirred somewhere within her again. Another boy who had been shot, another boy whose blood had touched her. It came with fleeting impact like a late night dream recalled suddenly in the middle of the next day.

Thump!

A bullet shredding skull, spewing brains and bones from its path. The memory faded, replaced again by thoughts of her grandfather. She had helped him with the cows; milking them, tending them. The farm was far from town and secluded, leaving the animals as her closest friends. There was a horse only she could ride, a blind dog sleeping his old age away at the foot of her bed. She'd let it crawl under the covers with her at night. In the morning she liked to watch her grandfather shave. Sometimes he would scrape a hand layered with green, sweet-smelling after-shave across her face.

Hedda turned back to the matter at hand. She had to move while the night was her ally. Steal a boat or commandeer a plane to take her to one of the many friendly sites she had developed over the years. But to get anywhere at the outset, she would have to walk and carry the boy, slowing her to an unacceptable degree. A vehicle, then, she needed a vehicle. . . .

She carried the boy in her arms as gingerly as she could. He stirred a few times, and Hedda flirted with the notion of giving him a sedative to keep him from coming round. Her path through the woods had brought her within view of the road, and she sat back to wait. It was five minutes before the car pulled over to the side. Three figures emerged from it and fanned out through the brush.

A fresh jet of adrenaline surged through Hedda at the sight of her pursuers. The fools were too well dressed for this sort of work. Even more stupidly, the routes they chose took them out of eye contact with each other. Their search was perfunctory, motions gone through and no more. They probably thought she was dead. Hedda gazed back toward the car. She could reach it and be gone from here before any of them was the wiser. But the theft of the car would be reported minutes later, and Librarian would respond accordingly. She would have gained nothing.

The men had to die. It was as simple as that. Not for herself—for Christopher Hanley, whose life depended on it.

She decided at last to inject him with a sedative. This done, she readied both her killing knife and strip of garroting wire. The kills would have to be fast and silent. Hedda left the boy cloaked by the brush and flowed into the dark. She used the knife on the first and the third man, the wire on the second. She wasn't even breathing hard as she eased Christopher Hanley into the car's backseat and drove off into the night.

Christopher Hanley had come awake halfway into the boat ride that formed the next leg of their journey. His piercing scream had shaken Hedda from her perch at the bridge. She rushed below to find him sobbing and moaning, the victim of sedative-induced nightmares as well as the real ones that had nearly stolen his life. He clung to her and she let him, the feeling distant and foreign but somehow welcome.

"How does your leg feel?" she asked him.

"Numb. Stiff."

"Can you walk?"

"I . . . don't think so."

"Then you won't have to."

He had looked at her fearfully. "I remember the shots. I was shot, wasn't I? What . . . happened?"

"It doesn't matter. I'm going to get you home. Just do what I tell you and I promise I'll get you home."

The boy hugged her again. Hedda's large frame swallowed him.

The boat had enough fuel to get them to Syria, where she enacted the next phase of her plan. The boy indeed couldn't walk, so she rigged a crutch for him and taught him how to use it. The key to disguise was to make use of what was available, and in this case they easily adopted the cover of a woman with a crippled son. Hedda even showed him how to beg so he would fit in perfectly with the natives through the limited time they would spend finding safe haven.

They docked in Syria's port city of Latakia an hour past dawn. The open-air market there sold far more than just fish and produce. The right price bought Hedda and the boy space on a transport plane east into Qatar. She and Christopher arrived at the Gulf Hotel in the capital city of Doha. The doorman's eyes flashed briefly with recognition and her check-in to the Gulf was expedited. A bellhop brought her and the boy straight to a secluded room on the hotel's seventh floor without ever having to appear at the front desk. In Doha discretion was everything.

The afternoon shifted toward night, and she managed to grab sleep in fitful bursts that actually left her more tired. She had gotten this far and knew she and the boy were safe. By the same token, though, they were trapped. Doha provided sanctuary but offered no handy escape route.

"Can't you just call my father?" the boy asked her.

"They'll be watching and listening."

He hesitated. "The ones at the bridge, you worked with them."

"Yes."

"But they tried to kill us."

"And they will again, if we let them."

"There are so many of them." He sighed.

"Less now," Hedda replied, thinking of the three she had dispatched back in the woods the previous night. She wanted to elaborate, but there didn't seem to be a way without alarming the boy even more.

His eyes were glistening with tears again. "But if you can't call my father, how can he come and get me?"

"There's a way," she assured him. "There's a way."

Hedda composed the note carefully, a half-dozen drafts before settling on one that would do the job. It was not possible to say everything. The trick was saying enough.

MR. HANLEY:

    I HAVE CHRISTOPHER WITH ME AND HE IS SAFE. SOMEONE BY NOW WILL HAVE TOLD YOU THAT HE IS DEAD. THAT IS UNTRUE. HE IS SITTING BESIDE ME AND SAYS HE HOPES YOU HAVE BEEN WORKING ON YOUR BACKGAMMON GAME. I WAS ASSIGNED TO RETRIEVE HIM FROM HIS KIDNAPPERS, BUT MY SUPERIORS BETRAYED ME AND YOUR SON WAS CAUGHT IN THE MIDDLE. I WISH ONLY TO SEE HIM SAFELY RETURNED. BUT YOUR LIFE MAY BE AS ENDANGERED AS YOUR SON'S. DO *EVERYTHING* AS YOU WOULD ORDINARILY AND THEN TOMORROW . . .

                        A FRIEND

The note went on to specify where and when they would meet. It was sent by fax to a contact in London with specific instructions pertaining to delivery: when Christopher Hanley's father opened his newspaper that evening or the next morning, he would find an envelope taped to the business section. If all went well, he would have his son back tomorrow afternoon and Hedda would have a greater understanding of the reasons behind what had happened on the bridge.

* * *

"I don't know how to thank your for this."

"Don't thank me yet," Hedda told the man by her side in Doha's open-air market. "You've got lots more ahead of you, and little of it will be pleasant."

They strolled about listening to the vendors make their pitches in the afternoon heat. The market was nothing more than an alleyway covered with a ramshackle corrugated tin roof. The more fortunate vendors were housed in actual store-fronts rimming the alley. But the great majority had laid their wares out on blankets or small tables. The enclosed nature of the market trapped the smells and sounds within, the result being a constant throbbing clamor and assault on the nostrils from the pungent scents of spice and fresh fish.

"You're sure we're safe?" Lyle Hanley wanted to know. He had come alone, as requested. If he hadn't, Hedda would not have approached him.

"They'd stand out if they were here."

"Just like we do."

"That's the point."

"What about my son? Where is he?"

"I don't want you seeing him until you understand what you're facing."

"Just tell me, is he hurt? Your note . . ."

"He was wounded the night before last."

"Wounded?"

"Shot."

Lyle Hanley wavered on his feet. "By whom?"

"It doesn't matter. What matters is taking steps to insure it doesn't happen again. You're both liabilities to them. They can't afford to let either of you live."

"I followed your instructions. Nobody knows I left London."

"Somebody knows. Somebody always knows. But that doesn't matter because you're not going back."

"*What?*"

"Not for a while. You're going to take your son, sir, and disappear."

"I'm not prepared, not—"

"That's the point, Mr. Hanley. From here you'll go somewhere where no one knows you. You'll remain there for three weeks to a month. Use intermediaries to get a message to your wife. Have her join you. Immediately. The three of you must disappear, perhaps forever."

"My *God* . . ."

"I'm sorry, Mr. Hanley. You have to hear this. They tried to kill your son, and they'll try to kill you. And now you're going to tell me why."

Lyle Hanley stiffened.

"My superiors told me Christopher was kidnapped by Arabs because you worked for Aramco," Hedda continued. "But Christopher tells me you're an organic chemist, and I know now that his kidnapping seems to have been arranged by my own people. They tried to kill me two nights ago, Mr. Hanley. They tried to kill your son."

"They gave me their word!" Hanley had raised his voice enough to draw stares from the booths they were passing before. "My son was to be safely returned when my role was done. I was given assurances."

"Role in what?"

They stopped near an alley where there was no shop or stall. Hanley swallowed hard and made sure to lower his voice before resuming.

"They came to me because of my work in toxic materials used mostly in agriculture."

"I don't understand."

"Much of my career has been devoted to developing pesticides that linger on plants and crops to kill insects and parasites over a long period of time. In itself that's nothing new. What was new was that in my versions, the poisons were transdermal."

Hedda looked at him questioningly.

"Meaning that the compound is absorbed through the skin or outer shell," Hanley explained. "In all other cases pesticides had to be either inhaled or digested by the pest. Transdermal means that simple touch was all that was required to produce the desired effect.''

"Death.''

"Yes.''

"And someone wanted your formula in exchange for the return of your son?''

"Not exactly.''

"What then?''

"They wanted a transdermal toxin that works on people.''

"I don't understand,'' Hedda said.

"The principle's been around medicine for some time in the form of patches that gradually release their medication through the patient's skin. They wanted a poison that worked similarly, that could kill by mere contact with flesh.''

"And you gave it to them.''

"What choice did I have? They had my son. They had Christopher. Yes, I gave it to them. A more complicated offshoot of one of my pesticides was all it was.''

"But equally deadly.''

"At least. Potentially more so.''

"Then you produced it.''

Hanley nodded. "And supervised the process. It was a liquid I called TD-13: TD for transdermal and thirteen for the fact that it took me that many lots to get it right. We're going back several months now, and they've all been hell. Because, of course, they had Christopher to hold over my head. They provided letters occasionally, tape recordings.''

"Who were 'they'?''

Hanley snickered. "Why are you asking me? You said it was *your* people who kidnapped my son.''

"Assume it was. How could they make use of this poison?''

"The quantities of TD-13 produced weren't sufficient to do damage on a truly extensive scale. I mean we're talking about a toxin with severe limitations placed upon it. It can't be spread from one person to another because it's not a bacteria or virus. Direct contact is the only way to be infected.''

Hedda tried to think with him. "What if it were used on an item that is touched by a large number of people?"

Hanley shrugged. "If you sprayed it on every front doorknob . . . No, given the toxin's limitations, I can't understand why anyone would have gone to such great lengths to obtain it."

"But somebody did."

"Your people . . ."

"Only as intermediaries, soldiers in the employ of someone else. The man who kidnapped Christopher." She paused. "Me."

"You could have turned him over to them and you didn't. They would have killed him, wouldn't they?"

"That depends."

"On?"

"Whether you still held any value to them."

"Production of the toxin was shut down nine days ago."

Hedda nodded. "Both of you would have been killed then, at the time Christopher was to be returned."

"My God, what kind of people are these?" Hanley asked through quivering lips.

"People you produced your TD-13 for, Dr. Hanley. The trick is to find out what they're going to do with it."

CHAPTER 10

THERE was no easy place to start the search Peet had sent him on. The best Kimberlain could do was Brown University, which was the closest location where Leeds had chiseled an identity. As Professor Alfred Andrews, he had performed an autopsy on a living female senior who had been one of his students in full view of a forensic pathology class. In addition to that, though, in Leeds's year at the university an additional five coeds disappeared, committed suicide, or were found murdered. None of these could be positively linked to him, but the connection was unavoidable, at least to Kimberlain's way of thinking.

The nearly four-hour drive to Providence was made with Leeds as Kimberlain's traveling companion. He remembered the monster as he had been in court three months before. Leeds was of average height and build. His dark eyes drooped and looked prematurely old. He was fifty and looked every year of it. The only notable feature Kimberlain could recall was the awful dye job he had done on his hair. Colored it jet black with what looked like shoe polish that glistened under the hot court lights.

Watching him, the Ferryman thought of Peet and so many others whose physical attributes mirrored the scope of their twisted aims. But Leeds looked weak and sallow. What powered him came from deep within, something dark, twisted, and

77

ugly; a slithering, eyeless slug residing where most people kept their souls.

Road maps directed him to Brown University, where he found a parking space in the fenced-in shadow of a rising dormitory. The cool chilled him, and he realized he had brought the wrong jacket for the weather. He followed the rest of the directions as best he could to the office of Dr. Ryan Fields. Fields, now an assistant professor, had years before been one of Leeds's advisees in his guise as Alfred Andrews. Fields's office was located on the third floor of the bio-med center. He was grading lab reports for students enrolled in summer session when Kimberlain knocked on his open door.

"Dr. Fields?"

Fields stood up and removed his glasses. He must have been in his early thirties now but looked ten years older. A bald spot spread outward from his crown. His eyes looked tired and lifeless.

"Call me Ryan, please. You're Kimberlain, I assume."

The Ferryman reached the desk and thrust his hand across it. "Thank you for seeing me on such notice and on a Saturday."

Fields started to sit back down again. "You're the one who finally caught Alfred Andrews."

"Andrew Harrison Leeds," Kimberlain corrected.

"Changing a first name to a last name. Is that common practice for them?"

"For who?"

"Serial killers. Madmen."

"Is that what you think Leeds is?"

"Don't you?"

"I came here to listen."

"I think he was a terrific professor. It's painful to say this, but I learned more from him than anyone else I ever studied under." Fields paused. "I read where his IQ is in excess of two hundred. How many different identities did he have? Four was it?"

"Five that we know of anyway. There are probably others, one or two at least."

"How can you be sure?"

"Because I found all the people he pretended to be, but I never found Leeds himself."

Ryan Fields gazed up at the wall clock. "I'm due at the hospital in a half hour. Please, sit down." The Ferryman did, and he went on. "Exactly what is this about, Mr. Kimberlain? You were very vague on the phone."

"Leeds escaped from the sanitarium three nights ago."

Ryan Fields's eyes bulged in surprise. "I hadn't heard, hadn't read anything. . . ."

"It was kept secret from the press. No sense starting a panic. If we get lucky, he'll be back in custody before anyone has a chance to notice," Kimberlain added, trying to sound convincing.

"And if you don't?"

"I'm here to make sure we do. I'm looking for hints to the identity we're missing. If I find what links his others together, I'll have a starting point."

Fields cleared his throat. "What is it exactly that you want from me?"

"Your impressions mostly. Of all the people I'll be talking to, you probably spent more time with Leeds alone than anyone else."

Fields suppressed a shudder and leaned back in his chair. "We had many talks. His office was right across the hall from where we are now. Actually he did most of the talking."

"About?"

"Any number of things. He was a remarkable man, knowledge-wise. Many of our discussions were strictly technical; a few, well . . ."

"Go on."

"He had ideas, visions, on the way society was going to end up if it didn't correct itself."

"Coming from a forensic pathology professor that didn't seem strange to you?"

"No, because he clearly enjoyed his ramblings. Lots of times I didn't pay close attention. Other times I'd listen and feel uneasy."

"Such as?"

Fields seemed to be searching for the words to describe it. "Well, one recurrent theme of his was that maybe America had it backward. Maybe the crazy people and convicts should be kept free and the rest of us imprisoned. After all, if we're trying to keep them out of our world, what could be safer? They'd be breaking in instead of out."

"Go on."

"I acknowledged the argument had some validity, but Andrews—Leeds—took the issue further. He kept asking what if the poor, the mad, and the depraved were all that was left? He had all kinds of theories of what kind of world that would be and why it would be better. He suggested I make that the topic of my thesis. Even had a title: 'The Ninth Dominion.' ''

"Meaning?"

"Apparently, he had a theory that eight previous times in history great personalities had tried to rule the world, but each had failed." Fields's eyes turned to gaze out his door at the office across the hall that had remained unoccupied since the truth about Professor Alfred Andrews became known. "I remember him sitting in there telling me where they had all gone wrong."

The Ferryman's mind drifted, the scent of Leeds strong enough here to make him wonder if he might be hiding in his former office, listening. "What does that have to do with madmen and criminals?"

"According to him, purity. Madmen and criminals were the only pure humans because they weren't afraid to express themselves. Nothing holds them back. They envision something and they make it happen. In the ninth dominion, the world would be made theirs."

Something cold slid down Kimberlain's spine. "Did he say how?"

"I don't think he knew. Yet."

"Yet?"

All the color had drained from Dr. Fields's face. "I was close to him, Mr. Kimberlain, closer than anyone else at the university. A week before he killed that girl, he asked me to speculate on how long an anesthetized subject once gutted would live compared to an unanesthetized one.''

"A proposition . . .''

"In a continuing series. Only it wasn't until that last day that I realized he'd made good on every one of them.''

In a daze Kimberlain walked back to the spot where he'd parked his Pathfinder. His mind was swimming with the words of Dr. Ryan Fields, measuring them beside what Winston Peet had said.

By finding his purpose, the truth behind what brought him into The Locks . . . and what brought him out.

The ninth dominion . . . a world left to the criminals and the mad, with the maddest of all at the helm. The Ferryman could see Leeds planning for that, living for it. And if so he was seeing only part of the picture here, and a very small part at that.

He reached the Pathfinder and opened the driver's door. Shadows from the dorm construction site danced in the street, cast there by the street lamps that gave the shadows the illusion of motion. The heavy equipment parked on the street about him looked like great yellow dinosaurs waiting to be awakened. Kimberlain climbed in behind the wheel, closed the door, and jammed his key into the starter.

A huge shadow crossing over his rearview mirror alerted the Ferryman to the fast-descending shovel an instant before impact. Enough time to throw himself low beneath the dashboard before the bone-jarring crash came. The entire top of the Pathfinder caved in and crumpled under the shovel's massive weight. The vehicle shook on its wheels, and Kimberlain felt his teeth gnash together.

He was going for his gun when the Pathfinder was hammered by a barrage of bullets. Glass shattered and metal gave, the raging bullets piercing steel in the coffinlike confines. Kimberlain's right hand swept beneath the floor mat, and at last he found the latch hidden there. He shifted the latch all the way to the right and then pushed hard, as bullets continued to pierce the Pathfinder. The angle at which he was bent threatened to make the effort impossible, but finally the hidden door slid free, and an escape hole opened into the night beyond.

Captain Seven had helped him install the floor panel in the Pathfinder and reinforce the lower part of the vehicle's frame with an extra inch of galvanized steel. He never expected really to need either and hadn't up until this moment. They were simply two more precautions among so many others.

But these two had paid off handsomely.

As the automatic fire continued to blister the upper part of the frame, Kimberlain pushed off with his legs in order to angle his body through the hole in the floor. The night and the gunmen's attention on their firing would shield him well enough. There were three of them, one on the driver's side of the Pathfinder, one at the front, and one at the rear. This left the passenger side for him, the side flanking the sidewalk and the chain link fence enclosing the construction site. He would have little room to maneuver, but he wouldn't need much; his mind had already pinned the location of the gunmen within inches.

Kimberlain emerged through the open floor panel headfirst. His arms trailed quickly behind and positioned themselves to support his weight as he lowered the rest of himself out. From there he pulled himself toward the sidewalk and slid out onto it.

Its top crushed, the vehicle would provide him no cover once he rose. He would have to shoot and keep shooting, relying on surprise to buy him the seconds he needed.

At last the machine-gun fire ceased. Kimberlain rose into a crouch. He was pressed too close against the Pathfinder's shell to see any of the gunmen, but he had glimpsed all three sets of their legs from underneath the truck. He held his ground as one of the gunmen approached slowly from the driver's side. The Ferryman waited until the approaching gunman had reached the remains of the door, waited until all his attention was focused on peering in to check for the victim's body. Then Kimberlain sprang, rising up over the crushed form of the vehicle. He shot the man at the Pathfinder's rear first and was rotating the barrel fast around even as the man's head snapped backward. His next three shells slammed into the gunman at the front. By this point the closest of the assailants had lurched back from his inspection of the demolished cab, finger on the trigger. The instinctive maneuver actually placed him square in the Ferryman's sights. Kimberlain fired twice, both head shots, and the man crumpled with his face reduced to pulp.

Kimberlain's breathing steadied. He hesitated briefly and then emerged from behind the Pathfinder's remains to inspect his handiwork. The muted sound of a shoe heel grazing the asphalt reached him. He was airborne in the next instant, his body vacating the area where a hail of automatic bullets rained down.

There had been a fourth gunman!

Machine-gun bullets traced him and coughed shards of asphalt into the air. He tried to right himself to get off at least a token shot, but another flurry of bullets from the gunman ricocheted off the Pathfinder's carcass. One of them clamored against his Sig Sauer and sent it flying. He flailed for it briefly before another barrage forced him into a second dive.

He found himself against the chain link fence now with only one place left to go. The pause in gunfire told him the yet unseen gunman was changing clips. Kimberlain hurled himself over the fence and onto the brief bit of hard ground that rimmed the shell-like dormitory building. He took cover behind the site's construction trailer. Before him was an unfinished doorway that lacked even a threshold of steps. His mind calculated his options and found only one.

Bullets chewing the air around him, the Ferryman lurched into the unfinished building.

Inside, he pressed himself against a wall and waited, in case the last gunman elected to follow him through. The wail of sirens was in his ears now. Perhaps the prospect of arriving authorities had led his final assailant to flee, but Kimberlain didn't think so. More likely he had entered the cavernous, dimly lit building through another doorway and was stalking the Ferryman now.

With that in mind, Kimberlain began to move. His pursuer had no reason to rush. He knew the Ferryman was weapon-less, that the only thing working against him—both of them, in many respects—was the promised arrival of the police. But Kimberlain had something else he could turn in his fa-vor:

The unfinished dorm building itself.

The first floor, and all those above, he imagined, were com-prised of large room suites; a series of bedrooms around a larger living area. Many had walls or parts of walls missing, in effect creating a labyrinth. The ceiling was present in parts, missing in others. There looked to be five or six floors in all. Kimberlain was able to see up through all of them at some openings in the corridor.

Sawdust and what might have been the remnants of fiber-glass insulation stuck to his eyes and then threatened his nose. The Ferryman covered his mouth and kept moving. An unfin-ished staircase rose before him, and Kimberlain took it, careful with his steps. The stairs angled to the left and then lifted straight again. He glided toward the second floor.

The sounds of screeching tires and slamming doors reached him from below. He heard garbled reports over radio sets and walkie-talkies coming toward the site, footsteps crunching over rock and gravel.

Don't come in here! he wanted to yell out to the approaching policemen. *Don't come in!*

Kimberlain leaned over, very close to verbalizing his warn-ing.

A hail of silenced bullets coughed splinters from the wood around him, fired from the *basement* of all places. His pursuer had found a route down into it and had been trailing him, shadowing him, this whole time, from below. The Ferryman spun onto the next set of stairs and climbed faster, legs churn-ing as if to kick the bullets from their path.

"Help me! Please help me!"

The shout echoed up from below; the gunman wanted to draw the police inside.

"I'm on the first floor. . . . *Please hurry!*"

"We're coming in!" one of the policemen shouted as more continued to arrive.

"No!" Kimberlain screamed down, but it was too late.

Automatic fire echoed from three floors down. Screams of pain and death followed instantly. The ill-prepared policemen had been dropped in their tracks. No more would follow for a while now. The killer had what he wanted.

Kimberlain scrambled up to the fifth floor and stopped inside an open space the size of four unfinished rooms. Huge table and band saws rested atop massive piles of sawdust, the residue of the most recently completed work. Too bad they were too bulky to hoist and use as weapons.

That thought gave him a idea. He dragged a table saw closer to the doorway he had passed through and covered the blade with handfuls of sawdust. Next he made sure the plug was out and flipped the power switch to ON. Then he scampered to the electrical outlet the plug rested by and had just reached it when the footsteps of his adversary could be heard down what would eventually be a corridor.

Kimberlain glimpsed the figure passing into the darkness, the meager light in the hallway just a memory. He continued to glide forward warily, machine gun sweeping before him. His steps made a swishing sound as they grazed over the construction debris layering the floor. Kimberlain counted the seconds until he would cross through the doorway near the table saw.

The killer had drawn up even with the saw when the Ferryman jammed the plug back into the socket. The table saw spun with a grinding wail, coughing the sawdust away from it in waves that crested in all directions. The gunman maintained the presence of mind to bring only one hand up to his ravaged eyes, while the second stayed on the machine gun. But Kimberlain was in motion by then.

The gunman saw him at last and brought the gun round. Kimberlain locked a hand on its stock and forced it down. The clip drained into the floor, as his other fist slammed into the man's jaw. The Ferryman felt the teeth give and jaw retract. The man gasped and uttered a scream inaudible beneath the constant raging of the saw.

The gunman gave up on the machine gun and whirled in against Kimberlain. The two were equal in size and, as Kimberlain discovered, in strength, too. Locked against each other, they twisted across the floor in a bizarre pirouette. Kimberlain continued to pound the assailant's face, but had his ribs thrashed in return. He felt his feet teeter on the edge of a rectangular cutout in the floor where someday a stairway would descend. In the haze of semidarkness, the assailant tried to thrust him over the side, but Kimberlain twisted and slammed the man backward into the nearest wall.

The entire structure seemed to quiver. The assailant took the full brunt of the impact and spun away from the wall, the Ferryman's control over him gone. Kimberlain turned from one blow, but a second pounded his kidney and a third buckled his knee.

The pain sent electric shocks through him. Kimberlain righted his balance and kicked out with his legs, but another blow hammered the rear of his head. Then he was being slammed forward, directed toward another wall, he thought, until he saw the still-churning table saw.

His hands grasped the table and held just before his face met steel. His nose flirted with the spinning saw, oil and more remnants of the sawdust spitting up into his eyes. The assailant shoved onward, sensing the kill now. It took all the strength the Ferryman could muster just to hold his ground, and this left his position virtually indefensible. He couldn't maintain the stalemate for much longer. A precarious shift in position was his only hope.

Kimberlain spun his entire body around in a sudden motion. Face to face with his assailant now, his arms jammed into the man's shoulders. The man shoved hard, and the back of the Ferryman's head flirted with the spinning blade. Dead eyes glared at him, hands struggling to summon enough strength to force him the rest of way down.

Kimberlain jabbed his right arm into the assailant's windpipe, found his Adam's apple, and squeezed. The man gave ground backward, which allowed Kimberlain to sweep his left hand toward the saw's on-off switch.

Click.

The assailant's savage, enraged thrust wedged Kimberlain against the blade just as it spun to a halt. The Ferryman twisted his Adam's apple some more.

The man wailed and hoisted Kimberlain upright. The Ferryman went with the motion. The assailant probably thought he had him, right up until Kimberlain's hands locked onto him, grabbing hold of his lapels with both hands as the momentum brought him forward. Still holding fast, Kimberlain ducked down and jammed his own shoulders against the plywood floor with a foot wedged in the man's midsection. The assailant could do nothing to thwart the maneuver, and he was pitched airborne. He twisted to brace for the fall and then realized too late that he was heading for the empty hole where the stairwell was to be. His arms flailed desperately for something to grab but came up empty. His scream split the night, ending with a thud six floors below.

With the screech of more police sirens drawing ever closer, Kimberlain slid toward a rear exit and escape.

He called Talley's number from a pay phone in a café a half mile south at the corner of Brook and Wickenden streets.

"Problems, Lauren," he said as soon as she came on.

"Are you still in Providence?"

"At Brown, more or less."

"Leeds?"

"Not exactly." Kimberlain detailed in rapid fashion what had happened.

Lauren Talley accepted it all calmly. "I'll have agents from our Boston office there in an hour. They'll use discretion."

"Tell them not to bother."

"Can you get to the airport?"

"Soon as I grab a car."

"There's a plane leaving for Atlanta in thirty minutes. I'll have them hold it until you get there. Go right to the gate. Sorry I can't send the Lear.''

''I suppose you need it yourself.''

''I don't want you going to Georgia on your own.''

''I didn't know I was going at all.''

''We talked about it this morning.''

''I said later, Lauren.''

''And that's what it is now, Jared.''

CHAPTER 11

''**D**AISY, Georgia,'' Lauren Talley recited, reading from the yellow legal pad held on her knees. ''Population 115.''

''Mostly black,'' Kimberlain said from behind the wheel.

''Almost all. Sixteen white residents; thirteen of them comprised three of the town's nineteen families.''

Kimberlain gripped the wheel tighter. Talley had been waiting at the Savannah International Airport, where a private plane had taken him from Hartsdale. Her rental car was parked on the tarmac, ready for the half-hour drive to Daisy.

''Do you think that means anything?'' Talley asked him.

''The ratio in the other town was almost the opposite, but, no, I don't think race has anything to do with how he's selecting them.''

''You read the files.''

''Skimmed them.''

''They tell you anything I wasn't able to?''

''He likes what he does, Ms. Talley.''

"You can keep calling me Lauren, you know."

But Kimberlain's mind was otherwise engaged. "This has become a game for him, a challenge—maybe the ultimate challenge."

"How so?"

"Killing so many without being seen and leaving so little time in between his strikes. The others I've gone after, even Leeds and Peet, were tacticians, strategists. Every move they made had a method to it leading toward a definitive end, however repulsive. But Tiny Tim could be in this strictly for sport. Contemplation of the act and then reflection back on it isn't enough for him, like it is for the others I've dealt with. Either his appetite for killing is insatiable, or . . ."

"Or what?"

"Something about the way he's choosing the towns necessitates that he hit them with as brief an interlude as possible."

"Because he's afraid of being caught or wants to be caught?"

Kimberlain eyed her tensely. "That's the behavioral science profile, isn't it? Well, I don't think it fits in this case. No, if his targets aren't random, he's got a very logical rationale for not spacing out his strikes."

"And if they are random?"

"Then maybe he opens to a page in a road atlas of the nation. Maybe throws darts at a map. That'll make it impossible for us to break into his pattern."

"Meaning?"

"We'll have to catch him based on what he left behind."

Daisy came up suddenly in the night. One minute they were on the dark, country road, and the next they were on the main street of a town that would never wake up again. The Georgia Highway Patrol continued to leave a man stationed at both main entry routes twenty-four hours a day to discourage the morbidly curious and tourists with their autofocus 35-millimeter cameras. Lauren Talley flashed her ID, and they were passed through.

"Dixon Springs depended on seasonal skiing for its survival," she reminded Kimberlain. "But Daisy was a working town. The ones who weren't farmers drove maybe twenty, thirty miles to their jobs." They were proceeding down Main Street. "Some of the houses are pretty isolated. Nice view of the mountains and a lake during the day. He started with those."

Talley slowed the car to a crawl. On her right was a restaurant-bar called Belle's. A municipal building containing the post office, sheriff's substation, and bank lay directly across the street. There was a general store and livery. Between them stood a few small specialty shops that had catered more to outsiders and those passing through off the highway. There was a rooming house above what had been another restaurant. But Kimberlain could tell it had been boarded up even before Tiny Tim paid Daisy a visit.

A cool breeze greeted them when they stepped out of the car. Unseen shutters flapped in the night. Somewhere a stray door was creaking open and closed. The Ferryman moved toward the entrance to Belle's and stopped at the yellow DO NOT CROSS tape.

"How many?" he asked.

Talley consulted her legal pad, raising it close to her eyes to read the writing in the dark. "Five, including one bartender. The cook had already gone home. He doesn't live in Daisy. We don't know whether Tiny Tim killed them first or last be—"

"First," said Kimberlain.

"Why?"

"Because they were regulars and he knew they would be there, just as he knew they represented his greatest threat. The phones weren't dead, were they?"

Talley went back to her legal pad, flipping pages. "In Dixon Springs yes, but not here in Daisy. Too many underground cables, believe it or not."

"He knew that."

"Not terribly difficult to ascertain."

Kimberlain moved a little toward her, gazing down off the porch. "How'd he take the phones out in Dixon Springs?"

"Incoming wires off the line. Three. No," she added, correcting herself after finding the right page. "Four."

"He cut any here?"

"No."

"Not even the ones he could have."

"I don't see what—"

"His casing of these towns is more elaborate than you thought. He didn't bother with the wires in Daisy because he knew the underground cables serviced a good portion of the town. He doesn't like to waste effort."

"So he hit the bar first."

Kimberlain stepped down and walked past her. "And any other areas of congestion where people were still up."

"It was late, remember. There weren't many. In fact," she added after a rapid skim of some pages, "this was the only one."

"No."

"Excuse me?"

"People at home would have been watching television, reading, talking on the phone. Maybe they hear or see something, make a call that could put a crimp in Tiny Tim's plans."

Talley let the legal pad drop a little. "The randomness . . . we couldn't account for it. He gets to the town and he hits one house but doesn't come back for the others on either side of it for over an hour."

"He got the houses where people were awake first."

"How?"

"Let's take a walk, Lauren, and I'll show you."

It was like strolling through a nightmare version of Oz. Instead of following the yellow brick road, they followed the line of yellow DO NOT CROSS strip barriers. Some had already given in to the elements and flapped in the wind like party streamers. Talley found she was quite cold, even though Kimberlain had given her his jacket. Even so, the Ferryman looked hot. Sweat had spotted his shirt and soaked it over his midsection. They came to a house that had been among the first Tiny Tim had entered. It was two solid-looking stories. Dull green in need of a paint job, with a walkout basement.

"Parents and two teenage children. Mother was a teacher at the school in Harnell where kids from Daisy are bused. Father owned a filling station on the highway," Lauren Talley read from her pad. "All awake at the time of entry. Three silenced bullets for each. None of them struggled. Blinds were drawn. We don't think he could have seen much from outside."

"Sight had nothing to with it."

"You said he knew they were awake when he made his pass by."

"Not because of what he saw; it was what he heard."

Talley was looking at him very closely now. She followed him around to the side of the house and a window well off the ground.

"You find any of his boot imprints here?" he asked her.

She had to check the legal pad and looked surprised at what she found. "Yes. Just about where you're standing. But he couldn't have heard enough to—"

"Not with the naked ear. He had help." Kimberlain stretched his hand toward the window. "Brought a listening device with him. Attach it to the window with a suction cup and it would be like he was in the same room as anyone talking."

"Suction cup," repeated Talley, realizing. "He might have licked it."

"Almost surely. It's been how long now?"

"Three days."

"Traces?"

"Maybe still present. He couldn't have wiped all the secretions off the glass. I guess it depends on how much moisture's been in the air since. I'll have the lab here by morning to find out." She paused. "How could we miss this?"

"Watch," Kimberlain told her. He stretched to the tips of his toes and still could barely touch the glass of the window. "I'm almost six-two. Whoever used that suction cup has to be at least six, probably closer to eight inches taller."

Talley pictured it in her mind and shuddered. "We knew he was big, but . . ."

"Can you type his blood from what's left on the glass?"

"At the very least, if there's anything still there."

"Blood type, size, military background somewhere, knowledge of sophisticated electronics."

"Don't need a lot of knowledge to wedge home a suction cup."

"You do to build one yourself."

"You think that's what he did?"

"Tiny Tim wouldn't have used it otherwise. Too easy to track down suppliers, follow a trail. I'd imagine he'd love to have you wasting your time following it up anyway."

"You haven't said anything about his malformed foot."

"Because it won't help you find him. Forget about it being congenital."

"Why?"

"No branch of the service would have taken anyone with such a defect, especially the kind of people that trained this boy. It happened postentry."

"In the field?"

"Could be. But you've checked the records and found nothing of the kind, right?"

"The search is ongoing."

Kimberlain was looking at the ground now, trying to imagine Tiny Tim doing the same thing three nights back. "He doesn't walk with a limp, does he?"

Talley gazed at him in amazement. "Lab people can find no evidence that he does but feel, given his handicap, he must."

The Ferryman shook his head. "He doesn't. He might have once, but he doesn't anymore. Having a limp is weak, and this boy would never accept weakness of any kind. For him strength is crucial because strength means power, and power—well, power is everything to him."

Kimberlain looked up. The window held not the slightest reflection in the night.

"He shot the ones who could still threaten him, who were awake," he went on. "Used gas on most of the ones who were sleeping."

"But he always entered the house."

"Man like this would need to watch his victims die one way or another."

"And he used a knife," Talley reminded. "A few times, anyway. One in particular." She flipped madly through the pages and then went back when she realized she had passed the one she wanted. "Family on the other side of town. He mutilated them."

"On his first pass."

"No. He got to them near the end."

"Doesn't figure," Kimberlain told her. "Something like that he'd do early to a family he came in on while they were awake. You're saying there were no other mutilations?"

"None."

"What about Dixon Springs?"

"No, but . . ."

"But what?"

"He burned some of the houses. We thought it was to attract attention to what he had done. Maybe it wasn't."

"Have your lab people head back up there with the best equipment they've got. Tell them to focus on the remains found in the burned houses. Tell them to look for evidence of mutilation on one of the families."

"You think that might be a pattern?"

"It might be too late in Dixon Springs to find out, and even if it isn't I don't know what it means. All I know is it may be something."

"More than we had when we got here."

"There may be more. Let's keep going."

Two hours more of reconstructing the last night in the life of Daisy, Georgia yielded no further clues. Talley had been to the town on several prior occasions, but never at night. Worse, as their tour lingered it seemed Kimberlain was drifting further and further away. A few times she gazed over and imagined it was Tiny Tim himself she was seeing. Their return to the car came none too soon for her.

The mobile phone started ringing even before she turned the key.

"It's for you," she said, handing it to Kimberlain.

"Hello, Captain," he said, since Captain Seven was the only person he had told how to contact him.

"Where the fuck you been, boss? Been trying you for hours."

"Looking for ghosts."

"Find any?"

"Don't know yet."

"I did, and eighty-four of them had plenty to say."

"The Locks?"

"Get your ass up here, Ferryman. I got this son of a bitch licked."

THE THIRD DOMINION

Renaissance

Sunday, August 16; 1:00 A.M.

CHAPTER 12

"Is it you, Hedda? Is it truly you?"

Hedda accepted the hug of the diminutive man who might now be the only one who could help her.

"Ah, excuse my manners. Come in out of the rain. You're soaked."

Hedda stepped into the restaurant, and its tiny owner Jacques, half-Vietnamese and half-French, slammed the door behind her. She cringed at the sound.

"You're on edge. And you're starving."

"I can't stay."

"Nonsense. Jacques can tell you are famished. I have stew, venison, chicken, all fresh. Please, it will take me only a minute to prepare a splendid meal for you."

"I—"

"I'll have no more of this protesting. Sit. Warm yourself, while I prepare your meal."

With the boy safely back in his father's hands, Hedda was free to chart her own course. Her own people, The Caretakers, were part of something that had called for her death. Her only chance for survival lay in tracing down what they were up to and how Lyle Hanley's TD-13 toxin was part of it. Her lone hope in this regard was to find Deerslayer. After all, he had been the one who kidnapped Christopher. He would have to know something, and that was more than she knew.

99

She reached Paris without incident and drove directly to Le Jardin D'Amber. Located just outside the wall of the palace at Versailles, Jacques's small restaurant catered almost exclusively to "soldiering" types as he put it. The building's facade was stucco, with more than one missing chunk attributed to German shrapnel in World War II. The interior was only about fifteen by thirty feet, allowing Jacques, who doubled as the cook, the freedom to roam about his seven tables greeting most of his patrons by name.

He had been making his rounds when Hedda arrived early Sunday morning. She found that, as always, most of the tables were occupied, at this hour by drinkers rather than diners. The inevitable stares cast her way were now receding, the men returning to their glasses or cards secure in the knowledge she was one of them.

Jacques emerged from the kitchen with tray in hand. He set it down on a stand and placed a thick bowl of soup in front of her.

"I need to speak with Deerslayer," Hedda said softly, as he leaned over her to put a basket of bread on the table.

"I saw him just the other day."

"Then he's in the city?"

"As far as I know." Jacques wiped his hands on his apron. "Trouble?"

"Bad trouble."

"How can I help?"

"Make sure no one finds out I was here."

"Of course."

"And tell me where I can find Deerslayer."

Deerslayer's latest residence was located on a dingy back street called *Rue du Chat qui Pêche* on the Left Bank in Paris's Latin Quarter. Hedda slid past block after block of the decrepit buildings, wondering why on earth Deerslayer had chosen such a place to base himself. She could hear babies crying through the open windows, screams and shouts, too. Kids roamed about in packs even at the late hour. A few regarded her briefly, then shied away as if jolted by an electrified fence.

Deerslayer lived on the fifth floor of an apartment building with no lights outside it or within the entrance way. Where a lock had been there was only a hole. The inner door's window was missing. Hedda held it so it would not squeal upon closing and began her way up the dark and dingy steps. Light from a single bulb spiraled down from the fourth floor, barely enough for even her well-trained eyes to see by. She found Deerslayer's door and froze; the latch had been shattered. Shards of thin wood hung from the useless door. Hedda eased it open with a hand pressed against its ruined frame.

She stepped through the doorway and pushed the door shut behind her. The room's only illumination came from the sputtering beams of a neon light across the street sliding through the half-drawn blinds. The room was a shambles. Furniture had been tipped over and shattered. Pools of drying blood soaked the floor, and splashes of it decorated the walls. Hedda leaned over and touched the blood. Barely an hour or two old by the feel of it. She moved on.

The room was a perfect square, unpainted and poorly furnished. The acrid stench of spilled blood became stronger in her nostrils. The blood was thickest in a splotchy line across the floor toward the rear wall, where a single inner door led into a bathroom. That door was open just a crack. She found the knob and pulled it toward her. The invading rays of the neon sign reached inside the bathroom.

Deerslayer was lying on the floor, right hand clinging to the soiled toilet bowl in a death grip. The volume of his wounds was incredible. Drying blotches of blood painted his midsection. A portion of his throat was torn, and the arm still by his side had been shattered.

Hedda backed out from the bathroom and inspected the room more carefully, seeing it all happen in her mind. There had been between four and six attackers. They'd crashed through the door and come in firing. Taken by surprise, Deerslayer had still been able to make a fight of it. The trail of blood near the bed she identified as the first to be spilled. He must have lunged for a gun with the enemy's bullets slamming his midsection. One had caught his neck and sprayed scarlet across the bedspread. Deerslayer would have emptied a clip, and now Hedda's attention turned to the ink-blotch patterns against the front wall. He'd killed two and probably wounded another, lunged into the rest with knife in hand when his bullets were gone. He'd been too weak to use it, though, and one of the killers had turned it on him, after a desperate struggle had left Deerslayer's arm shattered. That's where it had ended, and then for some reason the killers had dragged him into the bathroom.

Hedda realized her breathing had become thick and rapid. Deerslayer was a link to whatever The Caretakers were involved in, and he was dead. She was a link, and they had tried to kill her.

Her mind shifted in midthought. Time must have been of the essence here. The kill had gotten messy, and the surviving assassins would have wasted no time in fleeing with their wounded and their corpses.

Then why had they bothered dragging Deerslayer into the bathroom?

The answer struck her with a chill: they hadn't dragged him; he had dragged himself. He hadn't been dead when they left. He had crawled into the bathroom to, to . . .

To what?

Had he sensed Hedda was coming? Had he understood what happened to him and wanted to leave her some sort of warning? The cleanup crew would find it if left in plain sight, the floor or wall for instance. But where in the bathroom could he have—

Hedda returned swiftly to the bathroom and looked down at Deerslayer's corpse, strong and ominous even in death. His hand was cocked near the cracked porcelain of the toilet bowl.

Hedda edged closer. She looked down at the back of the tank. Nothing. She checked the toilet seat. Also nothing. Then she leaned over and inspected the back of the toilet bowl itself. There was blood there, long etches of it in symmetrical designs. No, not just designs—letters, numbers, a message!

Hedda had to get down on her back to read it. She eased Deerslayer slightly away. His upright hand slipped from its perch and touched her cheek. Hedda tried to read the message, couldn't in the dark, and so chanced turning on the single dangling bathroom bulb.

Deerslayer had penned the message with a trembling hand.

17 Rue Plummet—6A

An address and apartment number. Deerslayer was sending her there for answers, for help, for vengeance perhaps. Whoever lived at the address would know something.

Thump . . .

A sound in the corridor, on the stairwell perhaps. There was nothing else to hear. Then suddenly heavy, staggering footsteps and raucous laughter. Drunks were stumbling home.

No!

If they were drunks, she would have heard them earlier from the floors below. The men approaching had slipped into this guise after one of them had tripped and made the noise that alerted her.

Laughter echoed through the hall beyond Deerslayer's apartment.

Hedda quickly smudged the blood-scrawled message and bounded to her feet. They knew she was here; they had probably been waiting for her. She charged into the living room toward the window that opened onto the fire escape. It came up with a squeak and Hedda slid through it.

Four floors lay beneath her. The steel supports were rusted and wobbly. She began to descend, holding fast to the rail with one hand, pistol in the other.

Pffffft . . . pffffft . . . pffffft . . .

The silenced gunshots from below clanged off the steel around her. Hedda managed two rounds in their direction as she ducked low and turned her eyes upward. Through the still-open window in Deerslayer's apartment, she heard the door crash open. The men posing as drunks would be charging for the window even now. She was boxed in.

More gunshots, from below. Shapes darted down in the street. Now she couldn't go up or down, which left only sideways. The apartments neighboring Deerslayer's were accessible by a second decaying fire escape.

Glass shattered above her. One of the drunks plunged onto the fire escape platform, machine gun in hand. Hedda shot him and spun round. Five stories beneath her a pair of gunmen had moved into the open. She dropped them with four bullets, which left her seven in this clip. Enough. The moment was hers, and she seized it.

Hedda fired off five more shots at the shattered window to cover her rush to the rickety fire escape rail. It nearly gave under her weight but held long enough for her to leap outward and grab hold of the neighboring rail. With bullets already tracing her again, Hedda transferred the momentum of her leap into a swing. She kicked out toward a window just beneath her to the right. The glass shattered easily on impact, and she crashed through it into an apartment over and down from Deerslayer's.

The glass had pricked and scratched her arms and face, but she had managed somehow to hold on to the pistol. She burst into the corridor with a fresh clip jammed home and started for the stairs.

Hedda slowed. The stairwell was a death trap. The enemy owned it. She could make this floor the battleground, but eventually the opposition would wear her down. No, it had to be escape, but how? *How?*

Built into the corridor wall on her right was a waist-level door that opened from the top. This building must have once been a hotel, complete with laundry chutes on every floor. Of course! Why Deerslayer had chosen to base himself here was suddenly clear to her. The chute would drop into the basement, and from the basement—

Hedda had yanked down the hinged latch just as doors burst open on either side of the hall. In the next instant, she had squeezed herself through the narrow opening and was sliding downward for the basement. At first she managed to slow her descent with hands and feet pressed against the wall, but the last two floors came at a breakneck clip. Impact took her breath away.

Hedda rolled onto her stomach and made it up to her knees. The basement's blackness was broken only by what little street lighting penetrated the painted-over windows. She began to crawl across the floor with her hands in front of her.

Where was it? It had to be here, had to be!

Near the far wall, her hand scraped against a latch on the basement floor. She knew it! Knowing he was in trouble, Deerslayer would have chosen this building only if it possessed an entrance to the tunnels used by the French Resistance in World War II. It was the way Caretakers were trained to think. Hedda grasped the latch with both hands and began to lift. The hidden door started to give, then held. Hedda let go and tried again. She was running out of time; it would be only seconds more before her pursuers located the basement door and charged down.

Hedda yanked harder this time, and the hidden door broke free. The stink of must, mold, and rot flooded her nostrils. Before her was a ladder, and next to it a flashlight Deerslayer had fastened into place. She had grasped the flashlight when footsteps pounded down the basement steps. Hedda lowered herself onto the third rung and was reaching up to close the hidden door when the rung broke under her weight. She plummeted a dozen feet and slammed her head hard against the ladder's base. The flashlight slipped from her grip. Its glass cracked and it rolled sideways, casting a spiderweb pattern of light about the cavern. The pistol was gone, too. Above her, shapes were already beginning to appear around the open doorway. Hedda grabbed the flashlight and staggered off.

The tunnels of the French Resistance were a combination of long-abandoned sewer lines and channels linking them together. Some were actually open for public tours, but others, like this, had been forgotten and untraveled for decades. Accordingly, the stench was revolting.

Behind her brighter flashlights pierced the darkness. The sound of footsteps sloshing through wet muck mixed with the clacking of expensive shoes against the still-hard surface of the tunnel. Weaponless, Hedda could never hope to defeat all of them. Nor could this labyrinth of tunnels and channels protect her forever. In trying to lose her pursuers, in fact, she might very well become lost herself.

For now she had no choice but to keep moving. Afraid the flashlight would give her away, Hedda switched it off and felt her way along the wall. A hiding place perhaps. If she could find a hiding place—

The floor in front of her suddenly dropped off, and Hedda fell into a roll. The drop leveled off, and she found herself in what seemed to be a cavernous pool with a stink that nearly choked her. The air was thick with stray sewer gases that must have been collecting here for years. Exposure for more than a few minutes could result in fatal poisoning. A methane explosion was also a very real possibility.

Hedda stopped in her tracks. An explosion! Of course! She began moving faster through the cavern, counting the seconds it took to reach the other side. She reached the upward slope and scaled it just as the sounds of some of her pursuers echoed through the cavern. Hedda squeezed herself against a wall and tore the lower portion of her shirt off. She turned the flashlight back on and pressed the cloth against the exposed bulb. Her fingers were singed through the material almost instantly. When the cloth began to smoke, she laid the flashlight down on the cavern's slope and backed off, after making sure the cloth was tight against the bulb.

She saw a small flicker of flame before she turned and ran. There was nothing but darkness before her, and she moved with her side scraping against the wall for guidance, rounding corners until she came to a large alcove.

She had barely ducked into the alcove and pressed herself against the inside wall when the explosion sounded. It was deafening. The wall she was lodged against began to crumble, and she turned away in time to see a massive bluish-orange flare shooting down the path she had taken from the cavern.

Hedda felt the incredible surge of heat and thought she was melting. The bright flash poured toward her, and she threw up an arm as if to block it. Then a pool of darkness swept over her, and Hedda plunged into it.

CHAPTER 13

THEY found Captain Seven sitting atop the main control board outside the entrance to The Locks' maximum-security wing.

"Nice of you to show up, Ferryman."

"Get off that!" Dr. Alan Vogelhut ordered.

Captain Seven eased himself down, careful to skirt the various knobs and switches. His sandals clacked against the floor.

"Take it easy, Vogey. Chill out."

Vogelhut swung toward Kimberlain. "I want this man out of here! As soon as he explains whatever it is he's discovered, I want him out of here!"

"Glad to go now, Vogey," Seven said to him, reaching back to the control board for his bong. "Just let me grab one toke for the road. . . ."

Captain Seven lowered his lips to the bong's top and sucked down into its water-filled chambers. Instantly the bubbling water produced a misty smoke that vanished quickly into his mouth. He held his breath until his features began to redden, then exhaled.

"Ahhhhhhhhh," he said with a smile.

"Jesus Christ," Vogelhut said.

"Just trying to collect my thoughts, Vogey. You should try it someday. Anytime you want a hit, just—"

"Get to the point, goddamn it!"

Captain Seven shuffled forward. The bottoms of his faded bell-bottom jeans scraped at the floor. He was wearing a tie-dyed shirt and had captured his wild hair in a ponytail.

"Better make that two hits," he said with a wink to Kimberlain. "I'm starting to like it here, Ferryman. Might think about renting one of their many vacant rooms."

"I'm not going to stand here and listen to all this," Vogelhut shot out.

He had started back down the corridor when Captain Seven hit a switch that activated all twelve of the television monitors on the wall before him. The glare bathed the corridor in dull light as the pictures came to life. Vogelhut stopped and turned around.

"Look familiar?" Captain Seven wanted to know.

Displayed on the screens were various shots of the prisoners who had escaped from The Locks still in their cells, seen as they had been that last night just prior to the blackout. Vogelhut drew closer and scanned them quickly.

"We make tapes," he said. "Standard procedure."

"And this is a recording of the night in question?"

"Right."

"Wrong, Vogey."

"What do you mean?"

"Leeds and the others were long gone before the power went south. Thing was, your boys didn't know it."

"Let's start at the beginning," Seven said over Vogelhut's insistent protests. "What time were your animals fed that evening?"

"According to the logs, between six and six-thirty."

"And the blackout occurred at . . ."

"Eleven-thirty, give or take a few minutes."

"So that gave our boys a roughly five-hour time frame in which to disappear."

"But I saw them," Vogelhut argued. "I saw them in their cells when I got back."

"You saw them in their cells, Vogey, but they weren't there. You told me your standard procedure is to make tapes.

Twelve cameras means twelve tracks. Pretty complicated stuff.''

"It's a complicated system. Most technologically advanced in existence.''

"Not quite. NASA's version has a few yards on yours and so does mine. You coulda done better. Too bad you didn't.''

"Why?''

"Because it gave Leeds and the others their way out,'' Captain Seven continued. "See, there's a recording device about four times the size of a normal VCR built into the guts of your circuit panel. Tapes are about three times the size. You want to check the animals the next day, you tell the computer which cell you want to peek into and that's the view comes up on your screen.''

"I know that,'' said Vogelhut. "It was designed to my specifications.''

"Bad specs.''

"What?''

"Flaws. Weaknesses.''

"This is crazy!''

"No,'' Seven said, tapping the main control board, "this is shit. Seventh grader could have put a better one together for his science fair, you ask me. Jesus Christ, you really don't get it, do you?'' the captain continued. The three men were bathed in the haze of the dozen television screens that flickered around them. "Somebody dipped into your system, Vogey. Somebody did some rewiring that turned your monitor recording equipment into a player.''

Kimberlain followed Seven's finger to the main control panel, which looked like that of a sophisticated VCR. The MONITOR/RECORD button was engaged, not the PLAY button. "Then what we're seeing now . . .''

"Is exactly what the guards and Vogey were seeing four nights back. 'Cept it was no more real then than it is now.''

"No,'' Vogelhut gasped, as if he'd had the wind knocked out of him. "The system checked out. Nothing like what you're describing was found.''

"Because it was switched back after the fact, well after possibly, since your check wasn't conducted till nearly a day following the escape." Seven pushed POWER and the screens went dark. "I switched it back for purposes of this demon-fucking-stration. Piece of cake really. Like changing a light-bulb. This tape came from probably a week ago, long enough for your monitoring people not to remember anything that might stand out and make them think twice about what they were seeing. Perps could even have spliced a number of nights' tapes together."

"Then we're looking at an inside job," Kimberlain concluded.

"For more reasons than one, Ferryman."

"When did they get out?" Vogelhut asked, turning suddenly from the darkened screens. "*How* did they get out?"

"Funny you should ask." Captain Seven smiled. "Let's work backward." He propped himself up on the control board again, this time with no protest from Vogelhut.

"With the blackout and systems failure," Kimberlain suggested.

"Which occurred at precisely eleven twenty-nine according to the log. Tells us much of what we need to know."

"How?" Vogelhut asked.

Seven grasped his bong and drew a deep hit of smoke into his lungs. "It's like this, Vogey. The twelve-track tape your system takes can only run three hours per cassette. So when the tape hit the end and the screens went goofy, even your simple-minded monitors might figure what was up." He drained the bit of smoke remaining in the blue plastic bong's main chamber. "Unless, of course, that moment happened to coincide with a total electrical and backup systems failure."

"Lights come back on and everybody's got other problems on their minds," Kimberlain concluded. "Empty cells, for example."

Vogelhut paced nervously. "So you're saying they escaped between eight twenty-nine and . . . when?"

"Well, Vogey, got to give your boys some credit for sealing the island as quick as they did when the power came back. So we got to figure Leeds and his boys were long gone by then. By my figuring that means they were out of their cells by ten forty-five at the latest. Could have been as early as nine.''

"That still doesn't explain how.''

"Yeah. The best is yet to come.''

They were inside the MAX-SEC cell block, Captain Seven pointing up at one of the surveillance cameras.

"Remember now, boys, those babies weren't broadcasting anything, and security precautions dictate no guards active on the halls. So Leeds and the others had free reign of the corridors inside MAX-SEC.''

"Only if they could get out into them,'' Vogelhut reminded.

"Nice system. Allows you to open any individual cell, an entire floor, or all floors at once. Dinner gets distributed one floor at a time between six and six-thirty. Meals passed through slots in the door,'' Seven said, fingering one of them. "Christ, like a drive-through window. I'll take a quarter pounder and two large fries!'' Seven shouted into the slot.

"Where is this going?''

"Slots have locks on 'em like the doors. Single switch controls each floor from MAX-SEC central station.''

"So?''

"So, Vogey, the relocking mechanism on the meal slots was jimmy-wired into the unlocking mechanism on the doors. Soon as dinner was over, every door in MAX-SEC was open to the world and none of your boys would be any the wiser to who was stepping out.''

"Which gets them into the corridor,'' concluded Kimberlain. "Then what, Captain?''

Seven pointed a thin arm back in the direction of the trio of main entry doors. "I think we can safely rule that way out. I mean, Vogey, even your boys probably would have noticed eighty-four loonies walking right by them. That leaves us with the door at the other end of the staircase on each of MAX-SEC's four levels.''

"Solid twelve-inch steel with cobalt-reinforced seals on both sides,'' Vogelhut said. "Has to be opened manually from the other side of the corridor. The inner stairwell, which provides the only link to the levels of MAX-SEC, is accessible only from above, and that door is guarded by two men all the time. Leeds and the rest of them never passed by them either, which, according to you, means they never got out of MAX-SEC.''

"According to *me*?" Captain Seven looked to Kimberlain. "Did I say that, Ferryman?" He resumed before Kimberlain could respond. "Boy oh boy, Vogey, I'd say you were putting words in my mouth, but I'm not sure you could find it."

"Just tell me how they did it!"

Captain Seven led the way down the corridor and up the four flights of stairs, speaking as he walked. "Thing you gotta understand, Vogey, is that this whole escape was planned on the outside, not the in."

"By Leeds's people?"

"By Leeds *himself*."

"I . . . don't understand."

But Kimberlain was starting to comprehend, and it showed in the taut expression on his face.

They had reached the top of the stairwell, one floor above the uppermost level of MAX-SEC. Around them the walls were solid concrete. Before them was a white-steel security door that looked like it could weather a nuclear explosion. Captain Seven's eyes gazed up at the ceiling.

"Give me a boost, will you, Ferryman?"

Kimberlain propped the captain on his shoulders. Seven's hands played about the ceiling.

"Haven't checked this out myself yet," he said down to them. "Figured it'd be more fun to find it together. . . . Yup, here we go."

Seven pushed up hard and a square section of the eight-inch-thick ceiling seemed to disappear. Above him, in the crawl space running between floors, only darkness was visible.

"Voilà," the captain said, as Kimberlain lowered him back down. "Private elevator serving MAX-SEC was closed for repairs that evening, right, Vogey?"

"Yes."

"But nothing was really wrong with it. According to the

plans you furnished me, I'd say Leeds and the others used this crawl space to reach that elevator shaft. Then your former inhabitants simply rode down a few at a time and left the building into the storm. Once outside they met up in a predetermined spot."

"The guards would have seen them, I tell you!"

"Not if they slid around and used a few of the side entrances in the less-secure wings. And in that storm who could have seen anything once they were outside? We're talking about eighty-four men escaping over roughly a two-hour period. Plenty of time to be patient, Vogey."

"They still had to get off the island," Vogelhut reminded.

"We're coming to that."

The sun had burned through the clouds by the time the three of them reached the rocks forming the jagged shoreline of Bowman Island. They walked in the cold wind for forty minutes on the side of the island facing away from Watertown on Lake Ontario, before Captain Seven's constantly sweeping eyes stopped.

"Here," was all he said.

Kimberlain crouched low enough to feel the salt water spray on his face and reached his hand into a small pool between a pair of rocks.

"Is it there?" Seven wanted to know.

Kimberlain was about to say no when his hand grazed against something thick and circular. He found two others before standing up.

"How many?" the captain asked.

"Three," the Ferryman replied.

"Three what?" Vogelhut demanded.

"You'll find five or six others all about this area."

"Other *what*?" Vogelhut demanded again.

"Steel spikes," Kimberlain replied. "Driven into these boulders so rafts could be tied down to them."

"Rafts?" Vogelhut asked uncomprehendingly.

"Ten or so men in each one," Seven elaborated as he gazed

at the blank expanse of sea. "A tight squeeze, but they didn't have far to go."

"Leeds and the others got off the island in *rafts*? I don't believe it. It's impossible. They would have still been at sea after eleven-thirty when we threw a dragnet over the area. We would have found them."

"By that time they'd already been picked up."

"No aircraft could have done the job in that storm, no helicopter either."

Seven had come close enough to the edge of the rock for the water to lap up over his sandaled feet. "Not an airplane or helicopter, Vogey, a submarine."

"*A sub—*"

"Another tight squeeze, but again, they wouldn't have far to go." The captain spoke into the wind, his words blown backward from his two companions. He turned to face them. "It's worse than I thought."

"Submarines, rafts, electronic bypasses, elaborate plans to this whole complex." Vogelhut shook his head in frustration. "Even Leeds couldn't have planned all this after he was put away."

"No," Kimberlain told him, "he planned it before he ever got here."

He looked to Captain Seven, who nodded in affirmation while Vogelhut continued to speak, obviously confused.

"That's, that's just not possible."

"I caught him because he let me, Doctor, because he wanted me to, because he knew he'd be sent . . ." Kimberlain turned back to the fortresslike structure of The Locks. ". . . here."

"So he could *escape*?"

"With the others. From the inside. It was the only way."

"Toward what end? What purpose?"

Kimberlain looked at Vogelhut. "I don't know, Doctor." But he did, sure now of what he had only suspected before. The ninth dominion . . .

For Andrew Harrison Leeds it wasn't just a mad vision; at least, it wasn't anymore.

* * *

Kimberlain had the captain transfer all the available videotapes of Leeds in his cell onto one master for viewing. This tape ran forty-five minutes, and the Ferryman was watching it for the fourth time. There was no sound to accompany the picture, but his mind added it by the third showing. A scratching sound when Leeds rubbed his head. A slight squeaking as he shifted on his bed frame. A deep hiss every time he glared into the camera, his teeth bared in a wolfish snarl.

Leeds was not a big man in any respect, but Kimberlain had to remind himself of that as the tape unwound before him. It was as though the madman were reaching outside the camera to make the viewer see what he wanted him to see. Or, perhaps, the viewer was influenced by the scope of Leeds's intentions, the breadth of his evil. If size were measured in deeds and ambitions, no cell at The Locks would have been large enough to hold him.

The black-and-white tape suited Leeds's pale and colorless features. His hair was jet black and slicked straight back over his head. His eyebrows were thick and speckled with white. His face was gaunt, almost skeletal, with eyes that were sunken, a corpse's eyes. They looked black, too, but Kimberlain knew they were actually dark brown. Leeds was wearing the standard-issue white Locks outfit. He had rolled up the sleeves of the shirt to reveal a pair of sinewy forearms and long, gentle hands that looked baby soft.

In not a single frame did Andrew Harrison Leeds reveal himself to the camera. He was a showman, on stage constantly because he knew that at any time someone might be watching. The Ferryman watched, searching for an instant when Leeds's guard dropped and a glimpse of the true self could be caught. Kimberlain wanted and needed to understand him. But there was no moment when he gave up any truth to the camera. Leeds did not just employ a persona, he vanished into it. His various identities must have been, must *be,* like hotel rooms to a traveling salesman: he kept checking into the one that was most convenient.

"The phone, Mr. Kimberlain."

The voice of Vogelhut's receptionist made him shift in the

chair abruptly. Startled, the woman clutched for her mouth.

"I'm sorry. I didn't mean to . . . It's just that you have a call. I tried buzzing but—"

"Thank you," the Ferryman said, and picked up the phone as she took her leave.

"Kimberlain."

"Talley."

"And how are things in Daisy?"

"You were right," she told him. "Tiny Tim used a suction cup on the window. We've already typed his blood, and we're hoping the remaining secretions yield even more. I've also obtained a court order to exhume the burned remains of the victims from Dixon Springs to check for mutilation, just like you said."

"But that's not why you called."

"No."

"News from Providence, I trust."

"Washington IDed the corpse from the shoot-out as one Donald Dwares. Killed five school teachers in Miami and was sentenced to death."

"I'm losing you, Lauren."

"Then try this out: Donald Dwares, the man you killed last night, died in the Florida electric chair five years ago."

CHAPTER 14

IT was not until early Monday morning that Hedda at last reached the address Deerslayer had scrawled for her in his bloody bathroom. The explosion in the underground tunnels had knocked her unconscious for a time, and she woke up with one ear useless and the other ringing. But the alcove had provided enough cover to save her life, and after feeling her way through the darkness for a time, she found a route out into the basement of another building. She stole replacement clothes from a clothesline and bathed herself as best she could in a public fountain.

The apartment building at 17 Rue Plummet overlooked the Bois de Vincennes and proved a stark contrast to the one Deerslayer had died in the night before. It was a magnificent six-story brick building. She would need a subtle means of entry here; slip in only when the doorman was distracted.

Twenty minutes into her vigil a building resident arrived by cab with a half-dozen shopping bundles. The doorman hurried out to help, and Hedda simply walked through the door past his vacated post.

Not wanting to wait for the elevator, she moved for the stairs and took them quickly. Apartment 6A was located well down the hall, and she passed the other doors along it warily. None of them had peepholes. She reached 6A and rapped twice.

"Who's there?" a voice called out from within.

Hedda recited the woman's name from next door in the hushed, whispery tone of an older woman. The label on the door had been handwritten in an old-fashioned, spidery hand.

"One moment."

She heard something like wheels churning and then the locks were being undone. The door creaked open.

"Good morning, Mrs.—"

The wheelchaired speaker looked at her and his eyes bulged. Hedda gazed back transfixed.

"No," the old man in the wheelchair rasped. *"It's impossible! . . ."*

It was her grandfather!

"You're dead!" the raspy voice blared at her. *"You're dead!"*

A bony hand flailed out in an attempt to slam the door closed. Hedda easily pushed by it and entered the room; the wheelchair rolled backward across the rug. Hedda closed the door and relocked it.

"What are you doing here?" he gasped fearfully. "What do you want?"

Hedda's hand trembled as she moved it from the latch. Her mind swam in confusion. So often in the past, in stressful moments, she had sought solace in the peaceful memories of the past. The farm, her grandfather—the contemplation of them set everything right again, rebalanced her thinking. But this man staring in red-faced fear at her now could not possibly be her grandfather. Just a coincidence, she tried to tell herself, but she felt it was not that simple.

"Get out of here," he wheezed, "before they come."

"Before *who* comes?"

"Don't be a fool. They got Deerslayer, but somehow you escaped them and now you're pressing your luck."

"You knew Deerslayer. . . ."

"I knew all of you."

"All of *who*?"

"The Caretakers. I created you, Hedda," he said, using her name for the first time. "I created all of you."

Hedda felt unsteady on her feet. She leaned back against the door.

"Who *are* you?" she asked suddenly, feebly.

"We could leave me as your grandfather. Easier that way, more pleasant and acceptable."

"A lie."

"But, you see, there is no truth. There never was, not for you or any of the others."

"What are you talking about?"

The old man gazed about him. The living room was beautifully furnished with antiques; the magnificent Oriental rug was marked with the lines of the wheelchair's most recent routes. The sun streamed in through a large picture window. Hedda shuddered inwardly at the thought that someone, anyone, could be watching them through it now.

"It would be much easier if you left now, Hedda," the old man said with his eyes on the door. "Not for my sake, but for yours. You must believe that. Listen to what I have to say and you walk out of here a different person, one you never knew existed."

A chill ran through her. "I want the truth."

"Forget truth. I told you, it doesn't exist. Truth is an illusion we create, a myth we perpetuate to fool ourselves even in the normal world. Religion, spiritualism, need, want—look at them all. Truth is not what we see; it is what is provided for us to ease the pain of existing in a vacuum."

"Like what I've been existing in, you mean."

"No!" he insisted. "Never! Truth for you was what you needed it to be."

"But you were in it. Your image, your picture."

"Walking upright. Strong and vibrant."

"Yes! Yes!"

"My truth as it can never be. If I can never walk again myself, then at least I can walk in the minds of you and the others."

"Why? Who *are* you?" Hedda repeated.

"A name?"

"For starters, since somehow you know mine."

"August Pomeroy."

Hedda's face turned blank. "I've never heard that name. I feel I've known you all my life and I've never heard that name."

"I was only part of a block for you."

Hedda started to feel weak at the knees. "What are you talking about?"

"I'm talking about obstacles placed in your mind to prevent conscious recall of past events."

She moved closer to him, wanting to deny the words but knowing she could not. Perhaps her unconscious had always known what her conscious mind was learning. "Sometimes I have pieces of thoughts run through me, like dreams that slip away before I can recall them."

"Thanks to the blocks. Something comforting, something soothing for the mind to turn to as an alternative to the pain of actual memory."

"Your image on the farm, as my grandfather."

"Chosen for practicality, as well as ego and extension. For the block to be effective it had to have at least some substance in reality. If not a true event or happening, at least an actual person to be transposed onto an illusion. Like a character filmed in front of a fake background for a moving picture. There was so much work I had to do with you that I seemed the natural choice for that character."

"You're saying my entire memory is a lie. You're saying I have no idea who I really am."

"Your life as Hedda began four years ago."

"And before that?" When Pomeroy remained silent, Hedda drew closer to him. "And *before that*?"

August Pomeroy gazed at her for several moments before responding. "This is your last chance to choose the door, Hedda. From here there will only be more questions, and the answers will get progressively more unpleasant."

"I've got to hear them, Mr. Pomeroy."

"*Doctor* Pomeroy. In the kitchen, then, over tea."

* * *

Pomeroy set the water to boil himself. Hedda sat watching him, hands twisting and turning atop his thick oak kitchen table.

"I am a psychiatrist," the old man said as he wheeled his chair toward the table. "For many years I was quite respected in my field, quite well known for my area of expertise."

"Memory?"

"Not precisely. Pain: when people's lives had been ruined by guilt or sadness over a particular event, a wrong choice made, perhaps a loved one's loss. I dedicated my life to relieving that specific pain, to soothing it and repairing it the same way a surgeon does a damaged knee or broken limb. I set it right again so the mind could regain its symmetry." His voice tailed off slightly. "I married an American woman and relocated my practice to the United States where my work prospered. Then my wife died tragically and I found myself in need of my own medicine. Physician, heal thyself, is 'the phrase, I believe. I was lost, and in that state men came to me with a challenge that could make my life worthwhile again."

He stopped and cleared his throat. On the stove the teakettle had begun to rattle.

"Work in the field of memory suppression was accepted and well documented. But what these men wanted to accomplish was the total suppression of a person's past and its replacement with transparent screens and backdrops."

"My memories of . . . you, the farm, peacefulness."

"Exactly. You see, Hedda, an area of the brain called the hippocampus is responsible for the formation and recall of long term memories. What my work essentially did was short circuit the hippocampus' ability to send signals to other areas of the brain which would have ordinarily summoned memories. Once the signals were received, the false memories—the blocks—I had implanted would rise to prevent disorientation and soothe the mind."

"Madness!"

"Anything but, I'm afraid. I was charged with furnishing

subjects who had no past, only a present.'' The old man sighed. "Subjects for a project called Renaissance.''

"Subjects . . . How many?''

"How many Caretakers are there?''

"I don't know.''

"Neither do I. But it could be hundreds. Other psychiatric specialists were brought in and taught my system.''

"By whom, Doctor?''

"Would you believe me if I told you I did not know?''

"No.''

"It's true. I have my ideas, of course. A private army, a renegade faction of the American intelligence community. It doesn't matter, really. I did what they asked in order to ease my own pain. Who they actually were didn't matter to me, Hedda. It might be one of the reasons why I'm still alive.''

"And also the reason why millions of people might be about to die.''

"What are you talking about?''

"TD-13, a transdermal poison someone tied to The Caretakers was in their possession. Deerslayer and I were part of the operation that obtained it, one they were determined to erase all trace of.'' A bolt of realization struck Hedda. "That's why you were surprised to see me. You knew Deerslayer was dead, so you thought I would be, too! That's it, isn't it?''

"He . . . came to me.''

"Deerslayer? He came here?''

"Twice. The first time because the blocks had begun to erode for him. He caught a glimpse of me in the park and followed me back. He wanted answers.''

"And you gave them to him.''

"Just like I'm trying to do for you now.''

"Who was he before Renaissance? Who was *I*?''

"I don't know.''

"You must!''

The teakettle began to whistle. Before Hedda could move, the old man had wheeled himself backward toward the range. He pulled the kettle off as he spoke.

"How much do you know about the original Caretakers?''

"Original? You mean there's more than one group?"

August Pomeroy set the two cups of tea down on the table and wheeled himself back to his place. "An organization of the same name preceded yours and flourished from just after the end of the Vietnam War to the early eighties, when it was brought down by one of its own. Jared Kimberlain, known as the Ferryman and presently the last survivor of the original members, was betrayed by his own people, and it was he who exposed The Caretakers as a result. It was not until five years ago that other interested parties rechartered the organization."

"Renaissance . . ."

"But there was more, Hedda. The term renaissance also applies to the means by which their operatives were to be chosen. You know what you've been asked to do repeatedly for them. You know the kind of person they needed."

Hedda remained silent

"You, Deerslayer, the others—all killers par excellence. But they didn't train you to be that way, they merely refined you."

"What are you saying?"

"You don't want to hear this."

"Talk!"

"You and the others were chosen for an already demonstrated capacity to commit violence. You had all shown you were good at it, and more, that you liked it."

"Bullshit!"

"No, truth. That's what you wanted and that's what you're getting. You and all The Caretakers were salvaged from prisons, asylums, stockades. Your 'release' was arranged so you could be reborn to do their bidding for them. You and all the others were taken to an island where I was waiting."

"And you proceeded to erase our pasts."

August Pomeroy shook his head. "I merely eliminated your memories, so you could start with a clean slate. Where chaos had once ruled all your lives, I made it possible for order to take over. The propensities were not changed. The capabilities and abilities were not changed, only the way they were channeled. The people over you wanted ruthless killers, but they wanted to be in control of them.''

Hedda felt her heart sink. "I see a boy sometimes. Who is he? Did I kill him?''

"I was never told specifics. Not of you, not of Deerslayer, not of any of them.''

"How old am I? Where am I from?''

"I don't know! I don't know!''

"What is my name?''

"I don't know!"

"Why Hedda?''

"The original Caretakers, as I understand it, were all given names out of Greek mythology. The new Caretakers, of which you were a part, were named after famous characters from literature. You, for instance, were named for Hedda Gabler.''

"You told all this to Deerslayer. . . .''

The old man nodded. "The first time he came, yes. Four days ago.''

"What about the second?''

"He came back again the day before yesterday to leave me a note.'' Pomeroy's red-streaked eyes held hers. "A note for you. He knew you'd be coming.''

The old man wheeled himself back toward the refrigerator. There, affixed to it with a magnet, was a plain white envelope. Like Poe's purloined letter, Deerslayer's message had been hidden in plain sight.

"He told me to give this to you. He said you'd know what to do.''

Hedda accepted the envelope. Its thin contents consisted only of a single newsclipping concerning the dramatic resurgence of a Massachusetts-based plastics manufacturing company called PLAS-TECH.

"Do you know what this means?" she asked August Pomeroy.

"I haven't looked at it. I don't want to. Deerslayer said it required no further explanation.''

No further explanation . . . And yet there was no mention of transdermal poisons or deadly plots undertaken by some force who had enlisted the aid of The Caretakers. But somehow, clearly, PLAS-TECH was connected to whoever had demanded her death and Deerslayer's. He had figured that much out and had left it for her.

"What will you do now?" Pomeroy asked her.

"Find whoever's behind the TD-13."

"They'll kill you."

"Kill Hedda, you mean. You already killed the person I really am. They might be the only ones who can tell who that was."

"I used drugs; they use bullets."

"So do I, Doctor."

THE FOURTH DOMINION

Andrew Harrison
Leeds

Monday, August 17; 2:00 P.M.

CHAPTER 15

"**C**AN you hear me, young man?"

Arthur Whitlow could not clear the frog from his throat. "Yes, sir," he croaked.

"I await your report."

On one of the twenty-four television monitors that formed the wall directly in front of T. Howard Briarwood's desk, a youngish looking man with glasses could be seen fidgeting in his chair. Whitlow was understandably awed. After all, in seven years with the company he had not met another executive who had even spoken to the head of the massive, multibillion-dollar conglomerate directly.

Briarwood Industries maintained holdings in virtually every sphere of American business, all of them overseen by the company's leader himself, albeit from afar. The twenty-four television screens before him formed his link with his domain beyond the top floors of his executive tower. No less than five hundred similar transmission devices had been placed all over the world. Briarwood could activate them at any time he desired and peek in at the goings-on at his various holdings. Some would call it spying or eavesdropping. Briarwood called it good business.

Of course, Whitlow was aware of none of this. He knew only that the most important meeting of his life was being held with a television camera and a phantom voice that reached him in the room through an unseen speaker. The young man spoke at last with his eyes glued to the paper before him.

"The final shipment from PLAS-TECH was shipped yesterday. I am told the installation process has gone exceptionally well."

"Splendid. It's good to see Uncle Sam accepting the worthy advice of a willing nephew. Tell me," the voice continued through the speaker, "have you seen any of the production process firsthand?"

"I have, sir. It's most impressive."

"And is the Kansas facility on schedule?"

"Ahead, actually. So much so that storage capacity was exceeded, forcing a preliminary shipment to three of the major distribution sites."

Something in the voice changed. "Why was I not made aware of this sooner?"

"The shipments are being held back from distribution until the date previously arranged."

"You're quite certain of that?"

Whitlow nodded toward the camera, confused by the line of questioning T. Howard Briarwood was pursuing. "Yes, sir."

"And you're equally sure that the services of PLAS-TECH are no longer required?"

"The contract has been fulfilled to everyone's satisfaction. Additional orders have already been placed, of course, but for now—"

"You'll be going back, won't you, Mr. Whitlow? To the Kansas facility, I mean."

"I could, sir."

"I wonder if you might videotape their end of the process. I'll arrange the proper clearances. You'll do that, won't you?"

"Certainly, sir."

T. Howard Briarwood's finger crept to a button on his console. "Then again, perhaps it would be a better idea if you didn't."

He pressed the button and watched on the screen as Whitlow's body spasmed horribly. His hands and feet twitched in twisted symphony, as the electrical current continued to surge through his body. Then finally it was still.

The chair had been one of Andrew Harrison Leeds's first inventions, and he had never shied from using it. As he watched Whitlow's body smoke, he tried to imagine the scent of singed hair and flesh. Pity Whitlow had to die. The man had been nothing but loyal to T. Howard Briarwood. Too bad he knew too much about the plan of Andrew Harrison Leeds.

Leeds turned his fingers back to the sophisticated control panel on his desk and began scanning the screens, changing them like an impatient TV viewer with an overactive remote device. Locations in fifteen different countries swept by his eyes. Empty conference rooms, jammed hotel lobbies, a television studio. Leeds lingered on no screen long enough to see anything in its entirety, and yet he missed nothing. The contents of the screens belonged to Briarwood; to fully capture the scope of his holdings a thousand more would have been required.

A single screen in the vast wall remained blank until Leeds pressed the PLAY button that was within easy reach of his hand. Instantly the screen filled with a long shot of a man standing in a motor launch as it neared a dock. Leeds fast-forwarded to the point where a close-up of the man's face filled the screen and froze it.

"Kimberlain," he muttered. "I'm not going to let you catch me this time, not this time."

Leeds advanced the tape in slow motion, studying each of the Ferryman's moves, his every mannerism. He had been about to rewind the tape and view it yet again, when something snapped him alert.

"Ah," he said out loud, "the meeting."

He rose quickly and moved to the conference room door. Its electric eye caught him, and the door opened automatically.

Andrew Harrison Leeds stepped through into the opaque darkness of a windowless room.

"Good afternoon," he announced to the figures gathered around the central conference table. "And a very good afternoon it is indeed. . . ."

Andrew Harrison Leeds killed for the first time when he was ten years old. He had reached out to pet a neighbor's dog and the animal bit him. Leeds felt the sharp pain and yanked his hand away. The dog snarled, daring him.

Leeds snarled back.

That was the first time he had felt the raw, untapped rage that had driven him to reach the heights he had attained. But the rage was controlled. He did not lash out at the dog then. He returned to his house and stole a sharp knife from the kitchen, along with three slices of cold cuts from the meat drawer. Leeds watched the dog saunter off into the neighboring woods and headed after it. Finding it just inside the cover of trees, he extended the meat as a peace offering. So convincing was he, he scarcely admitted his intention to himself. The animal hesitated only slightly. Before its jaws had even closed on the balled-up cold cuts, Leeds pounced, driving the knife home.

He heard the cries and liked it.

He smelled the blood, *felt* it, and liked that, too. He remained calm through it all, never even breathing hard.

He killed other animals later, but it was never as much fun. A person would be much better. Leeds let himself fantasize. In his mind the act was always so simple, so . . . fulfilling. And for a time the fantasies were enough. Somewhere there was reality, but it didn't seem to matter as much anymore. Reality was what you made it. Leeds had already discovered that in school. He knew how smart he was, far smarter than the brainless twits that taught him. But he never let on, kept his true self covered, exposing it to no one.

He began to see a younger girl from the neighborhood hanging around the woods a lot. She was often dirty, and sometimes she had bruises on her face. She said she was running away. Leeds said he would help her.

Thinking back now, he would have to say it was very much like the dog. He brought the girl food on the pretext of gaining her trust, and while she ate he looped a rope around her neck and strangled her. After burying the girl's body near that of the dog's, Leeds went home and listened to the radio.

He was twelve years old.

His parents never realized how smart he was. No one realized, because Leeds concealed his intelligence. They saw only what he wanted them to. Leeds could make people love him, hate him, follow him. He could frighten them, humor them, win them over, beat them down. They were playthings, toys. But they fueled his fantasies and kept him from needing to visit the woods too often.

He exposed his true potential only upon reaching college, because he saw it as a quicker route to dominate. Domination, after all, was what life was all about. Killing was about domination. Leeds could kill the body, but he could also kill the soul. By the age of thirty, three dozen people had perished under his hand. He was careful how he chose them, avoided patterns at all costs. It wasn't enough, though. He lived off his fantasies, but to continue to make them viable he needed to merge them with reality.

He took a job as a junior high school science teacher. Three glorious months spent gaining trust and seeing the end as it was going to unfold. He made sure that the authorities could easily find the bus, making it all the worse that the bodies of the twenty-six students would never be seen again.

His stint as a doctor came next, a similar number of victims but with infinitely more pleasure since they were spread out over time, the same method never used twice. The causes of death always looked normal initially, and Leeds was gone before the police ever realized the connection. He found he could live off fantasy for only so long now, his mind like a parking meter ticking away a quarter's worth faster and faster.

His psychiatrist identity proved unfulfilling and frustrating. He hated listening to his patients talk, complaining of the dark

evils that haunted their lives. Surrender! he wanted to tell
them. Give yourself up to the evils, and only then will you
realize your true self. . . . Leeds knew they never would have
listened, so after three months of practicing, he ended the
problems of his therapy group forever.

Later, as a forensic pathology professor, he was disappointed to find that his brilliant students cared more for bet-
tering their grades than expanding their minds. Was this what
the world was going to be left to, this horde of the living dead?
It was that very thought that gave Leeds the idea for his exit
from that identity. He wondered if anyone bothered to see the
symbolism.

His brief tenure at the university reaffirmed his conviction
that madmen, misfits, and outcasts were the people most fit to
inherit the world. The dream began to take shape over the next
several months; he needed only the means to bring it to be.
And when the means to accomplish it were found, during his
tenure as the Candy Man, Leeds had barely been able to re-
strain his excitement.

In order to accomplish his goals, though, he needed to be
placed in The Locks. Only from within its walls could the final
strokes be brushed onto his portrait of the future:

The world was going to be turned inside out. The madness
he had previously needed to flee into would be there for him to
reach out and touch.

And so he had outwitted the foremost adversary he had ever
encountered by turning that adversary's greatest strength into a
weakness. Let him have the thrill of the pursuit. Give Kimberlain just enough to be sure he would pick up the trail and
follow it. A brilliant ploy in all respects.

But the Ferryman was still out there, and there would be no
rest for Leeds until he was out of the way at last.

"Where should I begin?" Andrew Harrison Leeds continued.

Two of the four walls in the conference room were covered
by maps of the United States. The other two had maps of the
world. Thin track lighting aimed at those maps provided the

room's only light, so that its darkest point was actually the conference table where eight of the nine chairs were occupied by silent figures. Leeds moved to the unoccupied chair at the head and sat down.

"With apologies, of course. I'm sorry I'm late, my fellows, but it couldn't be avoided. My work is almost complete. Shipment from Kansas begins in a matter of a few weeks and distribution soon after. All that is left is the waiting, waiting for a rotting society to be cleansed of its weaknesses."

Andrew Harrison Leeds clutched the end of the table with his hands. He waited for one of the eight figures gathered about the table to speak. None did.

"What, my fellows, no words? No words of congratulations or commendation? But no. I understand. You are so full of admiration for my schemes you remain speechless. I will succeed, after all, where you have failed. You each tried to found a dominion based on your personal vision, yet in the end each of you was defeated. The ninth dominion will be different, because I have determined the way the world was always meant to be and have discovered the means to make it so."

Leeds rose slowly, then paced to the right side of the table and peered more closely at the figures around the table, as if waiting for them to speak. But they didn't. The figures Leeds had assembled were all wax replicas of formerly great commanders and visionaries, ranging from Caesar and Genghis Khan to Charlemagne, Napoleon, and Hitler. These were the only leaders Leeds believed could approach him in purpose and mentality.

Leeds stopped at the last figure seated on the right. "You, Genghis Khan, could have controlled all of Asia, the Orient, and beyond. But your thirst for violence frightened off your inner circle, and you paid with your life."

The wax figure of Genghis Khan did not argue, did not stir. Andrew Harrison Leeds moved on.

"And you, Alexander, were limited by your own satisfaction and contentment. You thought you had conquered enough, and what you failed to accomplish became the seeds of your undoing.''

Leeds touched the waxen shoulder of the next figure. ''Ah, Caesar, destroyed on the verge of great achievement from within your own ranks, those you considered closest. You let them get too close, for men like you and I can ill afford such a luxury.''

He moved on to a uniformed figure with hair tight to its scalp and a carved-off mustache. ''Adolf Hitler. You among us had the least reason to fail, and yet you failed quickly after coming so close to a dominion that would have changed the course of history. But obsession ruined you. You saw only guarded images through a tunnel of your own making. You did not see the whole, and this destroyed you.''

Andrew Harrison Leeds gazed at the remaining four but did not address them as he moved back toward the head of the table past Catherine the Great and Attila the Hun.

''All of you must be commended for seeking to shape the world in the image you had of it. But in the end it was the error of your vision that condemned you to failure. The ninth dominion will be different.'' Leeds paused and took a deep breath. ''In the ninety day period commencing September 1, the United States will become a virtual wasteland. A minimum of ninety-five percent of her population will be dead with no damage whatsoever done to the structures and technology. No nuclear fallout, no biological toxins floating about in the air— nothing so crass and final. I will inherit what is left and forge it as my dominion with those I have deemed worthy to populate the wasteland. The rest of the world will follow shortly, unable to resist the tide I bring forth.

''My ninth dominion will be peopled from the ranks of the outcasts, those that society has shunned and have shunned society in return. The prisoners who thirst inside for a freedom that will allow them to express themselves without fear of chastisement and alienation. It will be their world to do with as they please.''

Compassion filled the face of Andrew Harrison Leeds. His eyes grew watery.

"How I feel for you, who could not see your visions reach fulfillment. But you can still succeed. Come with me, my fellows. Come with me as I embark on a journey into the abyss of man's soul, as I turn the world inside out so it may at last be right and proper. The time has come to rise from the crevices, to crawl up from the cracks where society has stowed those of us who understand life well enough to express it. The world will bury us no longer." He grabbed the waxen hands of Hitler and Catherine the Great, seated on either side of the table's head. "Join me on a crusade that will see over two hundred and fifty million people perish in the blink of the eye, be swept away by a vision that will see itself denied no longer."

"*What about the Ferryman?*" Leeds thought he heard one of the figures ask.

Leeds's face began twitching. His left cheek pulsed and seemed to be rising toward his sunken eye. His breathing picked up. The waxen limbs he held in either hand began to compress under his grip.

"He is being taken care of."

"*You already missed your chance.*"

"*You should have killed him. You should have waited at his house and killed him.*"

"*He can bring you down. He's the only man that can.*"

Leeds released his grip, and the waxen mounds that had been finely chiseled hands thumped to the table. The voices of the failed conquerors seemed to be converging on him, smothering him with their accusations.

"*What about the woman?*"

"*She's very dangerous because she knows about—*"

"Enough!" Leeds screamed. His hands clutched the underside of the conference table and, with an incredible burst of strength, lifted it up and over. The heavy table crashed down and scattered the wax figures in all directions. Hitler's head snapped off and rolled across the floor. Catherine the Great's arm jumped into the air and flopped back to the floor.

"I'll kill the Ferryman, do you hear me?" Leeds demanded. "I'll find him and kill him. The woman, too! Is that enough for you? *Goddamn it, is that enough?*"

"*When?*" the voices seemed to ask in unison.

"Tonight!" Leeds ranted before his voice grew eerily calm. "Tonight."

CHAPTER 16

GARTH Seckle slept outside, sometimes in a tent, sometimes under the stars. The air was thicker tonight but pleasantly cool for summer. Too cool would have made him uncomfortable and perhaps necessitated a brief fire. But he didn't want to start one. Nothing that might draw attention to him. He was alone and had to stay that way. Leave no trail, nothing to follow. He hadn't yet and didn't plan to.

He had carried many names through his life, but none of them meant as much as the one the country was calling him now:

Tiny Tim.

Imagine that! The press was so creative, naming him for an innocent little crippled boy who wouldn't harm a fly. Well, he would harm flies as well as crippled boys and make no distinction between them.

He had lost a big chunk of his left foot back then when his

life changed for the first time. Some nights the cold wind made his bad foot hurt more than usual. Tonight the wind felt soothing. He liked to take off his sock and look at the foot, because it was the only thing that reminded him of who he really was and the task that remained before him.

Seckle twisted on the grass and pulled his pack over to use as a pillow. The night was warm enough that he didn't need to use his sleeping bag as a blanket. He never slept inside it. Too confining, especially for a man six-foot-ten-inches tall weighing nearly three hundred pounds. Seckle had never liked to be confined. He had the instincts of a wild animal. A man who lived alone and hunted alone.

Seckle stretched beneath his blanket of stars. His bad leg and foot throbbed. There was always pain, not a second without it.

The two towns had gone easy for him, four blessed hours in each when death stood by his side and cheered his every move. Enter the first house, silenced machine gun in hand. Parents' room first, then the kids'.

Pffft . . . pffft . . . pffft . . .

And the bodies jumped a little, then stopped. Sometimes blood sprayed. Sometimes it didn't. A few times his victims managed a glance at him before he dispatched them. A few times they even managed to move or start a plea. Seckle saw them through the deep haze of his night-vision goggles.

Some layouts required the use of the poisoned gas canisters he wore attached to his commando belt. A high-tech gas mask that made him look like something from a science-fiction film hung from his belt. He always saved his hands for near the end, the innermost section of what Seckle called his death circle. Snap the necks quick or squeeze the life out of them and watch their eyeballs bulge. Seckle liked the look when they gave up and knew it was finished. He wished he could make that moment linger.

Of course, the bulk of these victims meant nothing to him. They were no more real than black and white cardboard silhouettes on a shooting range. They were nonentities, meaningless in death as they had been in life. His only true satisfaction lay in a single stop on each of his visits. For these he used special means and could have left it at that. But this was a game for him, and he wanted to see if there was anyone out there good enough to play along.

Of course there was one man, and Seckle couldn't wait to see how long it took him to catch on to the true essence of what he was doing. By now the FBI would have called that man in and the race would be on. Perhaps in one of his upcoming visits the man would be waiting, and that would suit Seckle just fine.

Tiny Tim . . .

Seckle loved reading the news accounts of the utter randomness of his visits. Two in just over a week now, and the entire nation was cowering in fear. He had read that National Guardsmen were being stationed in small towns all over the country. Did they really think that would stop him? Even if they knew the locations of his remaining ten visits his fury could not be stemmed. It had simmered through the dead years when his life had been confined to an eight-foot square. He had known all along his time would come, and when it came he did not hesitate.

Seckle moved his pack about, trying to find a comfortable position for his head. The forced inactivity of this night was making him restless. He pulled his Gerber MKII killing knife from its sheath on his belt and held it up like a scepter drawing power from the night.

The hunger that drove him fluttered about the pit of his stomach. He wet his lips with the saliva bubbling from his mouth.

It was time to pay his next visit.

CHAPTER 17

THE Prince Edward section on the Canadian side of Lake Ontario looked like a desperate hand rising out of the water. Its curled fingers formed jagged peninsulas lined with docks and small-town life. Kimberlain was well into his second day of driving the thin roads that wrapped around the coastline in search of the place where the submarine carrying Andrew Harrison Leeds had docked.

"I figure Leeds got it down to the lake in one of them iron ore boats," Captain Seven had explained back at The Locks. "Nice World War II job, and it wouldn't be hard to camouflage either. Think about it, boss. Sub picks up Leeds and the others off the rafts and brings them to shore somewhere. Running a diesel engine in rough seas wouldn't be anyone's idea of a Sunday sail. That thing goes down and you got shit to chomp on with your teeth instead of chewing gum. Wanna run it as little as possible, say in a straight line."

"Prince Edward?"

"Yeah, the Canadian side of the lake. Short and sweet. Dock and be done with it. About a thousand possibilities, and in that storm not likely anyone would have known what they were looking at even if they saw it."

"It's worth a try," Kimberlain had said, but now he was beginning to doubt that he would ever track it down after many unsuccessful searches. As he had feared, the storm that night

141

stole away both visibility and witnesses. What would Leeds have been thinking? If the operation had been carried out to his specifications, there would be order, precision—not randomness.

Kimberlain tried Bloomfield Cove next, a lip of land shaped like a smiling bear with a mouth of dangerous shale. The dock was tucked into the lower jaw, land shield on three sides and open water on the other. Kimberlain pulled over and walked the last hundred yards to the dock. The breeze was chilly, more late fall than summer. He reached the cove and swept his eyes about. A dangerous trek but not an impossible one, especially for a submarine riding on the surface with no fear of being seen in the night. He reached the dock and saw a bulky shape seated there in plaid mackinaw jacket with a shotgun laid over its legs. Not wanting to startle the figure, he made sure to kick plenty of stones as he approached.

The figure turned lazily, not seeming to mind him. A chubby, emotionless face gazed at him beneath an old work cap that barely contained a limp mop of auburn hair.

"I'm waiting," the figure told him, and turned back to its vigil.

The voice that emerged slowly and hoarsely was female. The eyes dropped, bored and uninterested, but they weren't old. Kimberlain knew the woman suffered from some form of retardation. Thirty or so chronologically, but little more than a child. She wore denim overalls that were dirty at the knees. The shotgun she held was layered with dust. The breech was cracked open and Kimberlain could see no shells were chambered. He approached tentatively and waited for her to become aware of his presence again before speaking.

"Waiting for what?"

"I'm not supposed to tell." She looked up at him for a brief instant and then hung her head back down. "They didn't believe me."

"You saw something."

She nodded. "Uh-huh."

"What was it?"

She shook her head. "Uh-uh. I'm not supposed to tell."

Kimberlain sat down next to her. The woman-child shifted slightly away.

"What's your name?"

"I'm not supposed to talk to strangers."

"But you already have—" He smiled. "—haven't you?"

She smiled back. "Yeah, yeah. My name's Alice."

"I'm Jared, Alice."

"*J-a-r-r-i-d,*" she spelled out.

"*J-a-r-e-d,*" he corrected softly.

"Only one *r.*"

"Right."

"And an *e,* not an *i.*"

"Yes."

"I like to spell things."

"Alice, I want you to know something. I believe you."

Her eyes glowed. "You do?"

He nodded. "I'm looking for the thing you saw."

"The sea monster?"

"I don't think it was a monster."

"It was!" Alice flared, pushing herself away from him. "You said you believed me!"

"I believe you saw a boat, the kind of boat that travels underwater. It's called a submarine."

"I don't know how to spell that."

Kimberlain spelled it for her. Then they spelled it again together.

"I'd like you to tell me what you saw that night, Alice."

"Promise you won't laugh?"

"I promise. I believe you, remember?"

Her eyes gazed at him, wanting to trust. She moved back closer to him.

"I was sitting by my window. I live up there," Alice said, and pointed up the hill toward the house closest to the water. "I like to watch storms. Storms are fun. Do you like storms?"

"Sometimes they scare me."

"No. I'll bet they don't."

"When I was younger, I mean. Was this a fun storm to watch?"

"Oh yeah. Lots of lightning in the sky, the kind that looks like thin fingers."

"And how many nights ago would it have been?"

"I don't know."

"Five or six maybe?"

"Yeah. That's right. I saw the monster first when the lightning came. It was black. I saw it swimming toward shore. I thought I'd better call for help but my mom wasn't home. I tried to use the phone but it didn't work."

"What did the monster do?"

Alice regarded him suspiciously. "You said it was a sub-ma-rine."

"Tell me what you saw and then we'll know."

"It came up to the dock and then the dock had people on it. Lots and lots of people getting wet in the rain. I saw them best when the lightning came. I guess they came because of the sub-ma-ronster," she said, proud of herself for combining the words as well as the thoughts.

"Lots and lots," Kimberlain repeated. "Did you count?"

She looked down. "No."

"They left the dock."

"And went toward the trucks. I saw them, too. Only they didn't have their lights on, so it was tough."

"And the sub-ma-ronster?"

"It was big and black. Long, too. But I think it might be coming back. I'm not gonna shoot it. I just want to talk to it. Do you think it's coming back?"

"Maybe. But only if it comes by tomorrow."

Alice seemed to remember something. "Somebody wrote on it. Somebody wrote on the sub-ma-ronster."

"A word you mean?"

"I don't know. I'm not sure."

"Can you spell it?"

"I can try." Her face squeezed itself taut. *"M-a-r-l-i-n."*

"Marlin?"

"Yeah, mar-lin. Is that how you say it?"

"That's perfect, Alice."

The woman-child beamed and rolled her head proudly. "Do all sub-mar-ronsters have names, Jared?"

"Yes."

"Why?"

"So we can find them, Alice, when they get lost."

Captain Seven said he needed an hour to research the *Marlin*, so Kimberlain called back from the same general store in Bloomfield Cove sixty minutes later. The Ferryman knew that Seven's computer was tied into virtually every major data bank in the nation. The captain had the access codes and passwords for all of them. And what he didn't have, he could get.

"Okay," Captain Seven opened, "here's what I came up with. The *Marlin* was sold to Spain off the military down list in 1962, where as far as I can tell it has remained ever since."

"Until now."

"Whoever got it back here knew how to cover their tracks."

"And where might they have covered the *Marlin*?"

"Thought you'd never ask. Got a couple possibilities there. First they could moor it on the surface somewhere under some pretty heavy camouflage."

"Too much risk when all they'd really have to do was sink it."

"Bad idea, boss. Have to use explosives to do the job right, and that would have drawn the attention of the various search parties."

"Okay, so what did they do with it?"

"How about hiding it in one of the five biggest scrap yards in the whole country, which just happens to be located in Oswego, New York?"

"Across the lake from where I'm standing now . . ."

"Almost. See, they dock it the same night after depositing the passengers. Spend the rest of the night with some underwater cutting tools, and by morning it's in pieces hidden all over the yard."

"Meaning someone at this or some other scrap yard would have had to be involved with Leeds."

"Abso-fucking-lutely."

"You've outdone yourself again."

"Just getting started. Got something else you might be interested in." Captain Seven paused long enough to call up a new screen on his computer. "Fact that Donald Dwares who tried to waste you in Providence was supposed to be dead got me thinking. I ran a check on maximum-security prisons going back five years to his supposed execution. Lots of inmates conveniently got sick and died. Seemed to afflict only the most violent; lifers, a few on death row."

"You got a list?"

"Growing by the minute. Damn unsavory bunch, specialists in brutal violence, lots of it random like with Dwares. Plenty of the names will be familiar to you."

"How many?"

"Sixty-five already. Whoops, make that sixty-four; I forgot to cross off Dwares."

"Sounds like an army."

"Not far from it."

"I go after Leeds, Dwares comes after me," Kimberlain said, thinking it out for himself. "Meanwhile, Leeds springs eighty-three more to add to the list."

"An army, Ferryman, just like you said."

"The question is, what is Leeds planning to do with it?"

"Don't know," Captain Seven said. "Maybe the *Marlin* can help us find out."

CHAPTER 18

KIMBERLAIN waited until well after dark before approaching the Gerabaldi Scrap Yard in Oswego, New York. He figured a more clandestine approach was called for on the chance that someone at Gerabaldi was connected to Leeds. The scrap yard turned out to be a massive place located on the outskirts of the small city, off Route 104 four miles from Lake Ontario. The acres and acres of junk stretched farther than the eye could see. Finding no sign of guard dogs, he sliced through the chain link with his razor knife and entered the yard.

Directly before him, the corpses of home appliances rose in columns between twenty and thirty feet high. Many of the machines sat with their innards exposed, disemboweled for parts and left to rot. There were washers and dryers, rusting and brown, cursed by curled and warped metal. There were refrigerators with doors either missing or chained, seeming to make them prisoners of their own demise. There were stoves, the oldest of which might have dated back a generation.

Watching over the scene stood a trio of man-operated loaders Kimberlain knew were called two-tonners after their maximum payload. All of nine feet tall, the machines had the look of massive steel skeletons. All three possessed the arm and leg extremities of a man, with slots for an operator to wedge his

147

hands and feet into to control them in maneuvering the ancient appliances about. The arms were especially impressive, fitted with pincer apparatuses for hands. The orange-colored things stood naked and ominous, like guards over a treasure of rusted brown steel. Kimberlain noticed they were named after the Three Stooges.

Passing out of the appliance graveyard, Kimberlain found himself swallowed by mountains of brown steel drums. He smelled oil and figured that was what they had once contained. Now they were bleeding it from their bottoms, and the ground was soaking it up. They rose silent and defiant, stacked to fifteen feet tall, rows and rows of drum towers stretching for the sky.

The Ferryman continued on. The next section, containing the yard's huge cache of junked cars and trucks, was much larger than the previous two sections. Cars flattened in the crusher had been piled atop each other like playing cards. Those still reasonably whole lay squeezed together as if in some bizarre parking lot. Worn out tires were stacked in a mountain. Hubcaps were piled in a bulging, square heap.

Squeezed amid the clutter were the machines of the trade. Kimberlain noted a pair of massive black steel front loaders. He passed by the man-sized tires of one and noted the lighter rusted color of its six-foot prongs. The rust, Kimberlain thought, might have been blood collected from its snared victims.

His stomach rumbled slightly, and he pressed on past a loader with oscillating arms for agile manipulations of its pay-loads. It was smaller than its cousins and was colored a deep, shiny red. Kimberlain saw that scrawled in black letters across the loader's side was the word SCARLETT.

Squeezed ominously against the fence further back, detached and indifferent, was the portable crushing apparatus. The loaders would deliver the wrecks into the open slot and back off while the crusher flattened the heap for easier storage. Kimberlain imagined the sound of popping glass and tearing steel.

The scrap car piles stretched on for over an acre, but none of the mounds of junked cars seemed the right place to hide the severed pieces of the *Marlin*. That task would be better served in Gerabaldi's last and largest section, which was lined with piles of commercial scrap and salvage. Moving closer, the Ferryman could see a massive stack of disassembled rides from an amusement park. A huge clown's head peeked out from near the middle. The standards of what had once been a roller coaster leaned against the pile and towered above it.

An equally large mound of steel salvaged from demolished and burned out buildings lay directly across the way. There was no real order here in this section as there had been in the others. Instead, everything just seemed to have been heaped up. Much of the steel was twisted or scorched black. It seemed to be hoping for a second life, but by the rusted, worn out look of things that had already been long in coming.

Beyond the steel refuse, past a yellow loader even more massive and ominous than the black ones back in the auto yard, lay the boat scrap. Some looked reasonably whole, while little enough remained of others even to distinguish what they had been. There were tops with no hulls and hulls with no tops. Chunks of decks and gunwales. If someone at Gerabaldi had wanted to hide the remains of the *Marlin,* this was where it would be. Hidden from sight, though, probably within another mound that might show evidence of being shuffled about.

The Ferryman made his way toward a wide, haphazard stack of junked smaller craft. He could pick out the remains of pontoons and speedboats, cabin cruisers and outboards. They had been lost to accident, neglect, or simply to age. With no value left they had ended up here. Kimberlain could picture the monstrous pronged payloader he had just passed shoveling away huge masses of the pile to make room for the *Marlin's* remains and then sealing the hole up again.

When a scan from the ground gained nothing, he located

firm footing and began to scale the mound. It was much like rock climbing, only with steel that bit into your flesh and footholds that wobbled beneath you. Halfway up, Kimberlain's foot slid down a slope of curved steel. He grabbed hold of the remains of a foredeck to halt his plunge and steadied himself, breathing deeply. He gazed upward.

The fragment that had almost sent him plummeting was black and narrowed down to a thick point at the end. It was almost like what a bullet might look like if it had been cut into segments and then sliced in half.

A bullet or a submarine.

The Ferryman pulled out his flashlight and inspected the black steel more closely. He shoved the empty hull of a speedboat aside far enough to give his head and shoulders room to pry through. His flashlight illuminated a series of numbers, white outlines jumping out from the black surrounding them. Kimberlain felt his neck prick with excitement; they were the last three numbers in the *Marlin*'s register. He peered further into the pile with his light but found nothing else. No matter; he had what he came for, a link that might help take him all the way to Andrew Harrison Leeds. Someone at Gerabaldi would know something. His next task, tomorrow, was to find out who and what.

He retreated down the mound and had placed his foot on an upside-down cruiser hull just above the ground when the lights snapped on directly before him. Kimberlain threw up a hand to shade himself from being blinded and heard a powerful engine roaring to life. He realized it was the monstrous yellow loader bearing down, and he readjusted his balance to leap from its path.

The loader slammed into the hull he had been standing on. Its powerful prongs cut steel like butter. The loader pulled back from the wreck with the sounds of grinding and twisting metal marking the path of its withdrawing prongs. Kimberlain was moving away now, staying close to the line of boats. The loader turned his way and started coming after him.

The Ferryman quickened his pace, but the yellow loader's

driver had chosen an approach angle that cut him off. Its prongs reached for him, and Kimberlain desperately scaled the pile of boat wrecks.

The steel ends sliced effortlessly through steel just beneath his dangling feet, then drew back for another try. The driver raised the prongs and angled them upward, then threw the machine forward once more. Kimberlain managed to dodge to the side this time; his legs kicked furiously while his hands clung to the frame of an ancient Bayliner. The loader drew backward once more and pulled part of the mound directly beneath him with it. Kimberlain was left dangling.

The loader charged again, and Kimberlain swept his lower body away from its thrust, swinging with one arm above the up-angled prongs. The prongs shredded steel and then crunched back out. The loader didn't draw back much at all this time, just came straight forward and sliced through rusted steel boat hulls when Kimberlain twisted away again. He saw the loader buckle a bit as it tried to back away, the monstrous tires spewing a cloud of junkyard dirt behind them as the prongs refused to give up their hold. Looking upward, he got his first clear view into the cab.

It was empty. The loader had no driver.

The immediate ramifications of that struck him hard. His gun would do him no good now. This was a machine he was fighting, seven or eight tons probably and all of it steel. But someone was controlling it.

Andrew Harrison Leeds must have been anticipating his every move, lying in wait for him, toying with him from the time he left the note stuck to his cabin door. . . .

With the robotized loader still struggling to free itself, the Ferryman seized the offensive. He pried a shard of twisted steel free from above him, then pushed off and dropped onto the loader's right prong. The machine pulled free at last and continued backing up as if unaware of his presence, then started to raise the assembly to force him off. Kimberlain turned the resulting momentum to his advantage, sliding down the prong onto the top of the loader's hood section.

He raised the piece of rusted metal he still held high overhead and thrust it downward with all his strength, denting the loader's massive engine grill. He slammed the steel shard down again, then a third time, and a fourth. At last the grill gave, exposing the rear section of the engine.

The machine lunged forward madly, gears whining as if to protest the invader atop it. Kimberlain braced for the collision he knew was coming by pressing himself as close to the loader's empty cab as possible. Its freshly straightened prongs stabbed the pile of boat wrecks and continued forward until its engine section was flush against it. When this maneuver failed to dislodge the Ferryman, it backed off and slammed forward again.

He was jarred loose from his precarious perch and might have tumbled off if the loader had tried the move a third time. Instead, it retreated only slightly and began to raise its prongs upward, attempting to bring a section of the boat wrecks up and over to crush him.

Turning toward the cab again, Kimberlain's hands swept into the exposed engine section. He swiped and jabbed with the steel shard to no avail. The piece was too thick to permit enough access and maneuverability. So he abandoned it and jammed his bare hands inside the loader's turning insides.

The prongs were coming up with a collection of wrecks, shedding a few to the sides while the rest buckled and settled against each other. This was his chance, here and now.

The Ferryman felt about the hot, revving engine, as the heap behind him continued to rise skyward. He knew that if he grazed a churning belt he would lose a finger or hand. Touch the wrong spot and he'd be burned horribly. His hands closed on rubber that felt like spark plug wires, and he pulled them free.

The loader sputtered, engine grinding, but its prongs had almost reached a forty-five-degree angle and were still coming. Kimberlain's hands found what felt like a fan belt. He pulled out his right hand and grasped the steel shard once more. He guided it into the hole in the hood and jammed it hard against the fan belt, producing a squealing sound. The smell of burning oil reached his nostrils an instant before smoke began to pour up all around him. The loader's engine died. The prongs stopped moving, a rusted outboard dangling from their grasp.

Kimberlain slid off the loader's hood and eased himself to the ground. He stood there with shoulders against its black steel.

It was Leeds! Leeds had done it all!

He wondered how the madman had pulled it off, but nothing should have surprised him when Leeds was involved. Best to get out of the yard now while he had the chance. He had what he came for; Leeds couldn't take that away from him.

Kimberlain jogged away from the loader's corpse. He would retrace his steps and be gone from here before the madman could throw any more tricks at him. He passed back into the auto yard and heard the rumbling an instant before the lights caught him. The rumbling turned into a roar of two monstrous engines, as the twin black loaders advanced toward him.

CHAPTER 19

KIMBERLAIN knew he could not outrun the loaders, and if he tried to dodge them, they would alter their routes and trap him anyway. So he stood his ground, wondering what the loaders would think of that if they could see.

But someone could see, someone controlling them from afar.

Leeds . . .

"Try this, you sons of bitches. . . ."

With the loaders all but upon him, Kimberlain hit the ground where he had been standing. His move came at the last possible instant before the loaders would have crushed him, too late for the driverless machines to react. They smashed into each other, sparks flying as their prong assemblies smacked together. Flat on his stomach, on the ground between the monstrous tires, Kimberlain heard the gears screaming in protest. He crawled out from beneath the rear loader and scampered away.

The twin iron monsters hit reverse simultaneously to pull back from the collision. But their prongs locked, providing the Ferryman with time to escape. A grinding sound made him turn their way again, and he watched as the loaders separated at last. They spun toward him side by side.

There would be no escaping until they were incapacitated. He needed a weapon, but what?

His eyes fell on *Scarlett* when he was halfway to it. The fact that the smaller, red loader had not joined its two larger brethren seemed to indicate that Leeds did not control her. And if Leeds didn't, well . . .

The Ferryman lunged into *Scarlett*'s cab as the larger loaders gained ground fast. This smaller loader had an entirely different front assembly: pronged, yes, but with oscillating joints like elbows that could twist and bend in humanlike articulation.

Kimberlain jammed a small device that looked like a rounded hairbrush against the ignition. He pressed a button on the device's back that sent electrical signals designed to "fool" any machine's starter system.

"Come on, baby! Come on!" the Ferryman shouted as he twisted his universal starter to find the proper charge.

Scarlett roared to life, as one of the black loaders pulled ahead of the other and bore down on the smaller machine. Its bright lights poured into the cab. Kimberlain's hands located the joysticks that controlled *Scarlett*'s arms, as he gassed the accelerator and shoved the stick forward.

Scarlett lunged at her larger enemy and Kimberlain had just enough time before impact to twist the front assembly perpendicular to the ground. As the black loader closed, he braked hard and applied gas at the same time. The result was to force *Scarlett* into a fishtail that took her from her bigger cousin's path. At the same time, Kimberlain worked the joystick to bring her cocked front assembly down hard to the left.

It clipped the big loader in the front quarter panel just beyond the left side prong. Impact threw the bigger loader wildly off course, slamming straight for a neatly stacked pile of car wrecks that tumbled down upon it as it plowed through.

Kimberlain swung round in time to see the second loader almost upon him. This time he turned *Scarlett* to face it head on. As the enemy charged in, Kimberlain pulled *Scarlett*'s oscillating assembly up toward his cab, bending its steel arms inward at the joint. He snapped it out and down at the last, relying on momentum and impetus. He was not disappointed. Impact on the larger machine forced the loader's prongs to their lowest point at near ground level. Its bulk slowed in response time considerably, and the black monster was helpless when Kimberlain drove *Scarlett* forward and slammed her front assembly into the larger machine full throttle.

The loader's front steel section buckled and bent. Smoke poured from its grill. Kimberlain moved to strike at it again, but it drove forward. He tried to parry its ascending prongs, but they soared up and over him. They lashed downward against *Scarlett*'s oscillating assembly and pinned it before the Ferryman could pull away. Steel ground against steel with a horrible shriek. Kimberlain tried to pull back, but it was no use. The best he could manage was a stalemate as the two iron monsters struggled for position, spinning, with dirt and scrap yard debris hurled behind their tires.

Out of the corner of his eye, Kimberlain saw the other loader burst through a pile of flattened cars, climbing atop the last few stubborn ones en route to the battle. If the loader he was hooked up with now could merely maintain the stalemate, *Scarlett* would be finished.

The freed loader was heading straight his way, certain to try to sandwich him between it and the one he was battling. The things fought like great beasts from a prehistoric era of steel. Their engines snorted and huffed, with clawlike prongs whistling against each other.

The second loader had angled itself for a charge against *Scarlett*'s rear. Kimberlain could sense it coming and needed only brief glimpses to adjust his timing. When only ten yards remained between them, he spun *Scarlett*'s wheel and floored the accelerator. The resulting momentum carried *Scarlett* around the loader she was locked against, switching their positions too late for the second loader to stop its charge. It rammed its prongs through its twin's engine and cab compartment. The dying loader bled smoke and oil. Flames sprang up from its already-mangled hood top.

With *Scarlett* freed, Kimberlain drew her backward. Although her arms were locked in place, the delicate controls stripped by the battle, Kimberlain didn't hesitate. The second black loader had just extricated itself from its twin's smoking carcass when *Scarlett* smashed into it at full speed. The loader was driven sideways and back against the impetus of its own churning wheels. The impact threw Kimberlain forward, but he held fast to the controls. The final loader tried futilely to right itself and had almost succeeded when *Scarlett* slammed its back side into the car-crushing apparatus and held it there. Almost instantly, the top section of the crusher began its descent.

The enclosed cab section of the black loader compressed on impact. Glass shattered and flew outward. The loader's heavy steel back resisted briefly, forcing the crusher to rev higher, and then gave up the fight. Two of the huge tires exploded under the pressure and blew out all the glass in *Scarlett*'s cab. Kimberlain managed to duck low just in time, and when he looked up, the crusher was rising in its slot to reveal the flattened black loader.

He climbed down from *Scarlett*'s cab and walked off cautiously. The scrap yard seemed endless, as he slid by the still-smoking corpse of the other loader and crossed through the rest of the auto yard.

The section dominated by tall stacks of rusted oil drums was darker and more malevolent, but he welcomed the silence. He decided to take a more roundabout route to the appliance graveyard in order to stay hidden. By lingering in the open he had already helped Leeds twice, and Kimberlain didn't want to make it three times. There was just enough room for loading equipment to operate between the neatly stacked rows of oil drums. The setup provided him with cover, as well as views toward the scrap yard's main artery.

Thump . . . thump . . . thump . . .

The sound of what might have been heavy footsteps rose in the night.

Thump . . . thump . . . thump . . .

It came again, louder and more pronounced. Something was

coming, something that made no effort to disguise its approach.

The Ferryman cut back down one of the aisles, where towers of rusted brown keg drums rose toward the sky. He reached an intersecting row and backed into it for cover.

Thump . . . thump . . . thump . . .

Louder still. Whatever made the sound was coming up on his aisle from the yard's primary area. Kimberlain peered out down the aisle. A huge dark shadow loomed directly ahead of him. Clanking and clamoring, one of the two-tonners pounded its way across the dirt. A thousand pounds of orange steel carved in the outline of a man.

Though it featured the extremities and torso of a man, its head was a simple cage designed to protect the operator. When it walked, flexing at the knee joint like a man, its arms did not move or sway. Those same arms could be manipulated in virtually any direction and had been fitted with delicate yet powerful pincers to serve as hands.

The two-tonner passed out of sight toward the next row, and the Ferryman made sure of his breath before ducking that way toward it. When he eased around the cover of the drums to peer out again, he found the thing standing straight and still directly before him. Kimberlain started to duck back behind cover, but not before he saw the two-tonner's solid steel extremities coming up.

My God . . .

It had known he was there. Leeds, wherever he was, must have had hidden cameras placed all through the scrap yard. Kimberlain sensed what the two-tonner was going to do and burst into a dash to avoid it. He stumbled on the poorly packed, oil-rich gravel of the yard, just as the thing's powerful arms smashed against the closest pile of drums. Instantly, the steel kegs began to crumble, spreading not just down a single row, but also out in the direction Kimberlain was fleeing. He felt the drums thundering down in heap after clanging heap. It was like running from fire, the noise burning his ears.

Crack!

Kimberlain realized the columns he was rushing for were

now tumbling in a second avalanche. The walls of loosed steel seemed to be closing in on him like tidal waves sprung by a hurricane. He bolted down the center of the yard with the drums tumbling in his wake, as if his sprint were pulling them down behind him.

He finally got beyond the avalanche, but the two-tonner appeared from behind a newly formed mound of kegs directly in front of him. He could read the name *Moe* painted on its midsection. It lashed at him with a heavy steel arm, and Kimberlain ducked to avoid it, never breaking stride. The things were huge and capable of incredible lifting strength, but were generally slow and lumbering. A second two-tonner labeled *Larry* moved sideways to block his path. *Larry*'s arms snapped up to right angles, and its pincer apparatus turned. The machine seemed to be challenging him. *Moe*'s approach from the rear ruled out retreat that way, so the Ferryman chose the next best alternative. He leapt up onto a heap of drums the two-tonners had spilled over. The machines spun his way, but the Ferryman was already lunging from drum to drum, toward the appliance graveyard and escape.

As he reached the appliance graveyard, far outdistancing the pursuing two-tonners, he froze. Before him the tall neat columns of scrapped appliances had been tumbled into heaps blocking his way in all directions. The two-tonners must have done all this during his battle with the loaders back in the auto yard. Leeds had been taking no chances, and now Kimberlain was trapped.

Where was *Curly*?

He had barely formed that thought when a grating sound made him duck and twist. He avoided the brunt of *Curly*'s blow, but it nonetheless pitched him airborne and he slammed into a mound of gutted stoves. He slid sideways as *Curly* advanced toward him, eating up ground in huge gulps.

With no other path available, Kimberlain lunged onto the heaps of splintered appliances. He began leaping from one to another in a random path back toward the hole he had cut in the fence.

Curly plowed a more direct path, shoveling the piles of appliances effortlessly aside. A glance to his rear showed Kimberlain that the two-tonner had slowed long enough to grasp an ancient stove and lift it upward. It was airborne in the next instant. The Ferryman threw himself down on a mangled drier and the stove sailed over his head. The Ferryman clawed his way back to his feet and charged on until a refrigerator tilted under his weight. He went down hard and felt his foot catch between a pair of washing machines. *Curly* moved toward him at its top clip, the mounds of scrap receding in its path. It climbed atop the appliances nearest him and grasped what looked like half a refrigerator door in its pincers. The door came overhead and whistled down at Kimberlain, just as he yanked his foot free and backpedaled desperately. The door smashed brutally down on the spot he had just vacated. *Curly* drew it back for another try.

The Ferryman was on his feet again, still moving backward when the door swished by, inches from his face. *Curly* climbed atop the debris and followed him across the endless heap, pulling back for another blow as the trailing pair of two-tonners furrowed through the scrap at converging angles. Kimberlain assessed the situation between blinks and chose the only response available to him.

He scaled a higher peak of appliances and leapt down on *Curly*. The two-tonner spun wildly, like a bronco trying to throw its rider, but Kimberlain found enough purchase on its steel hull to hold on. He was not in a position to wedge his arms and legs into the slots provided. He could, however, reach some of the controls, including the one that was responsible for the thing's right arm. The one still holding the refrigerator door.

Kimberlain pressed the PINCER RELEASE button while he manipulated the arm back and then in a quick cut sideways. The refrigerator door whirled outward like a frisbee, straight into the line of *Moe*'s approach. The Ferryman heard the *thud* of impact, but only glimpsed *Moe* going down as *Curly* continued to spin in an attempt to shed him.

With *Larry* still advancing, Kimberlain at last found the

main control panel. He strained to reach the ON/OFF button, but *Curly*'s twisting kept him from depressing it. He wrapped his dangling feet tight around the two-tonner's extremities and tried to better his angle for the switch. At last he found it and pressed.

Nothing happened. *Curly* kept fighting, slamming him backward into a mound of washers and driers. Kimberlain reached out to cushion the impact with his arm and shredded more of his flesh on a sharp piece of a washer's exposed frame. He managed to close his fingers around the steel and tear it free while *Curly* spun and slammed him into a pile of refrigerators.

Once again, impact knocked the wind out of Kimberlain. But he maintained his grasp of the yard-long steel shard. The two-tonner was trying to reach back for him with its pincers, and he seized the opening provided to jam the pointed end of his shard into the control box. Sparks flew. He could smell smoke and hear a popping sound.

Curly twitched wildly but still tried for him with its pincers. Kimberlain jammed the shard in deeper and wrenched it up and down again. There was a fizzling, staticky sound. *Curly* stopped in the midst of reaching for him and keeled over backward. The Ferryman tried to twist to prevent being crushed under its weight. In the end, though, the best he could manage was to avoid the major brunt of impact. The two-tonner's carcass came down on his legs, pinning his lower body beneath it, leaving him for *Larry*.

The last of the two-tonners was almost upon him. It shoved a huge section of rusted debris from its path and continued to advance. Kimberlain fought to squeeze himself out, and when this failed tried to lift *Curly*'s frame from him. It was no use. The two-tonner weighed too much even to budge from this angle. *Larry* was coming. If Kimberlain was going to mount yet another struggle, it would have to be from down here.

With what, though?

No weapon was within his reach. He had only his hands to use from an inferior position against a machine that could snap

his spine with a single squeeze of its pincers. He saw it looming over him, pincers turning and snapping together like an
alligator's jaws. He kicked desperately to free his legs from
beneath *Curly* but succeeded only in pinning himself deeper.
Larry stood over him and hesitated, as if it could see he was
finished and wanted to savor the victory—as if it were seeing
with Leeds's eyes. At last, one of its massive arm extensions
raised upward and started whistling down.

Kimberlain might have closed his eyes if something long
and black hadn't whirled before him. There was a metallic
clang, and the two-tonner's hydraulic arm was knocked upward again. The Ferryman turned to see the impossible in the
form of a monstrous bare-chested shape lunging forward between him and the two-tonner.

Winston Peet!

Peet had never looked so big to him, even when measured
against the huge shape of *Larry*. The giant swirled a massive
square steel beam around again, smashing the two-tonner's
cage assembly atop its torso. The thing turned his way then,
and Peet squared to face it, weapon back level with his midsection.

The two-tonner advanced on him, its hydraulic legs bending
at the center with each step over the uneven terrain of scrap.
From his angle, the thing looked to Kimberlain like an ani-
mated monster from a science fiction film. Peet was big, but
the two-tonner towered over him by nearly two feet. Its pincers
came forward and lashed out at Peet's steel beam. The giant
pulled it away as if to tease the machine, careful to place his
feet on as firm a foundation as possible.

The two-tonner struggled briefly up a rise, and Peet slammed
his beam into one side of it and then up around into the other.
The thing wobbled but steadied itself.

"The knee!" Kimberlain screamed. "Go for its knee!"

Peet must have realized it at the same time, because his next
blow was already whirling that way, impacting squarely
against the joint.

Clang!

The sound was deafening. Peet brought his beam back and slashed it round once more.

CLANG!

Louder, harder. The two-tonner's leg bent inward and locked there. Peet went for the other one, but his precarious balance betrayed him and the two-tonner was able to grasp the beam within one of its pincers. It jerked upward but, incredibly, the giant stood his ground. *Larry* thrust its other pincer out, and Peet blocked it with the end of the beam he still controlled. The two-tonner shoved with all its force, and Peet went flying, the steel beam tumbling to the scrap-strewn mound after him. His massive bald head slammed into a stove and he lay there still.

"Peet!" the Ferryman shouted, still struggling unsuccessfully to extricate himself from *Curly*. "Peet!"

Larry moved for the kill, its left leg bent inward and dragging. Its good leg kicked aside the relics in its path, and it climbed the steep hill of junk. The two-tonner's pincers angled themselves forward and down.

Kimberlain watched Peet's fingers close on the steel beam from his downed position in the instant the two-tonner loomed over him. The bald giant started the beam in motion, even as *Larry* swooped in low with its pincers.

The deadly pincers stopped inches from Peet's face as he drove the beam into the *Larry*'s midsection. The intent of the move was not clear to Kimberlain until he saw an explosion of dark ooze spray outward onto Peet.

Oil, hydraulic fluid! Peet had smashed the two-tonner in the one place it was truly vulnerable. Without the fluid pumping through it, *Larry*'s flexible parts seized up almost instantly. It seemed to hang there in slow, surreal motion before it keeled over backward, frozen in the same attack position it had assumed just seconds before.

Peet regained his feet and moved toward the Ferryman. As big as he was, his stride was light and graceful as a dancer's. His massive chest and shoulder muscles rippled beneath the splattering of oil. Wordlessly, he reached down and hoisted

Curly up, allowing Kimberlain to drag his lower body out.

"Can you walk, Ferryman?" he asked as he eased an arm beneath him.

"I'll manage."

Kimberlain was almost upright when his legs gave way. Consciousness had faded even before Peet caught him halfway to the ground. The giant leaned over and hoisted the Ferryman effortlessly upon his shoulder. Something made him stop at that point and turn about. His gaze turned upward. Mounted on a light standard high above the junkyard was a camera watching him through the darkness like an eye.

Andrew Harrison Leeds jumped to his feet, the wheel-based desk chair jetting backward across the floor. The face peered through the camera at him and then was gone.

It couldn't be! He was dead! Winston Peet was dead!

But Leeds could not be mistaken. The face on the screen had been that of Winston Peet.

He had watched in awe as Kimberlain battled his machines. The man truly belonged with him here, not in the old world so soon to perish. In the end, when the battle with the two-tonners began, it was all Leeds could do not to root for him to win. Then, when the Ferryman's death seemed certain, something had gone wrong just out of camera range. Now he saw what that something had been. Peet had intervened and destroyed the two-tonner that had been about to kill the Ferryman.

Winston Peet! Imagine the possibilities. . . .

It must have been ordained that the battle in his scrap yard would end this way. After all, if there was one man besides the Ferryman that Leeds truly admired, it was Peet. His one great rival whose efforts were nearly a match for his own. But Peet had escaped from The Locks and drowned in Lake Ontario. At least that was what they said. Obviously, though, he had survived and had joined forces with Kimberlain—a match better suited for hell than heaven. It was another potential allegiance, however, that Leeds's mind strayed to.

"Winston," Leeds said to the screen, "can you hear me, Winston?"

He fancied that the bald giant paused as he neared the edge of the camera's range.

"You belong with me, Winston. You belong here. We belong together."

The possibility set Andrew Harrison Leeds trembling, as Winston Peet vanished into the night.

THE FIFTH DOMINION

Lucretia McEvil

Wednesday, August 19; 9:00 A.M.

CHAPTER 20

Aɴᴅʀᴇᴡ Harrison Leeds sat before his wall of video monitors, his own reflection a dull outline on each of the screens. At last he leaned forward and activated one of the monitors.

A shot of Chalmers sitting rigid in a chair filled the screen. Chalmers gazed up at the camera mounted before and above him, as if he knew it had been switched on.

"What are we to do with you, Mr. Chalmers?" Leeds asked him.

Chalmers made sure the speaker attached to his throat was facing the camera.

"Out of . . . control," he said.

"Meaning your operatives, of course. All having gone the way of Hedda, is that it? There's something I think you should listen to."

Leeds pressed a button. Instantly a pair of voices filled the room where Chalmers sat alone in the darkness.

"Who are you?"

"We could leave me as your grandfather. Easier that way, more pleasant and acceptable."

"A lie."

"But, you see, there is no truth. There never was, not for you or any of the others."

Leeds stopped the tape. "Recognize the voices, Chalmers?"

Chalmers's face had paled to match the color of the

socket sprouting from his throat. "Hedda," came his mechanical wheezing rasp, the syllables more of an effort than usual.

"And Pomeroy, of course. We've already dispensed with the old man, a regrettable fact necessitated by your inability to eliminate Hedda as ordered. Hedda, meanwhile, has become even more dangerous to us now. Your failure has forced me to expend my own resources to deal with her."

"I can find . . . her."

"She is my problem now. But a much more pressing problem is that you would have me believe that the others I entrusted to your care have turned rogue as well."

"Everything . . . has broken down. . . . They won't come . . . in."

"And how hard have you tried to tell them to?" Chalmers made no reply. "I had high hopes for you, Mr. Chalmers. You are someone who could have stayed by my side through the magnificent restructuring of society that is soon to take place." Leeds's finger moved to the red button that was apart from the others on his console. "But now you have failed. And for failure there is a price."

Leeds pressed the red button. Chalmers's body lurched horribly in his chair. His speaker fell to the floor, and his limbs twitched spasmodically.

"A pity," Leeds said out loud. "A pity."

And he turned off the monitor screen.

Chalmers waited several minutes before opening his eyes, wanting to be sure T. Howard Briarwood was no longer watching. Disconnecting the wire that fed current into the chair had been a simple matter, as was rigging the same wire to a bulb across the room. When the bulb lit up Chalmers knew it was time to play dead.

The possibility that Briarwood might want to dispose of him had always been very real to Chalmers and had grown increasingly more real as of late. Ultimately Chalmers had elected to force the issue; his apparent death would give him the freedom to enact the remainder of his plan.

He checked his watch: just a few more hours before the next stage would be upon him. Chalmers climbed out of the chair and moved toward the door, eyes lingering on T. Howard Briarwood's camera for the last time.

"I'm sorry, miss," the policeman said as politely as he could manage. "The whole area's still closed off until we're sure it's safe."

Hedda tried not to show any reaction besides dismay. "What happened?"

"Plastic plant burned down to the ground. Air's still polluted with chemicals."

Hedda shrugged and turned her car around. Inside, fear tugged at her. She knew which plant it was without being told; she had known since catching the first scent of a harsh burnt odor several blocks back. She had come here to Leominster, Massachusetts, on a two hour drive straight from Logan Airport, where she had flown in from Paris. The drive on top of the flight had left her fatigued until the sharp acrid stench of an inferno's aftermath revived her.

Hedda parked her car on a nearby street and approached PLAS-TECH on foot. Pinned to her sweater was the press badge she carried to permit access where it might otherwise be denied. She carried a notepad and pen to further flesh out the charade.

A fireman with a soot-blackened face was sitting on the sill of his truck as she passed. Hedda stopped and came back his way.

"When did it start?"

"I been here twelve hours."

"Arson?"

"Could be we'll never know."

Hedda jotted some notes and spoke again. "How many dead?"

The fireman regarded her with disdain. "Where you been, lady?"

"They sent me up from New York."

He stood up. "Then let me give you the scoop. Employees were working a full shift in there when the building went. Every last goddamn one of them was trapped."

There had been four survivors. By morning, one had already died, and the three others lingered in critical condition. The least critical of these, Hedda learned, had been transferred to the burn unit at Mass General Hospital.

The morning edition of the *Boston Globe* told her pretty much everything else she needed to know, not just about the fire but about the background of PLAS-TECH as well. The company was a plastics manufacturer that was doing just fine with the space program until NASA's bottom dropped out after *Challenger*. It retooled and rebuilt but lost a fortune along the way. Then a subsidiary of the massive Briarwood Industries conglomerate bought out PLAS-TECH, and rumors abounded that the company had been granted an unspecified government contract. Whatever the case, the stock soared and the company was well on its way to recovery when the fire struck last night. Tragically, it was reported, all indications were that the sprinkler system was never activated.

Tragic but not surprising, Hedda reckoned. Somehow PLAS-TECH must have been linked to whatever plot was to employ Lyle Hanley's transdermal toxin. Hanley had produced it while remaining unsure until the very end how it was going to be dispensed. Perhaps the answer lay with PLAS-TECH. Perhaps something they had manufactured had been treated with TD-13.

At Mass General, Hedda incapacitated a female security guard, left her in a storage closet, and emerged in her uniform. The survivor from the deadly fire was named Ruth Kroll. Hedda found her room and cringed at the sight. The form lying in the bed of ice barely resembled anything human. Only the eye and cheek on the left side of her face were free of bandages. The rest of her body was encased in white gauze.

"Mrs. Kroll?"

The eye turned toward Hedda slowly.

"We need to talk, Mrs. Kroll. I know you're in pain and I'm sorry, but the fire last night wasn't an accident. It was set to wipe out all traces of whatever you had been working on at PLAS-TECH. It was set by people who plan to kill far more people."

Ruth Kroll's eye glistened with tears.

"Will you help me?"

No response. But the eye regarded her, asking questions of its own.

"I can get to those people, Mrs. Kroll. I can stop them. It's what brought me here. But I need your help."

The woman's bandaged right hand rose off the bed of ice. Hedda came closer and placed a pen in it. The hand grasped it as best it could. Hedda held her notepad in front of it.

Who? Ruth Kroll asked.

"I don't know yet."

The eye blinked in frustration.

Who? Ruth Kroll scrolled again.

"Who am I, you mean. The same people who did this to you tried to kill me. They'll try again unless I find them."

Ask, the bandaged hand wrote in wide strokes.

"What had PLAS-TECH been working on since being purchased by Briarwood Industries?"

Contract.

Hedda flipped the page. "Yes, a government contract. I know that. But what were you producing?"

The writing took longer this time, letters lengthening and overlapping themselves. *Micro-thin plastic strips. Monofilament design. Meshlike. Millions of them.*

"For what?"

Don't know.

"Were they destroyed in the fire?"

No. Already shipped.

"Where?"

Ruth Kroll waited for Hedda to turn to a fresh page. *Three production plants.*

"What kind of plants?"

Paper.

Hedda was as frustrated with that answer as the poor woman seemed with the whole direction of the questioning. It made no sense. Assuming the shipped plastic strips had been treated with TD-13, why had they been shipped to paper mills?

"Did all this have something to do with the government contract PLAS-TECH was working on?"

Strips did, the woman scrawled.

"How?"

Don't know, she wrote. *Secret even from us.* The ice sloshed about her as she shifted painfully.

"Who might know? Is there anyone I can talk to who can help me find out the secret?"

O'Rourke, the woman jotted.

Hedda recalled the name from the news clipping Deerslayer had left for her in Paris. The clipping had to do with Briarwood Industries' acquisition of PLAS-TECH. O'Rourke had been the lone Briarwood official quoted.

"Where can I find him?" Hedda asked.

When phone calls to O'Rourke's Boston office yielded nothing, Hedda learned from Briarwood Industries' central headquarters that he was at his vacation home in Stowe, Vermont. She drove north and called his number when she was a half hour away, announcing herself as a Briarwood administrative assistant who needed him to sign some papers immediately. The woman who answered informed her that he had taken his kids to the Alpine Slide and would be back early that evening.

The Alpine Slide recreational complex was located another ten minutes from O'Rourke's home. She would have to rely on the picture from Deerslayer's news clipping to recognize him. Though it was black and white, the shot was clear enough for her to know he was a tall man with thick salt-and-pepper hair. She'd know him once she saw him at the complex. The presence of his kids could complicate things, however. After all, there was the very real possibility that O'Rourke was in danger as well.

All the more reason to seek him out, Hedda told herself. Everything pointed to the fact that Lyle Hanley's TD-13 had been implanted on the plastic strips produced at PLAS-TECH. O'Rourke was her only chance at this point of finding out what the three paper mills were going to do with them.

Why three? Why not just one to ease security problems?

The answer lay in the government contract O'Rourke would be able to enlighten her on.

The Alpine Slide complex was crowded on such a perfect summer day, and Hedda studied the faces for O'Rourke's. She rotated her search among the shops, restaurant, water slide area, and the Alpine Slide itself. She could see people on colored sleds barreling down the last of the Alpine Slide where it spiraled down the mountain like a white marble fountain. Actually it was formed of asbestos asphalt, a surface most conducive to jetting down its banked structure. To the right of the slide was a complex of water slides filled with splashing children.

The lines for both attractions were long, and Hedda continued to loiter. As she made her way once again through an area of small sheds featuring displays of candies and crafts, she suddenly spotted her quarry. There, standing with two boys near a hut called the Fudge Factory, was O'Rourke. She recognized him instantly from the photograph.

Before she could approach him, O'Rourke was dragged by the boys back toward the line for the Alpine Slide. She would follow him up, then, and speak to him up on the mountain where there would be fewer people around.

O'Rourke and his sons boarded a tram car which would carry them to the drop-off point for the slide. Hedda rode alone in a car a dozen back from her quarry's. She wondered if O'Rourke was in danger even now, wondered if the presence of his sons had been the only thing that had saved him. A warning would be necessary after they spoke, just as she had warned Hanley.

By the halfway point in the climb, the sloping angle hid O'Rourke's car from view. Judging by his head start, he would reach the unloading platform a minute or two before her and then take his place with his sons among those patrons waiting for a run down one of the twin tracks.

The beginning of the tram ride had shown her more of the asbestos asphalt track that swirled and dipped through the mountainside. Closer inspection of the plastic sled hanging from her car revealed wheels on its underside that could be lowered or raised by manipulating a center gear lever. The lower, the faster. Pull the lever all the way toward you and the sled would grind to a halt. Push it all the way forward and the wheels would be forced down flat against the track; the effect would be akin to flying down the mountain.

Hedda could see the unloading platform clearly now, and with that checked the Sig Sauer holstered well back on her hip beneath her light windbreaker, hoping it would not be required. Her tram passed under a sign instructing her to raise the safety bar, and Hedda obliged as her car slid over the wooden unloading platform. A white line told her when to ease herself from her seat, and she followed a streak of white arrows to the right off the platform. Before her, a pair of teenage boys who'd ridden the car immediately ahead of hers grasped plastic sleds from a nearby ramp, and Hedda did the same to blend with the scene.

A pair of long single file lines had formed starting to the platform's right, composed entirely of sled-bearing patrons awaiting their turn to plunge down one of the Alpine Slide's twin chutes. Hedda joined the left-hand line and peered ahead in search of O'Rourke's salt-and-pepper hair.

The line was moving quite slowly. Hedda was close enough to the chutes now to hear the grinding sounds of sled tires being lowered to the slippery asphalt track surface, as riders disappeared around the first bank at regular intervals. Fifteen places ahead in line, a tall man leaned over to tie his sneaker, and

Hedda's eyes locked on the salt-and-pepper hair that had been hidden up until then. She should approach O'Rourke now, while they were safe up here. His sons were in line in front of him, meaning she could even wait for them to begin their drops before making her move.

"Excuse me. I'm sorry."

Hedda was jostled to the right as a man slid by her toward the front of the line. A parent looking for a child perhaps, she thought, since he wasn't carrying a sled.

Something made her turn to her rear. Other men had taken up posts through the area of the lines, none with a sled in hand. One met her stare, and his eyes wavered uncertainly, hand creeping inside his jacket.

It was too hot a day for anyone to be wearing a jacket unless they had something concealed within it, as she had.

They had come for O'Rourke!

Hedda discarded her sled to the side and threw herself forward just as the man who had jostled by her yanked out a machine gun. A woman screamed nearby, and O'Rourke swung round. The man fired a burst, and blood leapt from O'Rourke's midsection. Hedda crashed into the Gunman from behind. He pitched downward, machine gun flying from his hand.

"It's her!"

"Hedda! . . ."

The screams reached her ears from behind as Hedda drew her own pistol and lunged toward O'Rourke's shrieking children. She took them down and covered them in the instant before indiscriminate automatic fire opened up from the gunmen posted amid the lines. The screaming intensified. Bodies dropped everywhere, impossible for her to tell whether from bullets or for cover. She fired six times in rapid succession, aim shunted by the innocent bystanders attempting to flee. At least the children were safe, though, now that the killers had her as a target to focus on.

She could not possibly work her way back to the tram line, leaving only one possible escape route: the slide itself.

To reach it, she had to make the chaos work for her instead

of against her. Rising into a crouch, she fired off another rapid burst of six shots and moved toward a sled sitting empty at the top of the track.

CHAPTER 21

SHE leapt on the sled and shoved it forward along the brief straightaway that led into the slide's first drop. Jamming the hand lever all the way forward for maximum speed with one hand, she steadied the Sig Sauer with the other and turned back around as the sled jetted down the slide. She drained her clip in the general direction of the gunmen gathering above her, which bought her time to drive the sled into the first curve and out of sight.

She had just steadied herself in a normal riding position when a figure hurled itself with a scream over the track's side atop her. Hedda saw the man's knife in time to ward off the first strike and launch a vicious elbow into the face now level with hers. The man screamed again and went for Hedda as the sled slid into a steep drop. Hedda had managed to wedge a leg forward against the lever to keep the wheels lowered all the way, but had yielded position to her assailant in the process. The man rose over her, and when Hedda turned to focus on his knife, his free hand cracked into her chin. Hedda felt her head being forced over into the track whistling by beneath them.

That certainly further fueled her desperation. Her own people were out to do the job they had failed to do in Lebanon.

Hedda fought to jam one hand into the attacker's face while the other locked on the wrist bearing the knife to keep it away from her body. Trees and bushes sped by, and the sled rolled precariously up on the track's side, nearly sliding off onto the adjoining turf. The man continued trying to force Hedda's head down, and she managed to maintain the stalemate. Her advantage was that she was in control of the sled. Steadying her leg against the control lever, she dipped her shoe to the lever's far side and jammed it toward her instead of pushing it away. Instantly the wheels were pulled back with brakes lowered in their place. A grinding screech found her ears, and her assailant was lifted slightly forward. Hedda was ready for the sudden stop, but the man wasn't. She twisted out of his grasp and maneuvered on top of him.

Maintaining her control of the man's knife hand, Hedda shoved his head sideways until it came into contact with the curved track siding. At the same time she jammed the control lever all the way forward again, wheels lowered as the sled dipped into its steepest drop yet. Her ears were stung by the sound of the man's skull scraping against the asphalt, a trail of blood left in his wake. Straining every muscle, she heaved him off the sled into the brush rimming the track.

By the time Hedda's sled was moving again at top speed, she heard gunshots behind her. Another pair was pursuing her on sleds, firing at the same time. The shots were errant, though, both because of the movement and the awkward firing positions.

Hedda grasped the lesson in that and reached beneath her for her Sig Sauer. After snapping a fresh clip home, she tucked it into her waistband within easy reach. Then she stood up and found an uneasy balance, as the sled sped into a straightaway where a banner read SLOW!

Hedda saw that the sides of the track had lowered to almost nothing. Her sled wavered fitfully as she struggled for an uneasy equilibrium with right foot working the control lever. She kept it pressed as far forward as it would go and rode the track standing fully upright like a surfer on a huge wave.

The track banked into a sharp curve that sent her listing almost parallel to the ground. The sled righted in the other direction and Hedda compensated by shifting her weight, gun now steadied in one hand. The pursuers dropped into the straightaway and caught clear sight of her standing form for the first time. The one on her track fired from a crouch with his machine gun, but another curve came up fast and Hedda disappeared around it. When the gunman swung round the same curve, Hedda's gun was trained on him. A bullet spun the man around and lifted him airborne, and he flew off the track through the air.

Hedda turned forward again in time to shift her weight to jibe with the bends of an S curve that featured a smiling wooden figure between the tracks holding a sign urging CAUTION! She swung fast at the sound of wheels speeding down the other side. The other man had risen, too, but was unable to maintain his balance. At the instant he pulled the trigger a sharp curve threw him from the sled, and Hedda watched both sled and rider fly from the track as bullets stitched the air.

Hedda, meanwhile, had no idea where precisely on the track she was. She knew sight of a blue water slide on her left would mean the final stretch was coming. She took a curve hard, and again her sled flirted with the edge of the track. Behind her the grinding *whoooossssh* from around the bend to her rear signaled another pair of attackers closing fast, one on each track. They broke into the open, and from her sideways standing position Hedda could see both had settled into crouches that permitted them to steady their machine guns across the front of their sleds. The staccato bursts pierced the warm air and echoed along the brush of the mountainside. Hedda did her best to aim through the turns and curves, but the bullets from her Sig were faring no better than the opposition's automatic fire when it came to hitting targets. Her next squeeze of the trigger brought a click, signaling an empty clip.

Her pursuers' automatic weapons provided them with a much fuller sweep, and Hedda presented an easier target for them than she would have wished. She took advantage of a thickly wooded area rimming the track to reload her Sig and was ready when she re-emerged into the open.

Twisting to her rear, Hedda snapped off a series of rapid bursts as her opposition's automatic fire fought for a bead on her. One of her bullets ricocheted off the asphalt track siding and grazed the enemy on her track. His sled wobbled fitfully, and he was pitched headlong over the side, thumping across the ground. The gunman across wavered as well, and again Hedda widened the gap between them.

Hedda knew he had no choice but to go all out to catch her, and she elected to let him. She negotiated through an especially difficult bank turn to the left and chose it as her spot, since it would come equally as hard for the gunman speeding her way.

His sled rolled up and nearly over the track's edge as he swung into the bank. Hedda saw his body wavering from side to side in the last instant before she fired the final two bullets in her clip. Impact tossed the man upward into the air from the track, while incredibly his sled held to its position and continued straight on, slowing by itself.

Hedda ejected the spent clip and extracted a final one from her jacket pocket.

The squealing approach of a sled running with wheels all the way down on the adjacent track alerted her to yet another attack. She turned and saw a large man thundering for her, machine gun in hand. If her count of the men atop the mountain was correct, this was the last one she'd have to contend with. He opened fire, and one of his bullets bounced off the asphalt and stung Hedda's wrist, numbing it. She lost her grip on the fresh clip she had yet to slide home into the Sig. It fluttered in the air, and she snatched at it futilely before it dropped to the ground behind her. There would be no outgunning this final adversary now. Outrunning him seemed equally impossible.

The track! Think of the track!

It swerved to the left toward the blue of the water slide en route to the final straightaway leading to the foot of the mountain. She caught glimpses of the crowd fleeing in a panic brought on by the gun battle. Cars thundered from the parking lot. Sirens wailed, drawing closer.

Hedda realized where her only chance lay and crouched low, readying her legs to spring as she wrapped the hand she could still feel around the control lever. She didn't need to look behind her; her ears told her everything she needed to know about the enemy's position.

Bullets singed the air above her, and a few pounded the asphalt at the lower rim of the track. Above her, the attacker dropped into the sharp turn that banked into the final straightaway, machine-gun fire drawing a closer bead.

Now!

She jammed the control lever toward her, brakes meeting the asphalt surface with an ear-wrenching screech. She braced herself to avoid the violent forward thrust of stopping short and rose to stand erect as the gunman whizzed toward her. Her sudden stop had spoiled his aim, and he worked frantically to diminish his own speed.

Hedda leapt when the man's sled drew even with hers. Impact drove both of them through the air, their progress stopped when they slammed into the rim of the water slide. The machine gun was still held to the man by a strap slung round his shoulder, and he fought to gain control of it again. Hedda had expected him to do precisely that. She wedged the gun against his body with her numb hand and pounded his face with her other. The man managed to twist away after the third blow, slippery and lithe as a snake as he tore himself from Hedda's grasp, almost free.

The sounds of water rushing by in the slide gave Hedda the idea for her next strategy. Grabbing hold of the man's hair, she yanked violently and propelled both of them all the way over the rim into the water slide itself. The pair, inseparable now, crashed down the jetting currents with Hedda on top and the man struggling to relocate the trigger pinned beneath him.

Hedda ignored the gun; grasping a thick handful of the man's hair, she bashed his head against the frame of the water slide. Then she twisted it around so that his face was pressed into the swirling waters as they dipped and darted through the S-like design. Hedda kept the pressure up with all her might, the man's flesh taking the brunt of the contact with the water slide's bottom. They hit the pool at the slide's end hard, and Hedda jammed the man's face down one last time to force as much water into his lungs as possible.

He sank slowly to the bottom, and she bounded out from the pool. Around her the chaos was everywhere. She rushed for the parking lot in the hope she would be able to join it.

"You!" a scream ran out behind her. *"Stop!"*

She had been seen, then, identified as one of the parties in the battle that had raged up on the mountain. Before her in the parking lot cars continued to scramble away. Perhaps she could reach one just as its owner was inserting his key, or yank a driver from behind the wheel.

She was charging forward with that intention, when a trio of police cars blared into the parking lot and headed straight for her. She spun around to flee in the opposite direction and saw an old sedan hurtling toward her. Hedda lunged out of its way, and it screeched to a halt beside her. She caught a glimpse of the driver and couldn't believe her eyes.

"Get in!" Chalmers ordered.

CHAPTER 22

FOR a long moment, she couldn't move.

This was Librarian, her control! He had set her up in Lebanon, deceived and then tried to kill—

"I said . . . get in!" the speaker wedged against his windshield blared.

Bullets slammed into the ground around her, and Hedda jumped into the backseat.

Librarian jammed the big sedan into reverse and floored the accelerator before she had gotten the door all the way closed. Just as it caught, the sedan's rear end slammed into a pair of police cars speeding for it. Librarian spun the wheel and floored the gas pedal in a desperate move to escape. Bystanders dove from its path as the car tore forward, jumping the curb and clanging hard to the pavement. Its back window exploded and showered Hedda with glass. She could hear Librarian's labored breathing, coming from his speaker, she thought, and not his mouth.

The slight head start Librarian had gained over his pursuers wouldn't last long. In hopes of foiling the pursuit, he spun the big sedan onto an unmarked, unpaved road a mile down the main drag before the police drew back in sight.

"Listen to me," he rasped, turning around to look at her.

"The road!" she screamed, as the car left the road and headed for the trees.

Chalmers looked back too late. He managed to swing the wheel to avoid a head-on collision, but impact was nonetheless jarring. Hedda kicked her door open and moved around to his. The radiator was hissing from the white steam that was rising from beneath the crumpled hood.

"Come on!" she screamed at him, finding her feet. "Hurry!"

Chalmers mouthed, "Can't."

Hedda stooped and grasped a rock. "Look away," she warned, and then smashed what remained of the driver's side window. Still not understanding why Librarian had chosen to rescue her, Hedda eyed him warily, then reached inside to grab him. His leg was pinned between the crushed door and the seat. Hedda pried it free and hoisted him out.

She gazed back up toward the road, over two hundred yards away. "I don't hear them yet, but they'll be coming. We've got to move."

From the ground, Librarian mouthed, "My speaker."

Still eyeing him with caution, Hedda reached inside the car and found it lying on the passenger seat. Then she hoisted him to his feet and began to drag him away. When it was obvious he couldn't walk well enough to cover any ground, Hedda effortlessly placed him over her shoulders. None of her own wounds were serious, but there wasn't a part of her that didn't ache beneath her slowly drying clothes.

She brought Librarian as far into the woods as she thought necessary to avoid pursuit from whoever found the car. For some reason, he had helped her escape, even though the Gunmen back at the slide might as well have been the same ones from the Litani River Bridge. She set him down and gave him his speaker.

"Time to talk, Librarian," she ordered.

"Chalmers," he mouthed.

"What?"

"My name is . . . Chalmers," he mouthed again, reaching for his speaker.

"You saved my life back there."

A nod.

"Why? You tried to kill me first, and then you save me. Why?"

He fumbled the speaker as he drew it upward. Stretching the cord out, he found the pronged end and raised it obscenely for his throat. Three holes peeked out from the discolored patch, looking like bites from a vampire. Chalmers felt his way and jammed the prongs into the proper slots.

Instantly a wheezing sound emanated from the speaker, a wet gurgle like that of a man bleeding to death inside.

"No," emerged through the wetness.

"Bullshit!"

"I let you . . . escape in . . . Lebanon."

"Your men shot at me! They hit that boy!"

"But you lived . . . You got away . . . like I knew . . . you would."

"What are you saying?"

"They wanted you . . . dead. I couldn't . . . do it. Not . . . after Deerslayer."

"No! You had him killed!"

Chalmers's expression looked pained. "Like killing . . . a piece of . . . myself." He shook his head. "I wouldn't . . . do it again. . . . Not to you . . . not to the . . . others."

"The Caretakers?"

Chalmers nodded. "They were mine . . . You were mine. . . . I couldn't hand . . . you over to . . . him."

Hedda felt chilled. "To who?"

"Not yet," Chalmers said, shaking his head.

Hedda grabbed him at the shoulders. "Now!"

"You're not . . . ready yet. . . . Trust me."

"Why should I?"

"Because I . . . saved your life . . . twice now."

"But you lied to me. You lied to Deerslayer. About the boy. All of it, lies! His father wasn't Aramco, he was an organic chemist." Hedda stopped. "Wait. If you arranged the boy's kidnapping, why'd you need me to get him back?"

"Screens . . . fronts . . . everywhere . . . the Arabs held . . . the boy for us. . . . But then they . . . wouldn't give him . . . back. We tracked . . . them down and . . . sent you."

"So you could kill him?"

"No. Just you."

Hedda slid backward, suddenly wanting to put distance between herself and Chalmers.

"I would have . . . returned the boy . . . to his father."

"You expect me to believe that?"

"I expected . . . you to do . . . what you did. . . . I knew you . . . would save the boy. . . . I let it . . . all happen . . . because it was . . . the only way I . . . could keep you . . . alive."

"Why bother?"

"Because you . . . are the best. . . . That's why I . . . need you now."

"Need *me*?"

"It may be too . . . late to stop him."

"Stop *who*?"

Chalmers seemed to be catching his breath. Hedda spoke again before he had a chance to reply.

"Lyle Hanley's son was kidnapped to force him to create a poison deadly to the touch. My God, that's what this is about. Whoever it is you suddenly want to stop has the poison! That's it, Librarian, isn't it?"

Chalmers nodded slowly.

"What else?"

"I don't . . . know."

"I do. The way the poison is going to be delivered is somehow connected to a plastics company that burned to the ground yesterday. I think the poison was placed in plastic strips and then shipped to a trio of paper mills as part of some secret government contract. But what is it that's coming out of those mills?"

Chalmers's face twisted in puzzlement. "I don't know. . . . I never did."

"But you do know millions of people are going to die, don't you? You know that's what The Caretakers were involved in the whole time. I've seen Pomeroy, Librarian. I know *what* I am, what all of us were. But I still don't know *who* I am, Chalmers. Who am I?"

"You don't want . . . to know."

"I *have* to know. You said you need me, but I'm not going to help you until you tell me *who I am*!"

Chalmers regarded her thoughtfully. She didn't realize he was speaking again until she heard the speaker's rasp coming from next to his lap.

"Only name that . . . matters," he started with strange evenness, "is the one . . . you were . . . wanted under."

"Wanted?" Hedda waited with breath held and stilled heartbeat as Chalmers's next words emerged.

"For murder. They . . . called you . . . Lucretia McEvil."

The memories came flooding back as pieces of her story emerged through the speaker in rasps and gurgles. Hedda didn't need to hear it all; enough was returning on its own, triggered by the name.

Lucretia McEvil . . .

The name for her the press had used a dozen years ago. It was all coming back to her, and she realized with terrifying starkness that August Pomeroy had been right: she indeed *did not* want it to. The easiest memories to suppress are those the conscious mind would prefer to smother. Pomeroy had said that was what made her a willing subject. So much she wanted to suppress. Becoming a different person was infinitely preferable to staying the one she had been.

Fragments of a fractured life came back to her in large chunks, fitting themselves together as Chalmers continued to speak. Her eyes left him and focused on the speaker in his lap, but soon they saw nothing other than what her mind had denied her for years.

Chalmers's words concerned the events of 1979, but the fragments of her life before that time were returning as well. There were five of them in all, friends from the sixties who missed the fire of those times and decided to bring it all back. The raw, untempered violence that had been expected for a time, even condoned. Where had it gone? Vietnam was finished, along with the cause and the rationale it brought. But who needed a rationale when you came right down to it? Revolution was revolution. You didn't need a cause; you needed a desire.

Hedda and the others called themselves the Storm Riders, after the song "Riders on the Storm" by the Doors. They planned to ride herd on the storm, sweep the nation away in its vortex and show it that God might be dead, but His wrath sure the fuck wasn't. Their group was spawned from the remnant waste of the Weathermen and SDS, fringe dwellers who had almost remade society and got buried for it in the end.

They took their names from famous songs from the times that had spawned them. Hedda was Lucretia McEvil from Blood, Sweat and Tears. Bob Calhoun was the Reaper from the Blue Oyster Cult tune. Frank Webb was Major Tom courtesy of David Bowie. Ian Swenson was the Sandman from the song of that name by America. And Paula Rebb became Eleanor Rigby, who was buried along with her name.

The Storm Riders took themselves seriously. Maybe it had started as a game, but it hadn't ended up that way. They'd robbed banks, depositories, even a casino once. Their specialty, though, was kidnapping. At first they chose their victims politically. Before long politics changed to economics. Only the facade of activism remained.

The boy had been thirteen years old, Hedda remembered now. His name was Ricky Baylor. They'd grabbed him after school while he was waiting for the bus. Son of a rich Washington lawyer who had actually defended a number of fringe dwellers back when revolution was more fashionable. Hedda had just walked right up and snatched him, shot up the bus a little to discourage anyone from playing hero.

Though a woman, she was actually the tallest of the Storm Riders and equally as strong as the men. Naturally attractive she deliberately worked against her good looks, for the Storm Riders didn't care about how they looked. That was buying into the system. Thinking products from Revlon or Max Factor could change your life was bullshit. You wanted change, you went out and did it, went out and *made* it.

The Storm Riders weren't really changing much, except maybe themselves. If Calhoun and Webb couldn't transport themselves back to the sixties, maybe good old LSD could. They started eating the stuff and seeing zoo animals everywhere. Paula went sex crazy, fucking everything in sight, including, perhaps especially, her .44 magnum. She chambered a single bullet once and played her own version of Russian roulette. Spun the cylinder and stuck the gun up into herself, pulled the hammer back and fired.

Click.

Said it was the best come she ever had. Ian and Hedda stayed clear of the drugs and the weird stuff, and through it all, somehow, they fell in love. They would lie in bed hugging while in the next room Bob would be freaking out over some inside-out acid dream where the world changed color and only he could see it. And next door down Paula was screaming in ecstasy with God knew what jammed inside herself.

It was all coming apart, but none of them could see it. They made up their own rules, and if the rules changed that was okay, too. The Baylor kid would make everything all right for a while. They needed to disappear, burrow underground to recharge the fringe batteries that had drained dry on excessiveness. Make themselves a cool mill on this one and ride into the sunset on a horse with no name.

But Bob the Reaper fucked up. Got himself IDed buying groceries; never even saw the FBI man who was one of five hundred showing pictures around the Washington area where their van had been found. Goddamn Frank was supposed to torch it, but he forgot the detonators and just drove it into a ditch instead.

"This is the FBI. Come out with your hands in the air. We know you're in there. The house is surrounded."

Hedda was the only one who heard this first challenge over the bullhorn. Ian was asleep, Bob and Frank were tripping, and Paula was painting the inside of her vagina with cocaine. Hedda reached the window just as the spotlights came on, the house hit by a sudden patch as bright as day. They were everywhere, more guns than people, barrels attached to figures lost to the night.

"What the fuck?" Bob wondered, as he stumbled down the stairs with a pair of pistols in hand.

"Wow," Paula said, emerging from painting class in the kitchen.

"We're fucked," Hedda heard Ian say.

"I repeat. We have the house surrounded. Come out with your hands up, surrender the boy and—"

"Ah, fuck you!"

Frank's booming voice shattered the night, rising even over the bullhorn. Automatic fire from one of the upstairs windows followed, and one of the cops' windshields exploded. Instantly the fire was returned, peppering the house and chewing it apart.

"Ahhhhhhhhhhhhh!"

Hedda was conscious of her own screaming, and for a brief time nothing else. But then something happened. The Storm Riders got their collective sense back. The five terrorists who at that time occupied five slots on the FBI's most wanted list coalesced once more into a fighting group. Bob took charge.

"Sandman, back up the Major upstairs. Rigby watch the back. Lucretia, get the kid from the basement. He's still our ticket out of this!"

They grasped rifles from closets and corners first, and then went for grenades and belt fed machine guns. The house continued to shake under the fusillade of bullets pounding it, but now the fire was being returned in kind. Death had already knocked. Thing was to trip it up after you opened the door.

Hedda held her hands cupped over her ears as she descended into the basement. She found the boy tied up and blindfolded where she had left him, undid his bonds with her knife and replaced them with a powerful arm around his chest.

He fought for breath, unable to speak. Hedda dragged him along with one hand while the other tightened on an M-16 turned to full auto. Upstairs the feds had tried tear gas, but Reaper had already passed out gas masks, even one for the kid. On the second floor, Major was firing forty-millimeter grenades from his MK-19, blowing the shit out of the cop cars and laughing through all of it. A few of the feds crashed through an attic skylight and turned the Major into a pin cushion. Hedda heard it and charged up the stairs, pulling the trigger as she rounded the top and carving the two of them up.

"We got the kid!" Reaper was screaming to the feds outside. "Just back away and leave us the car. You fuck with us, he dies!"

And he would. Lucretia McEvil had no doubt about that. Outside the firing stopped.

"All right, you got it," the bullhorn voice came back. *"Just don't hurt the kid."*

It took ten minutes before the arrangements were set to Reaper's satisfaction. He turned to Hedda.

"You take the kid, Lucretia." He handed her a pistol. "Keep it against his head. It's my Colt special, just for you. Rest of us will bring up the rear."

"Wow," Eleanor Rigby muttered. "Wow."

Her hands had seemed to find the bloody splotch in her midsection for the first time. It had soaked her shirt and was dripping down the crotch of her khaki pants.

"Wow," she said one more time, and crumpled dead.

"We're coming out," Bob the Reaper screamed. "Don't fuck this up!"

Hedda went first into the spill of bright lights, the boy held in front of her with the barrel of the Colt special against his head for all to see. She had to squint to make her way. Sandman and Reaper followed closely behind, both cradling M-16s.

"Take it easy," the bullhorn voice said.

The car was parked on the lawn, as ordered.

"Kid comes with us," Reaper yelled. "Try anything 'fore we get where we're going and he's gone."

Of course they didn't know where they were going, not yet. Maybe to a pizza joint. Reaper was the brains. The planning was up to him.

Hedda took the steps gingerly, feeling her way, the boy a shield before her.

"Get the fuck back!" Reaper shouted to a few stray cops looming in front of their bullet-ravaged patrol cars. "Get the fuck—"

Pffffffft . . . pffffffft . . .

She heard the silenced gunshots an instant before Bob groaned. The next burst pinned Ian against the porch post, his face gone and limbs twitching horribly. Sandman! . . . She swung back to the light, shaking.

And her gun went off.

The hair trigger on Bob's Colt special was to blame, a cruel accident. The Baylor boy's brains smashed into her and blew her backward. His blood was all over her, and what saved her in the end was the fact that the feds thought she had been shot and not the boy. Only when they rushed forward did they see the truth. The boy's face was miraculously intact, but the rest of his head was gone, showered over the dazed Lucretia McEvil.

Page-one news. A media trial. Yes, it was all coming back. . . . She would have been sentenced to death, had not the death penalty been recently overturned by the state supreme court. As it was, four one-hundred-year terms to run sequentially eliminated any possibility of parole. She would be in prison for the rest of her life.

Yet here she was now, no clear memories of prison at all, and no idea of how she had been taken out for service with The Caretakers as part of what Pomeroy had called Renaissance. The memories she did have hurt, hurt *physically*. Within the pain, though, there was relief. Questions at last answered, gaping holes at least partially filled in.

Her rescue of Christopher Hanley had stirred her mind to recall the Baylor boy in fits and starts, one incident triggering another similar one. She had glimpsed parts of that final shootout in the street in which her gun had gone off and showered her with the boy's brains. But the blocks had kept her from seeing it all as anything more than an unpleasant lingering dream. Now Hedda supposed similar memories would be given life by other associations. The blocks August Pomeroy had implanted were eroding, washed away by the actual life she had led before The Caretakers.

Chalmers's words had evaporated into wheezing. He had spent himself, couldn't summon the energy to make the words emerge anymore there in the woods. Hedda sat facing him as the rest of her past filtered back. The ground dirt stuck to her wet clothes. The day's midsummer warmth did nothing to relieve the chill surging through her.

Something new fluttered through her head. Something more about that last day of the Storm Riders, about herself. She searched for the memory, but it eluded her. Not blocked by August Pomeroy, blocked by herself. Something that would hit her like a blade to the belly if she found firm hold.

What? What was this last fragment she couldn't recapture? In all that pain, could there have been something beyond what she was now facing?

"I was convicted. Sentenced to prison for life," she said finally, hoping to distract herself from considering the answer. "What happened?"

"We came and . . . got you," Chalmers managed to get out through his speaker. "You . . . fit."

"Fit what?"

"The profile. You . . . could kill. You did . . . kill."

Hedda looked at Chalmers's lips as he nodded and began to speak again. She imagined that the words were emerging from his mouth with each gurgled rasp through the speaker.

"You were all . . . proven killers. No . . . conscience. No . . . hesitation. We . . . wanted that, needed . . . that."

"The island," Hedda muttered. "Pomeroy mentioned an island."

Chalmers nodded. "Devil's Claw . . . Where you and . . . the others were . . . taken. Where you . . . were born. Where . . . we must go."

"You and I?"

"And oth-ers."

"Who?"

"The rest of . . . The Care-tak-ers."

"They're *alive*?"

Chalmers's tired eyes drooped. He sighed. "I wouldn't give . . . the others up to him . . . after Deerslayer. . . . I couldn't. I hid . . . them because . . . I saw what had . . . to be done."

"The island . . ."

"It must be . . . destroyed . . . He is there. The . . . rest are there."

"Rest of what?"

"An army, all like . . . you. His army."

"*Whose* army, damn it!"

Chalmers looked at her closer. "Name would mean nothing to you."

"But he has Hanley's poison, doesn't he? And he's going to use it."

"Not if we . . . stop him at . . . the island."

"We . . . How many?"

"Seventeen and . . . me."

"Against an army, as you put it. An army that will be expecting you now."

"No," Chalmers said.

"Why?"

"Because I'm . . . dead."

THE SIXTH DOMINION

Tiny Tim

Wednesday, August 19; 8:00 P.M.

CHAPTER 23

KIMBERLAIN never remembered the long drive to Captain Seven's from the scrap yard; he barely recalled Winston Peet easing him into the backseat and driving off. He came to sporadically over the next eighteen hours. Pain rocked him everywhere. The pounding in his head drove him back into oblivion each time he reached for consciousness. When he at last managed to keep his eyes open, Peet was there by the bed, his massive bulk squeezed into one of Captain Seven's patchwork armchairs.

"How?" he mouthed more than said.

The giant grasped the intent of his question without further words. "I came to your friend because I felt you were in trouble. He sent me to the scrap yard."

Kimberlain's mouth was sandpaper dry. "At the cabin, you said you couldn't help."

"I could not help you in your pursuits because doing so would mean crossing over again into the dark world I have abandoned and forsaken. But what we face now, what you faced in the scrap yard, threatens to reach out and drag me back. That is what I felt, and it left me no choice but to intervene."

"The ninth dominion," Kimberlain followed. He explained

that its goal was for misfits and madmen to take over the world under the guidance of Andrew Harrison Leeds.

"The hints were there when you visited me," Peet said when the Ferryman was finished.

"But you didn't say anything."

"Because you weren't ready to hear."

"And now you think Leeds is prepared to make the ninth dominion a reality."

The giant shook his head. "Not think. I am sure."

"How?"

"I felt him."

"Felt him?"

"Before we left the scrap yard, I felt him watching me through one of the cameras. In that instant I touched his soul and all was clear."

"Not to me, Peet."

"The lack of clarity is Leeds's greatest advantage. You see the ninth dominion from your perspective, not his. It is real because he sees it as real. And if I do not help you stop it, I will be drawn into its domain."

"A world inherited by the mad, the violent, and the depraved," Kimberlain elaborated. "What happens to everyone else?"

"Washed away. Plowed under and lost forever. I feel it about to happen, Ferryman. Leeds has the means to bring it about. I felt his confidence through the camera."

"You're sure he saw you?"

Peet nodded. "I felt him reach out his hand. Part of me wanted to take it, Ferryman."

"That's behind you, Winston."

"Only if life were linear. But it is circular. From one perspective, behind is actually ahead. The swirls are everywhere. Order is tenuous. If the ninth dominion is not stopped before Leeds finds me, I lose everything I have gained these past few years."

Kimberlain's thoughts were a jumble now, and it hurt his head to think. Too much pain. Too much pounding.

"How, Winston?" he wondered out loud. "How could Leeds have come up with a means of destruction that spares his chosen lot?"

"Good question," Captain Seven said from the doorway. He was wearing a ragged bathrobe and holding a bag of Cheez Doodles in his hand. "I don't have the answer yet, but I've learned some things that might help us find it."

Leeds ran the tapes again in slow motion. His cameras had caught extraordinarily little of Winston Peet's battle with the two-tonner. In fact, the only clear shot of the bald giant was the one where he gazed at the camera after raising Kimberlain upright. Leeds stopped the tape there and zoomed in. Peet's head, turned slightly to the side so only one eye was completely in view, filled the entire screen.

Leeds imagined Peet was actually there in the room, ready to join him. If anyone was made for the ninth dominion, it was Peet.

He would have to find him first, though, and Andrew Harrison Leeds was certain he knew just how to go about accomplishing that.

"You sure you don't want any, big fella?" Captain Seven offered, holding his bag of Cheez Doodles out to Peet.

The giant shook his head.

"Sorry, boss, can't offer you any till I'm sure you're ready to hold food down."

"How bad is it?"

"Does it hurt to sit up?"

"Yeah."

"That bad. Seriously, you've got a slight concussion, bruised ribs, six alcohol ounces worth of cuts and lacerations. Fuck, I always preferred blowing people up to putting them back together."

"What'd you find out?" Kimberlain asked.

"Been able to confirm that starting five years ago at least seventy-five maximum security prisoners have disappeared without a trace and another sixty apparently died. Add to that count another fifty or so who came out of you-know-where.''

''The Locks?''

''Bingo.''

In the chair between them, Peet had stiffened.

''What is it, Winston?'' Kimberlain asked.

''I should have known all along. . . .''

''Known what?''

His liquidy dark eyes sought out Kimberlain. ''They came to The Locks not long before you did all those months ago. They . . . observed me.''

Kimberlain managed to sit up. ''Who?''

''Names were never exchanged. They asked questions I did not answer. They took a lot of notes. Besides you, they were the only ones besides Locks personnel who were ever allowed into the wing where I was kept.''

''Then Vogelhut knew them,'' Kimberlain concluded. ''That son of a bitch was a part of this from the beginning!''

''Fuck me,'' Captain Seven muttered. ''Nice if we knew what Leeds was going to do with all the eggs he's pulled from the cuckoo's nest.''

''They're going to serve a purpose for him, at least he thinks they are,'' said the Ferryman. ''Play a role in his vision.''

Peet nodded in agreement.

''Thing is,'' Kimberlain continued, ''now we may know enough to track him down.'' He started to stand up and then thought better of it. ''Hand me your phone, Captain. I think I'll ring my young friend Talley. . . .''

It took two or three minutes for the bureau switchboard to locate Lauren Talley for him. The agent came on the line sounding ragged and hoarse, uncomposed for the first time.

''Sorry to wake you, Lauren,'' said Kimberlain.

''I'm wide awake. I've been trying to find you for almost a day now. Jesus Christ, where have you been?''

''Long story.''

''Mine's a short one: Tiny Tim struck again.''

A chill wracked Kimberlain's body. "What was the town this time?"

"Not a town, Jared. A hospital. In central Massachusetts. You'd better get down here."

CHAPTER 24

"**W**E'VE managed to keep it out of the news so far," Lauren Talley explained when Kimberlain arrived on the scene. She had sent a helicopter to whisk him the bulk of the trip to Auburn, Massachusetts. A car was waiting to speed him the rest of the way off something called the Purple Heart Highway west along Route 20 past a heavy concentration of small businesses and industries. The hospital itself was situated on a hill and was clearly visible from the road, not secluded or hidden like the first two towns had been. Tiny Tim's work this time had been carried out in full view of a highway, albeit late at night with all the nearby businesses long shut down.

"The patients . . ."

"Just like I told you on the phone. A hundred and twenty-seven bodies this time. A new record."

The Auburn Medical Center was a four-story structure painted in rustic browns and tans in an effort to make it seem less clinical. Talley led Kimberlain through the white spill of portable floods set up on the neatly manicured front grounds that enabled investigators to work through the night.

"This is where we laid the bodies out yesterday," Talley explained. "Rows and rows of them, arranged by hospital floor with tags attached to the tips of the bags. Made them look like luggage."

Talley looked haggard and worn. Clearly she had gotten no sleep, and yesterday's makeup was long gone. The lack of it made her look younger and vulnerable for the first time. Kimberlain could see the hardened exterior was all show. Beneath it now her true self showed through. He wanted to tell her to let it out all the way, but Talley spoke again before he had the chance.

"I've had the building cleared. I wanted you to experience the inside without distractions."

"I don't know what I'll be able to tell you."

"It's got to be more than what the forensics team has been able to. You were the only one to pick up any clues in Daisy, and this scene's fresher."

"When?" Kimberlain asked, as they moved past a collection of bureau personnel clustered near the front entrance.

"Yesterday between midnight and three A.M. or so. Same as with the other two. Hospital doesn't maintain a round-the-clock emergency room service, so he didn't have to worry about unwarranted entries. Doctor coming back to pick up a lab report made the discovery. He isn't doing well."

"What's the lab been able to tell you?"

"Not much besides where he entered, the order he did it, where he walked out. Grand goddamn fucking tour."

Her use of profanity surprised him. "You're letting it get to you, Lauren."

"You haven't been inside yet."

"You let it get to you and you never find him."

"I haven't been doing such a great job as it is."

"It's not your fault."

Talley's eyes peered upward toward Kimberlain's. "Try telling that to the brass at behavioral science. Once television gets ahold of this, there won't be a person in this country who feels safe. Before, ninety-nine point nine percent of the population felt insulated by the fact that they didn't fit the pattern.

Guy's going after small towns in Hicksville. Who gives a shit? But now he hits a hospital. *A hospital, goddamn it!* What's next? An apartment building? A hotel, maybe? How about a school, or maybe the passengers on a goddamn 747, or the patrons of a restaurant sitting down for dinner?''

"You're straining."

"You're damn right I'm straining, and what do you think the country's going to do? Start vigilante groups. Arm themselves to the teeth probably, buy Uzis, shotguns, make homemade grenades in their basements."

"They wouldn't help against this guy."

"It won't stop folks from trying." She stopped just before the door. "You know I got here an hour before dawn yesterday, and I couldn't wait for the sun to come up. I knew it wouldn't change anything except make me less scared."

"Quite natural. Evil owns the night is the popular perception."

"And is it true?"

"It is with Tiny Tim."

Talley's dark, rich eyes were empty. "Why a hospital?"

"Plenty of reasons, except none of them jibe with the profile based on his previous attacks. Tiny Tim broke his pattern, Lauren, and he broke it big time. He could have been seen, at least noticed. If someone had made it out of the hospital and sprinted down the hill, then the whole world would know what was going on in a matter of minutes."

"You're saying there was risk involved this time."

"Plenty more than in Daisy and Dixon Springs, anyway. And that means something had to make the risk worth taking, something beyond the pattern itself." Kimberlain thought briefly. "I want a list of all the victims from the hospital and the first two towns. I'll give you a number to fax them to."

"You think this is about individuals *within* his targets?"

"The targets have something in common, Lauren. We find out what and we find Tiny Tim. Maybe that's what takes us where we need to go."

"Let's go inside."

* * *

Garth Seckle lay in the field, gazing up at the sky. Clouds had covered the stars long before, swallowed their light just as he had swallowed the lives of his victims only a day before.

Seckle knew he wouldn't sleep tonight; he seldom did in the days immediately following one of his visits. He could imagine the experts clustered around a table offering theories as to his methods and psyche. None of them would ever stop to consider that the roots of his work were found in reason. In his own mind it was justifiable because of what had been done to him.

Before. Long before.

His unblinking eyes held on the sky and imagined the clouds as blood scarlet. Just thinking of the color made him quiver. And there would be more blood soon, much sooner than anyone expected. The pieces were all falling into place, the symmetry so pleasing to his innermost thoughts.

It was time to close his eyes so he could go back to the hospital in his mind. Renew the pleasure by rerunning the actions while they were still fresh. That way they would stay with him until a new set replaced them.

He had parked his van in the building's rear not far from the service entrance. But that would not serve as his route in. No. In order to maximize the use of his time he must use the entry where his presence stood the greatest chance of being noticed. He hugged the building to avoid the spray of the hospital's outdoor lights as he slid round to the front and approached the one entrance open at such a late hour. . . .

"It's the only door they keep open after midnight," Lauren Talley explained, holding it open for Kimberlain to pass through.

"Not very accessible for a hospital."

"Just the way they want it. Without an emergency facility, the last thing they want is drive-in business."

The Ferryman entered and had the feeling he was stepping into hell. Inside the small reception area and lobby, fingerprint dust was evident on the counters and desk, as well as the walls.

Kimberlain could see sprinkles of it on the floor, too, the shape of a massive foot filled out.

Talley pulled out her memo pad and flipped it open. From behind her, Kimberlain could see many of the pages were full of chicken-scratch scribble.

"He entered here," Talley started, consulting the fourth page of her notes, "and shot the nurse once in the head. Two security guards slain as well, both with shots to the chest and midsection. Silenced automatic. Shell casings not found. He then proceeded to the—" Talley flipped a page. "—fourth floor."

"Work his way down," Kimberlain said. "Makes sense. More likely to be hurt by someone coming down than up."

Talley reached the stairwell. "He used the stairs. The fourth-floor nurses' station was not manned at the time," she continued as they began to climb. "Duty nurse was checking a loose heart monitor. Floor nurse was dispensing meds."

"Good assumptions," Kimberlain said.

Talley looked at him gravely. "Not assumptions. We found their bodies in the respective rooms."

Kimberlain pulled open the door leading onto the fourth floor.

"This floor had twenty-two patients, eleven pairs of two," Lauren Talley said as she stepped out behind him. "Eight rooms vacant. No evidence he ever stepped into any of the empty ones."

"Door labels," Kimberlain pointed out, noticing one just down from the elevator. "Only the occupied ones had them. Acted like invitations for our boy."

"All elderly on this floor, many invalid or infirm. Not much ability to fight back, even if he'd given them the chance."

Kimberlain nodded ever so slightly. "Tiny Tim is no sportsman. The kill is both end and means. He doesn't need build-up, because each kill serves as build-up for the next. He visualizes the next act while still in the midst of the current one. In other words, the person he's killing doesn't mean anything compared to the one he's going to kill next. And so on, so on, and so on." The Ferryman hesitated. "Makes perfect sense in explaining him."

"Explaining him how?"

"He can't be satisfied. No matter how many he kills, he's always thinking of the next victim until there are no more victims left. He can't help it any more than you or I can help breathing."

"Don't pull this psycho crap with me," Lauren Talley flared.

"You can't catch him if you don't understand him, Lauren. You've got to see the way he thinks if you ever want to see him captured."

Talley nodded, trying to understand as Kimberlain spoke again. "Now show me where he started on this floor."

The hospital was a microcosm of the shitty world that had scorned him. Garth Seckle found it more orderly than the towns he had visited previously. The old people were on the top floor, as if it had taken all their lives to climb up there and now they'd never be coming back down. He hated them, hated the lingering smell of slow death that struck him when he stepped out of the stairwell. He could hear the hum of a few televisions, moans and sobs from those who were beyond entertainment. The true object of his visit here lay on the floor below, but Seckle needed to leave his mark, and that would begin up here.

Tiny Tim went from room to room, never using the same method twice. Got to be quite challenging near the end, especially when he killed one old geezer without waking the roommate. He broke a neck, crushed a larynx layered with liver-spotted flesh, smothered one with a pillow.

In contrast to earlier kills, these deaths didn't refresh him. He felt drained, unfulfilled. Tiny Tim wanted to be done with it, wanted to move on and finish with the true reason for his being there so he might enjoy the rest of his visit. He completed his work on the second half of the fourth floor quickly and made for the stairwell that would take him to the next level down.

"Standard rooms on this floor," Lauren Talley told Kimberlain as they descended the stairs. She had turned her memo pad open to a fresh page. "Adult patients in for tests, evaluations, minor surgery, orthopedic work. Physical therapy wing's up here, too. Thirty-five rooms in all, twenty-six doubles and nine singles. Two of the singles had a second bed wedged in."

He opened the door just ahead of her, and the bloodsplattered nurses' station greeted him.

"There were three on duty," he heard Lauren Talley reciting. "One was on rounds, the other two were here. We're almost certain one of those managed to push the security button when she saw him. Just a quick press before he got her, barely enough to stir the guard downstairs from his nap."

Her eyes aimed further down the corridor, and Kimberlain adjusted his angle in order to see the elevator. The floor before it was stained by a dark red pool. The elevator doors themselves had a series of scarlet splotches embossed upon them.

"Automatic weapon," Talley said. "Upward of ten silenced rounds. After he killed the nurses, he must have heard the elevator coming and waited for whoever was going to come out."

"He waited for more than that."

"Excuse me?"

"That blood on the outside of the doors. He must have given the guard time to get out, probably even draw his gun."

Talley's eyes widened. "It was still in his hand when we found him. We thought . . ."

"Thought what?"

"That maybe he came close to getting a shot off."

"Not a chance. Tiny Tim just wanted to have some fun."

"Sound of a gunshot would have risked everything. Patients wake up, reach for their phones."

"He never risks anything. The nurses?"

"The two behind the station were shot and one was mutilated postmortem, we believe after he was finished with the rest of the floor."

That struck a chord in Kimberlain's memory. "There was a mutilation in Daisy, too. You were supposed to check the burned bodies from Dixon Springs."

"We did. We are. Nothing conclusive yet."

"Assume it is. Who did he torch in Dixon Springs?"

"You want names?"

"Specs will do just fine. Whatever your memory has handy."

"A couple, the occupants of a rooming house, a—"

"Stick with the couple. It was a family in Daisy, wasn't it?"

Lauren Talley nodded. "Children included."

Kimberlain drew closer to the formerly white counter. Much of the blood had sprayed atop the trays holding the patients' charts, as if Tiny Tim was wiping out what had brought them here in addition to the people themselves.

"Just the one nurse?" he raised.

"Yes."

"Anyone else on the lower floors?"

"No."

"Strange."

"Why?"

"Say he set the fires in Dixon Springs to hide the mutilation of that couple. Then he goes after an entire family in Daisy, and finally a single nurse here. It doesn't jibe with the rest of his thinking." Kimberlain's mind returned to the setting and the matter at hand. "Run it through for me on this floor."

"It got messy for him. He wasn't expecting a third nurse, and she appeared at the wrong time. From the contortions of her mouth in death, we believe she managed to scream. That drew some patients from their beds. Tiny Tim dispatched her, and them, with the same rifle he used on the other nurses and the security guard. Then he made rapid work of the rest.''

"Poison gas?"

"How did you know?"

"The smell. It's almost tolerable. Somebody had the windows open for a time.''

. ''We had to. The toxicity levels were still too high when we got here.''

"Any idea how he released it?"

"Canisters. He was kind enough to leave them behind."

"I'd like to see them."

"Of the homemade variety, though. Forget tracking him down through army surplus.''

"Not so sure you're looking for a soldier anymore, Lauren?"

"Like you said originally, he's something else, something . . .''

"More?"

"To use your phrase, yes."

"And what would your phrase be? You've seen his work firsthand now. Still think you're dealing with a man?"

"I don't believe in monsters, Mr. Kimberlain."

"You probably don't believe in Santa Claus either. But if you saw him sleigh and all on your roof, you might reconsider.''

"No one's seen Tiny Tim, including you."

"But I've seen Peet, Leeds, a half-dozen others maybe."

"None of whom was behind anything like this."

"Oh, they had the capability. They just didn't elect to employ it. The killing was more personal for them; that's where the pleasure from the act originated. For Tiny Tim, it's detached, like target practice. I doubt he even considers his victims to be living in the first place. At least not worthy.''

"Worthy of what?"

"To occupy the same plane of existence as he does. He thinks of killing the same way the rest of us do swatting flies.

The act has no meaning, just as his victims have no meaning for him."

"No," Lauren Talley said, "you said he enjoyed it."

"That's not meaning in itself. The act becomes its own justification. The more he kills, the more he has to kill to continue the fantasy that he's doing what's right. Only . . ."

"Only what?"

Kimberlain looked suddenly uncertain. "That's why the mutilations don't fit, especially if he tried to hide his first one in Dixon Springs."

"Care to speculate?"

"Not at the moment, Lauren. Right now I want to see the second floor.

"No," Talley told him. "You don't."

CHAPTER 25

Tɪɴʏ Tim reached the door leading from the stairwell onto the second floor kicking on all cylinders. Not only had his work with his primary target gone brilliantly, but the emergence of some of the patients into the corridor had confronted him with a challenge. Imagine if one of them had cried out or somehow else alerted the floors below what was coming their way. . . . Expediency was demanded, precision achieved against the possibility of discovery and disaster. His heart was still hammering away inside him when he took the stairs downward.

He felt cleansed, refreshed. He had completed his mission.

Now he could take his time and enjoy the remainder of this visit, make them live up to the towns. The towns had been so fulfilling, enriching even. Each house had brought a new challenge. Each home had been filled with its own smells, its own vitality. The act of killing kept renewing itself, as he moved from one to the next. The variety was striking, the challenge constant. The third floor of the hospital had provided him with at least a semblance of that, albeit one that promised to fade quickly. His victims here seemed no more than cardboard copies of one another. The rooms were the same, as were the very clothes of those whose lives he was snuffing out. The result was the feeling that he was repeating the same act over and over again instead of expanding and building upon the experience from one kill to the next. But the feeling that had reached him behind the door leading onto the second level indicated things were about to change for much the better.

Garth Seckle quivered in the night air, the brush rumbling around him. The sky was bloodred in his mind in that moment, his memory of the next acts as real as those acts themselves.

There were children on the second floor! *Children!*

Something stirred in him in a rush so powerful that he felt his heartbeat quicken and breath grow rapid. He stilled himself just behind the door and leaned against it to prolong the moment. In his present state, a single jolt of his shoulders would send it crashing inward, but Tiny Tim held his ground. Nothing could go wrong on this floor, no distractions that might detract from his pleasure. He grabbed the knob, turned it loudly without giving the door any pressure. Then he rapped loudly against the steel.

"Hello . . . Hello! Is anyone there?" he called.

Alone so much, he spoke almost not at all, and when he did the sound of his own voice was foreign to him.

"Coming," a nurse's voice returned.

Tiny Tim worked the knob again. "Door's stuck," he said to her through the door.

"Just give me a moment," he heard her say trustingly. And

then the door was coming inward, and Tiny Tim lashed out for where he knew her face would be.

The massive shape of his right hand swallowed it from chin to brow. She tried to scream, tried to flail out, tried to kick, but he jerked her upward and held her there with her feet swiping at the air. Tiny Tim drew the nurse further into the stairwell and slammed her against the wall. It gave on impact, plaster shredding inward as the nurse's head was embedded into it. Her limbs spasmed horribly with the rupturing of her brain. She was still twitching when he left her stuck there and emerged onto the second floor.

At this point his memories became jumbled. He remembered rooms and faces in no particular order. Most of the children were asleep when he entered. He took the first of them quickly and quietly, but the next he made sure were awake as he stole their lives from them. That way he could see the look in their eyes as the daring hope of youth that had withstood whatever had brought them to this place of sickness was extinguished. Children did not show fear in any way like adults, holding perhaps to that same youthful resilient surety that it could not end for them this way. Only in the last seconds did they finally realize with pleading sadness what was happening to them.

It had been over much too fast. Emerging into the corridor from the last occupied room, though, Tiny Tim had heard a sound. A muffled wheezing reaching out to him from somewhere ahead.

Crying.

Smiling tightly, Tiny Tim moved off toward the nursery and maternity wards.

"I'll be the judge of that," Kimberlain had told Lauren Talley before moving ahead of her onto the stairwell.

"Pediatrics and obstetrics," she said from behind him.

The Ferryman stopped, suspended between floors and worlds.

"Go on," she urged him. "You have to see it, don't you?"

Kimberlain turned toward her but didn't speak.

"I studied you, Jared. I studied each and every one of your cases and each and every one of the monsters you brought in. But I never really understood you or them until tonight, until now. And I'm scared of you almost as much as I am of the monster that did this."

"Regretting that you came up to see me in Vermont, Lauren?"

"I just feel a lot older now than I did then."

"And you want to blame me for that, as well as this. You hate and you fear and you need something to focus all that on." He took two steps closer to her. "Well, wake up, Lauren, wake up and smell the blood. This is the real thing, away from the books, the classrooms, the reports, and the promotion ladder. This is reality, and this is where I live. You came up to Vermont full of ambition. I help you catch Tiny Tim, and you end up making points at behavioral science. Section head maybe. First woman ever in that department, correct me if I'm wrong."

She didn't bother to.

"Well, Lauren, take the call letters of your grand department together and you get BS. Fitting, don't you think? Because all those attempts to assemble portfolios and profiles are bullshit. When I walk through that second-floor door, I'm looking for traces of the person. I find them because I can climb into their heads and think just as perversely as they can. You said you didn't understand that before. Congratulations. You just grew up. Might even be able to do it yourself someday."

"Please," she shot back, showing disgust.

"Please," Kimberlain echoed. "You didn't use that word in Vermont, but you might as well have. 'Please come and help me catch Tiny Tim. Please help me get the bureau off the hook from a country living in fear. Please help me become a department head.' Now I'm helping, and you don't fancy what that looks like."

"I'm . . . sorry."

"No, you're not. And if you're sorry about anything, it's about getting involved at Quantico in the first place. That's to be expected. When this is over, ask for a transfer. I'll write you a nice recommendation."

"You're angry."

"Damn right."

"Not just with me, though."

"It's him, Lauren, Tiny Tim. He's in my head now, and that makes him a part of me I don't want. But I can't get rid of him until I find him."

Lauren Talley slid down the stairs until Kimberlain's features, lost in the stairwell's dimness, were clear again. "The years in your file that are blank, before the paybacks . . ."

"Should be accessible somewhere on the bureau's data bank."

She shrugged. "Not to me."

"I did what the monsters do," he told her. "On orders."

"Oh," she muttered.

"And every time I walk into a scene like this, it comes back. I can't be rid of it until all the monsters are gone. But they'll never be gone. That's reality, and that's why you're scared of me all of a sudden. I'm sorry, Lauren. Really I am. I tried to tell you as much in Vermont, but you kept at it, and now you know the truth."

"We'd better get moving," she said, advancing ahead of him with a stabilizing breath.

Kimberlain followed her down the remainder of the steps. A patch of blood outlined a deep oval-shaped crack in the wall on the right eight feet off the ground.

"It was the nurse, wasn't it?"

"He lured her in here somehow," Lauren Talley confirmed. "She was the only one on duty. Night maternity nurse was on break downstairs in the snack bar. That left him with free reign of the hall."

The door creaked open, and they advanced onto the pediatrics and obstetrics wing. Kimberlain moved slowly down the corridor, passed the rooms without entering a single one or even seeming to look inside. Talley hung back, afraid to draw any closer. There was no need for explanation; the signs left in the pediatric rooms were very clear.

"He heard crying," the Ferryman said suddenly. "He stepped out of this last room after he was finished, and he heard crying."

"Thirty-eight bodies on this floor up to this point," the woman from the FBI reported. "Thirty-nine including the nurse back on the stairwell."

"How old?"

"Does it really mat—"

"How old!"

Lauren Talley flipped open her notebook again. "Four to fifteen. Twenty-two girls, sixteen boys. We've got their medical files if you want—"

"I want to see the nursery, Lauren."

It was almost too much for Garth Seckle. Standing there at the window, it seemed as if the babies belonged to him. After all, they were his to do with as he pleased. More than any of the others that night, they were at his mercy because they lacked the capacity to grasp what he was. When he stepped through the door, the ones who were crying continued to cry. The ones who were sleeping continued to sleep. His presence, though perhaps detected, was not affecting.

He found their helplessness to be a metaphor for the other victims he had taken. None had stood a chance against him, but it was much worse because they could grasp what was happening to them. Tiny Tim moved up and down the rows of cribs, certain that death could hold no meaning for these since life had yet to form into any coherent shape.

A few more seemed to be crying now. He wondered if somehow the smell of blood had awakened them. Had some primal, instinctive sense alerted them to the scent of their mothers' blood on his clothes? Avoiding the blood had been impossible considering the way circumstances had demanded he dispatch the women.

Until that moment, Tiny Tim had considered leaving the infants as they were, since their utter indifference provided him no satisfaction. Now he saw them as no more than extensions of those he had just visited in the adjacent rooms. His work could not be considered complete if they were left alive.

"We aren't sure whether he came here first or to the mothers," Lauren Talley said as the nursery came into view.

"The mothers. He would have liked to maintain the order of things. You haven't gone in there, have you? To where the mothers were, I mean."

"No. I . . . couldn't."

"He would have used a knife on them. Opened them up in the same area where the baby had come from to attack the canal of life itself."

"Yes," Lauren Talley muttered, and swallowed hard.

"How powerful it would have made him feel," Kimberlain continued. "As if the power of life was his to dispense."

"Death, you mean."

"Indistinguishable for Tiny Tim. Death *is* life, you see; at least that's the only way he can accept it. Order and precision. Everything balanced."

"Does he think that way consciously?"

"No more than the rest of us do. We are what we are. Tiny Tim kills because it makes him feel stronger, invincible. He has no reason to believe anyone can stop him, so his own order is the only one he has to acknowledge."

The nursery began as a windowed wall on the corridor's left-hand side. The lights were still on. As Kimberlain approached he could feel his blood run still and his breath form into a big lump in the center of his throat.

The nursery was . . . empty. That was all he could say. The cribs lay unoccupied, blankets barely ruffled. It looked undisturbed, almost pristine. Even the name tags taped to the appropriate slots on each crib were untouched.

"The infants," Kimberlain muttered.

"They were all found alive. We know he was in here, but he didn't kill them. A show of humanity possibly. Maybe there's a limit to what even this monster can bring off."

The Ferryman was sliding about the room between the empty cribs. "No," he said distantly. "Tiny Tim was prepared to kill them, but then he heard something." He swung toward Talley. "Something that startled him from downstairs."

She flipped feverishly through her notes. "Yes, here it is. There was a code blue in the intensive care ward downstairs. A crash cart tipped over and took a few trays of bottles with it. Lots of noise."

"Distracted Tiny Tim. Made him head in that direction."

"Downstairs," she acknowledged. "The first floor."

The noise from below had shaken Tiny Tim just as he was about to begin his work in the nursery. Had someone discovered what he had left on the floors above and brought that panicked message down? He could not risk that eventuality. A change of strategy was essential.

Peering out from the first floor stairwell, he realized the noise had come from something else entirely. No one was rushing about. People were simply going about their business. This level would prove the most challenging for him. Not only did it contain the intensive care unit, but also the snack bar along with the doctors' lounge where those on call waited for a page. Lots of individual places where victims would be waiting for him. Four doctors garbed in white coats were on duty this evening, all presently on this floor. Add these to the four nurses on around-the-clock duty, and things promised to be complicated.

Tiny Tim checked both his silenced Uzi submachine guns and emerged from the stairwell. There was no longer a need to act quietly. The first person he spotted was a bespectacled doctor walking with his eyes fixed on a chart. He never saw Tiny Tim. A burst blew him backward and splattered blood upon a receptionist working the phones. Tiny Tim shot her next and watched her body disappear under the desk. Then, almost mechanically, he moved on toward the wing marked NO ADMITTANCE and under that DOCTORS ONLY.

The double doors came open as he approached them, allowing a pair of nurses to rush out in the wake of some emergency. Tiny Tim used a burst from each Uzi on them, and the women's white uniforms leaked red. He burst through the doors to find the remaining pool of on-duty nurses and doctors clustered around a bed on the right. The rest of the ICU cubicles had their curtains drawn. This one alone had been yanked open.

"Clear!" one of the doctors ordered, pressing the wands of a defibrillating machine against the patient's chest.

There was a thump, and the chest heaved.

"No pulse," one of the nurses reported.

"We're losing him," someone else said.

"Clear!" the doctor handling the defibrillator instructed again.

Tiny Tim liked the sound of that. He waited until the shocked chest jumped one more time before speaking.

"Clear," he said loud enough for all of them to hear and swing his way. "Lost," he followed before he opened fire.

The bodies crashed into the monitoring machines, spilling them over. Several IV hookups tumbled as well, and the sound of glass shattering echoed through the unit, along with the clamor of metal striking tile. The ICU patients were stirring now; the ones who could were screaming, and Tiny Tim moved for them with his submachine guns. Incapacitated as they were, it was over very fast. Most died with tubes still pushed up their noses or needles stuck in their arms. The doctors who had been in the on-call room rushed through the double doors just as Tiny Tim was finishing up, and he used the rest of one of his clips on them. Nice stroke of luck. Saved him a trip into their lounge.

His research indicated the hospital's two sublevels contained a number of labs, pathology, and the morgue. At this hour there might be a few strays left down there, and Tiny Tim headed down to finish his sweep.

* * *

Lauren Talley had shown Kimberlain the intensive care unit last, keeping with the theorized chronological progression Tiny Tim had taken. On the floors above, walls had separated the killings, cushioning the shock and disguising the scope of the truth. But ICU was little more than a ward, beds separated only by curtains and rollaway partitions. Some of these had been toppled, a number of the curtains shredded.

And the blood was everywhere, dried and dark; on the floor, on the walls, on the bed sheets waiting to be removed. Kimberlain didn't want to know the number of victims down here. The exact number was a useless piece of information. The only reality was the river of red.

"This is as far as we traced him," Talley was saying, "probably as . . . far . . . as—"

Her broken speech had Kimberlain moving toward her an instant before she started to drop. He caught her in midswoon and felt her press against him.

"I'm sorry," she mumbled.

"No need."

"It's just that I haven't been able to sleep." She eased herself away. "Even when there's time, I can't sleep."

"He's inside you, Lauren."

She looked up into Kimberlain's ice-blue eyes. "And how do I get him out?"

"We catch him."

CHAPTER 26

"**D**R. Vogelhut, this is Rembart down in the LW. You'd better get down here, sir."

"Something wrong?"

"You have to . . . see it."

The intercom page reached the chief administrator of The Locks in the midst of his usual morning rounds, which ordinarily would not have included what Rembart referred to as the "LW." The basement wing of The Locks was known in the vernacular as the lost ward, but Vogelhut preferred to think of it as hell. The lost ward contained those incarcerates who had lost all touch with reality. Most had come there in that condition. A few had evolved into it after spending time in one of the facility's other levels. Either way, those who came to the lost ward were truly the forgotten. No appeals were pending. No lawyers made contact. No psychiatric students sought audience for research.

Dr. Vogelhut heard the inmates' sounds as soon as he emerged from the elevator. Cries and screams combined with desperate howls and wails. There were animal sounds and loud, angry sobs. A regular pounding as one of the inhabitants repeatedly threw himself at the door.

Vogelhut took a deep breath and headed down the corridor toward the monitoring station each of the floors contained.

222

This one was the antithesis of MAX-SEC's, however. Only a single video monitor screen and communications apparatus, along with a panel that controlled the operation of the doors along the ward floor. Nothing fancy because the lost ward didn't require it any more than hell did. Vogelhut swung left at the hall's end and entered the monitoring room.

It was empty, the desk chair pulled out and left askew.

Through the glass partition he noticed a door on the long, straight ward hall was open. Damn it! Didn't anyone follow procedure anymore?

Vogelhut leaned over and flipped the microphone to the PAGE position.

"Rembart, this is Dr. Vogelhut," he called, hoping his voice would carry over the sounds of the inmates. "Are you there? What's going on?"

He could not hear his own words echoing through the hall at all and tried again. When there was still no reply from Rembart, he decided to enter the ward himself. Obviously there was something wrong with the inmate in the open cell. Summon security down here and he would have to file another report. In the wake of the mass escape of not even two weeks previous, that was the last thing he wanted to do. Vogelhut was beginning to fear for his job. If a scapegoat was required, he was the logical choice. Vogelhut would lose everything.

He entered the proper code into the keypad, and the single door leading onto the wing slid open. He passed through and sealed it behind him. Instantly he felt chilled. No longer muffled by the door and walls, the mad sounds of the hopelessly crazed scratched at his eardrums. They were sounds he could never get used to, no matter how often he heard them. There was a rancid stink in the corridor as well; feces and urine, vomit and stale, unwashed bodies. Vogelhut focused on the echoing clip-clop of his shoe heels as he made straight for the open cell the guards had clustered in for some reason.

"Rembart? Rembart, it's me. What's happening in—"

Vogelhut swallowed the rest of his words when he reached the door and peered in. Rembart and the other two guards, along with the inmate, were inside on the floor unconscious, legs and hands bound. Vogelhut had started to back away when a voice echoed through the hall.

"Good morning, Doctor."

A chill grabbed for Vogelhut's spine, and he turned back into the corridor. "Who is it?" he asked. "Who are you?"

He wondered if he could be heard above the screams, wails, and cries of the lost ward. Not wanting to seem frightened, Vogelhut pounded his way back down the hall for the door. He got there and keyed in the code.

Nothing happened.

He took his time and pressed the proper sequence into the pad once more.

The door still didn't open. Vogelhut pounded it in frustration.

"I reprogrammed the code, Doctor."

The familiar voice emerged through the speaker, pushing its way past the sounds of madness down the hallway.

"Who is th—"

"An old friend, Doctor. I've come for a second opinion."

"Open this door right *now*!"

"As soon as we've talked."

"Who are—" But Vogelhut had realized even before the familiar face appeared briefly in the lone viewing window beyond. "Kimberlain . . ."

"It's nice to be remembered."

"Let me out of here!" Vogelhut screamed over the sounds of the lost ward.

"I will. After we've talked."

"You'll pay for this! God, how you'll pay! . . ."

"I don't think so, Doctor. See, the debt sheet's heavily balanced against you. I know about the game you've been playing for the past five years or so. I know about the faked deaths and patients you arranged premature departures for."

"I don't know what you are—"

A clamoring thump sounded on the corridor.

"I just threw back the bolts on the last four doors on the hall, Doctor. Shouldn't be long before your charges figure out they've been set free and step into the corridor."

"Please, you can't!"

"I already have. How do they feel about you down here, Doctor? Not a place I'd like to be stranded. Wait . . . on the monitor, I think I see one of the doors opening."

Vogelhut swung round and jammed his shoulders against the heavy door; he pressed himself tight against it as if trying to melt through. The very last door down had indeed opened a crack, and as Vogelhut watched another showed a break.

"What do you want to know?" he raised pleadingly.

"You were involved. You were a part of it. Yes?"

"I had no choice. This is a federal institution. It was government business."

"The *government* was behind these faked deaths and reassignments?"

"Open the door. *Please.* I'll tell you everything."

"You'll tell me everything from where you're standing right now."

"One of them's coming out! God, can't you see? I beg you, don't do this!"

Another thump sounded over the mad rantings, as Kimberlain opened another quartet of doors along the hall.

"Stop stalling, Doctor. No one's coming to help you. Everything's reading A-okay on all the boards upstairs. Captain Seven showed me how to do it."

"He's coming this way! Another one! Oh God, there's another one! . . ."

On the screen before him, Kimberlain saw two inmates, one tall and lanky, the other short and very fat, sliding tentatively up the corridor. They moved as though each step were a struggle, with hands pressed against their respective walls as if to hang on.

"Talk!" the Ferryman ordered.

"Yes, the government! There was a project. I was briefed

but never informed in detail. My God, this is my career we're talking about. If I tell you, I'm finished.''

"In one piece, though. The same might not be said if you have to face all your guests down here.''

"I don't know what they wanted them for. That's the truth!''

"But you knew the profile they were looking for. Peet, for instance.''

"The most violent. The most unsalvageable.''

"Taken from here so they might be salvaged.''

"For what, I don't know. You've got to believe that!''

"Keep talking, Doctor.''

"What do you want to know?''

"Were your inmates actually recruited?''

"They weren't given a choice. That's the way I was told it would be. Now open the door! Listen to them! . . . They've seen me! Oh God, they're coming this way! . . .''

On the screen Kimberlain could see a man with patches of hair torn from his head stepping into the hall, then a bearded mountain of a man emerging from the other side. All four of the men moved tentatively, as if they expected the world to snap back at them like an angry dog they reached out to pet. Another two who might have been twins were slamming each other into the wall. A man who looked to be all bones advanced, feeling about the air, perhaps checking for invisible barriers.

"What happened after they left here?'' Kimberlain asked.

"I was never briefed.''

Thump!

The remaining doors on the right-hand side were open now, allowing hands and feet to probe tentatively outward. Meanwhile, the first four inmates to emerge were drawing nearer to Vogelhut, thirty feet away and closing slowly.

"All right, all right! As far as I know, they were taken from The Locks to be reconditioned. Hypnosis, new drugs, memory suppression. The project was called Renaissance.''

"Rebirth . . .''

"Only partially. Whoever was behind it wanted individuals

who had the capacity to commit incredibly brutal acts without conscience or regret. They wanted to preserve that part of their minds while at the same time being able to control that same part."

"Who were 'they,' Doctor?"

"Conduits, liaisons—that's all I ever dealt with. I suspected the intelligence community the way things were handled, but I can't say for sure. Please, let me out. You've got to let me out. . . ."

"Where were your inmates taken after they left here?"

Vogelhut's lips trembled. His eyes gazed fearfully behind him.

"Don't make me repeat myself, Doctor."

"All right! It was an island off the coast of North and South Carolina. I don't know the name. The references were vague."

The corridor had filled now, and all of the madmen seemed to be converging on Vogelhut. Kimberlain opened the door and yanked Vogelhut free of the hands tugging and tearing at his clothes. The closing circle of madmen resisted, trying to strengthen purchase on their claim. But they were too busy battling each other to stop the Ferryman from stripping the chief administrator of The Locks away. He forced back the hands that had managed to poke through the door and slammed it behind them.

Vogelhut bent over at the knees. He seemed on the verge of collapse when Kimberlain grasped him at the shoulders and slammed him back against the communications console.

"What else can you tell me about this island?"

"Nothing!"

"Who did you speak to from the government? Answer me!"

"No one, not directly. Just contacts, liaisons, like I said. It was one of them who mentioned the island. I don't even know if he was telling the truth."

"Then I'll have to find out, won't I?"

"You don't know what you're doing, I tell you."

"And you don't know what you've done, you stupid son of a bitch!"

"I'm a government employee. I had no choice."

"The government had nothing to do with this and never did."

Vogelhut regarded Kimberlain quizzically. "No, that can't be. Everything checked out."

"Sure. Officials in the right places were probably bought off, enough of them to make this whole charade possible and keep it thriving."

"*What* charade?"

"You're not listening, Doctor. You didn't before and you're not now. You simply followed orders, just like the wardens of all the prisons convicted killers were sentenced to spend their lives in."

"*Others?*"

"Hundreds. Whoever's behind this found their subjects in plenty of areas beyond The Locks."

Vogelhut's eyes swam fitfully. "Why should I believe you?"

"Because I'm the only one who's telling the truth. Don't you see? It all fits. Leeds never could have escaped without considerable help from the inside, and now I understand how it was set in place."

"Leeds? What does he have to do with this?"

"Everything, Doctor. He wants to create a world where only those who meet his particular standards can exist. He wants to turn things inside out, bequeath society to the same kind of person he got himself placed in here to bust out."

"Placed here?"

"All part of the plan. He wanted, needed, to empty MAX-SEC, because whatever he's plotting is going to happen soon, and those eighty-three inmates must have some role to play."

Vogelhut straightened tentatively. "This is madness!"

"Your specialty, doctor."

"I'm telling you the people I dealt with had all the right credentials. We had phone conversations. I called their offices!"

"You called the numbers they gave you. Before I leave I'll give you some new ones. None of the people on the other end will have ever heard of them or their operation."

Vogelhut's face sagged, his features seeming to melt. "I released all these madmen to their custody. I covered the truth up."

"You were guilty of being stupid, and my guess is you were played by experts. At least one person who'd been on the inside of the game, maybe more."

The inmates of the lost ward were clustered before the entry door now, those closest pounding their fists raw against it. For a brief instant Kimberlain saw the world within the ward as a microcosm of what Leeds endeavored to make. A world where there would be no door to bar the lost and no cells to confine them. Leeds would be back for these and all the others like them. They were his legion. He would set them free.

"Lock them in tight, Doctor," he told Vogelhut. "Lock them in tight."

Kimberlain tried to reach Lauren Talley from The Locks, but she was in transit between the hospital where Tiny Tim had struck and Quantico. It would be another hour before she would be accessible, and, no, Kimberlain didn't want to talk to anyone else in her place. Instead he used the empty time to call Captain Seven.

"So what happens next?" the captain asked after the Ferryman had briefed him on what he had learned from Vogelhut.

"My young friend Talley helps put a search party together to find this island. Any ideas?"

"Well, boss, you probably remember that techno plan our old D.C. buddies asked me to draw up to protect the East Coast from submarines. Along the way they sent me the most accurate maps possible of the whole fucking seaboard from north to south. Give me ten minutes to find some possibilities on them and five to tell you what I came up with while you were paying the doctor a house call. . . ."

"You pausing for effect?"

"What I got here's too much for even Hawaiian lava bed to mellow. You were right about the mutilating being a key, boss. One per site, sure as sunrise."

"Not confirmed in Dixon Springs yet."

"Far as I'm concerned it is. Old couple named Snead, right on the master list you gave me."

"Snead?"

"They were parents, boss. The ones in Daisy were a brother and his family. The nurse in the hospital was an ex-wife. Relatives all, closest living from what I can tell."

"Whose relatives?" Kimberlain asked in confusion.

"The original Caretakers, Ferryman. That's who our boy is going after."

CHAPTER 27

KIMBERLAIN'S head was still spinning when he finally got Talley on the phone.

"This time it's you who sounds shaken," she said, before he had even begun to relate everything he had learned.

"With good reason. I think I know where Leeds and the others are." He swallowed hard. "I can also tell you how we can go about catching Tiny Tim."

"Should I be heading for my superior's office yet?"

"You should hear it all first. Better sit down, Lauren. This may take a while. . . ."

* * *

Actually, it took only ten minutes for the Ferryman to summarize everything. Each minute to him was one more that brought Andrew Harrison Leeds's ninth dominion closer to fruition. But it could be stopped now. Find the island where Renaissance was headquartered and they would find Leeds.

"What do we do?" Talley asked in the end.

"You go to your superiors, Lauren, and you get them to authorize a major recon mission. Probably have to call in the army, but that shouldn't be a problem. Captain Seven will narrow down our field of choices, and we send the cavalry in."

"You'll have to come down here for a full debriefing."

"Send the Lear to Buffalo. I can be there in two hours."

"What about Tiny Tim, Jared?"

"I'm going to have Captain Seven fax you the complete files on all The Caretakers. Track down the closest living relatives of the eight others and you'll know where to look."

"Nine others including you."

"I've got no relatives. That means he's probably saving me for last."

Kimberlain ran it through his mind over and over on the way to Buffalo and while he was waiting on the tarmac for the bureau's Learjet to arrive. Who could have held a grudge against The Caretakers of the magnitude to justify what Tiny Tim was doing? One of The Caretakers, yes. God knew Kimberlain and the others had left plenty of enemies in their wake. But *all of them*? It made no sense. There was only one time the entire dozen had actually worked together, and that, well . . .

The island of San Luis Garcia . . .

It had been the one time all The Caretakers had been summoned as a unit, the one time Kimberlain had actually laid eyes on the others who were considered to be on the same level he was. The interests of the nation years before had required the assassination of the island of San Luis Garcia's despot ruler and the installation of a puppet government in his place. To the dismay of all, the puppet leader, an American general, elected to start pulling his own strings. General Travis Seckle, it seemed, had his own ideas of what was best for the island and they were in direct conflict with those of the United States. Worse, he threatened to reveal the embarrassing truth about the assassination if he were deposed.

The Caretakers had parachuted down to the island just after midnight and made their way to the hilltop palace. Seckle had done a decent enough job of positioning his troops to guard against such a maneuver, but there was only so much he could do in a short period of time. And against a small, precision group with the skill level of The Caretakers, the entire complement of San Luis Garcia armed forces might have proven insufficient.

Their advances along the palace's outer perimeter had gone smoothly and quickly, but there was no disguising their presence once they reached the courtyard. A bloody battle ensued that eventually spilled into the palace itself, where Seckle had been killed. Kimberlain had been charged with holding the perimeter at that point and never actually entered the palace. Two Caretakers who did had been wounded, and one would never be able to fill missions again. But the cost was worth it. If the truth about San Luis Garcia and Travis Seckle had ever gotten out, the cost for both the U.S. government and The Caretakers would have been incredibly high.

But Seckle was dead, everything connected to him was dead. Something else, then.

The Lear arrived two hours after Kimberlain got to Buffalo Airport, and Kimberlain walked onto the tarmac to meet it. He was halfway to the jet when the door opened and the stairway was extended down. Seconds later a well-dressed man descended.

"Kimberlain?" he called over the jet's still-roaring engine.

The Ferryman nodded.

"Let's go."

Kimberlain climbed on board and found a second agent waiting to greet him.

"I'm Special Agent Greeley and this is Special Agent Hawks." The two men flashed their IDs. Hawks went back to the task of closing the door. "We've got com link with Washington and Quantico. No reason to waste the trip. We'll get started on the way, if you don't mind."

Kimberlain sat down and fastened his seatbelt. This Lear was a technological marvel even Captain Seven would be proud of. There were three television screens, two fax machines, four telephones, and a pair of computers that were obviously attached to modems.

"We can start with where Leeds can be found," the Ferryman began, as the jet streaked into its takeoff.

Captain Seven had narrowed the field to remarkably few prospects, one of which stood out above the rest: an island called Devil's Claw located forty miles out to sea due east from the border of North and South Carolina. Isolated and undeveloped, it was technically not part of either state but at various points had been possessed by both. Its topography and jagged, rock-strewn shoreline made it uninhabitable, and with a hundred more desirable islands within close reach of the shore, no one paid any attention to it anymore.

The name Devil's Claw referred to the island's general form. It was a massive range of hills with a single flat plane five hundred acres large sitting square in the middle. Five tall hills dominated the area enclosing the plane, as the captain described it, each coming to a narrow peak that might have been a talon. From above, the single plain looked like a palm of an upturned claw.

"That can wait," the agent named Greeley was saying, after twisting in the seat ahead to face Kimberlain, "until the director is on line."

The Lear was banking upward through puffy white clouds as thin as the jet's exhaust plume in—

Something scratched at Kimberlain's spine. They hadn't refueled the jet at the airport before taking off again. No way the Lear could have enough fuel to manage the return flight to Washington. . . .

The agent named Hawks was leaning forward in his seat, working one of the television's controls.

"I have the director now," he said, and a staticky picture appeared on the screen. Then it sharpened in the same instant Kimberlain's seatbelt retracted and dug into his stomach. His hand was halfway to his gun when he realized the belt had trapped it against his body. He was struggling to extract it when another pair of men lunged from concealed positions in the rear of the jet and steadied machine guns upon him.

"Welcome," said the image of Andrew Harrison Leeds that now filled the screen before the Ferryman. "It's so nice to have you aboard."

THE SEVENTH DOMINION

Devil's Claw

Thursday, August 20; 11:00 P.M.

CHAPTER 28

From Vermont, Hedda and Chalmers drove west toward a secluded estate overlooking the Hudson River in Highland, New York. Two of the other Caretakers were already present when they arrived, and the rest trickled in over the course of the next six hours, as a cool summer night replaced the day. They had flown into the country from safe houses where Chalmers had stashed them in cities all over the world. One after another rental cars slid into an old barn on the outskirts of the property and the drivers made their way to the main house.

Finn, Ishmael, Kurtz, Marner, Iago . . .

They were a group like none other Hedda had ever encountered. At first glance utterly different in appearance, they were alike in the way they carried themselves and in their eyes, hollow and blank, impossible to read. They were her eyes, predator's eyes she had looked at in the mirror, but never really seen until now.

This was what she was. . . .

But she had been someone else before. Chalmers had steadfastly refused to tell her anything more about her true self, and Hedda realized it was pointless to press him. He was holding the truth hostage; she would get it only if she played her role on Devil's Claw.

When all The Caretakers were accounted for, the group adjourned to the living room of the large house, which had been emptied of furniture except for a large table. On it rested a detailed mock-up of the island. Clay formed the five hilltops that rose over the single flat plain. Miniature wooden buildings represented a small town complete with roads and traffic lights. A dangerously short airstrip lay on the edge of the plain beyond the buildings.

The Caretakers gathered around the table. Hedda wondered if any of them knew more of the truth than she did, but guessed they didn't. After all, only she and Deerslayer had been involved directly with Chalmers's operation. To the rest this might have appeared just another mission.

"You were all on . . . this island . . . once," Chalmers told the assembled group. "You became . . . who you are . . . on this island. . . . I know none . . . of you remember . . . it. It's been . . . two years since . . . I was there. . . . But it must . . . be destroyed . . . if all of us . . . are to survive." He turned her way. "Hedda?"

"The hills," she proposed, without missing a beat. "We wire them with explosives to cause an avalanche. Entomb the buildings and the people."

The Caretaker named Finn ran his fingers over the model town, stopping at the airstrip. Hedda noticed they were long and slender, like a piano player's.

"Then this strip would be our only way off the island. Means we'd have to secure the town and bring a plane down for pickup once the explosives are ready."

"How many?" one named Bloom asked Chalmers.

"Depends. Several . . . hundred at . . . least. Even more . . . perhaps."

"Like us?"

"Some worse. Many . . . worse."

The Caretakers gazed about the room at each other.

"But we . . . may be too . . . late to get . . . them all."

"Why?" Hedda asked.

"Because they . . . may have already . . . been dispatched. . . . But he'll be . . . there. I know . . . he'll be there."

"Perimeter security?" a Caretaker named Marlowe asked.

"Nothing we . . . can't bypass."

"But a direct land or sea approach is out of the question."

"Yes. Of . . . course."

"Then our first requirement," Iago said, "is a means of access."

"Followed by immediate securing of the airfield and surrounding area," Kurtz added, "while the hills are mined with whatever explosives we elect to use."

"Trenching dynamite," Fagin said. "I've worked with it before."

"The problem," Chalmers broke in, "is . . . that I don't . . . know what security . . . they have in the . . . hills. Once they . . . know we're there . . ."

"Two teams, then," Hedda concluded. "One takes the airfield and secures the town while the other plants the explosives. That way, if we trip something up on the hill we can hold back any emerging force."

"We'll need the plane to be circling," Finn said. "A beech 1900 can take us all; it can handle a short runway. Fuel might be a problem, though, depending on how long we're in the zone."

"Do we blow it from the air, then?"

"No," Fagin responded. "The runway, once we're all on board . . ."

The plan continued to evolve through the night, the give and take constant. Discussion of the general plot gave way to specific team assignments. They would have only until the following morning to complete the logistics; the rest of the day would be needed for obtaining supplies and making final arrangements. The raid would come that evening.

The late morning found Chalmers and Hedda alone long enough for her to probe him once more.

"Why?" she asked him.

He gazed at her questioningly.

"Why are you doing this? Is it for you? For us? I want to understand, Chalmers, because maybe it will help me understand myself."

"You were mine . . . all of you. . . . An experiment."

"What do you mean?"

"To see how well . . . the reconditioning . . . process worked."

"The island . . ."

"Yes, after you . . . left. It was . . . my idea. I had . . . recruited you . . . you and the others. . . . I had done . . . it before . . . a long time ago."

"I don't understand."

"There were other . . . Caretakers before . . . you. Different . . . but the same."

"Pomeroy told me."

"I recruited . . . them too." Chalmers touched the socket plugged into his throat. "Until this. I . . . was relieved. . . . But then I was . . . needed again."

"To recruit us," Hedda picked up. "But you went against whoever was controlling things. You saved us."

"Because I . . . figured out . . . what you were . . . really wanted for . . . I couldn't allow . . . it. You were mine."

Hedda suddenly felt chilled. "The TD-13! We were supposed to have something to do with the poison, weren't we?"

"No. After . . . the poison."

"How?"

Chalmers shook his head. "Not time to . . . hear it yet."

"When?"

"After we're finished . . . on the island."

Fragments . . .

That's all Kimberlain's mind could grasp. A room, small and windowless. Voices without context. Chains lacing his arms and legs to a small cot, heavy chains fastened into concrete walls. And darkness interrupted only by flashes of memory.

His last clear thoughts came aboard the Learjet. Andrew Harrison Leeds, smiling ear to ear, had appeared on the screen.

"How nice to see you again, Ferryman."

Kimberlain had given up going for his gun and raised his arms in the air. He waited for an opening, already sensing it wasn't going to come.

"I know it's rude of me not to greet you personally," Leeds told him, "but circumstances dictate I be elsewhere."

"Your ninth dominion, Leeds?"

The madman's eyes filled with genuine admiration. "Most impressive, Ferryman. You make me regret my attempts to dispatch you before we could at least talk. I must try to enlist you in my legion, mustn't I?"

"So long as you're prepared to be disappointed."

"You could never disappoint me, Ferryman. You are the only man who approaches my level—you and Peet, of course."

Kimberlain's eyebrows flickered.

"Yes, I know you and he have joined forces. He told you that, of course."

Kimberlain said nothing.

"Your eyes speak for you, Ferryman. I must say I am most jealous, but I am taking steps to alleviate that. I know where you have been hiding him. A few brief moments with me and I'm sure he will return to his old ways. And there's also the matter of that FBI agent. . . ."

"Talley . . ."

"Yes. Most attractive, isn't she? A shame I must use her for my plan."

Kimberlain calmly pushed his arms outward in an attempt to break his bonds, but the seatbelt gave not an inch. His eyes never left the screen. He knew that a camera was broadcasting his picture back to the madman, wherever he was.

"You have no one to blame but yourself, of course," Leeds continued.

"How?"

"I simply tapped her access lines. I knew you would be calling to provide my opportunity, but I never expected you would actually discover my island." Leeds's eyes scorned him. "You should know better than to drag anyone who doesn't belong into our world. Only bad things can happen to them. Must I always be teaching you lessons, Ferryman?"

"I'm a slow learner."

"Apparently so. You didn't learn when I enlisted your services back when they called me the Candy Man. I knew you would cooperate. You would never suspect that someone would be able to control you. The final lesson is that your true place is with me.''

''And if I don't come with you, you'll kill me like all the others who don't fit into your grand scheme, right?''

Andrew Harrison Leeds smiled. ''How worthy you are, Ferryman. . . .''

''And where are you taking me?''

''Just where you wanted to go, of course: Devil's Claw Island.''

The Ferryman watched the screen as Leeds's face broke into a grin. At the same moment he felt one of the madman's henchmen jab his arm with a needle. He felt groggy almost instantly but never really passed out. His mind slid through different dreamlike levels of consciousness, all sense of time and perspective lost. How he had gotten from the plane to this windowless room he could not say.

Now he realized that the sedation was at last wearing off, meaning Leeds had other plans for him. Toward that end, he tried to focus his mind on the room he was confined to and devise a plan to act on when his bonds were removed.

Kimberlain's eyes cut through the blurriness and at last focused. The room he was confined in was a perfect replica of the cells of MAX-SEC back at The Locks, right down to the six-inch meal slot cut into the door. The lighting was low, no exposed bulbs anywhere. Of course not; they were potential weapons. Kimberlain tested the irons holding his arms behind him and found no give whatsoever. Even if he managed to free himself, it wouldn't matter, because somewhere in this room would be a camera through which Leeds would be viewing his every move.

Just as Leeds's moves were viewed during his brief incarceration at The Locks.

''Ah, Ferryman.'' The madman's voice filled the small

room. "I see you've awakened at last. I hope you find the accommodations acceptable."

"I've seen them somewhere before."

"As have I, for the two months I spent in The Locks, thanks to you."

"You mean, thanks to yourself."

"To both of us, working together. But now you are seeing things from my side. What does it look like, Ferryman? How does it feel?"

"Like you belong in here with me, Leeds, just the two of us."

"With your manacles removed, of course."

"That would be my thinking."

"How many people have you put in places like this, Ferryman? How many souls have you denied expression to?"

"How many killers have I stopped from killing, you mean?"

"But now I have freed them and put you inside. The world needs to be set right, and this island is where the process starts. I wanted you to see things from this perspective so you might consider stepping out onto the other side where you have always belonged."

"Go to hell, Leeds."

"A short walk, Ferryman."

And Kimberlain heard the door's locking mechanism snap open.

CHAPTER 29

Leeds himself stepped through the door first, followed by six of the most intimidating men Kimberlain had ever seen. He recognized none of them right away and knew that they weren't the same men they had been when they came to the island.

Renaissance . . .

Leeds had had his way with them now. They belonged to him.

The madman himself was dwarfed by them. He wore a white outfit that was almost identical to standard issue at The Locks. He stepped forward with his hands clasped behind his back, as if they were bound as well. His black hair shone like shoe leather in the room's meager lighting. His eyes were gleaming.

"How long I have waited for this moment," he said.

"Excuse me for not sharing your enthusiasm."

"You can if you wish, Ferryman. Just say the word."

"I'm afraid not."

Leeds nodded knowingly. "Yes, you are afraid, not so much of me but of yourself. I have a grasp on your true essence, the raw unbridled power that drives you. Give yourself up to that and you at last become the person you were always meant to be."

"And I suppose you can show me the way," Kimberlain said, realizing this might be his only chance for escape.

"Precisely why I am here, Ferryman. Let's take a walk."

Leeds's half-dozen henchmen unclasped Kimberlain's chains from the wall. He felt a hard tug and knew he had effectively been placed on a leash. Pulling free was conceivable, though it would probably not gain him anything with Leeds's guards enclosing him on all sides. They spun him around so that he came face-to-face with Leeds.

"Come, Ferryman, and view my work."

There was a tug on his leash, and Kimberlain stepped into the corridor just behind Leeds. Doors lined the corridor every ten feet or so. Leeds touched a button on the wall, and the overhead lighting snapped on. Corridors adjoining this main one became visible. Leeds began to walk and beckoned Kimberlain to follow him. Again the Ferryman flirted briefly with the notion of launching an attack.

The madman approached one of the doorways and stopped. Kimberlain felt a tug on his leash and stopped as well. Leeds flipped a switch next to the door frame, and the lighting inside snapped on. There was a man stirring something on a stove. Kimberlain could see the stove wasn't plugged in. He wondered if the pot was empty as well.

"I believe you know this man as Chef Fred," Leeds said. "Poisoned an entire community of college students. Well over a hundred died, and investigators were able to connect him to fifty more deaths in restaurants and cafeterias. Arsenic was his poison of choice, but it was discovered during the investigation that he placed assorted other extras in the food he cooked over the years."

"Sentenced to The Locks. One of the eighty-three you took out with you."

"Yes. They're all still here."

"How'd you organize it all? Never mind the logistics, I'm talking about getting all the inmates to cooperate."

Leeds smiled. "Simple, Ferryman. I speak their language—when it's necessary to speak at all."

Leeds flipped the switch and pressed on. He stopped two doors down and turned on another. The first thing the Ferryman saw was heavy, commercial-strength furniture that had been broken up and lay in pieces everywhere. The next thing he saw was a monstrous, shirtless black man snapping wooden fragments with his hands.

"Randford Dobbs," Leeds announced. "Family man with a bad gambling habit. Football team he had bet on blew a ten point lead in the last two minutes. Dobbs killed his wife, three children, and six neighbors before the police shot him. He thinks the game is still going on."

Kimberlain followed Leeds toward a room on the opposite side of the corridor.

"Here's one of my favorites," the madman announced, peering through the one-way glass.

Inside was a teenage boy with rock-star long, blond hair. He sat on a couch with his face squeezed by headphones connected to an elaborate stereo system that almost filled the far wall.

"Jon Goldberg," Leeds recited, "young rich boy who got himself addicted to thrill killing. He and two other boys killed five younger boys with baseball bats. Then one day his friends slept over, and Jon killed them. That was three years ago. He was transferred to The Locks on his eighteenth birthday, just a month before I arrived."

"I've seen enough," Kimberlain said.

Leeds frowned in disappointment. "We're only just getting started."

"These are the people of your ninth dominion, Leeds? Not very stimulating for a man of your standards."

"Because I haven't finished with them yet. Come, there really is one more thing you should see. . . ."

A door at the far end of the corridor opened onto another, shorter hall with rooms on one side. Once again one-way glass permitted viewing, but all of these rooms were unoccupied. Each had one chair or two. Some of the chairs had straps.

"You did it here," Kimberlain said knowingly. "Renaissance."

"Yes," Leeds said, standing closer to him, almost close enough for Kimberlain to risk an attack. Dying would be acceptable, if he could take Leeds with him. But he had to wait for the odds to be better than they were at present.

"In the early stages," Leeds continued, "several years ago, we used advanced mind conditioning. Deep hypnosis and what might be referred to as brainwashing. Alas, the results have not proved to be longlasting enough. Several of the subjects recall parts of their pasts, and in a few cases all the memories came back. Chaos results. The mind rebels. Such a waste . . ." They moved on slowly down the corridor. "More recently, we have been successful in erasing memory by exposing the hippocampus and those segments of the cortex where its component elements are stored to direct microwaves via a probe. Fascinating work. Expedites the process remarkably."

"And after their pasts don't exist consciously anymore?"

"We implant false memories, enough to provide a sufficient cushion for consciousness. But only the memories themselves are erased. The essences are preserved, allowed to expand and flourish."

"You make them in your own image."

"In *their* own images, but yes, you have grasped the concept."

"Tools, Leeds, robots."

Leeds swung toward him in a violent motion. "No. Men and women allowed to express their true natures, their energies channeled where they can best be utilized."

"But there's more, Leeds. Your ninth dominion won't be theirs until everyone else has been pushed out of the way. Just how does that come to pass?"

Leeds nodded. "A fascinating means really. I think even you would approve."

"Tell me."

"I will when the time is right, providing . . ."

They had come to the final room on the hall. Leeds stopped and gestured for Kimberlain to peer through the one-way glass. Inside was the most elaborate room of all, sterile and high tech. Kimberlain couldn't identify most of the devices inside and wondered if even Captain Seven would be able to.

"It would happen in there, Ferryman. You would step out a different man than when you stepped in. Free of the moral dilemmas that bind you to a life of discontent. Free of everything except your elemental nature. You can't deny that. You can't even try."

"I won't bother."

"I am offering you freedom, Ferryman, freedom from what has always enslaved you. I can take your past away and leave you free to express yourself as you were born to."

"I was born to stop you, Leeds."

Leeds's eyes chided him. "Really? How well do you think you really know yourself, Ferryman? Are you really this naive?"

Kimberlain gazed through the glass again at the operating room. "Why ask my permission? Why not just strap me in and have your people go to work?"

"Out of respect, Ferryman. I could not force *you* to take the chair. Not you, not Peet. The others are my soldiers. You could command by my side. Join us."

"Us?"

"A small surprise I'm saving until later."

Kimberlain shook his head. "I'm sorry, Leeds. There is no later."

"Purity, Ferryman, raw essence—that's what I'm offering you and what you deny. And in so doing you deny who you are. Accept it for your own good, as well as mine."

"No."

"Then we must remain as victor and vanquished."

"We do what we have to, Leeds."

"Always."

* * *

The four cigarette boats cut their engines and slowed to a drift when Devil's Claw was two miles away. Each carried four Caretakers; Chalmers and one other were left to fly the Beech 1900 that would pick them up when their operation was complete. Hedda was in the boat farthest to the right. With the engines cut, none of The Caretakers needed to be told what to do. Each had his assigned task and went about it with precision.

Hedda's task was to ease over the side and hook into place black hang gliders attached to parafoils. Running on autopilot, the cigarette boats would hoist The Caretakers into the air on chutes. Once sufficient speed and height had been attained, they would disengage themselves from the parafoil apparatuses and reach the waters near the island by glider. The logistics were not at all exact. They could only hope that the wind would cooperate enough to bring them within easy swimming distance of the island.

With everything in place, Hedda donned her wet suit. She strapped her equipment and armaments inside a waterproof wrap and eased herself over the launch's side into the chilling water where the three other Caretakers from her boat waited. She belted herself into her glider, fastening buckles around her waist and under each arm. The four-foot-long skis accepted her feet, and she tightened them in the slots. When she was sitting ready, buttocks to the water with the black wings poised behind her, she nodded to Iago. Iago flashed the proper signal to the other boats and had it returned in kind. Then he activated the remote control device in his hand.

The autopilot engaged instantly. In the next moment, the cigarette boat's sudden burst of speed jerked her to her feet and nearly upended her. Hedda managed to right herself and almost immediately was airborne. The wind current was straight and easterly, just the direction they wanted to go.

The boats were spread far enough apart to leave a comfortable distance between the four groups of Caretakers. Behind each boat, though, occasional wind swirls caused the four being dragged to be pulled dangerously close to one another.

Hedda had to manipulate her parafoil on several occasions to keep it from becoming snarled with another.

The Caretakers waited until the cigarette boats hit top speed and the rope links attaching them were fully taut before disengaging the gliders from the parafoil spreads above them. Hedda dropped suddenly before the wind grabbed firm hold of her and drew her upward again. She felt incredibly light. She picked up more speed than she had been expecting and worried that she might overshoot Devil's Claw altogether. But she leveled off and saw the island coming so fast that she was late picking up the signal to dive. As a result, she overcompensated and dropped too fast. The glider smacked the water hard, and Hedda sank under the surface, weighted down by the apparatus. She fought off panic, as she clawed back to the surface for breath. She stripped off the glider and began to fight her way through the surging swells toward the rock-strewn shoreline.

Around her only a few of the other Caretakers were visible, but this was of little concern; they would be rendezvousing at a prearranged point before breaking into two teams and going their separate ways. So far Hedda had no indication that perimeter security around the island was anything more than Chalmers had predicted. Still, she swam cautiously, eyes never straying from the shoreline.

Finally she climbed over the last of the rocks and reached the shore. Finding a plateau on the ragged expanse of low hills, she joined the rest of her team in inventorying their supplies. Everything had remained dry, most importantly her portion of the trenching dynamite Fagin himself had made back at the estate in Highland.

She was part of the demolitions team that would string the trenching dynamite around three of the rising devil's claws—enough to ensure an avalanche big enough to bury the town on the flat, palmlike plain below. They would work in four separate groups of two each, one to plant the dynamite and the other to set the fuse. All the fuses were rigged into an electronic transmitter each of the eight carried in case only one survived to detonate the explosives. Hedda estimated it would take between twenty-two and twenty-five minutes to wire the hillsides as specified. During that time, the eight additional Caretakers would secure the town and airfield. Meanwhile, Chalmers would be in the Beech 1900 with Bloom piloting. Pickup would come approximately eight minutes from the time the hillsides were wired, assuming all else went as planned.

Hedda stripped her wet suit off and strapped her packs and belt into place. Her ammo vest held four fragmentary grenades and extra clips for her M-16 and Uzi. All The Caretakers were similarly outfitted, the ones charged with securing the perimeter carrying even heavier firepower. By now those two teams would be approaching their positions. It would take Hedda and those charged with the demolitions duties several minutes more to scale the hillsides of Devil's Claw and begin to lay the explosives. Communication would be via voice-activated, headphone-style walkie-talkies with a chip added to each of them that made eavesdropping or jamming impossible.

Four members of the demolitions team had already headed off. Hedda checked her weapons one last time and gave the ready signal to the three men with her. Eight minutes into their climb Fagin signaled her and Ishmael to break off toward their sectors. The vantage point allowed her a clear view of the plain below. The real settlement was virtually identical to Chalmers's mock-up. Clearly, most of the buildings had been added after the original construction, as demand for space grew. The prospects of that were chilling. How many like her resided here still, waiting to be summoned for a purpose Chalmers had yet to reveal? But it didn't matter, because after tonight none of them would be leaving.

"Come in, Hedda."

"Here, Iago," she whispered into her walkie-talkie.

"My team is sweeping the town. Everything quiet. No sign of anyone outside."

"Finn," Hedda said to the Caretaker in charge of securing the airfield, "where are you?"

"Approaching western rim of the strip now," he said.

"What's wrong?" Hedda returned, sensing something in his voice.

"Recent stress fractures in the tarmac indicate lots of planes have been landing and taking off from here lately. Also the hangar's empty."

"Chalmers, did you copy that?"

A burst of static preceded his response, indicating his plane was almost out of range of the walkie-talkie. When he spoke, the words sounded hollow, and Hedda could picture him holding his speaker against the microphone.

"Yes. Proceed . . . as planned."

"This is Iago," came a sudden call from inside the town.

"Read you. Is your sweep—"

"This place is empty."

"Say again."

"I say there's nobody here. The target's been abandoned."

Hedda had her binoculars pinned against her eyes. What she saw seemed to confirm Iago's report. The settlement was a wasteland, no sign of life or movement anywhere.

"Chalmers"—Hedda had lowered her binoculars and raised her walkie-talkie—"what should we do?"

"Continue . . . as planned."

"But—"

"Do as I . . . say."

"Iago, did you copy that?"

"Roger, Hedda."

Hedda brought her binoculars back to her eyes. She swept the town again and stopped at one of the twin guard towers that rose at either end of the single street. Even in the darkness, she could see something was wrong with the picture.

"Iago!" she roared into her walkie-talkie. "Get down! Take—"

Hedda heard the powerful staccato bursts echoing in the wind and through Iago's walkie-talkie. She was steadying her binoculars again when Iago's screams found her ears. In the town below, heavy-caliber machine guns were firing in all directions. The two mounted in the towers swept the street, while what might have been a dozen others spit fire, each in a specific grid.

But Hedda could find no trace of any man firing.

"Hedda!" the hollow voice of Chalmers demanded. "What's . . . happening?"

"First teams are under attack. No gunmen visible, just weapons. They must have tripped something."

"I should have . . . known. . . ." The rest of his words were garbled.

"What was that? Say again?"

"Underground . . . I said they . . . must be underground! . . . Continue mission . . . as planned."

"Finn, do you copy?" Hedda said into her walkie-talkie.

"Under heavy fire. But it's centered in—the towers on the airfield! Jesus, *the towers*!"

"Finn?"

Nothing.

"Say again," came Chalmers.

"He's dead!" Hedda screamed.

"Please re—"

"This is Hedda. I'm heading to the airfield. Repeat, I'm heading to the airfield."

CHAPTER 30

"**W**ELCOME to my theater, Ferryman."

Leeds led the way into a sloped room that had the look of a college lecture hall, minus the chairs and desks. They had gone down two flights of stairs to reach it, so Kimberlain assumed it was actually some sort of subbasement.

"Behold."

The madman flipped a number of switches, and the lighting changed from dull to bright. At the lowest point of the room, a man-size cage attached to the high ceiling by a steel cable rested on the floor.

"If you do not change your mind, Ferryman, this is where it will end for you."

"In a cage, Leeds? I would have thought you more sporting than that."

Leeds was smiling again. "Oh, but I am. I'm still clinging to the hope that you won't make me prove it to you."

He had barely finished speaking when a rattling sound reached the chamber from above. Heavy machine-gun fire, Kimberlain realized, intermixed with explosions.

"Looks like your private world is under attack, Leeds," the Ferryman taunted. "And from the look on your face I'd say you weren't expecting it."

"A minor misjudgment," the madman said through the obvious dismay on his features, "one that is more unfortunate for you at this point than me."

Leeds nodded, and the men holding Kimberlain's chains dragged him down toward the cage. Drawing closer, he saw it was like an antishark cage, accessible through a hatch in the top. Two of Leeds's henchmen lowered the cage onto its side and opened the hatch. Leeds was keeping a safe distance.

"I'm sorry I won't be able to stay for this, but I think you'll find it most interesting," he told the Ferryman. "I'm even going to give you a chance to survive, though not much of one, I admit."

Kimberlain's eyes fidgeted.

"Please, Ferryman, do not even contemplate any desperate lunges. I gave you plenty of opportunities earlier and you passed on every one. Get into the cage."

Before Kimberlain could respond, the guards holding him yanked brutally down on his chains. He dropped hard face first against the floor. They dragged him backward, keeping his bonds taut as they shoved him feet first into the cage. On the hatch hung a lock; one of the guards turned a key in it, then popped the key back into his pocket. Then the others stood the cage upright.

The Ferryman watched as Leeds flipped a switch on the wall. Instantly, the cage began to rise toward the ceiling, with the madman and his henchmen gazing upward to follow its ascent.

"I'd give you one more chance to change your mind and join me," Leeds said, "but I know your answer would be the same."

"So instead you leave me up here to die slowly. Maybe cling to the hope that I can find a way out."

"On the contrary, Ferryman, I am going to activate a control that will lower you slowly back to the ground. And . . ."

Leeds paused, as another of the men flanking him tossed a key up through the bars. The Ferryman caught it and gazed down again.

". . . This is the key to the irons on your hands and legs. I do wish to make it interesting for you."

"You can do better than this, Leeds."

"No," Leeds said over the sound of a stampede of feet approaching, "I don't think so."

A trio of doors opened, and Kimberlain watched as the eighty-three escapees from MAX-SEC spilled into Leeds's theater.

Kimberlain had his chains off by the time the cage stopped ten feet from the ceiling and dangled there. Thirty feet below the escaped inmates of MAX-SEC shook their upraised hands and fists at Kimberlain. From this distance they were indistinguishable from one another, little more than a white blanket of madness spread across the floor.

Andrew Harrison Leeds stood directly below Kimberlain, watched by his half-dozen guards.

"I believe they know who you are, Ferryman. Won't be pretty when they get their hands on you."

The cage had begun its agonizingly slow descent. Leeds lingered in the doorway briefly, then smiled.

"Good-bye, Ferryman."

He disappeared into the darkness, and Kimberlain turned his attention to escape. He shook the top of the cage to test the strength of the lock securing the hatch in place. It didn't give in the slightest, which meant his only chance lay in picking the lock. The mechanism was simple in design but would nonetheless require the usual pair of implements: one to maintain pressure on the pins and a second to work those pins into the proper slots. Kimberlain gauged his rate of descent and estimated he had another minute-and-a-half at most before his cage came within reach of the madmen below. Allowing fifteen seconds to pick the lock, that gave him just over a minute to come up with reasonable facsimiles of pick tools, but where to find them?

The key that had opened his irons was useless, though not so the ring it was attached to. It took all the Ferryman's strength to bend the ring open at the slight gap where the key had been squeezed through. He kept bending until the ring was the shape of a rounded "L"; this would be thin enough to squeeze into the hatch lock to apply pressure to the pins. But he still needed something to pop the tumblers.

Nothing he could see in the cage held the answer. Something he couldn't see then . . .

The escapees from MAX-SEC were screaming now as his cage descended toward them; it was at the halfway point now. The distant bursts of gunfire convinced Kimberlain that this entire island complex must be located below underground. He could picture some invading force trying to blast its way in past whatever security Leeds had left on the surface.

He looked up and focused on the hook holding the steel cable that was lowering him from the ceiling. It was held to the cage by a long cotter pin jammed flush through a tailored slot. The cotter pin would make the perfect second tool. Pull it all the way out, of course, and he would run the risk of sending the cage plummeting. If he could break it off, however, he would have the implement he needed.

Standing on his toes, he was just able to reach the cotter pin. He bent it toward him, then back away. Toward him, then back away . . . It didn't seem like it was giving at all, but suddenly . . .

Snap . . .

Just like that, a two-inch fragment of the cotter pin broke off in his hand. Kimberlain took the key ring from his mouth and probed it up through the hatch. The lock itself was on the outside, meaning he would have to work blind. No matter. He had picked plenty of locks in the dark, albeit without the desperate time constraints confronting him now.

The Ferryman squeezed his other hand through the bars and felt about the lock with the broken-off cotter pin. It slid in easily just ahead of the bent key ring. Feeling the perspiration dripping into his eyes as he gazed upward, Kimberlain located the tumblers with the curled section and applied the sideways pressure necessary to prepare them for his work with the cotter pin. His hands were sweaty, and the angle made the job especially difficult.

Below him, some of the inmates had climbed on other's shoulders, and they were almost able to reach the cage. Explosions sounded from above and shook some of them back to the floor. The cage wobbled. Kimberlain's hands trembled slightly, and his fingers tightened.

Click . . .

The first of the lock's four tumblers fell into place. Kimberlain moved on to the second, fighting against the impulse to rush and risk the cotter pin bending in the lock. He felt the second tumbler give.

Click . . .

Beneath him, inmates were scratching at the cage's bottom. Kimberlain stamped their fingers with his feet. One managed to grab hold of the cage's side and hang from it, trying to pull himself up, and Kimberlain kicked him in the face through the bars. The man fell to the floor.

The move broke the Ferryman's concentration and pushed the cotter pin off the third tumbler. He found it again quickly and wasted no time in sliding the pin home.

Click . . .

As Kimberlain eased the cotter pin to the final tumbler, he stole a glance downward. The cage bottom was brushing the outstretched fingers of the tallest MAX-SEC escapees. He could recognize several of them now, the monstrous Ranford Dobbs and the hulking Jeffrey Culang most prominent among their figures. Leeds was using Kimberlain to feed their madness. But he could get out of this. Damnit, he *would* get out of this!

Click . . .

Hands were probing through the bars toward him, when the fourth tumbler gave. Kimberlain pushed the hatch open. He got a firm hold on the bars above and barely managed to kick free of the fingers grabbing at his ankles. At last he pushed himself upward through the hatch.

The screams of the escapees grew enraged now. An object of insane desire was slipping from their grasp. Those who had lived with killing for so long and been denied it since incarceration had to confront the fact that they would have to wait still longer to kill again.

Their wails sounded inhuman, as Kimberlain began to scale the cable toward the ceiling. Just to the right of the ceiling bracket was some sort of ventilation shaft covered by a grate.

A potential route out.

Beneath him, mad furious hands had tugged the cage all the way to the floor and some of the inmates were climbing atop it. A few jumped to swipe at him and narrowly missed. He was halfway to the ceiling, when the cable began to swing wildly from side to side. A gaze down showed a half dozen inmates shaking it, determined to tear his grip away.

Kimberlain climbed faster. His head start was sufficient to reach the ceiling with room to spare. Once he got there, though, there was still the matter of getting the ventilation shaft open and pushing himself into it.

The closest MAX-SEC inmate was fifteen feet below him when the Ferryman reached out to his right and grabbed the steel grate covering the shaft. He pulled hard. When the grate refused to give, Kimberlain hammered it with his fist along both sides to loosen it. This time it wobbled when he pulled, and on the next yank it came free.

Its weight almost tore Kimberlain's balance from him and sent him plummeting. As it was, he was able to hold fast to both the coil and the grate. Beneath him, meanwhile, the closest inmate was only a yard away. Kimberlain took aim with the cover and dropped it directly on him. Impact stripped the inmate's grip from the cable and he tumbled downward, taking the four men directly beneath him along for the ride. Kimberlain swung himself into the ventilation shaft, which possessed enough of a sill to give him a foothold. With pursuit coming yet again from below, he leaned outward and jimmied the cable. The ascending inmates may have thought he was merely trying to shake them off, but his true goal was to unhook the cable. It came free, and Kimberlain let it drop downward toward a white sea of writhing, screaming inmates.

The Ferryman slid back into the ventilation shaft and studied what lay before him. The darkness turned to utter black just a few yards ahead, but those few yards showed him the shaft was steep but mountable. He began to climb with hands pressed against either wall for stability.

The shaft finished two hundred feet later with another grate, which Kimberlain effortlessly knocked out with a single thrust of his shoulder. Night air rushed in, along with a sound like a constant thunderclap rolling his way. The entire island seemed to be shaking around him. Fighting to steady himself, he climbed out of the shaft and found himself just below ground level in a rectangular basement with only part of a ceiling. No, the ceiling was retractable, as if, as if . . .

Kimberlain swung right and saw marks scorched into the floor. Then he turned left and smiled at what was waiting there for him.

Hedda glimpsed the shapes of Finn and the other fallen Caretakers as she descended the last bit of the devil's claw adjacent to the airstrip. The position of their bodies revealed the angle of fire, and her eyes flashed between the pair of twin concrete towers on either end of the field a hundred yards from her. If the rest of them were going to escape once the explosion was triggered, she had to disable those towers.

Hedda held her ground. Before her she could see the smoldering ruins of the town. Flames sprouted from several buildings, and other structures had collapsed, evidence of The Caretakers' failed resistance. Together they might have been able to defeat a small army. But against heavy weapons rigged with thermal heat sensors . . .

Hedda stopped and touched her vest. Packed inside were a dozen flares meant to light the runway for the Beech 1900 when the time was right. She pulled one out and moved to the edge of the airfield. In her mind she could picture the big guns locking on to her, alerted by their sensors. Then she lit the flare, waited a few seconds, and hurled it to the right.

Instantly the big guns began to chew up the tarmac. Hedda dashed forward. She was more than halfway to the first tower when the right-hand gun locked on her and traced her steps. Asphalt was sprayed in her wake. She reached the left-hand gun before it had even picked her up. Steadying her shoulders against its hard surface, she pulled a hand grenade from her ammo vest and yanked out the pin. She hurled it and covered up as best she could, stealing enough of a glance to see it was right on target. A shower of asphalt followed the blast.

One down and one to go.

Hedda pulled another flare from beneath her vest and threw it back toward the town. The second gun rotated in its tower and blew apart the remains of a building. Hedda lobbed the grenade as the gun's turret swung back toward her. It hit before the bullets came, and the entire gun assembly was blown out into the air.

"Airfield secured," Hedda said into the pen-size mike. "Fagin, do you copy?"

"Roger. We're on our way down. All explosives set. Estimate eight minutes to airfield."

"Chalmers?"

"We're coming . . . in."

The other seven surviving Caretakers reached the strip just as Hedda finished laying her remaining flares out along the runway. The Beech 1900 began its descent immediately. It touched down and sped to the end of the strip, coming to a halt with only ten yards to spare. Bloom spun it around so it was ready for takeoff. The side door opened, and Chalmers lowered the ladder. Hedda watched him climb down it gingerly and approach The Caretakers. He was holding his speaker.

"Get on board!" Hedda heard him order the other seven Caretakers, his eyes indicating she should stay as she was.

Chalmers met her at the edge of the airfield and gazed at the detonator in her hand.

"Let me," he said, and she handed it over.

Chalmers placed his hand over a button with a red light flashing next to it and looked back at Hedda.

"Finish it," she told him.

Chalmers pressed the button.

Directly behind him, the runway exploded in a blast of concrete and stone. He and Hedda had made it to the ground when the Beech 1900 erupted into an orange blanket of flames. Chunks of the strip continued to rain down on them, but Chalmers rose up to his knees amid it.

"No!" he moaned. "They're dead. . . . All dead! . . ."

Genuine sadness laced his voice, and Hedda understood what had transpired. The runway had been mined with explosives rigged to a universal detonator, so that any transmitted signal would trigger them. The ultimate defense, with one exception:

The explosives the now dead Caretakers had set had been detonated as well. A rumbling shook the ground. Above them the hillsides were tumbling in upon themselves to form a rolling mound of dirt, rubble, and promised death.

The helicopter was a Bell Jet Ranger, black and sleek like a bird of prey. Kimberlain figured Leeds must have fled the island in a twin that had, judging by the marks on the landing pad, been right next to it. The chopper started easily after one minute of prep time. Without any further warm up he lifted off the pad; the first bits of dirt and rock were flying over the edge. The machine fought him briefly and then jumped forward.

What he saw froze him. A massive avalanche was occurring on the island. What had been hillsides seemed to be melting before his eyes and rushing down toward a complex of shattered, flaming buildings. Whoever Andrew Harrison Leeds had left behind here would soon be entombed. But not him, not this time.

Kimberlain had just banked right toward the sea when he saw the two figures charging his way with the mountain of rubble chasing them.

He had no idea who the man and woman were, only that they might have been part of the raid that helped save his life. He pushed the chopper into a quick drop for one of the last level patches he could see. The machine wavered uneasily and he beckoned the approaching figures toward him. He threw open the Bell's right-hand door and watched the woman help the man up before climbing in herself.

"Go!" she said before she had gotten the door all the way closed.

And the helicopter lurched upward with a jolt that carried it over the rolling mountain of earth soon to cover the entire island.

CHAPTER 31

THE Ferryman turned on the chopper's lights and soared out over the water.

Hedda swung toward him. "Who are—"

But Chalmers cut her off. "Kimberlain."

Kimberlain looked his way long enough to see the cord dangling from his throat. He noticed the woman's face had filled with shock.

"Kimberlain!" Hedda exclaimed, recalling August Pomeroy's mention of the name. "But what—"

"Not now!" the Ferryman ordered, eyes on the gauges. "We're going down."

"*What?*"

"I didn't have time to fill up the fuel tank."

The power held just long enough for Kimberlain to settle the chopper into a drop. It smacked the water hard and sat there. Hedda helped Chalmers down and then followed him into the water. Kimberlain waited until they were both out before dropping out himself.

"How long a swim is it?" Kimberlain asked.

"Not very long at all," Hedda said, and she pulled the long-distance homing beacon from her soaked vest.

The autopilot mechanism of one of the cigarette boats would respond to the beacon's signal, just as long as the boat had stopped after The Caretakers had left it en route to the island.

Sure enough, four long minutes later, the boat coasted up alongside them. Kimberlain climbed in first and helped the other two up over the gunwale. Hedda moved immediately to the deck-mounted controls and took the wheel.

Kimberlain's eyes rotated warily between the both of them. "Who are *you*?" the Ferryman asked Chalmers. "How do you know who I am?"

"We met once. . . . Don't you . . . recognize . . . me?" Chalmers responded. His voice emerged even more broken and garbled than usual, thanks to the beating his speaker had taken in the water. "In Modesto . . . California . . . a long time ago. At . . . the beginning . . . The Ferryman's . . . beginning." Chalmers touched the cord running out of his throat. "The night you . . . did this to me."

A chill moved up Kimberlain's spine. "In the bar . . ."

Chalmers tried to nod. "You did it . . . with a chain. . . . You . . . remember."

Kimberlain remembered all too well. The night he had killed the members of the motorcycle gang who had murdered his parents, he had come back for the leader and found him in the bar's back room with another man. The man had drawn a pistol and begun firing. The bullets had poured into the biker leader when Kimberlain grabbed him as a shield. Then the Ferryman had stripped the chain from the corpse's midsection and lashed it outward. The sharp-pronged edge tore into the gunman's throat and came away coated with flesh. The man had gone down, gasping and gurgling, dead for sure.

Apparently not.

"But what were you doing there?" Kimberlain asked as the stiff sea breeze made him feel cold and clammy.

"Your parents' . . . deaths were . . . arranged by . . . me."

"*What?*"

"You were set . . . up. Everything was . . . set up."

"*Why?*"

"A test."

"You *bastard*!"

"You passed."

Kimberlain tried to compose it all in his mind. The very existence of the Ferryman was a lie. He had not acted on his own back then, any more than he had in the years that followed as a Caretaker. He had simply done their bidding. They had programmed him, and Kimberlain had performed. What did they have to lose, after all? If he had been killed trying to avenge his parents, they lost nothing. If he succeeded, they would be in a position to provide the only means available to free him from the stockade. What choice had there been? They had killed his parents to make him what they needed him to be.

Kimberlain moved a step closer to Chalmers, suspended between thoughts and intentions. "Maybe I should finish the job I started back then."

"Maybe. But . . . tonight finds . . . us on the same . . . side."

"I'm not convinced of that yet."

"But it's the truth," Hedda interjected. "I know who you are, too. I know you're the last surviving member of the original Caretakers."

"Original?"

"I'm part of the new Caretakers, the last survivor. . . ."

Kimberlain looked at Chalmers. "Recruited by him, too, I suppose."

Hedda nodded. "Under drastically different circumstances, though. I was in prison when he found me."

"Renaissance," the Ferryman realized.

Hedda jerked the wheel in surprise. Water lifted up over the gunwale and sprayed them all.

The term sent a shudder through Hedda. She exchanged glances with Chalmers, then spoke finally. "How much do you know?"

"Hundreds of convicted criminals, chosen for their capacity for violence, were taken from prisons and asylums to be reconditioned to serve in a twisted army run by the worst of them all. And you're one of them."

"What twisted army?" Hedda demanded. "Just who is the worst of them all?"

"Then there's something you don't know, isn't there?"

Hedda's eyes flashed between Chalmers and the night sea before them. "You know, don't you? It's what you wouldn't tell me."

"That and more," Chalmers confirmed.

"Including Andrew Harrison Leeds?" Kimberlain challenged.

Chalmers's face filled with confusion. "Who?"

"The man behind all of this."

Chalmers shook his head. "The man behind . . . Renaissance . . . was Briarwood."

"As in T. Howard Briarwood? The billionaire?"

"Yes."

And in that instant, everything was clear to Kimberlain.

"Briarwood Industries," Hedda muttered. "They owned the plastics factory that burned down."

"What are you talking about?" the Ferryman asked her.

"A trail I followed from the time my own people tried to kill me. . . ."

Starting there, Hedda told the story of her journey; from learning of Lyle Hanley's transdermal poison in Doha, to PLAS-TECH, to the mysterious toxic strips the ruined plant produced and then shipped to a trio of paper production facilities. By the end of her story, Kimberlain had grasped the total shape of what he had been pursuing. Everything had come together, and the shape was terrifying.

"TD-13," he muttered.

"It stands for transdermal, meaning—"

"Absorption through the skin. A poison that causes death by mere touch." He paused. "Hundreds of millions of deaths."

"No. Hanley said the quantities produced weren't sufficient for that kind of destruction. He said it was going to be more limited."

"He was wrong. This whole country's going to die, maybe the whole world in the long run."

"What are you talking about?"

"The ninth dominion," Kimberlain told her.

* * *

"Then Leeds, alias Briarwood, is going to use TD-13 to make his vision a reality," Hedda said when he was finished. "Only according to Hanley, he doesn't have enough to pull it off."

"The key lies in those plastic monofilament strips. Why send them to paper mills?"

"Because the finished paper is going somewhere else with the poisoned strips inserted within it." She thought briefly. "Magazines maybe, or newspapers."

"No. By your account, there isn't nearly enough of this TD-13 to infest even one city's supply of newspapers. And even if there were, most people don't read them. No, Leeds has figured out a way to get his poison into something *everybody* touches."

"Not everybody," Hedda said. "That's what his plan is all about. And that's where I come in, and the others like me, isn't it? Because it was Leeds who made me, made all of us."

"The guardians of his new order. He thinks he needs them to ride herd over the criminals and madmen he intends to let loose."

"Then the criminals and madmen are going to survive TD-13 when Leeds unleashes it on the rest of the country. But how?"

A thick sigh emerged from Chalmers's speaker. "It's coming soon. . . . He pulled them . . . off the island. . . . They must already . . . be in place. . . . Waiting. Except . . . for one." Chalmers looked Kimberlain tautly in the eye. "Tiny Tim."

"My God," the Ferryman muttered. "Then he's a part of Renaissance, too?"

"A part gone . . . terribly wrong. . . . Leeds must have . . . released him . . . from the island. . . . I didn't realize . . . it until the . . . second town. Then . . . I knew the . . . truth about . . . Briarwood."

"Leeds," Kimberlain corrected. "And you're saying he let Tiny Tim loose and set him on his way to find the closest survivors of the original Caretakers. Why?"

"Felt it was . . . justified."

"By what?"

"The past . . . San Luis Garcia."

"Travis Seckle . . ."

Chalmers nodded. "You wiped out . . . his family . . . including a son."

Kimberlain nodded. "Garth Seckle. Big brute who massacred a small village in Viet—" He stopped when the connection struck him, so obvious he hadn't been able to see it before. "He survived. . . ."

"Yes."

"Then Leeds let him out of the stockade so he could get his revenge."

Chalmers's eyes shifted rapidly between Hedda and Kimberlain. "And I know where . . . Tiny Tim is . . . going next."

"Which one of the other Caretakers is the target? Where's he going to hit?"

Chalmers turned away from Kimberlain and fixed his gaze upon Hedda. "That last night . . . of the Storm Riders . . . the night you . . . killed the boy . . . The piece you . . . knew was there . . . but couldn't identify."

"Yes," she muttered, feeling the truth now, almost close enough to touch it."

"You were pregnant," Chalmers told her. "Sandman's . . . baby. Delivered . . . six months later . . . just before the . . . trial. A boy . . . age twelve now."

"I have a son?"

"No," Chalmers corrected Hedda. "You *had* . . . a son. You . . . gave birth to . . . him. Nothing more."

"Where is he?"

"He was . . . adopted."

"The parents, do they know . . ." Hedda let her question tail off, the intent of it clear.

"They knew nothing . . . about you," Chalmers told her. "No one . . . knew. But you . . . have to know now. Whole family is . . . at a resort . . . in the Poconos. . . . That's Tiny Tim's . . . next stop."

"Wait a minute," Kimberlain broke in. "He's been killing families of the *original* Caretakers."

"And he still . . . is," Chalmers told the Ferryman. "I owe you for . . . what I did. . . . This is my . . . chance, my payback." Breathing replaced Chalmers's voice briefly through the speaker, and his eyes returned to Hedda. "Before Helena . . . Cain. Before . . . Lucretia . . . McEvil. Before . . . Hedda . . ."

"Finish it! *Who am I?*"

"Ellen . . . Kimberlain," Chalmers said with his empty gaze turning back toward the Ferryman. "His sister."

The Towanda Family Resort

Friday, August 21; 3:00 A.M.

CHAPTER 32

"*S*ISTER?" Kimberlain asked in disbelief.

He and Hedda stared hard at each other, wanting to deny the revelation but knowing they couldn't.

Chalmers continued. "We learned the . . . truth after . . . releasing you from . . . prison, Hedda. . . . It was quite . . . a shock to . . . us all. Briarwood . . . kept close track . . . of you. But . . . then it was . . . he who insisted . . . you be the . . . one I use . . . in Lebanon."

"Because you were a threat to him," Kimberlain said.

"No more than any of the others."

"Except you were related to me."

Kimberlain remembered his older sister had run away from home when he was six. She was never mentioned by name again, remembered only in the silent tears his mother shed when she was certain her father could not see her. His sister had become Helena Cain, then Lucretia McEvil of the Storm Riders, and now Hedda.

"Were we born this way?" Hedda asked Kimberlain abruptly. "I mean, think about it. Look at the two of us; what we are, what we've been."

"We're only what they made us." Kimberlain glanced toward Chalmers. "Him and all the others."

"No, you're wrong about that," she said. "They did it to *you*, not me. I joined up with the Storm Riders of my own

273

accord. Nobody forced the guns into my hands. I held them because I wanted to and fired them for the same reason. By the time Chalmers and the others salvaged me, I was already a done deal. You were manipulated. From the beginning.''

"None of that matters now," Kimberlain told her. "They made us what we are, and like it or not, we're going to need that to save your son. My nephew."

She looked at Chalmers. "Unless we're already too late."

"It's . . . possible."

"But if we're in time, we can save him. Call ahead. Warn the people at this resort to evacuate."

"They wouldn't listen. It might make them call in the authorities or put extra security on, but that would only make things worse."

"How?"

"Tiny Tim takes his time, likes to savor the moment. Put him against an army and he won't bother being subtle. Those families won't stand a chance. Your son won't stand a chance."

Hedda flinched at that. "You're saying he will otherwise?"

"If we can get his family out in time, yes." The Ferryman turned to Chalmers. "How long are they scheduled to be at the resort?"

"Three more days."

"We've got time, then."

"We go to the resort as soon as we get back to land, the fastest way possible," Hedda insisted. "Before we go after Briarwood, Leeds, or whatever he's calling himself."

"Of course," Kimberlain said.

Just as Chalmers nodded his acknowledgment, the cruiser's engine sputtered and died.

They were adrift for three hours before Hedda managed to get the engine working, but their speed was barely ten knots. It was ten A.M. before they pulled up to a dock on South Carolina's northeastern coast. All three were ravenous, and Hedda went into a dockside convenience store to get food.

She emerged seconds later with a newspaper in hand instead

of grocery bags. She skirted past Chalmers and Kimberlain, eyeing them furtively.

"Keep walking," she whispered, and they fell in behind her to a secluded bench beyond the dock area.

"What's going on?" Kimberlain wondered.

"This," Hedda told him, and handed over the newspaper.

The Ferryman opened it, and a headline on the lower half of the front page jumped out at him:

EX-COMMANDO SOUGHT IN FBI AGENT'S BEATING

"Talley," he muttered, and read on.

His name appeared in paragraph one. Next to a picture of Lauren Talley was a poorly drawn sketch of him. Talley had been horribly beaten and lay near death in a Maine hospital, found near a secluded cabin that —

Kimberlain's breathing stopped. Lauren Talley had been found in the cabin where Peet had been living. He could picture it all now: Leeds must have uncovered his whereabouts and lured Lauren there, after intercepting Kimberlain's phone call to her. Then he had arranged the evidence so all indications would point to the Ferryman as her assailant. Kimberlain read on. There was no mention of Peet in the article. Fingerprints would be checked, of course, and once Peet's were identified even more accusations would come Kimberlain's way.

But where was Peet now?

The only possible answer chilled him to the bone. Peet was with Leeds. Perhaps Peet had been Lauren's assailant; the way the wounds were described certainly made it seem possible.

What have I done?

Kimberlain looked at it all and blamed himself. Blamed himself for involving Peet in the first place. Blamed himself for letting Lauren Talley see inside the dark world he inhabited when the ultimate costs should have been obvious.

The Ferryman went back to the article. He was considered armed and very dangerous, the object of a massive national manhunt. He lowered the newspaper and handed it to Chalmers.

"There's nothing about the Towanda Family Resort, though," Hedda noted, "nothing about Tiny Tim. That means we've still got a chance."

Kimberlain walked away, speaking with his back to her. "Seckle will see the story. He'll strike tonight while I'm still at large."

"Why?"

"Because if I'm dead or captured, there's no sport."

"There's more," Chalmers said. "This . . . is Leeds's insurance."

"We get off the island and Tiny Tim kills us," Hedda followed.

"Or we get caught somewhere along the way trying to stop him at the resort."

"Either way Leeds wins."

"No, because there may be something he failed to consider."

Kimberlain called Captain Seven from a phone near the parking lot. It rang and rang. Which meant the captain was gone, out of the picture at least for now. Leeds had indeed considered him.

"We're in this alone," Kimberlain told Chalmers and Hedda.

"Without a single weapon, except my pistol." She pulled her gun from under her jacket. "One clip left. Fourteen shots. Not much of an equalizer against Tiny Tim."

"Then we'll have to get creative."

Garth Seckle's van sliced through the rain. Night was coming fast, the sky was already dark gray from the storm. The lights of approaching cars barely made a dent in it. Seckle shifted uneasily.

He had redesigned the driver's seat to accommodate his bulk. Too often in the past he'd had to squinch at the shoulders to keep the top of his six-foot-ten-inch frame from rubbing the roof. Seckle hated feeling confined; he liked to leave himself as much breathing space as he possibly could. He figured he had it coming to him after all those wasted years.

His home in the stockade had consisted of a single eight-by-eight windowless cubicle. Not that lacking a window bothered him. No. There was plenty to see inside his own soul, and it was there that Seckle's vision turned during those long years of incarceration.

Sometime in those months the passage of time lost meaning to him, at least in the conventional sense. He measured it not in hours and minutes, but rather in thoughts and visualizations. People were going to pay for San Luis Garcia, for his father.

His father had been a great man, misunderstood but wonderfully gifted. He had possessed a vision that allowed him to see what others could not. The island of San Luis Garcia was proof of what one man could accomplish.

Then The Caretakers had come, and Garth Seckle shivered everytime he recalled the bloody battle. He had badly wounded one, he was certain of it, when the room exploded all around him. He was blown through a wall and covered in debris. Unable to move, heaving in pain, he nonetheless never lost consciousness. He heard the screams, gunshots, and explosions, feeling each bullet as if it had penetrated him. The world of his father was crumbling around him, and there was nothing he could do.

Garth Seckle supposed the planning had actually begun then, in those stretched-out moments when he needed something to take his mind from the pain and loss. When it was over, there was no one to help him. His last reserves of strength were spent dragging himself from under the debris that had buried him. His wounds were much more serious than he had thought originally. It seemed certain he would die. The left foot, of course, was the worst, a chunk of it gone from the second toe across diagonally to the front of the arch. Pulp, sinew, and bone protruded where part of his foot had been.

But none of that mattered. Finding the bodies of his mother and two sisters, in addition to his father, tore his insides apart. Soldiers all, the way his father had made them in a dream come true. He found them broken and bloodied. A nightmare.

He supposed he would have died, too, if the mop-up team hadn't come upon him. The doctors put him back together in sloppy fashion, and he was taken to the stockade. Never a visitor. No one came except the stooges with his meals.

Garth Seckle didn't care. He took charge of his own rehabilitation, lived and breathed off the pain. They said his foot wound would make normal walking, much less running, impossible. But Seckle was walking about the cell in a month and running in place eight weeks after that. The sweat would pour off him in the stifling heat, and his mind would fight back the pain with the planning. He never considered for a single minute that he wouldn't someday be leaving the cell. To accept lifetime incarceration was to accept death.

Still, the means of his ultimate departure surprised even him. Strangers had simply come to his cell late one night. He was drugged and dragged off. When he awoke, a small man with eyes that looked pushed back into his head was looking down at him.

"Hello, Garth."

"Who. . . ?" he gasped. His mouth was too dry to speak.

"Who am I? Why, I'm the man who's going to give you back your life. And then some."

The man had sent him on his way with no conditions. He called it a test, insisted they would meet again another day. The files of the original Caretakers were provided to Seckle, and he began reconnoitering the sites where the closest relatives of The Caretakers lived and worked. It was the isolated nature of so many of the sites that led him to consider going beyond vengeance. After all, they hadn't just killed his father, had they? The entire world he knew had been destroyed. So it would be for the closest relatives of those who had brought it all on. He had done the same thing in Vietnam and felt fulfilled by the act.

But tonight was going to top that and all the others, because tonight Kimberlain was going to pay. Seckle wondered if the Ferryman would ever figure out that this visit was meant for him. It didn't matter. What mattered was that Seckle knew.

The van's windshield wipers pushed aside the pelting rain; fresh torrents hit the glass. Seckle liked the symbolism, for no matter how many lives he took, there would remain lives that demanded taking. Lightning threw shadows at him that disappeared instantly into darkness. Thunder crackled through his ears.

Tiny Tim drove on through the night.

Because of Kimberlain's fugitive status, the only completely safe means of transportation for them was by car. He detailed the elements of his plan after they had set out in the first of the four stolen vehicles that would take them up Route 81 to the Pocono Mountains of Pennsylvania.

"We'll have to make do with what we can salvage from gun and hardware stores," Kimberlain said in the end, "maybe a few—"

"No!" Hedda broke in. "A high school, even a junior high!"

"The chemistry labs," Kimberlain realized.

"And since it's summer, what we need will be neatly put away, stored and ready for the fall. Just a lock to pick, maybe an alarm system to bypass. Takes time to assemble what we need, though," she added. "No matter where we get it."

"There are shortcuts, less stable, but we're not in a position to nitpick." The Ferryman hesitated. "We've got other limitations facing us."

"The resort's layout, for example."

"We'll be coming in blind. He could have been there all day long, waiting for midnight like he always does."

"And we've got to assume Tiny Tim's going to be wearing state-of-the-art body armor, so regular bullets aren't going to stop him. Have to take that into account when we start assembling our wares."

"More than that, we've got to take him out surgically," Kimberlain reminded. "We can't unleash weapons that will help him do his job."

"No victims from among the vacationers."

"We won't do Tiny Tim's work for him, Hedda."

She seemed to relax. "Thank you."

"For what?"

"For calling me Hedda."

"You're not Ellen Kimberlain any more than you're Helena Cain or Lucretia McEvil today. The only life you know is your life as Hedda, and that's who I'm talking to right now." He hesitated and gripped the steering wheel harder. Chalmers was dozing in the backseat. "And Hedda has no son. Lucretia McEvil does, and she's dead, isn't she?"

"Her son isn't."

The rain caught them as they drew ever closer to Honesdale, Pennsylvania. The pounding downpour attacked the windshield wipers every inch of the way.

Hedda jotted down notes on paper salvaged from the car's glove compartment while Kimberlain continued to drive.

"I've made a kind of shopping list," she announced as they approached the Pennsylvania border with daylight a memory. "I figured we could divide it in half, save some time."

"Read it to me."

She did.

"Wow," Kimberlain responded. "I'm not sure we've got enough time for all that."

"It won't take as long as you think. There's nothing on this list I haven't worked with before myself."

"Under better conditions, I trust."

"Not always, not by much anyway."

Kimberlain flashed the highbeams to see if they improved his visibility. When they bounced back at him off the pounding storm, he went back to the lows.

"The key thing, if and when Tiny Tim shows up, is to keep

him away from the families. Make this a fight between him and the three of us."

"That's not what he'll want."

"Which is why we've got to dictate the terms."

Hedda was checking the map. "Carbondale is coming up in ten miles. Should have everything we need."

Hedda and Kimberlain decided that they would drop her at the Carbondale Area High School, located right on the Scranton-Carbondale highway thirty minutes from the resort. Then they would move into Carbondale under cover of darkness to obtain the rest of the items on her list.

Not a single car was visible in any of the one story, brick building's parking lots, and other than the outdoor floods no light burned. They dropped Hedda near a door at the school's rear out of sight of the road. She dashed through the storm's torrents and was soaked to the skin by the time she started on the lock.

Chalmers and Kimberlain waited until she had gotten the door open and vanished inside before they headed back down the drive.

"Eight-thirty," Chalmers said. "Most of . . . the stores we need . . . will still be open."

"A locked door and a closed sign in the window isn't about to stop me tonight."

"Because of . . . your nephew?"

"Because Seckle—Tiny Tim—has to be stopped. Period."

Chalmers gazed at him with his drawn eyes for a long moment. "The other . . . Caretakers . . . are all dead. . . . Not you."

"Luck."

"Not luck—under . . . standing. You lived . . . because you found . . . a way to live."

"It controls me."

"It saved you."

"From the world, Chalmers, but not from myself. In the end

that's the only person you've got to learn to face, and I can't do it yet.''

"Do you want . . . to?"

"Maybe not. A friend of mine tried and ended up the worse for it.''

"A friend?"

"Winston Peet, Chalmers." Kimberlain continued as a gasp emerged from Chalmers's speaker. "I thought you'd remember him. He was on Leeds's original list, but he ended up on my side. He saved my life, and I paid him back by giving him some land, a place to hide.''

"Where they found . . . the woman," Chalmers realized.

Kimberlain nodded. "Leeds got to him. Leeds brought Peet back to the other side, which means I'll have to kill him this time.''

"Like you should . . . have done before?"

"No, I did the right thing then. The wrong thing came much more recently. Peet is with Leeds now because I involved him. He didn't want to help me. He knew what it would mean, and then he did it anyway. So it's my fault.''

"No.''

"Yes. I gave him a place to live to pay him back, and then I wouldn't leave him alone. You see, Chalmers, I did the same thing to Peet that you did to me: I used him, and it stinks. I tried to convince myself that I did it for him. But it was for me. I'm the reason he's with Leeds." Kimberlain gulped down the lump in his throat. "I'm the reason Lauren Talley is almost dead.''

"What would you . . . change?"

"I need to stay alone. You're the one who cut me off from everyone, and now I see it was for the best. That's when it all started, when I was made.''

Chalmers shook his head. "You were already . . . made. That's why . . . we chose you. . . . We could have had . . . anyone, but we . . . chose you.''

"I guess I should feel touched.''

"Feel what you . . . want, but accept . . . it." Chalmers

tapped the socket wedged into his flesh. "Is what you did . . . that night made . . . less worthy by . . . the truth?"

"Not less worthy, only less meaningful. I thought I was acting for myself. Now I see I was acting because someone else who had pushed the right buttons wanted me to."

"You got revenge . . . on your . . . parents' killers. . . . That does not . . . change."

"Then I spent over three years working for the same people who had hired them."

"People you . . . brought down in . . . the end."

"What's your point?"

"You beat them. . . . You got even. . . . Another payback . . . perhaps the most . . . fitting of all."

"Without pleasure. Without satisfaction."

"But with success . . . You don't fail. . . . You *won't* fail."

"Against Leeds?"

"And Peet."

"He'll kill again if I don't stop him," Kimberlain said very softly.

"They both will . . . Ferryman."

Both the vacationers and the people who operated the Towanda Family Resort were suffering through the storm. Rain lashed against windows, accompanied by heavy roars of thunder. Sleep did not come easy for the guests in the forty cabins nestled in a pair of clearings. Those at the main lodge had resigned themselves to a night of complaints and impossible requests from the guests.

Lightning flashed over the rolling fields dotted with tennis and basketball courts. Down at the waterfront, the small white sandy beach had been swallowed by the resort's private Sunset Lake. Canoes and kayaks had been tipped off their platforms and lay piled in heaps atop one another. A single light had been left on at the tennis courts, and the dim glow it cast upon the inch-deep pooling water made the asphalt seem an ice rink, albeit one whose surface was melting. Trees shifted and bent as the wind buffeted them.

By ten o'clock the visibility was reduced to practically zero. The mountains that rose in the distance were dark specters without form. Those windows that looked into the storm were leaking, and they had been plugged with towels and sheets. In some cases, buckets had been placed on the floor to catch the water that poured in.

Just before eleven, lightning struck an electrical transformer in the center of Honesdale, Pennsylvania. The light over the tennis courts flickered once and died. The guests still up watching television or listening to tape decks worked the on-off switches as if that might have helped.

The Towanda Family Resort had been plunged into darkness.

CHAPTER 33

"MARBLES?" Hedda asked, as a small bag of them spilled out on the countertop. A few rolled off to the floor, and the Ferryman retrieved them near the trio of pump action twelve-gauge shotguns he and Chalmers had brought back.

"Last bag on the shelf," Kimberlain told her. "Like I said, we need a weapon that can penetrate Kevlar but won't hit bystanders."

"I'd rather take my chances with the twelve-gauges," Hedda said.

"I think you'll change your mind," he answered, and reached into a box at his feet.

Chalmers had visited the supermarket while the Ferryman

had gone to a hardware store and a toy shop. While they were gone, Hedda had worked much of her own magic in the Carbondale Area High School. The chem lab had proven to be a Disneyland of powders and liquids. She made a brief visit to the industrial arts section to fill a few gaps.

She returned to the chem lab with a dozen foot-long, inch-wide plastic pipes and a roll of heavy twine. Leaving them on the counter, she located a box of candles on a nearby shelf. These she placed in trays over Bunsen burners to met the wax for future use. Next she rummaged through the chemical storage area and found jars containing sulfur, charcoal, and saltpeter.

Hedda emptied the proper amount of each into a large bowl and mixed them until the colors of the contents swirled together. She brought over a fourth jar containing phosphorus packed in water and placed it near the mixing bowl before turning her attention back to the plastic pipes. One at a time, she brushed quick-dry cement onto their accompanying plastic caps and then sealed one end of each.

This done, she siphoned the proper portion of the fine, yellowish phosphorus powder into the pipes. There was enough for six. After packing the powder down, she poured a small amount of water on the phosphorus in all of the pipes. Then she grasped the tray of wax with a gloved hand and poured just enough inside each pipe to cover the water. After the wax hardened, she checked her handiwork by turning each of the pipes upside down to make sure nothing could leak out. Satisfied, she reached for the mixing bowl.

Her next task was to add the makeshift gunpowder to the half-dozen pipes. Then she drilled one-eighth-inch holes into another six plastic caps and affixed them to the pipes' open tops. Finally she cut a half-dozen eight-inch strips from the roll of fuzzy twine and let them soak in a bowl of concentrated potassium nitrate. She removed the strips after twenty seconds and laid them neatly on the counter to dry.

"What are these?" Kimberlain asked, as he removed a section of black iron pipe from his box and placed it near the eight-inch twine strips lying on the counter.

"The fuses for my pipe bombs. They should be just about ready now."

"Impressive," the Ferryman said. "Of course, I could have spared some of the fusing I got from town."

"No way I could be sure you would find any. Besides, I've worked with this version before."

She began forcing the twine fuses through the holes she had drilled in the top caps, twisting until they sank deep into the gunpowder.

"Okay," she pronounced when the last one was in tight. "Now tell me what you're going to do with these marbles."

Kimberlain picked up the yard-long, three-quarter-inch-thick black pipe. "Pretty similar principle to your bombs actually. Except the clerk at the hardware store was kind enough to drill my caps for me."

With that, Kimberlain screwed a steel cap into one end of the pipe.

"He didn't have any dynamite, but he did have this blast fusing. Chalmers?"

Chalmers had just finished cutting fuses to the prescribed lengths. Kimberlain threaded one through the bottom of his black iron pipe, much as Hedda had done with her smaller, plastic versions.

"Might not have been able to pull this off if the gun store we visited didn't carry black powder for old-fashioned muzzle loaders," the Ferryman continued. "Triple X."

"You only got one can?"

"More than enough."

Hedda watched as he siphoned a fifth of the can's contents into the first pipe, while Chalmers cut white chamois cloths into neat round pieces two-and-a-half inches in diameter and then wrapped a marble in each. Kimberlain jammed four wads down the pipe and worked them in tight.

"Voilà," the Ferryman said. "Light the fuse, and two seconds later the marbles are blown outward."

"With more force than a bullet . . ."

"Plenty more. I wouldn't want to try it at more than thirty

yards, but from that distance or less I doubt even Kevlar will stop them.''

Hedda's eyes wandered to the four kegs of kerosene still left over. "Then what are they for?"

Kimberlain pulled a pair of stainless steel, pressurized bug sprayers up from the floor to the table. "Flamethrowers."

The four kegs, as it turned out, were just enough to fill the two four-gallon bug sprayers.

"Hold a match or cigarette here," he said, pointing to the adjustable nozzle at the end of the brass wand, "and the kerosene rushing out catches fire. The result is a spray of fire as far as this thing would ordinarily shoot pesticide."

"Which is?"

"I'd say twenty-five, thirty yards."

"How accurate?"

"Won't know that until we try it."

The storm welcomed him, as Tiny Tim stepped out of his van into the night enveloping the Towanda Family Resort. Unlike the preparation he had made for his earlier visits, he had not done a thorough reconnaissance of the site, and much of what he saw was disturbing from a logistical standpoint. Most challenging was the close proximity of the cabins to each other. They were duplexes and triplexes mostly, separate entrances sharing a common screened-in porch. Wiping out the occupants of one without alerting the neighbors would be his greatest challenge. A panic-stricken site with parents and children running everywhere was not something he was accustomed to dealing with. But he would find a way to make that work for him. The true test of genius was improvisation, and Seckle considered himself a genius when it came to this evening's tasks. He had already disabled the cars in the resort parking lot, so there would be no escape.

His first job now was to locate the nephew of the Ferryman. The cabins were marked with numbers, and he could read them clearly through his night-vision goggles. Find the cabin the boy was in and he would find the boy. To accomplish that, he would have to break into the office and check the roster.

Then the fun would begin.

"My God," Hedda uttered after they had turned through the gate marked TOWANDA FAMILY RESORT, "it's huge."

The road had vanished three miles back to be replaced by hardpacked dirt that the pounding storm had transformed into thick mud. The track was so precarious and narrow they feared they were on the wrong route. Only skillful driving prevented them from going off the road or hitting any of the half-dozen deer that dashed in front of them, frightened by the storm. But finally their headlights had found the brown and white sign welcoming them to the resort.

The storm and darkness could not hide the size of the place. They made out a nine-hole golf course on the immediate right. Near the golf course was a grass parking lot lined with cars. Not a space to spare. The resort must be packed.

Turning up the hill leading into the resort, their highbeams briefly illuminated a seemingly endless series of fields and courts laid out further above them on the primary resort grounds. A huge flash of lightning revealed the shape of buildings, larger ones by themselves and smaller ones—family cabins obviously—in clusters.

"Notice anything else?" Kimberlain asked.

"What do you mean?" replied Hedda.

"No lights. Not a single one on anywhere."

"A . . . blackout," Chalmers's speaker crackled.

"You think he did it?" Hedda asked, aware that an affirmative answer could only mean that Tiny Tim had beaten them here.

"I don't know."

"I still think we should call the police. Take our chances."

"He'd kill them all and you know it. Make things worse because he'd be forced to speed up his process. Our biggest advantage is that he likes to savor his work."

Hedda nodded. She knew the Ferryman was speaking from

inside Garth Seckle's head, laying out the way he would do it if the roles were reversed. Her shiver came only when she realized she was thinking that way, too.

"We need somewhere to gear up," Kimberlain announced, continuing to snail the car forward. He killed the lights to avoid drawing attention as they drove further along the resort road. They swung right up a hill where a huge, wood-carved sign with the resort's logo flapped in the wind.

"Over there on the right," Hedda pointed. "A building."

"Ranger station," Kimberlain said. "Part of the resort must be on federally owned—" He stopped his words and the car.

"What's wrong?"

"The front door's open."

They stowed the car on the side of the building not visible from the main part of the resort. A green and yellow Jeep with federal markings was parked beneath the overhang that extended beyond the porch. The name STATION 61 was carved into a piece of badge-shaped wood that was nailed over the front door. Kimberlain saw the first body just when he cleared the last step up to the porch. Rain had poured in through the crack and soaked the uniform on the corpse up past the ankles. This ranger was a young man of nineteen or twenty. His neck had been snapped.

The Ferryman led the way in warily, with Hedda holding her pistol just behind him. Chalmers stood guard outside on the porch, a shotgun in his hands.

They found the second ranger in the doorway leading from what looked like a den into the front hall. He was an older man, his outdoorsman's hands lying in the pool of blood that had drained from the neat slice in his throat.

Tiny Tim had beaten them here!

Dread and fear, both unfamiliar and uncomfortable, raced through the Ferryman. How much deeper into the resort might Tiny Tim have ventured by now?

The Ferryman turned to see Hedda had disappeared. Before

he could call out to her, she had returned to the ranger station toting a large portion of their gear under both arms.

"I figured it was time," she said.

The office was located at the very top of the hill diagonally across from six of the resort's twelve tennis courts. Tiny Tim found it with little trouble. It was closed at this time of night, of course, but gaining entry was as easy as breaking one of the padlocks. He checked the phones to make sure they weren't functioning and then made his way through the door leading into the inner office.

Shining his mag light before him, he quickly located the daily manifest of cabin assignments posted on the wall. It was too good to be true, too easy. All the names right there on a detailed schema of the resort. The adoptive family of Kimberlain's nephew, according to the files he had been given on the island, was named Berman. The schema listed the Bermans in cabin 12½.

Twelve-and-a-half, Seckle thought. The resort didn't want to call it thirteen for superstitious reasons.

The irony made him smile. It was the bad luck of the family inside cabin 12½ that his work tonight would begin with them. Of course, his biggest problem remained what to do about the panic that would inevitably arise from his initial kills.

But he could make that situation work for him. Yes. Just beyond the office was a combination cafeteria and rec center, easily the resort's largest building. A gathering point, then, the place the panicked throngs were certain to come when they found their cars at the bottom of the hill disabled.

Tiny Tim decided to make a stop there. He had time to burn anyway. Indeed, the fire was all his.

"There's something else," Kimberlain said as they strapped on their gear. "The two dead rangers must have been off duty. That means there's another one or two patrolling the grounds."

"Radios?" Hedda asked.

"Might come in handy."

"Later."

"If there is one."

Tiny Tim glided away from the lodge, keeping close to cover. There were two separate clusters of cabins, north and south; basketball and tennis courts lay between them. The first ones to panic would run for their disabled cars, but he needed to herd them back to the lodge.

How could he get them there?

Garth Seckle had barely asked himself the question when the answer occurred to him. He shrank back into the shadows beneath the cover of a tree and inventoried his weapons. He counted his fragmentary grenades, along with his forty-millimeter charges for his M-203, a combination M-16 and grenade launcher. Last and most important, he drew his shoulder pack around to the front of his body and fingered through his claymore mines. He had plenty.

More than enough.

CHAPTER 34

Iɴ the ranger station, Kimberlain, Hedda, and Chalmers finished strapping on their gear. Special harnesses made it possible to sling the bug sprayers turned flamethrowers around the Ferryman's and Hedda's backs like scuba tanks. The black iron three-foot water pipes, minibazookas in effect, were slung by straps from their shoulders. Kimberlain had two, Hedda and Chalmers one each. They shared the six pipe bombs equally, and all three wore their twelve-gauges loosely across the center of their backs to maximize accessibility. Each needed to keep a dry pocket for extra fuses, lighters, and cigarettes or risk the possibility that none of their makeshift weapons were going to work.

"We've got to find out where the boy is," Hedda said suddenly when they were ready to venture back out into the storm.

"You'd head there first if you knew," Kimberlain concluded.

"Damn right."

"But we don't know Tiny Tim will. Remember, he didn't hit his primary targets first in any of the previous sites. It's him we've got to stop, Hedda, him we've got to find."

"We're talking about my son, your nephew!"

"Do you really want to know him?"

Her mind wavered. "I want to . . . save him."

292

"Then we stop Seckle."

"Should we split . . . up?" Chalmers asked, his speaker emitting barely a whisper in the driving storm.

"We stay together until we figure out how late in the game we're coming in."

"You think he's already started?" Hedda posed fearfully.

"It's time to find out," Kimberlain told her, and led the way back into the storm.

Tiny Tim had brought six claymore mines with him and used them all. Planting them took more time than he would have preferred to spend, but it would prove worth it.

Claymores were basically plastic explosives layered in a sheet with upward of seven hundred ball bearings. Seckle was using them as booby traps, with trip wires extended out in two directions. As soon as the guests fleeing for their cars jiggled the wire, detonation would result, forcing the survivors to swing back in terror.

Tiny Tim finished setting his final claymore in the soaked ground, careful to camouflage his handiwork with grass. He had set the mines along a perimeter those rushing from both clusters of cabins would have to cross to reach their cars. The thought of the tumultuous blasts and resulting shrieks of agony made him see clearly now how this visit was going to be quite different from his first three.

In the others chaos had been avoided in favor of a precise, orderly progression. Tonight was going to be just the opposite. Tonight he would use fear as an ally, as efficient as any bomb he could plant.

The change would be welcome, perhaps even preferred. Tiny Tim rose and moved on toward cabin 12½.

"Stop!" Kimberlain said suddenly, voice rising through the sounds of the storm.

"What?" Hedda started.

"Look down."

She did. Her eyes had trouble picking up anything in the rain-slick darkness, and she was about to look back at the

Ferryman when she saw the bulge. It looked like a small bubble in the wet ground, a portion torn up and then haphazardly replaced like a divot on a golf course.

"Claymore!" she realized. "But he never used mines before. What's it mean?"

"It means this site is different. He must be expecting some of the families to run. That's what the mines are for."

"Can you deactivate them?"

Kimberlain's wet gaze was noncommittal. "Never my specialty."

"I can, but—"

"Mine," came Chalmers's voice through his speaker on its last reserves. "My . . . specialty. In Nam . . . Demolitions."

Hedda exchanged glances with the Ferryman.

"I'll need a . . . knife," Chalmers said.

Hedda and Kimberlain yanked blades out and presented them, their motions mirroring each other.

"He must have placed them all in this area," Kimberlain told him. "But we don't know how many."

"I'll find them," Chalmers assured in a voice that sounded almost normal. ·

He handed over the pipe bombs he had been allotted and crouched down to go to work on the first claymore they had found, while Hedda and Kimberlain started on toward the two clusters of dark brown cabins nestled beneath the soaked trees.

"We should split up now," Kimberlain proposed. "I'll take the north row of cabins. You take the south, closer to the lake."

"He's going to start with the boy, isn't he?"

The Ferryman hesitated. "He hasn't before."

"I'm talking about tonight."

"Yes. I think he will."

"And if one of us finds him . . ."

"It won't take long for the other to know."

For an instant, just as he reached cabin 12½, Tiny Tim thought he heard something. Impossible to tell in a storm like this, with the trees shifting from side to side with each gust of the wind and the insistent hiss of the rain. Could even be the excitement that was beginning to fill him as he neared the completion of his revenge upon Kimberlain.

He gazed one last time in the direction he thought the sound had come from. The clear sight provided by his night-vision goggles revealed nothing. Satisfied the night was his, Garth Seckle stepped through the screen door onto the porch of cabin 12½.

Chalmers was working on the third of the claymores. Under ordinary circumstances, the task would not have been difficult. But tonight was hardly ordinary. Locating them proved the easiest chore of all, surprisingly. Garth Seckle had not been expecting anyone to be looking and must have been pressed for time, so he had not done a good job of camouflaging the mines' positions.

Chalmers still had to crawl on his belly to play it safe. He stayed there while he worked his knife under the slight mound marking each mine, unsettling the dirt in search of the blasting cap. Cut the wire connecting it to the main body, and the claymore was deactivated.

Chalmers severed the wire, disarming the third of the claymores. He lifted his face to the sky and let the storm wipe the sweat from it. Then, pulling himself along with hands clawing the muddied grass, Chalmers's eyes probed ahead for the next claymore.

Hedda palmed her pistol, afraid she was gripping it too tightly. Fear festered inside her, as she moved almost blindly about the cabins. What if Tiny Tim found the boy before she or Kimberlain found him? Would the first scream she heard on this night of terror come from the son she had learned of just hours before? Unseen, unknown, he was another part of her life scrapped and discarded forever.

I don't even know his name. . . .

She pressed on, with the storm doing its utmost to slow her.

* * *

Where was he? Where was the nephew of Kimberlain?

Cabin 12½ was fronted by a screened-in porch, beyond which lay three doors to three separate sections of a triplex.

Tiny Tim moved toward the first door he came to and found it unlocked. Once inside a short hallway followed, then a living room complete with television and air conditioner. Above him the blades of a ceiling fan churned slightly from the force of the storm pounding the roof. Beyond the living room were the bedrooms, three by the look of it. The flow of a flashlight or lantern snuck out from one, daylight bright through his night-vision goggles. Someone reading probably, maybe a mother secure in the certainty her children were safely asleep. Tiny Tim started that way and almost missed seeing the suitcases stacked neatly against the wall. He crouched and inspected the name tags.

Ramsey.

The Bermans would be in one of the other two, then. Tiny Tim exited as quietly as he had entered and moved on to next door.

Hedda stopped suddenly, fighting the storm for a clear view. A shape had appeared upon a porch of a cabin well down the row. She saw it ever so briefly, silhouetted between a pair of screen doors; one had just been closed, the other was being eased open.

A person going from one cabin to another. But if each cabin was reserved for a separate family . . .

Hedda began to run. The night and storm bled away in her path. The wind pushed her along instead of restraining her.

She readied her pistol. Close in, it remained the best weapon she had.

And close in was the way it was going to be.

The name Berman had been on a magazine Tiny Tim found atop a table within the den of the second cabin in the triplex. This time there were no lights other than what the night gave him, which was plenty because of his goggles. He could hear heavy snoring as he slid down the corridor. It was coming from the lone bedroom on the right. A man's snoring. Then the Berman children would be on the left, a single bedroom this time.

Tiny Tim reached the door and pushed it open, the huge killing knife struggling to shine in the darkness.

Hedda saw only a shape first, then the naked glint of steel in its hand.

"Stop!"

Her scream preceded her gunshots by milliseconds that proved enough to freeze Tiny Tim and make him turn. She fired the nine-millimeter Browning as fast as she could pull the trigger.

"Ahhhhh!" he screamed after her bullets had impacted with a series of thumps that blew him backward down the hallway.

But he never left his feet, and suddenly one of his submachine guns was coming round and flaring silenced orange from its barrel.

Pffffffft . . . pffffffft . . . pffffffft . . .

She dove, but her eyes never left the hall down which Tiny Tim darted. Suddenly a figure sprinted from the bedroom where Tiny Tim had just emerged. A boy in sweatpants and T-shirt. A fresh hail of fire sped toward him.

Pffffffft . . . pffffffft . . . pffffffft . . .

"Get down!" she screamed at the boy who must have been her son. *"Get down!"*

The boy dropped to the floor and crawled the rest of the way into his adoptive parents' bedroom. Hedda glimpsed two pajama-clad figures in the doorway who clutched the boy and pulled him into their room. More gunfire peppered the walls around them. Hedda fired blindly in the direction the shots had come from. The next staccato burst found her, and hot pain seared through her shoulder. She screamed in agony and fired five more rounds in the direction the orange glow of the shots had come from. Another bullet grazed her thigh. She felt herself crumbling, but still had the sense to fire back.

Click.

Her gun was empty. She hit the floor as a huge figure emerged into the corridor, nearly as tall as the ceiling. He saw her but didn't fire, moving for the bedroom door that had been slammed and locked just seconds before.

A window! If there was a window, maybe they'd escaped through it!

Tiny Tim raised a booted foot and kicked the door in with a single thrust.

"No!" she screamed, reaching to her belt for one of the pipe bombs.

"Seckle!" a fresh voice boomed and the monster twisted its way.

Kimberlain charged in from the living room area, one of his black iron water pipes leveled before him.

BOOM!

Hedda covered her head as the blast's reverberation blew the Ferryman down the hall. She glimpsed the massive shape of Tiny Tim rocketing backward into the air, straight through a window at the end of the hallway. Kimberlain darted by her, bringing his flamethrower's copper wand down from its upright position behind him. He approached the window Tiny Tim had crashed through with a lighter held to the nozzle, ready to ignite the pressurized kerosene as soon as he opened the flow. Hedda climbed to her feet and limped toward him.

"Shit," she heard him mutter when he peered through the shattered glass. And then she saw why.

The monster was gone.

CHAPTER 35

Tiny Tim was dazed, but he never lost consciousness. He cursed himself for not anticipating the presence of the Ferryman. Who else could it have been, after all? No one, no one! And the woman! She could only be . . .

How had they found him here? How could they have known?

Somehow they had joined up. Seckle had anticipated everything else but that. The damn woman! She had spoiled his work at the worst possible time. His knife had been about to begin its plunge when her bullets thumped into the Kevlar that enclosed every bit of his midsection up to his throat.

She had missed her kill shots, though, and he would have had her if not for the blast fired by the Ferryman. It was like getting hit head-on by a car, and whatever it contained shredded his body armor and broke at least one of his ribs. Seckle found himself coughing frothy blood as soon as he pushed himself up from the spot where he had landed outside. His insides felt rearranged. Splinters of window glass pricked his scalp and neck. It was all he could do to lumber away to find time to reorganize his thinking.

They'd pay for this. How they'd pay . . .

Kimberlain's nephew wasn't dead yet, but he would be. He would fall with the others, because Tiny Tim was going to kill them all, every last one. Just follow the screams, he told himself.

Follow the screams.

"I'm going after him," Kimberlain said, kneeling over Hedda.

"What about . . . the family?"

The Ferryman's gaze turned back toward the bedroom. "The window's open. They must have got out that way."

"Then they're outside. With him."

"I'll get Seckle," he promised.

"You can't. Not by yourself anyway. You already shot him, damn it! You blew him away and he still walked off."

"He's playing my game now."

She grasped for his arm. "Help me up."

"Stay here."

She didn't let go. "You can't do it without me, not against him."

Kimberlain shrugged and relented, easing her to her feet.

"The boy," she started hesitantly. "I . . . saw him. I—"

Her words were cut off by a thundering blast that shook sawdust from the cabin walls. Kimberlain had to grasp tighter to keep her from falling back down.

"Claymore," she muttered. "Chalmers didn't get it done, damn it!"

He pulled away from her. "I'm going after Seckle."

The panic had spread through the resort in a domino effect from cabin to cabin. A swarm of fleeing guests was converging on the slope down to the parking lot, just as Chalmers was approaching what he estimated to be the last of the mines. He cursed the timing, cursed the extra precision he had employed with the previous five sites. A few seconds faster with each one was all it would have taken. Now it was all for naught. The first pounding footstep that struck within a yard of the last claymore would blast dozens of people to hell. Worse, the blast's percussion might trigger the remaining claymores, even though he had deactivated their blasting caps.

No way he could find and deactivate this final one in time. No way at all.

Chalmers's decision was made in a millisecond, as the tide of panicked feet moved his way. He leapt, the motion carrying him directly over the last of the claymores. He lived long enough to record the dull thud his body made when it struck the soft ground. He should have been rigid, but he was strangely calm, hands pressing down into the mud.

And then he was gone.

The blast turned the panicked crowd back in the opposite direction toward the cabins. A few of those at the head of the pack had gone down after being struck by rocks or ground debris coughed up by the blast. Others were caught by flying pieces of glass from the shattered windows of those buildings nearest the explosion. Parents tended to children, dragging them to safety and searching for cover.

Tiny Tim had finally recovered his bearings, the pain in his chest a dull ache he swallowed down, when he heard the blast. He realized with great delight that the chaotic rush of parents and children for the parking lot would now be turned back in his direction. In no time he eased forward from the woods to an area between the two cabin clusters with a clear view of the lodge's entry doors. He leveled his M-203 combination grenade launcher and M-16 before him and waited for a congestion of targets to fire into. He could kill many of them this way, perhaps even the nephew of Kimberlain.

The first of the screaming throng raced his way, breathless and drenched by the storm. Tiny Tim brought his M-203 up and touched the trigger.

Kimberlain had just emerged from cabin 12½ when the rush swung back up the hill toward them.

"Over there!" Hedda pointed suddenly from just behind the Ferryman. "I see him!"

The Ferryman swung to follow her gaze. Garth Seckle was standing in the open, an M-203 poised in his hands.

"Like I said," Kimberlain promised, "he's mine."

He sped off around the back of the cabins to approach unseen. Still sprinting, he held a lit cigarette against the nozzle at the end of the copper wand. Closing on Tiny Tim, he readied to twist the nozzle, opening the flow of the kerosene. He knew the monster would wait until sufficient targets were gathered before him, knew that would give him the last bit of time he needed.

He was twenty yards away when, still in motion, he turned the nozzle. The initial gush of flames ignited in a wide burst, then steadied into a narrow stream.

Tiny Tim had only gotten off two shots from his rifle when the jet of flames found him. Kimberlain had been aiming for Seckle, but most of the flames hit the M-203. Then they seemed to reach outward and catch the monster in their grasp. Seckle was blown backward. Kimberlain turned the nozzle on his still-firing form, but Tiny Tim was already out of range. He darted for the woods with the fire dancing off him.

The Ferryman turned the nozzle counterclockwise. The jet of flames receded and was gone. He rushed forward in Tiny Tim's path and passed by the monster's smoldering M-203 on the ground where he'd dropped it. Hanging over it was the distinct scent of burned hair and flesh.

"I've got you, you bastard," Kimberlain said out loud to the shape charging up a path leading for the woods. "Now I've got you."

The Ferryman bolted after him, yanking one of the phosphorus-laden pipe bombs from his belt when he had cleared the length of the tennis courts. He touched the same lit cigarette to its twine fuse, which caught with a sizzle instantly. He rushed forward a few more steps before hurling it into the open area near the woods where Tiny Tim was headed. The pipe bomb exploded with a *poof!* and a dazzling flash that staggered Seckle. Kimberlain drew another, lit, and hurled it before Tiny Tim could straighten his path again.

This charge exploded closer to him and doubled him over. For an instant it seemed the hundreds of shards of ruptured plastic had done the job. He seemed almost to fall, his shape lost to the darkness of the storm. Kimberlain knelt to ready his second marble-loaded black iron pipe. He was flirting at the edge of its range now, but Seckle was an almost stationary target, too much to resist. Kimberlain lit the fuse and sighted down the pipe at a target now thirty yards away. Ready for the recoil's hard thump this time, he barely buckled as the marbles tore outward in a blast of orange smoke.

On target. Dead on.

Ears ringing, the Ferryman felt the certainty of triumph. The distance proved too great for his makeshift bazooka, though, and he saw the blast had instead shredded the base of a small tree not more than a yard to Seckle's left.

Not pausing to bemoan the miss, Kimberlain discarded the smoking pipe and followed Tiny Tim into the woods.

Garth Seckle had not known such pain in many years, not since the night The Caretakers had come and blown a chunk of his foot away. It seemed to be happening all over again, here on this night that should have belonged to him. The bulk of the damage had been done to his shoulders and back. He could feel his singed flesh bubbling and puckering. The pain was incredible, soothed slightly by the pounding rain soaking his exposed skin.

Once under cover of the woods, Seckle stripped off the gloves that had also been burned through by Kimberlain's makeshift flamethrower. His night-vision goggles, meanwhile, had been shattered by flying plastic from the pair of blinding explosions that followed him to the woods. But he could still see, and there seemed to be no damage to his eyes. Part of his scalp, though, had been ravaged by the blasts, and a section of his face was burned raw from cheek to temple.

He gasped as he tore the goggles off and tossed them aside. He grabbed for his canteen and dumped its contents upon his face and scalp. The relief was fleeting. The pain would not go away. He would have to use it like he used everything else. He started moving again, mired in the awareness that the Ferryman was closing fast from his rear, sure to have followed him into the woods.

What were these weapons the Ferryman was using?

Tiny Tim found himself wondering what else Kimberlain might have brought. He willed himself calm as he sank deeper into the forest. He reminded himself whatever Kimberlain might possess, his own arsenal remained infinitely superior. His task now was to lure the Ferryman into an area where he could use his weapons to finish him once and for all. He had a pair of machine guns left and plenty of grenades. Pistols on both hips and assorted other extras.

He felt himself grow even calmer. The resort still belonged to him. The families weren't going anywhere in this storm, and help was at least fifteen minutes away. An eternity for him to work.

Meanwhile, the families would be gathering in the lodge, secure in their numbers. That gave Tiny Tim hope. He could still win here tonight. He could still accomplish what he came to do.

But first Kimberlain.

The Ferryman entered the woods tentatively. He could tell from the weight of the tank on his back that his initial attack had consumed half its contents. Not that it mattered. Lacking the element of surprise, and in the confined space of the woods, the flamethrower's effectiveness would be negated. He still had both of Chalmers's pipe bombs in his possession, but finding the time to light their fuses under the circumstances seemed unlikely. Kimberlain reached behind him and pulled the twelve-gauge pump forward. The homemade weapons had taken him as far as they could. Seckle was wounded, in pain and perhaps fleeing. At the same time, though, like a wounded animal he was probably even more dangerous.

Thunder rumbled and a bolt of lightning illuminated the sky. His heart jumped. The woods looked alive, every shadow and tree sure to be Tiny Tim ready to fire. He could very easily be walking into a trap, but in one sense anyway that was a victory, for so long as Seckle was out here battling him, the families were safe.

Kimberlain edged on. He heard a branch snap directly ahead of him and threw himself to the ground. The move saved his life. A fusillade of bullets burned the air above him, chewing bark from trees where his head and chest had just been. He moved behind the cover of a huge pine tree and fired three rounds from his shotgun in the direction the bullets had come from.

Thump . . .

Kimberlain had heard the sound of a grenade striking soft ground often enough to know what was coming. He threw himself forward through the air to escape the reach of the first blast and skirted the second by diving into a small brook. The percussion stunned his ears, but this time he knew enough not to move. Sure enough, the next pair of grenades landed ahead of him, near where he would have been had he continued his motion. Water cascaded upward in fountainlike jets, splashing him.

Kimberlain gauged the angle the grenades had been lobbed from and lit his last two pipe bombs in rapid succession. He threw them within a second of each other, intending to enclose the target area rather than strike it directly, making Seckle expose himself so the remaining shells in his shotgun might finish the job. The bright flashes came almost simultaneously. No screams came in their wake, and no further fire either.

Where was Seckle?

A wild spray of machine-gun fire came his way, and Kimberlain dashed from the brook to the cover of a tree to avoid it. The bullets were still coming when he touched his lighter to the fuse of his last black iron pipe. The orange flame sped down the coil. Kimberlain spun out from the tree's cover with the homemade, marble-loaded bazooka leveled toward the origin of the still-raging barrage.

BOOM!

Impact jolted him backward as the marbles shot out. There was an echoing thud as they reached their target, and Kimberlain let himself hope Tiny Tim was finished at last. He came to his feet slowly and charged the area, his shotgun leading the way. He dared Seckle's bullets to take him and was certain he had won when they didn't.

The results of his latest blast showed him otherwise.

Neat chunks had been chiseled out of a tree that broke in two separate directions five feet up. Wedged through the center and strung to one of the rising branches were the remnants of a machine gun that had been blown apart by his blast. Tiny Tim had tied it into place and looped a support around its trigger so it would fire of its own accord, creating the illusion of a man behind it.

Garth Seckle was gone, circling around back toward the resort where only a wounded Hedda was there to stand between him and the families.

The clamor of heavy feet was pounding past Hedda, and she heard the repeated shout of instructions.

"The lodge! Everyone to the lodge!"

She caught a glimpse of a ranger in a storm-battered khaki uniform rushing about with revolver raised, shouting instructions to the panicked throngs and evacuating those still in their cabins. Everywhere families in soaked and muddied bedclothes rushed toward the combination rec center and cafeteria.

Hedda sat inside the screened-in porch, hidden from the activity. Cold and soaked, she shivered down her pain and cradled herself with her arms. She fought with the wind to distinguish accurately the sounds of the Ferryman's battle with Tiny Tim from those of the storm. Strange how she could only see him as the Ferryman and not Kimberlain, for to accept him as Kimberlain was to accept the tragic truth of her own past. He was no more her brother than the boy she had saved was her son. In name, perhaps, but nothing else.

"Move! Let's go! Move!"

And the parade of the desperate and terrified continued. She wanted to raise herself up to the screen in the hope of catching a glimpse of the boy again, in order to preserve some impression of him.

"The lodge, I said! The lodge!"

Gathering the guests together in a common area was the best way to ease their panic and protect them. An obvious strategy under such dire circumstances, one anybody would have chosen.

Hedda stiffened. If it was obvious to her, then surely it would have been obvious to Tiny Tim as well. He would have made a stop in the lodge prior to setting out on his night's work. Hedda pushed herself to her feet and stepped back out into the storm. She moved along as quickly as she could, falling into the wet muck only to regain her feet, muddied and even more desperate. She grabbed for the shotgun strung around her back and used it as a crutch to push herself along through the storm.

"Find a seat!" the ranger yelled through a bullhorn. "Please, find a seat and quiet down. . . . We've got to find out if any families or family members are missing. We need to know who's missing. Help is on the way," he finished.

The resort guests settled down as best they could. Mingling amid them, trying to restore calm, were the resort managers. They lived somewhat apart on the huge property, and had been called by the ranger via walkie-talkie.

Flashlights and a few powerful lanterns provided the sole light; a soft murmur and some scattered sobs were the only sounds that moved through the terrified crowd. Injuries, miraculously none serious, were inventoried and checked. Those with any medical experience at all moved about with what bandages and supplies they had been able to find in the resort's health center. Rumors of exactly what had transpired were flying, but those who truly knew were quiet.

The ranger and resort personnel were doing their utmost to avoid additional panic. That task became nearly impossible when one of the lodge doors crashed open. A woman, harried and soaked by the storm, with blood leaking from her shoulder, charged in with rifle in hand.

Hedda would have preferred to use a reasonable approach on the crowd, but she realized that only a shock would achieve her goal in the limited time frame available. A brief check underneath the building had revealed the final element of Tiny Tim's plan to her.

"Everyone out!" she screamed above the diminishing wails. "Everyone out *now*!" When they failed to cooperate, she brought the shotgun down level with her waist and rotated it about threateningly. "I said move! Get out of here and run, as far from the building as you can!"

The ranger was fumbling for his pistol when she turned the shotgun on him.

"Don't! Listen to me," she screamed to all who could hear her. "This building's going to explode. Now *get out*!"

After all that had transpired in the past few minutes, no one chose to doubt her. The next moment saw fresh panic overcome the lodge's inhabitants. Mad rushes were launched on every door. Screens were punched out and became emergency exit routes. The ranger pushed his way toward her.

"Who the fuck are—"

"Propane," Hedda told him. "He opened the propane tanks in the kitchen."

"I don't smell propane."

"Because it's collecting *underneath* the building. He crawled under, do you hear me? He crawled under and worked the lines outside. If he comes back here and ignites it, there won't be a building left."

A mixture of fear and uncertainty filled the ranger's face. "How come you know so much?"

"I came here to stop him."

"Jesus Christ, I don't even know if we had everyone in here."

"Just help me get everyone out."

Garth Seckle emerged horrified from the woods in the back of the southern cluster of cabins. The vantage point allowed him a clear enough view of the lodge to see it was being evacuated, his would-be victims slipping from his grasp.

It couldn't be true! It couldn't!

They scattered in all directions into the night, gone from the central gathering point where he had planned to finish them off. Seckle bellowed with rage as he rushed across the open area between the cabins. He pulled a grenade from his belt and yanked the pin out, each motion searing him with fresh agony. The reality of his failure brought the pain of his wounds beyond the point of denial. But the blast could help ease the pain, vanquish it even if enough of his victims were caught in the explosion. He was still running when he lobbed the grenade long and straight for the lodge, the seconds counted in his mind. It thumped to the ground and then rolled on beneath the building's underside.

Garth Seckle dove to the ground and covered his already scorched head.

The lodge exploded in a massive fireball, the loosed propane catching all at once. The flames leapt outward, the storm's fury unable to douse them. Shards of wood flew everywhere, and for a moment Tiny Tim let himself think the night had been salvaged. But the intensity of blast had forced the vast majority of the debris straight upward. He listened for screams of pain and death, but heard not a single one. He gazed at the flaming carcass of the lodge, and all he felt was empty and beaten. Beaten by both the Ferryman and the woman

With Kimberlain left behind in the woods, only she could have evacuated the lodge.

But he could make her pay for that. Seckle had one submachine gun left, an Uzi, and he leveled it before him. Most of the resort guests were fleeing toward the waterfront. If Hedda's son was among them, he would die there.

Tiny Tim counted his remaining grenades and threw himself into a rush.

"My God," Kimberlain muttered as he helped Hedda to her feet in the flaming shadow of the lodge. "You got them out. Jesus, you got them out."

She nodded halfheartedly. "But Tiny Tim's still loose. Somewhere."

The sounds of panic rose up through the night from the direction of the waterfront. "He likes that sound," Kimberlain told her. "That's where he'll go."

The Ferryman had seen the explosion when he was halfway between the woods and the lodge. Instinctively he dropped to the ground and covered his head with his arms. Dread anticipation drove him forward into the clearing where he found Hedda.

"They'll box themselves in down there," Hedda warned. "No place else to run from him."

"No place for him to run this time, either. I'll cut down to the lake through the woods. Either I'll run into Seckle, or I'll be waiting when he gets there."

"While I approach from the rear after you," Hedda followed.

"A cross fire," Kimberlain acknowledged, steadying his twelve-gauge. "Let's go."

The number of those who had stupidly gathered in the confined space of the waterfront surprised Tiny Tim. Several had climbed into rowboats or canoes, even kayaks and smaller playaks, to make their escape. But most simply huddled in small groups, figuring with the lodge blown up this night of terror must be over.

How wrong they were. Seckle still had five hand grenades and three clips for his Uzi just to demonstrate that. He knew he had to salvage something if this night was to be embraced again. He wanted to lie in his field, staring wide-eyed at the stars, and relive this visit. With nothing to relive, the very essence of his life was gone. He had to accomplish something to savor.

Tiny Tim pulled the pin from one of his grenades with his teeth and drew his arm backward. In the instant it started in motion, a loud report burned his ears and a segment of the tree nearest him exploded. A second blast struck him in the chest and blew him backward, some of the shotgun pellets penetrating flesh where his Kevlar had already been shredded. The grenade he'd been palming slipped from his grip and rolled slightly down the hill.

"Down! Everybody down!" he heard a booming voice cry out. Seckle took cover behind a tree at the start of the woods just before the explosion shook the beach.

The explosion sent the victims he had missed scurrying in all directions again. A young boy dashed near, not seeing him, pausing to catch his breath. Whimpering, sobbing. Alone.

Might this be? . . . Could this be? . . .

Close enough. Tiny Tim reached out and snared him in a bear-claw hand. Seckle let him scream and keep screaming, Uzi pressed against his head.

"Kimberlain!" he yelled through burned, bleeding lips. "I've got him, Kimberlain!"

Hedda watched it all transpire from Seckle's left flank, forty feet away with the boy between the monster and her. Was it her son? She couldn't see well enough to tell; she couldn't have been sure even if she could have seen him up close. With a decent rifle, even pistol, she could take Seckle out, but not with a shotgun. No chance.

"Where are you, Kimberlain? Come out, or I'll kill him! Kimberlain!"

Parents covered their children along the sandy beach at the water's edge. Others were crouched behind the cover of boats or shrubs. Cries of fear mixed with the chirping of crickets.

Hedda steadied her shotgun. Was this what Tiny Tim wanted her to do? A second boy lost to her bullet. Her son this time, maybe her son . . .

"Kimberlain!"

The Ferryman emerged from the woods on Tiny Tim's other flank, shotgun held before him.

"Drop it or I kill him!"

Kimberlain dropped the shotgun at his feet. Tiny Tim smiled at him through his charred and blackened face. The left side was raw and blistered, making him seem even more grotesque.

Hedda slid out of the woods and crept along the tree line.

Seckle moved the gun away from the boy's head and started it toward Kimberlain.

"Good," he said hoarsely. "Good."

As Tiny Tim brought the Uzi in line with the Ferryman's face, Hedda dashed forward. She grasped the boy and yanked him from Seckle's hold in the same instant he spun toward her. She covered the boy with her body as they both hit the ground. A volley of gunshots found her ears just ahead of the burst of pain exploding through her spine. The pain became pins and needles, and she gasped, heaving for breath.

Kimberlain dove for his shotgun and rolled, firing in the same motion. The pellets grazed Tiny Tim's side and he twisted away screaming, another shotgun blast barely missing him as he charged back into the woods leading up from the waterfront.

He had shot the woman, but Kimberlain was on his trail. He was running through the woods now, the uphill grade paining him. Branches scraped at his face, but Seckle felt nothing. He emerged in an open grove where wood benches had been laid out in circular fashion around a camp fire. Above him up a slight rise was the southern cluster of cabins, and beyond that the deep woods and escape.

Kimberlain had stopped over Hedda only briefly. He eased her onto her back, and blood instantly began to soak out of her wounds into the ground. Then he helped the boy whose life she had saved to his feet. The boy was standing limply, shock having overtaken him. An old couple rushed forward in their nightclothes and took the boy in their arms—his grandparents, obviously.

"Thank God," they muttered. "Thank God, thank God. . . ."

They were starting to speak to him when Kimberlain knelt down next to Hedda. Her face was ghastly pale. Her lips trembled. Her eyes were dying.

"I saved him," she moaned, "didn't I?"

"Yes."

Kimberlain saw her try to smile. Then her eyes reached up and held his.

"Get Seckle, Ferryman. Get him."

"Don't worry," Kimberlain promised, but Hedda's eyes had already locked open and sightless. He lowered his hand to close them and then bounded to his feet, rage filling him.

Wop-wop-wop-wop-wop . . .

The Ferryman was halfway up one of the dirt roads leading up from the waterfront when he heard the sound. He recognized it instantly and gazed up. Out of the darkness, a single floodlight over the lake broke the storm's control of the night.

Kimberlain caught sight of Seckle's massive shape struggling up the hill to the southern rim of cabins just as the helicopter began to descend. Its backdraft tore the ground out from under his feet before he could pull the trigger. Instantly automatic fire sprayed his way from within the chopper and chewed up the earth around him. Kimberlain waited until the helicopter banked into a rise again before breaking into a fresh sprint in Tiny Tim's path. But another barrage traced his movements, and only a leap behind one of the cabins prevented him from being shot.

By the time he crept around the cabin's front, the chopper was hovering over Garth Seckle. A rope ladder had already been lowered, and someone was gesturing for the monster to take it.

Kimberlain had four shells left, and he fired them all in the time it took Tiny Tim to grasp the rope and be lifted away. The storm, though, swallowed his shells, as the helicopter cut its floodlight and disappeared into the blackness.

THE NINTH DOMINION

TD-13

Saturday, August 22; 9:00 A.M.

CHAPTER 36

"**I**T'S a pleasure to meet you at last, Winston."

Peet sat in the center of the small, locked room. All the furniture had been removed prior to his being escorted into it. The room was empty, barren. The only evidence it had ever been occupied showed in the discolored patches on the floor where furniture had once been.

"We still haven't met, Leeds," Peet said without gazing at the camera over the door.

"Our spirits have. Years ago, perhaps even long, long before."

"You should have left me alone."

"As the Ferryman should have. Alas, we were engaged in a battle for your very soul. And I won."

"I own my soul."

"But you cast it with my lot. You would have chosen death, unless you truly wanted to be here by my side."

"To join you, you think?"

"To merely be as you are. And that, my friend, is with me. I do not seek to change you, Winston. I want you with me in your true light as we embark on a special mission to create a world you were born to live in."

"The ninth dominion . . ."

"Yes," Leeds said, surprise lacing his voice. "I see Kimberlain shared his discoveries with you."

"He will be coming, Leeds."

"I am expecting him. I thought you would want the pleasure of arranging his demise. A fitting finish to the circle, don't you think? So that a new one may begin."

"There is only one circle, Leeds, and it is continuous. To live is to be born not once, but every minute. Death happens only when birth stops."

"And it is time for you to be born again."

"In here?"

"Not at all."

Peet heard a click, and then the door before him began to open.

"I knew you'd be going to ground," Kimberlain told Captain Seven as he took the last few steps down into what might have been a massive gopher hole in the middle of rural Connecticut. "But I didn't realize you'd be doing it literally."

Captain Seven was there waiting for him at the bottom of the entry tunnel.

"It ain't much," he said as they stepped into a neat, square room. "And I don't even call it home. Can't even smoke my dope because the ventilation ain't adequate. This hasn't been easy, let me tell you."

"I was about to compliment you on the architecture," the Ferryman told him.

"Gaw 'head. Only thing worthwhile I stole from the gooks. Those fucking tunnels they had built underneath the whole country were masterpieces of construction. Even frags wouldn't shake the walls sometimes. Made a detailed study one day and brought the plans back with me." Captain Seven tapped his skull. "Up here. Lucky thing, too, since we might be spending considerable time here in the future." He lowered his voice. "Sorry about the way things turned out in Pennsylvania."

"Glad you finally became reachable again."

The captain had taken off as soon as the news of the attack on Lauren Talley and the alleged perpetrator reached him. He knew it could only mean that anyone close to Kimberlain was getting squeezed, and if Leeds could find Peet, Seven's railroad cars wouldn't elude the madman long.

"How's Talley?" Kimberlain asked him.

"Surviving, like the rest of us. Maybe a little better."

"That's something."

"You want to tell me more about Pennsylvania?"

"Later."

It still hurt Kimberlain too much to relive what had happened at the Towanda Family Resort. Hedda—his sister—was dead, but somehow he felt that was what she wanted. In at last discovering her true self, she had found there was nothing left to go back to. The existence of a son she could never know underscored the bleakness and futility. Getting her life back so quickly was like living the worst of it all over again. No way she could see it getting better. No way it could. At first he thought she believed the boy whose life she had saved in the end at the resort's waterfront was indeed her son's. On the way to Captain Seven's, though, he realized she knew it wasn't and didn't care. It might as well have been, because he was a stranger to her as well. It made no difference. That's what she had come to grips with, but the pain of it all must have hurt her as much as the bullets that had punctured her spine.

For his part, Kimberlain could still not manage a firm grasp on his own emotions. The past twenty-four hours had cast his entire life in a new light: a murkier, darker light that left him feeling his way without direction. He had lost his parents to a set of conspiratorial manipulations, and now he had lost his sister to the mad manipulations of a single man.

But it wasn't really his sister, was it? His sister had perished on that island to Leeds's reconditioning process, and somehow that made things worse. It nagged at him like a cut that wouldn't heal, and Kimberlain knew the only way to close it was to destroy what she had been meant to be a part of.

"Right now, I want to hear about TD-13," he said to Captain Seven.

"Bad news, boss. We're talking big time. This guy's even better than you thought."

"Let's have it, Captain."

"Okay. We got Briarwood Industries—your buddy Leeds—buying out PLAS-TECH right before the company wins a government contract to manufacture a certain monofilament strip. Once completed, these strips are shipped to three paper mills as part of the same government contract."

"To produce what?"

"Money, Ferryman. Cash money."

"As in dollar bills?"

"And fives, tens, twenties, and everything else. Currency, Ferryman. That's where Leeds has placed his TD-13, and that's how he's going to poison the country. Care to see how it works, up close and personal?"

"I think so."

"Right this way, Ferryman," Captain Seven beckoned. "Class is in session."

He led him through the well-appointed underground bunker, which virtually mirrored his train car. On a black table, covered by a glass dome, he had laid out a series of brand-new ten-dollar bills.

"I got these from the Federal Reserve Bank up in Boston. Not for general circulation yet, but a friend of mine took care of things. Part of the latest shipment out of a spanking new minting facility in Kansas. There's a plan to replace all the cash in this country with fresh currency."

"What?" the Ferryman asked.

"You heard right. Bear with me now, because here's where things get a little complicated." Captain Seven circled the dome containing the enclosed money as he continued. "Know what the biggest problem facing the treasury today is?"

"Off the top of my head I'd have to say cash hoarded for use by drug syndicates."

"Nope, not even close. The biggest problem, especially in the not-so-distant future, is counterfeiting. See, the next generation of laser copiers and printers is due out inside of two years, and they can make money even the banks would accept for deposit. So some bozo in the D of C figures we better come up with a simple way of identifying the real thing.''

''The plastic strips . . .''

''Abso-fucking-lutely. Based on an idea the Canadians used with their funny money. They put a kind of hologram in theirs. I think it's a naked broad but I'm not sure. Well, a hologram wouldn't work in ours because the paper's thicker, but a strip formed of monofilament mesh fibers would work just fine. Hold it up to any light and you see a pattern that looks like a tick-tack-toe board. No way to reproduce that with any generation of copiers coming in our lifetime.'' Captain Seven took a deep breath. ''So PLAS-TECH makes the strips and ships them to these paper plants.''

''Who, in turn, insert the strips into the huge rolls of paper that are then sent on to the Kansas Depository where all the new money is bring printed. But replacing all the cash out there now will take years.''

Captain Seven shook his head. ''Nope. Government has a plan to get all the old money out of circulation in less than six months, starting at the beginning of September.''

''What'd you find out about T. Howard Briarwood?'' Kimberlain asked, changing the subject.

''Would you believe he owns the Gerabaldi Scrap Yard in upstate New York where you mixed it up with those nasty machines?''

Kimberlain didn't bother to answer.

''You think that's good?'' Captain Seven resumed. ''Shit, it gets better. Let's talk Briarwood Industries, Ferryman, which happens to be the largest privately held conglomerate in the world, owned and operated by the Howard Hughes of the nineties, T. Howard Briarwood. Fucking recluse runs everything from a bunch of private offices all over the country outfitted with tech stuff that'd make me proud. Doesn't like people much, by all accounts.''

''I can understand why now.''

''Yeah, well check this out. In the just over two months Andrew Harrison Leeds was in The Locks, T. Howard Briarwood wasn't seen in public once. Another one of his reclusive stages, his people called it. Care to guess what some of his other reclusive stages corresponded to?''

"Murders committed by Leeds in one of his other identities," Kimberlain responded.

"You get an A for the day, boss. The scary thing is that this guy really is a fucking genius." Captain Seven cast his eyes admiringly on the ten-dollar bills laid out inside the glass dome. "Behold a masterpiece of modern science, as good as anything I could do myself, and that's saying a lot. You said the guy who created this TD-13 claimed he didn't produce all that much. Well, since money is handled by so many people during the course of its paper life, he wouldn't have to.''

"The poison won't lose its potency?" Kimberlain wondered.

"Sure it will—long after everyone is too dead to use it. See Leeds's people—*Briarwood*'s people—took the TD-13 and microencapsulated it prior to adding it to PLAS-TECH's strips.''

"Meaning?''

"Meaning the toxin will lie dormant until a certain set of circumstances are met. You got a dollar?''

Kimberlain handed him a twenty.

"To put it in your wallet or pocket, you gotta fold it first, right? Well, soon as you do that the encapsulation breaks and the poison is released. I'd say each bill's got a life span of a hundred owners or two months, whichever comes first.''

"And which would?''

"The hundred owners, almost for sure.''

"And just how many individual bills are we talking about?''

"In a normal year, the Treasury Department replaces fifty million pieces of currency. You can multiply that by ten or twenty in the case of what's already been minted in Kansas.''

"Past tense, Captain?''

"From what I've been able to gather, they're just waiting to ship the new currency en masse to Federal Reserve distributor banks on September 1." Captain Seven tapped the glass dome. "These are parts of an advance shipment to banks to make sure things get off to a smooth start. I gave them the full treatment. Great stuff, let me tell you. This TD-13 is a slow-acting, progressive nerve poison. Works on the internal organs until they just shut down. By the time anyone figures out what's going on, it's too late.''

"But the bills aren't available to the public yet."

"No. Instructions pertaining to that release date have been very precise."

"So the money gets distributed," Kimberlain concluded, "and whoever touches it gets infected by TD-13. What about people they go on to touch? Can it be spread that way, too?"

"Nope. This is a toxin, not a bacteria or a virus. And the way my simple mind has figured things, it's plenty bad enough on its own. Say a month at most before the entire country's been poisoned."

A chill crept up Kimberlain's spine as he moved away from the dome. "No, Captain, not the whole country. Not everyone touches money. Convicts and prisoners don't. Inmates in mental institutions and asylums don't."

"Right on, boss."

"The ninth dominion," Kimberlain said, "just like Leeds ordered it. A world left for the mad, the depraved, and the criminals, thanks to these new bills stockpiled at the Kansas Depository."

"I'd say less than five percent have been shipped so far."

"Makes it pretty clear what's got to be done," Kimberlain concluded.

"Already got the stuff brewing you'll need to pull it off. Delicate process. Got to give it time. Miss the proper temperature by a degree or two and the rats'll be eating our guts for breakfast."

"I blow myself up, or something along that line, you better be ready to call in your favors."

"I got numbers from the old days. They'll just love to hear from me again."

"Do you remember me?" Andrew Harrison Leeds asked the massive figure chained to the hospital cot.

Garth Seckle was still in the process of coming awake.

"Should I?" It hurt him to talk through his burned, scabbed lips.

"I should say so. We're brothers, you and I. I've been behind you every step of the way."

Seckle's stare scoffed at him. Then his eyes sharpened.

"The island," he muttered.

"Yes. I lifted you from the hell where you had been deposited so you might be free to express yourself in the manner you deserved. I supplied you with the files you needed and cheered you every step of the way."

"Who are you?"

"Who I am doesn't matter, Garth Seckle. What matters is that you passed your test brilliantly. What you did in those towns, the hospital; what you would have done in that resort, if Kimberlain hadn't disrupted you."

Garth Seckle's eyes filled with anger.

"Relax. You will have your opportunity to avenge yourself upon him. But he is meaningless to you and to us."

"Why am I here?"

"Because I need you. I had known about your imprisonment in the stockade for years, but waited until the time was right to arrange your release. Your potential was there. I only sought to bring it out to its fullest, to let the rage in you blossom so you might serve me better."

"Serve you?"

"It will be by your own choice."

Seckle tried to touch his face. The chain's wouldn't let him. "Last night, your helicopter?"

Leeds nodded. "Dispatched because the time has come to put your skills to infinitely better use."

"Where am I?"

"A facility I have appropriated for the time being. You haven't asked about your wounds."

"I can move. I can breathe. I can see."

"You can do far more than that, my good fellow. Besides one cracked rib, a shotgun graze in your side, and some very nasty burns, your wounds are strictly superficial in nature."

Seckle looked down and saw the white gauze bandages

wrapped around both his hands. He could feel the bandages over his left temple and above his eyebrow as well.

"I'm going to remove your chains now," Leeds told him. "They were put in place for your own protection until your situation could be adequately explained. Now that that has been done, you deserve to be released. You and I are alone in here. If you wish to kill me, I suppose you could be successful."

Without hesitating, Leeds used a key first on the manacles fastened around Seckle's ankles and then on the ones around his wrists. Tiny Tim stretched the life and blood back into them, rising slowly to a sitting position.

"What do you want from me?"

"Your participation in a new order of the world."

"Who *are* you?"

"The person who made you, Seckle. The person who lifted you out of the human scrap heap you had been dumped into, so you might have a chance to be even more than yourself again."

Tiny Tim looked interested now. "And this . . . new order?"

"Coming very soon. Yours to be a part of, if you so choose. It will be a world you were made for, my brother, a world that is made for you."

"Interesting."

Andrew Harrison Leeds smiled. "There's someone else I'd like you to meet."

CHAPTER 37

"SIGN in, please."

The driver of the large armored truck marked FEDERAL RE-
SERVE scribbled his name on the appropriate line and returned
the clipboard to the gate guard.

"You know the routine," the guard said.

"Oh yeah. This place gives me the creeps. Looks too damn
new."

"It looks new because it is new."

The Kansas Depository was one of only two facilities outside
Washington responsible for printing new money and disposing
of the old. Though construction was well underway before the
government opted for an elaborate money replacement program, the facility proved perfect for the task of minting the new
currency. Only slight modifications in the machinery were required, since Kansas was outfitted to take on a large measure of
the printing load anyway.

Of the nine levels comprising the facility, only four lay
aboveground. These contained the money presses and general
offices that were open for public tours on a daily basis. What
the public never saw were the five underground stories that
contained the massive storage facilities for freshly minted
money and the high-tech shredders and furnaces used for disposing of the old. The underground levels boasted ceilings in
excess of forty feet high, and two of them were literally

jammed with plastic-wrapped stacks of soon-to-be-shipped currency.

The complex was surrounded by a ten-foot-high electrified fence. Upward of fifteen men patrolled the perimeter at any given time, with another twenty serving inside the depository, many responsible for watching the workers. Floodlights streaming from the rectangular building's roof kept the outside brightly lit twenty-four hours a day. There were four machine-gun towers and a titanium steel gate at the entrance that could hold back a tank.

The midnight truck had been right on time, and with the clipboard back in his bulletproof shed the head guard activated the gate's opening mechanism to allow the truck to slide into the complex. The truck entered the building through a garage door on the first floor, where another security gate waited. Once this station was satisfactorily passed, the truck's contents could be unloaded under the watchful eye of ten armed guards who were in turn watched by two supervisors. The system had checks and balances for its checks and balances.

The bags of "dead" money were tossed from the truck and piled by one team, then dumped down a shaft that looked like a giant laundry chute by another. The chute formed the first step on the road to what depository workers referred to as "the ovens." To reach the ovens, the dead money first had to be dumped out onto conveyor belts that sent the bills through a massive shredder before the remains were burned. The depository was open twenty-four hours a day, but only for sixteen hours were the shredder and ovens operational. The shipping of new bills and receiving of old ones went on continuously.

On this night, deep inside one of the bags dumped down the chute from the truck making its midnight run, Jared Kimberlain shifted his frame. An oxygen mask drew air from a tank on his back, but precious little remained. He clawed the dead bills away from his head and chest area and climbed upward like a swimmer fighting for the surface. When his fingers felt the touch of canvas, he removed a serrated knife from his belt and sliced neatly through. The tear grew into a gaping hole easily big enough to accommodate his emerging shape.

The rest would be much easier. A backpack strung from both his shoulders contained a dozen canisters of the latest concoction Captain Seven had brewed.

"I call it GS-7," the captain had told him. "Short for Good Shit Seven. Best batch I ever made, if I do say so myself. What we got here is highly explosive aerosol of exceptionally high density, droplets less than a micron in size so they literally stick to the air. Toss a match in, and everywhere it's spread goes *poof*!"

Kimberlain's plan was to gain access to the roof where the air-conditioning evaporators were placed. There he would empty the canisters into the filtration system. In a matter of minutes, the whole building would be inundated with GS-7, spread through the labyrinth of air ducts. After the building had been evacuated, Leeds's deadly money would be a match-light away from destruction.

The Ferryman pulled the rest of himself from the tear in the canvas. He sat atop the heap of dead money and stripped off his mask and air tank. This was the third sublevel. On the floors below lay the shredders and furnaces used to dispose of money like this. Directly above lay the two floors where Leeds's poisoned bills were being stored.

It took Kimberlain's eyes a few seconds to adjust to the scant lighting of this level. He blinked rapidly to clear them and started to climb from the pile. As he moved he glanced around the room, and what he saw froze him in place.

Stacked against one of the walls were bodies, heaps and heaps of them, all dressed in the uniforms of those charged with guarding this installation. They had been murdered, which left one undeniable truth:

All the guards had been replaced by Leeds's men, who were now in control of the depository. Men who must be products of Leeds's Renaissance project, just as Hedda was, which made them formidable adversaries at the very least. And, of course, there was something else.

Leeds was here! In the depository!

And he must have known Kimberlain was coming.

* * *

Kimberlain assessed the situation. Even though Leeds was expecting him, there was a good chance the madman didn't know he was there yet. He clambered down the pile of dead money and moved for the elevator bank. The Ferryman touched the up arrow, and less than thirty seconds later the compartment doors started to slide open.

Inside, one of Leeds's six personal guards opened fire as soon as the doors were halfway open. Twenty of the submachine gun's thirty bullets sped out in a three-second burst, and the man lunged out to finish the job if need be.

Kimberlain had pressed himself against the wall alongside the elevator as soon as it came to a stop. He recognized the gunman as one of the six who had led him around on his iron leash back on Devil's Claw Island. The Ferryman rammed a fist into the man's throat. The gunman's Adam's apple broke free and lodged in his throat. Gasping, he tried to swing the gun round, but Kimberlain grabbed his head and twisted.

The man's neck snapped with a resounding thud. Kimberlain dragged him halfway into the still-open elevator compartment, so the doors would be unable to close, rendering the elevator useless. Then he moved for the stairs.

Another pair of Leeds's best-trained men were waiting on the ground floor when the sound of gunfire reached them. They tensed, Kimberlain's presence in the building apparently verified. Each drew his weapon. One tried the elevator. Nothing happened. It was stuck somewhere on the lower floors. The other gestured for the stairs, and they headed for them.

They took each level in utter silence, one advancing ahead while the other maintained cover. When they reached the third sublevel, they could see its exit door wasn't closed all the way. The two men moved to either side of the door and waited. They nodded in unison and burst through, one after the other with two seconds spacing, so that if an ambush awaited the second would have the shooter's location pinned down before he emerged.

There was no one anywhere. They were about to try the next sublevel when both noticed the guard whose gunshots they had heard lying half inside the elevator compartment. Together they moved toward him, wary of each step. When they reached the compartment, one turned his back to the open doors while the other yanked the dead man out so the elevator could be used again.

The body was halfway out when the Ferryman popped the elevator's ceiling hatch open and emptied the rest of the dead guard's machine gun into the two men beneath him. Then he lowered himself back down and pressed "3."

The guard waiting on the third floor heard the elevator coming and steadied his gun before it. The climb seemed to take forever, and he debated in his own mind whether he should open fire as soon as the doors began to part and risk killing one of his fellows.

His back tensed as the compartment locked home. There was a soft thump, and the doors started to open.

The guard still hadn't made his decision when Kimberlain burst through the stairwell and leveled a silenced Beretta nine-millimeter his way. Four bullets slammed into him and shoved him through the open elevator. The doors closed, the elevator staying just where it was.

Two more to go, Kimberlain thought.

And then Leeds.

Leeds's two remaining guards were under orders not to leave the fourth floor under any circumstances. The idea was to stop Kimberlain from reaching the roof if he made it this far. They formed the last barrier, and for this reason Leeds had chosen his best men for the post. One carried an M-16 with explosive-tipped bullets. The other handled a custom-made semiautomatic shotgun with a circular twelve-shot feed clip. A hit anywhere with it was a guaranteed kill.

They were standing at either end of the hall when the elevator began to rise their way. The one with the M-16 signaled the other to hang back. They had been well briefed long before on the capabilities of the Ferryman, and the fact that he had made it off the island indicated his reputation was well earned.

Take nothing for granted, Leeds had warned them, take nothing at face value.

The elevator opened, and the guard closest waited a beat before spinning toward the doors. His eyes regarded the entire compartment in the length of a heartbeat, noted the open ceiling hatch above, and . . .

"Shit . . ."

. . . the four bodies piled on the floor below, one still holding a pistol. The guard raised his hand and signaled the man on the other end of the hall to come this way. The man backpedaled to keep close eye on the stairwell at the same time, the only other route of access to this floor.

"They're all dead," he heard the guard at the elevator say. "They're—"

The soft spits came next, and the approaching guard spun around in time to see the Ferryman burst out from the cover of the corpses as the elevator guard crumpled. The approaching guard managed to get off two shots from his shotgun, both of which sailed wide, before Kimberlain's three bullets slammed into his chest.

Kimberlain held the gun leveled for a time longer, wanting to be sure. The pistol the first guard had glimpsed upon entering the compartment was actually held in *his* hand. The Ferryman hadn't even had to move to fire the first burst. It was the second that had worried him, and the other guard had cooperated brilliantly by doing just what he should have done.

"No chains this time, boys," he muttered to himself, and headed on down the corridor.

The exit door at the end of the hall led up to a ladder that accessed the roof. The Ferryman pulled it down and climbed up toward a steel hatch. He popped it open and hoisted himself onto the roof.

He had made it! But how much time did he have before Leeds realized his guards had been neutralized? He had to make it enough. . . . In any case, there was no longer a need to evacuate the building prior to detonation with Leeds's people the only remaining inhabitants.

The roof was lit irregularly by floodlights, and Kimberlain began his search right away. It didn't take long to locate the pair of central air-conditioning evaporators that were responsible for channeling cool air through the entire depository. The trouble, he could tell from this distance, was that the evaporators weren't running. Again something uneasy prickled his neck. He moved forward and touched his hand to one of the heavy steel machines. It was warm, almost hot. They had been in operation until very recently, perhaps even the last few minutes.

Leeds! It had to be Leeds!

Fortunately, the Ferryman had come with a contingency plan, albeit a less sure one. A number of ventilating baffles were situated across the roof, each connecting with a separate line of the building's duct work. There might be eight in all, ten even. Empty the contents of one GS-7 canister into each, and the explosive aerosol would drop downward eventually to envelop the entire inner shell of the building. An explosion less dramatic, but equally effective, would result upon detonation.

Kimberlain located the first baffle and pried it open with his screwdriver. It would take him fifteen to twenty seconds to empty each aerosol can manually. All he had to do was turn the top-mounted valve and hold it in place, according to Captain Seven's instructions.

Kimberlain turned the valve and started to ease it toward the open baffle. A slight hissing sound reached him as the GS-7 began to escape.

"Stay as you are, Ferryman," came the voice of Andrew Harrison Leeds.

Kimberlain swung round to see him standing just in front of the door to the roof where he must have been waiting. Tiny Tim stood alongside him with machine gun in hand and gauze bandages covering the many wounds he suffered at the Towanda Family Resort. As Kimberlain watched, the two of them eased across the roof, stopping halfway between the door and him. He calculated that the cover of darkness had prevented both his adversaries from seeing him place the draining can of GS-7 upon the sill of the nearest baffles.

"I'm so glad you could join us," Leeds continued. "There's

someone who's been most eager for the pleasure of your company.''

And through the door stepped Winston Peet.

"You disappoint me," Leeds said, coming forward in Garth Seckle's shadow, the monster's machine gun aimed straight ahead. Peet hung back behind them, empty eyes never leaving the Ferryman. "So predictable. I anticipated each and every one of your moves.''

"Tell that to the six guards I passed on the way up here.''

"Them?" the madman scoffed. "I left them for your enjoyment. I believe that you dispatched them in less than eleven minutes following your entry into this building. Splendid. I would have expected closer to thirteen.''

"I saved the last two minutes for you.''

"Did you now? You know, you really would have been much better off to let me dispose of you colorfully on the island. Now stand very still and remove the pistol from your belt with only two fingers.''

Kimberlain realized his calculation had been correct: Leeds could not see the canister. Its explosive contents continued to spread into the air over the roof. He removed the pistol from his belt.

"Now toss it in front of you.''

Again Kimberlain obliged.

"The backpack next," Leeds instructed. "Carefully, please.''

The Ferryman stripped it from his shoulders slowly, eyes shifting from Peet to Tiny Tim as he readied his next move.

"It doesn't have to end this way for you," Leeds told him. "You need only to give the word, and a place can still be made for you here.''

"With you?''

"Is that so bad?''

"I don't approve of your taste," Kimberlain said, looking solely at Tiny Tim.

Leeds's gaze tilted toward Peet. "Your friend has seen fit to join my order. You should follow his lead.''

"Sorry. Not my style."

"Really? Stop fooling yourself, Ferryman. You know you belong with us, but you do not admit it. Why don't you ask your friend Winston? He gave up the fight. He is where he belongs."

"That true, Peet?" Kimberlain asked.

"I'm sorry, Ferryman."

"It's my fault. I should have left you alone."

"Or killed me when you had the chance. It would have been the only way, because no one changes. Not you. Not me."

Peet had drawn closer to Tiny Tim while he was speaking. The sight of the two of them together flanking Andrew Harrison Leeds made Kimberlain see just how small and unimpressive the maker of all this was. Leeds's face was more gaunt and skeletal than ever. His thick dark hair was plastered back over his head, looking like paint sprayed onto his scalp.

"It's over, Leeds," Kimberlain said finally. "Give it up. You've lost. Even your giants can't help you finish this the way you wanted."

"Then I'll have to finish it another way, won't I?"

"This is a government installation, Leeds. When the morning shift comes on, you're finished."

"That is precisely my hope."

"That they find the bodies I did?"

"There are more you haven't found yet."

Kimberlain tried to make sense of it. Below him the hissing had stopped, the canister's contents spent. "The authorities get here and find the building ravaged."

"Security breached, an inexplicable tragedy. But the money, ah the money. They will have no choice, will they?"

And then Kimberlain realized. "It will be shipped immediately to the Federal Reserve Banks."

"But the banks haven't the facilities to hold it, so they will have no choice but to put the currency into circulation through member banks ahead of schedule." Leeds paused and breathed deeply. "The deaths will begin within a week at most. Unexplained, perhaps even unnoticed at first. Then they will multiply. Panic will set in. I will enjoy that."

Kimberlain's face wrinkled in disgust.

"You can enjoy it, too. You deserve better than what this world has given you. In my world you would belong. You are an outcast, Ferryman. The old world shuns you. You do the things you do to gain acceptance, but it will never come because you are not one of *them*." He gazed behind him at Peet and Tiny Tim. "You are one of us."

"Sorry, Leeds. The only thing we have in common is we both do the things we do to please ourselves. If we accept who we are, that's enough. I'm trying to. You can't."

"Is that so?" the madman posed, intrigued. "Tell me what you mean. Please."

"Fear, Leeds. You live and breathe off it because it forms a shield that keeps you from seeing yourself. You don't see yourself in the mirror; the only place you can see your reflection is in the eyes of your victims gazing back at you. Only when you look into them does your shape please you. You think this new world of yours, this ninth dominion, is going to please you? Forget it. Because you won't be feared, and without that you won't *be* at all."

Leeds took a step forward. "Why don't you ask your friend what he sees in the new order? Why don't you ask what made him see the truth?"

Kimberlain looked at Peet again. The bald giant had moved still closer to Tiny Tim. Why? His eyes seemed to dart toward the canister by the Ferryman's feet.

"Join us, Ferryman," Peet said.

"No can do, Winston."

"Very well," followed Leeds. "Have it your way. Kill him, Peet."

Peet started forward, then swung back toward Tiny Tim and smashed him across the face with interlocked fists. Tiny Tim's head snapped back in whiplash fashion. He maintained the sense to try to resteady his submachine gun, but by then Peet had already slammed against him, going for the trigger himself.

Kimberlain had meanwhile grabbed the backpack full of GS-7 and burst into a rush. He was halfway back to the skylight when Peet's hand closed on the trigger of the gun still held by Seckle.

"No!" Leeds screamed, realizing at last what was about to happen.

Peet aimed the burst from Seckle's machine gun forward and down, the heat of the bullets igniting the freed gas. Kimberlain had already thrown himself headlong behind a roof abutment when the shots rang out. The move shielded him from the fireball that blew a hefty measure of the rooftop off. The entire depository building trembled. The percussion of the blast cracked ceilings and walls. Flames from the roof jetted down through the cracks as far as they could reach, smoke billowing ahead of them. The fire alarm wailed. The building's sprinkler system snapped on to no avail.

Leeds landed near Tiny Tim, who immediately turned his weapon on the fleeing Peet.

"Kill him!" Leeds raged, watching the Ferryman dive through the skylight he had earlier used to reach the roof. "Kill him!"

Tiny Tim emptied his clip in Peet's wake as the giant hurled himself over the edge of the building.

"No! *Kimberlain*!" Leeds screamed. His eyes watched the Ferryman disappear through the skylight. "The money!" he followed, turning back toward Tiny Tim. "We've got to protect the money! That's where he'll go now. Stop him! *Do you hear me? Stop him*!"

CHAPTER 38

KIMBERLAIN dropped down through the skylight and hit the floor hard. Pain surged through his feet and ankles, adding to the beating his body had already absorbed from the percussion of the roof blast. His ears were still ringing, and he felt blisteringly hot all over. He moved down the stairs, braced against the wall.

Thanks to Peet, there was still a chance to stop the ninth dominion. If Kimberlain couldn't blow the whole building, at least he could blow those floors on which the money was located. Garth Seckle would be heading that way too, though, and success meant having to deal with him.

And what of Peet? He had glimpsed the giant lunging toward the edge of the building, perhaps to his death at last. He had saved Kimberlain and perhaps much more in the process by giving the Ferryman this opportunity to destroy the poisoned money.

Kimberlain came to a bend in the hallway, groping his way through the smoke, when he spied a huge figure just ahead. Instinct made him lunge for what he believed to be Tiny Tim. Instead a familiar voice found his ear.

"It's me, Ferryman."

"You had me fooled, Winston."

"Leeds, too, fortunately. After his people came for me at

337

the cabin, it was easy to make him think I had joined him, because that is what he wanted to believe. I knew you would be coming wherever he was, and I had to be there, to destroy him and whatever lurks within me once and for all.''

"You jumped off the building.''

"And landed on a ledge.'' Peet wiped the sweat and grime from his face. "We are meant to finish this together.''

"The money,'' Kimberlain said.

"Leeds showed me. We must destroy it, Ferryman.''

Kimberlain leaned against the wall and stripped the pack from his shoulder, the plan already formed. "You've got to go to the lowest level.''

"The ovens?''

"Turn them on. Turn them on so they'll ignite the aerosol I'm going to finish releasing through the building.''

The difficulty of the logistics was just beginning to occur to the Ferryman. Even if he were able to succeed on the roof in a second attempt, it would take several minutes at the very least for the GS-7 to spread through the ducts. Unless, unless . . .

Kimberlain reached into his pack and handed Peet one of the canisters. "Release this before you've turned the ovens on,'' he said. "When it blows, it'll carry the flames faster up to the aerosol I'm going to release into the building.''

Peet started off, still eyeing the Ferryman.

"Tiny Tim will be down there,'' Kimberlain warned.

"I know,'' the giant said.

Kimberlain and Peet had each gone their separate ways into the thick haze. The sprinkler systems continued to spray water throughout the building, dissipating the smoke to some degree. Cautiously, Kimberlain retraced his steps back to the roof, amazed when he got there at the damage a single canister had wrought.

The Ferryman found eight ventilation baffles still intact and spent seven minutes emptying his remaining GS-7 canisters into them. He would trust the rest to Peet, while he spent the few remaining minutes searching for Leeds. If the madman survived here today, the risk of the ninth dominion rising another day was all too real. Leeds would disappear into yet another identity and the preparations would begin anew.

The depository was a massive building, and Leeds could have been anywhere within it. But the Ferryman believed he knew where Leeds would head with his operation now in jeopardy, and he started for the stairs to join him there.

The videotape Arthur Whitlow had made had taught Leeds how to operate the massive printing machines contained on the first two aboveground floors of the depository. The entire process was computer keyed and controlled. The presses themselves looked like massive automatic-teller dispensers. Various lights flashed continuously as their huge slots spit out large sheets of bills and fed them toward the automatic cutting apparatus, which in turn passed them along to be stacked and bound.

Andrew Harrison Leeds turned all the switches to ON. A hum filled the air. The machines began to go about their business, as if there were business to do. In his mind, Leeds could see his death-charged money spewing from the presses in blinding fashion. He followed the imaginary process on foot to the cutting station where he envisioned the massive sheets cut sixty-four ways and fed along the belt. Excess edges were automatically swept aside into a shredder. Everything else moved on to be stacked and bound. His mind showed him piles a hundred bills thick appearing by the second and being sent along to be packed in bushels and wrapped in plastic.

Yes, he could see it all. He could *smell* it. The luscious smell of money that in this case meant death. The bushels the conveyor belt was now bringing to the lower levels were all his. Each and every bill had been touched by the grandness of his vision. In turn, the touch of them would bring on the final demise of the old world.

The smell changed. Suddenly the scent of money was gone from his mind, replaced by another he was coming to know all too well. The machines hid the sounds of the Ferryman's approach, but he did not need his ears to sense him. Leeds spun, firing his pistol, just as the Ferryman lunged. The bullet that thumped into Kimberlain's shoulder was not enough to stop his charge. Impact carried the two of them backward, where the conveyor belt transported them down toward the stacks of money clustered on the floor below.

Winston Peet reached the sublevel controlling the ovens by sliding down the shredding chute the dead money was dropped into en route to being burned. He had the sensation of being swallowed by a monster with terrible teeth in the form of the shredder's massive slicers, smelling of oil and thankfully inactive.

The shredding chute dropped onto a conveyor belt that transported the money's remains to their final demise. Peet rushed along the black tread in a crouch beneath the low ceiling. Finally he emerged on the bottom level where the shredded currency was equally apportioned toward a series of smaller chutes. These dropped directly into the ovens, which were contained in a subbasement beneath this floor.

Turn them on after first releasing the contents of his canister, and they would ignite the remaining deadly aerosol that, thanks to the Ferryman, would by now be spreading throughout the depository. The building would collapse in upon itself, the poisoned money reduced to dust.

Peet searched about the walls in the dim emergency lighting. The main control box was clearly labeled but locked. Peet shredded its steel bindings and tore the door off.

Inside lay a vast number of switches and knobs. Peet moved them to the ON position, firing up all the gas jets that formed the unseen fire pit below. Finally he twisted the hand-size spigots that released the gas. He imagined he could hear the hissing. Then he moved to one of the chutes that accepted shredded old money for the ovens and dropped his canister down into it. He elected not to turn the valve releasing the aerosol; allowing time for the can itself to explode would provide him with a few precious moments for his own flight.

As Peet turned away from the chute after letting go of the aerosol canister, a clack of footsteps made him duck and plunge himself beneath the cover of a conveyor apparatus. A hail of bullets meant for him slammed into the wall instead.

Beyond Peet's field of vision, Tiny Tim advanced. His eyes were trained on the machine behind which Peet was concealed, but what he sought lay on the far wall to the left: the controls for the furnace that the bald man had activated. The furnace had to be shut down if the installation was to be saved and the vision of Leeds realized. Seckle's steps were methodical, deliberate. He knew his foe's potential and knew enough not to put too much faith in either his weapon or the distance between them. Neither was insurmountable for Peet, just as neither was for him.

When Seckle reached the control board, he was forced to slide his eyes away from the bald man's perch in order to study the panel. The controls were elementary. He turned back toward Peet one last time before lifting his fingers to the buttons and knobs.

As he turned, a massive fist slammed into his face. Tiny Tim felt his jaw shatter under the blow. He managed to wonder how the bald man could have covered such a distance in only three or four seconds before a pair of powerful hands sought purchase on him. Seckle was able to level his machine gun forward and squeeze the trigger just before Peet kicked it from his grip.

One or two of the bullets grazed the bald man in the side, stunning him. In the time it took Peet to stagger two steps backward, clutching at the blood, Seckle had hit the ground rolling and tried to reach for the machine gun. Before his fingers could close on it, Peet kicked it aside and took a brutal blow to the knee that nearly tumbled him. Seckle found his feet as the bald giant wavered and the two slammed against each other, arms interlocking. Tiny Tim's eyes glared straight ahead.

Peet was smiling.

Even as Seckle thought one last time about the controls he had failed to deactivate, the can of GS-7 Peet had dropped down the chute was ignited by the rising flames. The explosion was deafening. Beneath the grappling giants, the floor receded to the tide of rising flames, and the two figures dropped toward them.

The bullet that entered Kimberlain's shoulder shattered his collarbone and left one of his arms useless when even two might not have been enough against Leeds. The madman fought on the conveyor belt like a female animal defending her young. Using his teeth, nails, fists—anything close to Kimberlain's flesh. Leeds's pistol had been lost somewhere on the conveyor, but the Ferryman gave up the search for it when it was clear he needed total focus to fend off the madman's attacks.

The belt dipped into its steepest drop, and the two of them slid off it onto the floor on the first of the two massive storage levels. There was a thud as Leeds's pistol hit the floor just behind the two men. Leeds thrust the Ferryman aside and lunged for the gun. He had it palmed and coming up before Kimberlain was able to move. His ravaged shoulder kept him from mounting a response. He lay on the floor struggling for breath as his blood spilled on the tile.

"I am destiny, Ferryman," Leeds said, eyes grasping the stores of money beyond Kimberlain. "I cannot be stopped."

"You'll stop yourself, Leeds. You *have* stopped yourself. It's over."

A broad smile glistened on his face. "Do you really believe that? You're the one who's failed, Ferryman. I will shoot you again, in the heart this time, and you will die a failure."

"If you're going to kill me, then do it and stop your games."

"Don't you know when you're getting complimented, Ferryman? It is so difficult for someone like me to find anyone worthy of my consideration. Perhaps you are the last. Kill you and that ends forever. But I suppose it must end, and I suppose—"

Leeds's speech was stopped when a thunderous explosion shook the floor. The ceiling blew out and the floor cracked. Walls crumbled inward.

Peet! Kimberlain realized happily. It had to be Peet!

Leeds rose and pressed himself against one of the many

ceiling-high stacks of money. Building fragments began to rain down on his cache of death-laden bills. Flames licked through the gaps.

"No!" the madman screamed. "Not now! Please, *not now*!"

While Leeds's attention was diverted and his eyes focused on the money, Kimberlain lunged forward. As he reached for Leeds, the madman again pulled the trigger of his gun. But this time a quaking tremble threw his aim off, and Kimberlain smashed into him amid the huge stacks of wrapped bills, which had begun to sway.

Peet felt himself falling, but his feet found some strange purchase in middescent. He realized he had been saved by a crisscrossing section of steel beams forming part of the building's foundation. But his survival might be short-lived, considering the certain combustion of the GS-7 Kimberlain had released once the rising flames touched it.

Peet swung to the right in time to see Tiny Tim coming at him with a massive knife glinting orange from the fire. Peet twisted from the path of the first strike and blocked the second with a piece of heavy insulated tubing his hand had locked on. Around the two giants, the jetting flames of the ovens continued to climb and surge. Their battle raged over a river of fire lapping ever closer to where they stood. The crisscrossing support beams formed a catwalk of sorts, and Tiny Tim's eyes followed it in the direction of the control panel. Despite the collapse of the floor, it remained in reach for a man his size. But to get there he had to get by Peet.

Tiny Tim lashed forward with his knife once more, and again Peet parried with his piece of rubber tubing. His free hand lashed against the burned side of Tiny Tim's face. Flesh tore, and Seckle screamed in agony. His bandage was gone now, revealing raw, scabby skin burned almost to the bone. His bad eye was half closed. He held his mouth open like an animal.

He came forward again, feinting with the knife to draw Peet's attention. When the bald man took the bait, Seckle lunged to a neighboring support beam that provided a direct route to the control box.

Peet realized Tiny Tim would succeed in reaching the panel first if he tried to leap across to the beam his adversary was already on and give chase. His only chance of cutting him off was to rush down the support beam he presently occupied, even though it ended several yards short of the one Tiny Tim was on. Peet charged forward, gathering as much speed as possible to fuel the leap now required to bridge the gap. Seven, maybe eight feet from one narrow catwalk to another—and he had to land *upon* Seckle.

The possibility that he might overshoot or undershoot his target never occurred to him, and he threw himself airborne. He smashed into Tiny Tim at full speed and took him down. Clutching for each other, fighting for control, their upper bodies hung over the side of the catwalk toward the rising flames.

But Peet's leap had left him on top. Not about to squander the advantage, he jammed a massive hand beneath Tiny Tim's chin and tried to bend his head back far enough to break his neck. Tiny Tim locked one of his own hands against Peet's to maintain the stalemate, while his other flailed desperately for the knife he had lost control of on Peet's impact. Smoke clouded both their eyes and the flames teased their flesh. But neither man felt anything besides the other. Peet continued jamming Tiny Tim's head back with the same hand still clutching the rubber tubing. He could feel it starting to give. Seckle's fingers were trembling when they at last closed upon his knife's hilt.

"Ahhhhh!" he screamed, and drove the blade hard into Peet's side.

Peet howled in agony, his life saved only when the blade bit into a rib and wedged there. Tiny Tim tried to yank it out to mount a killing strike, but Peet locked his hand over Seckle's to hold the blade in place. Tiny Tim twisted, turned it, and Peet bellowed some more, still holding firm. Seckle's head was coming up now, winning the fight against Peet's determined hand. At last Tiny Tim removed the hand that had been maintaining the stalemate from Peet's arm and began to slam him again and again in the soft side ribs.

The cracks sounded like gunshots as the ribs gave, but Peet wasn't finished. He released his hold on Tiny Tim's chin, and when the monster beneath him mounted the expected surge, he lashed him across the bridge of the nose with the tubing he still held. Tiny Tim greeted the blow with a burst of rage that allowed him to drive the knife stuck in Peet all the way through the bone. Peet responded with a wild strike from his hose that shattered Tiny Tim's teeth. He spit them up at Peet and buried the knife in him up to the hilt.

In the agony that resulted, forcing his teeth through his bottom lip, Winston Peet saw his only chance. When Tiny Tim tried to withdraw the knife this time, Peet let him, looping his piece of tubing through the gap in the catwalk and hoping it held. Tiny Tim lunged with the knife, and Peet simply went with the move, pushing off with his feet in the same motion. The knife made a neat, shallow tear just over his navel, and the two giants dropped from the catwalk together. The tubing stretched but held over the climbing flames, and Peet hung by it with his right hand. Beneath him Tiny Tim was clinging to Peet's belt with his left hand, his right still holding fast to the knife. He whipped it at Peet in wild swipes that drew blood on each occasion, until Peet dropped his free hand downward and did the only thing he could.

He grabbed the blade in his bare hand, accepted the agony and the blood, because now Tiny Tim was powerless. Peet began to thrash his legs wildly to throw him off. Tiny Tim lost his hold at last, and the blade tore from Peet's bloodied grip. Seckle slid downward and, in a desperate swipe, grasped one of Peet's feet, arresting his fall. The monster smiled as he began to climb up his leg, still clutching the knife.

Peet kicked both legs viciously but to no avail. Then, as he was trying to find another way to shed the monster, a huge gush of flames reached up and took Garth Seckle in their grasp, burning him black while he still held fast to Peet's leg. Peet never thought such screams could come from a man. When the death grip was at last relinquished, he gazed down into the inferno hoping to see Tiny Tim paying his final price, but the flames had swallowed the sight.

Peet bit down the pain in his sliced hand and ribs and pulled himself back up onto the catwalk. Around him the tallest of the flames engulfed steel. He charged through them for the shredding chute and clawed up its heavy tread. Peet emerged on the next level and burst into a sprint for the garage door. He didn't stop when he got there. His impact tore the right side of it from its hinges and he was greeted by the sight of fire engines streaming into the complex.

He turned back then toward the hot orange glow climbing ever higher through the building, knowing the final explosion was just seconds away and the Ferryman was nowhere to be seen.

Leeds got off four futile shots before Kimberlain was able to force the pistol up and away from him, the struggle flaring anew. He stared into the madman's rage-filled eyes and watched as they somehow turned bright red. It took him an instant to realize they had filled with the glow of a massive fire burst that rocketed the two of them through the stale scorched air. Kimberlain landed against heaps of fallen money bushels still clothed in their plastic wrappings, sight of Leeds stolen from him. Freed bills showered into the air, many blackened and already charring. Portions of the floor blew out to reveal an inferno raging in the second storage level below.

Only seconds left now before the entire building blew!

But where was Leeds?

The question was answered when his shape emerged staggering from a pile of loosed bills ten feet before the Ferryman. A half smile hung over his face. His trembling hand held fast to the pistol.

"It ends," he said.

Kimberlain could do nothing but watch as his finger tightened its curl on the trigger.

"You've lost, too, Ferryman."

Before Leeds could fire, though, massive segments of the ceiling and walls blew outward, tumbling the remaining stacks of money in the path of another fireball. The last the Ferryman saw of Leeds, he was standing statuelike amid the deadly money of his own making, his mad eyes fixed on the bills, as if welcoming them.

It ends. . . .

Yes, with the last huge bulk of the GS-7 soon to be ignited. But not before I get out, Kimberlain thought to himself.

The conveyor belt was still whole enough to allow for a rush back up it to the ground floor through the converging flames. The production area was a fiery shambles already. The machines Leeds had switched on were still whirling spasmodically, but gushed smoke instead of money. The Ferryman danced through the flames and debris until he reached the depository's lobby.

He burst into a dash for the glass doors forming the main entrance. Just as he reached them, a deafening blast projected him forward like a cannon shot. Crashing through the glass felt strangely like a sudden fall into ice-packed snow, albeit with something blisteringly hot breathing down his back.

Impact came with stunning abruptness, and the black night closed over him.

EPILOGUE

KIMBERLAIN came awake slowly to find a squat figure standing between his bed and the window.

"Who are you?" he managed.

"Jones will do," the man returned, as he approached with a trench coat folded under his arm.

"Washington?"

"Close enough."

Kimberlain's return nod was equally slight. He knew Jones was a fixer, dispatched by the powers that be to clean up a mess the government didn't want leaking out by any and all means available. His features were as nondescript as his job. Of medium height, he was slightly balding, his remaining hair was turning gray, and any muscle he might have had was a memory. When he was a yard from the bed, the Ferryman smelled drugstore after-shave.

"There are some matters that need to be cleared up," Jones said with the interest of a man already late for his next appointment."

"Where am I?" Kimberlain broke in. His throat was dry, and he had difficulty swallowing.

"Don't you remember?"

"Pieces. That's all."

"You're in a hospital. Better you don't know the name or locale for now. This wasn't the first hospital you were brought to. We had you moved after your ID came through."

"I wasn't carrying one."

"Your fingerprints were sent to Washington. When your name came up, they sent me."

"My wounds, how bad?"

"You were lucky. Collarbone needed surgery to repair. You suffered a severe concussion and broke your right ankle on impact with the ground. Assorted other bruises and lacerations. I can make you a list."

"Don't bother." Kimberlain swallowed as best he could. Even blinking his eyes caused pain.

"The money was all destroyed," the fixer went on. "The entire building was. No trace of Leeds either."

"How did you know about—"

"A rather unusual man sent by you reached one of the typical agencies with a most unusual story. He told them everything, as you and he assumed it to be."

Captain Seven, Kimberlain thought, following his orders when the Ferryman missed a planned contact.

"And did this agency believe him?"

"Would you?"

"No."

"They didn't either," Jones said. "But when word of your presence here and of the depository's destruction came in . . ."

Kimberlain tried to sit up and failed. "The money, some of it had already been shipped to—"

"Impounded earlier today."

"Checked?"

"In the process. I expect they'll find just what you destroyed in Kansas. We can't put a cloak on everything that happened. Probes are inevitable. The emphasis must be on minimalization."

"Of course."

"Toward that end, I have reached certain conclusions you need only confirm." Jones looked him closely in the eye. "It has been determined that one Winston Peet, believed to have died during an escape from Graylock's Sanitarium some years ago, was at the depository. Yes?"

Kimberlain wasn't sure how to answer until he observed the expression on Jones's face. "Yes," he said then.

"It is our contention that his escape from The Locks was engineered by Andrew Harrison Leeds at that time and that Leeds has been harboring him, along with numerous others, ever since. Yes?"

"I suspect so."

"And, lastly, we are led to believe that you were behind Peet's final demise within the Kansas Depository building. Yes?"

"I was," Kimberlain told him.

"Good," Jones returned.

"Devil's Claw," the Ferryman said.

"My next subject. You should know a resort community being built there perished in a massive landslide two nights ago. There were no survivors. The coast guard is making regular patrols to make sure no one strays even close to the island. And you might also be interested to know T. Howard Briarwood has apparently disappeared once again. We do expect this time it will be rather prolonged."

Kimberlain peered at Jones more closely but didn't get much past the trench coat. "Kind of you to come all this way to provide me with an update."

"Part of the cleanup process."

"There's a much bigger part you've got to undertake: finding all the monsters that came off the island to be stashed for judgment day. They're out there, Mr. Jones, and they won't be staying put for long."

"I'm afraid we have no firm evidence of their existence."

"Is it going to take one of them coming up and blowing your brains out to convince you they're real?"

"We deal in realities, Mr. Kimberlain, not suppositions."

"Of course," the Ferryman concluded, "because to acknowledge their existence would mean having to marshal forces and admit all this happened. Can't have that, can we?"

"I don't know what you're talking about. And yet . . . ."

"Yet what?"

"If a private contractor wished to work on this matter, we would lend any support he desires. All he would have to do was ask."

"That come from your superiors?"

"It comes from those who recognize your value and would like you to make use of it on our behalf."

"We've been through this before, Jones."

"Times change."

"People don't."

Jones lifted his trench coat and jammed his arms through the sleeves.

"I'll be back tomorrow," he said, and started for the door.

"Leaving guards in your place, Jones?"

The squat man stopped and turned back. "I'm not one of those people of yours. You're free to go anytime you feel up to it. Walk out of here, run if you choose."

Kimberlain settled back in silence.

"Think about my offer," Jones said, and then he was gone.

When Kimberlain awoke next, darkness filled the room except for areas of light from the parking lot sneaking through the half-drawn blinds. A huge shape stood there gazing out into the blackness.

"Hello, Ferryman," Peet greeted without turning.

Kimberlain smiled. "I didn't know if you were alive, if you survived the—"

"A cleansing explosion, fire ironically an element of purification, rather than destruction."

"In more ways than one."

"The fire department could not quell the blaze. It burned itself out."

"Again familiar . . ."

"I am free, Ferryman."

"You were free before all this, Peet."

The giant shook his massive bald head. Able to see a bit in the darkness now, Kimberlain made out the harsh red sheen on Peet's exposed skin, the cracked and bubbled places on his face from close exposure to the flames. In addition, a bulge beneath his shirt indicated a self-bandaged wound. One of his hands was wrapped thickly with gauze as well.

"No, Ferryman, I was prisoner on the property you lent me. Leave it and I feared everything would go back to the way it was before. I was a prisoner of who I had been, of my own persona. I am free of that now."

"Because you faced Leeds and stared him down, along with everything he represented?"

"Because I no longer have to run from the person I used to be. That person might still be out there, but he cannot catch me. I have at last learned how to emerge from unclean situations cleaner, to wash myself with dirty water."

Kimberlain shifted his head through the pain. "Does this mean you won't be using my cabin anymore?"

Peet looked at him deeply. "I must find my own woods, my own forest."

"They're still out there, Winston. Hundreds of them that Leeds sprung and then reconditioned."

"But left their essences intact."

"That was the point."

"It will make them easier to find on my way."

And then Kimberlain realized. "Give me some time to get healed and I'll tag along."

The giant shook his head. "Not this time, Ferryman."

"I was starting to think we made a pretty good team."

"We might yet again."

"You'll stay in touch."

"It won't be hard to figure out where I am."

"What else brought you back here, Peet?"

"The wish that you would not consider trying to join me. The hope that you will at last walk away from the world that torments your soul."

"I can't. You know I can't."

"Certainly not if you don't try."

"Leeds wasn't the first, and he won't be the last. Who would stop them?"

"Themselves—eventually."

"Not before plenty of people get hurt."

"You can't save them all, Ferryman."

"Because I'm not responsible, right?"

"You are . . . for yourself."

Everything was growing very clear, Kimberlain's mind splitting the darkness. "Not always. My parents were killed because of what some force wanted to turn me into. My first mistake was to let it. I'm not going to make a second by letting that go to waste."

"You pick up pieces that would be better left scattered," Peet told him.

"And aren't you about to do the same thing?"

"Yes, but for me there will be an end. I have found there can be closure. For you the cycle never stops or even lets up."

"And there must be a reason for that, don't you think? You see, Winston, I understand now that they tried to turn me into something that must have been there already or it couldn't have come out. I am what I'm supposed to be, and I'm at peace with that, now more than ever. I really don't want to change, Winston. I don't know what I'd be like as somebody else."

A slight smile spread across the giant's face. "From that which you want to know and assess you must depart, at least for a time. Only when you have left the town, can you see how high its towers rise above the houses."

"And do you ever come back?"

"Depends on what you find on the road."

Kimberlain tried to raise himself up and failed. "Travel well, my friend."

"You too, Ferryman."

About the Author

Jon Land is the author of *The Doomsday Spiral, The Lucifer Directive, Vortex, Labyrinth, The Omega Command, The Council of Ten, The Alpha Deception, The Eighth Trumpet, The Gamma Option, The Valhalla Testament,* and *The Omicron Legion.* He is thirty-five years old and lives in Providence, Rhode Island.

Be sure to read all the
Blaine McCracken novels by

JON LAND

from Fawcett Books.

THE ALPHA DECEPTION
Once again, Blaine McCracken—rogue, renegade, and
killer, feared by his enemies alike—must fight to return
sanity to a world gone mad... yet a world that must
survive.

THE GAMMA OPTION
From the treacherous depths of the Pacific Ocean to the
ancient city of Jaffa in Israel, from the Tokyo of a Bujin
warrior to the exotic alleys of Tehran, all the pieces fit
into one diabolical puzzle. At its center is Blaine
McCracken, the only man who can stop the awesome
momentum of a crazed conspiracy whose devastating
power will soon be unleashed against the world.

THE OMEGA COMMAND
Rogue agent Blaine McCracken is brought out of exile
to unravel the vicious mystery of Omega. Trapped in a
web of ever-escalating danger, abandoned by his superiors, McCracken is all that stands between a world and
its total destruction.

THE OMICRON LEGION
Washington, D.C....Rio de Janeiro...Boston...
Philadelphia...Tokyo... All the forces are in place for
the titanic battle that may shatter the globe.

Also available from Fawcett Books
by bestselling author

JON LAND

THE COUNCIL OF TEN
The shadowy, all-powerful conspiracy has but one aim:
total domination. It is fortified by an awesome super-
weapon that can render America helpless. And only a
desperate army of three can stop it.

THE EIGHTH TRUMPET
From New York to Washington, D.C., from London to
the Mediterranean island of Malta, and on to the frozen
wastes of Antarctica, the demented plot unfolds. It will
reach its terrifying climax on a day set aside for celebration—a day that may mark the end of humankind.

JON LAND

LABYRINTH
The most sinister conspiracy ever...Aimed at every man, woman and child in the world...Only one man can stop it. Only one man, Christopher Locke, an unsuccessful college professor, can expose the trail that begins with the brutal execution of every person in an obscure South American town.

THE VALHALLA TESTAMENT
Evil men envision the twilight of human freedom. A cruel yoke will enslave mankind,...if Jamie Skylar and Chimera lose the trail that is being erased beneath their very feet. Unless the final secret is revealed, no opponent will be powerful enough to defeat.